Monstrous acts

A novel

By J.R. Boelter

Nicole,
   Happy Holidays!
Hope you enjoy the Book!
      JR.

Acknowledgments

First and foremost, I would like to give a special thanks to Gabby and Rafael who created a fantastic cover for this book. You both rock! I would also like to thank Jason for giving me the strength and encouragement to keep on with the story. Did I ever tell you how amazing you are? Finally, I would like to thank the many people who stood by me during the times of doubt that I would ever finish.

Dedications

This book is dedicated to my mother, for she taught me the value of a great story. Thanks for being a shining light in a darkening world. I love you, mom.

Contents

Prologue

The crow watched from a crooked branch outside the window with its beady eyes. The cloaked woman inside the room lit a black candle and carried it over to a large basin against the wall. Above the basin hung an enormous canvas of a warrior woman dressed in armor. Three crows circled above her.

The cloaked woman knelt in front of the basin and began chanting. She reached inside her tunic and produced a dagger that shimmered against the candlelight. She raised the dagger up in both hands, as if offering it to the warrior woman. She took the knife and slit a small cut into her left palm in one swift motion. Blood oozed out of her cupped hand and into the basin in a steady stream.

The crow jumped from its position and landed on the windowsill, fluttering its black wings. It let out a shrill caw, and the woman turned toward the sound. She smiled upon seeing the crow. She got up gracefully and walked to the window, unlatching it. The window opened inward and a gust of wind sent a chilly night's air inside. The smell of dead leaves wafted into the room from the ground below.

The crow walked to the opening, then flew toward the basin, landing around the edge of the bowl. It cawed once more and craned its neck toward the painting. The cloaked woman walked back to the basin and started chanting again. The crow watched in fascination as the woman dipped a finger into the bowl and drew a symbol into the blood. She withdrew her finger and copied the same symbol on her forehead.

The crow cawed madly, and the woman stared at it for a moment. It fluttered its wings and dipped its beak into the bloody liquid. The liquid rippled outward and began to shimmer faintly. The shimmering became brighter, and soon, the red liquid was completely gone, replaced by an image of a young woman. The cloaked woman peered over the side of the bowl and watched intently as the image began to move.

The woman in the basin had fiery red hair with a short slender face. She was slightly freckled around the nose and cheeks and they clashed with her oval green eyes. The woman was talking to someone but the cloaked woman couldn't make out who.

"She's the one," she said aloud. The crow straightened its neck and cawed once more. She reached up and petted the crow gently, stroking its head and lower back. The crow cawed in response, then dipped its beak inside the basin again. The image changed, rippling out faster than before.

A faint whisper emanated from the liquid as the image came into focus. It was the woman from the painting, standing tall amongst a group of people cowering around her. She had a sword in one hand and the head of a man in the other. The whisper grew louder and the crow fluttered its wings in response.

Soon, the cloaked woman thought. *Plans were in motion, and soon they will return.* She smiled at the crow as the whispering stopped. The liquid in the basin shimmered and dissipated, returning itself back into blood. She bent down and gave the crow a gentle kiss on its forehead. The crow cawed once more, then leaped from the basin and out the window.

The woman looked up into the painting. "Soon," she spoke to it, then began to chant once more.

Chapter 1

Tara Bancroft moved to Seattle for a fresh start. The lovely city of Phoenix had not been kind to her during the last year she had lived there. Truth be told, it wasn't really Phoenix that hadn't been kind. On the contrary, she loved Phoenix with a fiery passion. She had lived there all her life and thought there was no better city in the world. No, Phoenix was not the cause of her grief. It was her husband, Kenneth Rogers.

She first met Kenneth on a homicide investigation, involving the death of a little Hispanic girl. Kenneth had been the only eyewitness to the crime. Upon meeting, she noticed he had the most amazing blue eyes she had ever seen. They went well with his short wavy black hair and chiseled jaw. He stood about 6'1, give or take, and he was well built in the upper chest area.

Tara had kept it strictly professional that day, asking Kenneth questions about what he had seen during his stay at the Desert Botanical Garden. She had jotted down his statement, in which he claimed he saw a white man hand a small boy, presumably his own child, a small sharp knife. He then witnessed the boy stab the girl repeatedly. He called 911. Later on, examination of the body corroborated his story.

Throughout the investigation and trial of the father and son, Kenneth and Tara became closer. It was a gradual closeness, first with meetings to go over his testimony in court, then later when Tara got enough nerve to ask him out. He said yes immediately with glee in his shiny blue eyes. They went on a couple of great dates involving sushi and movies. By the time the case was officially closed, and the father and son duo had been convicted, Tara had moved in with Kenneth. She had found someone who complimented her well. Tara was happy.

Two years later, Kenneth proposed. She graciously accepted and they got married in late February. A month later, Kenneth lost his job, due to cutbacks. He became sullen and depressed, drinking himself into a drunken stupor most nights. Tara did what she could to help him through that difficult time, but it wasn't easy. His demeanor changed. Kenneth became violent, and after an argument on leftover meatloaf, he punched her in the jaw, dislocating it.

Tara spent the next week in the hospital. The doctors reset her jaw, which was equally as painful as dislocating it. Kenneth was put in jail for assault. Her work partner, Detective James Spader let Tara stay at his place while she recovered fully. It was due to Spader that she considered moving in the first place. He had suggested she start fresh, in a new city, away from everything.

By midsummer, Tara had filed for divorce. Although she loved Kenneth, she couldn't stay with him; not after what happened. She was not going to be one of those battered women who constantly clung to their abusive husbands. She was raised to be strong and going back to him would make her weak. She moved out and found a new apartment that was Kenneth free.

The next couple of months really put Tara through the ringer. Kenneth stalked her, leaving pictures of him everywhere she went. Boxes of chocolates and bouquets of roses were left on her doorstep. He seemed to appear wherever she went; at the doctor's, in the grocery store, even on cases. She filed for a restraining order, but it did no good.

Kenneth broke into her apartment late one night and forced himself upon her while she slept. She fought him off, but only barely. He did outweigh her by at least 70 pounds, and it was by sheer luck she managed to stop him in time before he raped her. Luck and the fact that he had been drunk helped considerably. She subdued him and called 911. Kenneth was arrested and sent back to jail. Tara had enough. She decided to take Spader's advice and move.

Tara's captain gave her a list of transfer options. Seattle was at the top of the list. A week later, Tara's stuff was shipped off, and she boarded a plane to Seattle, leaving behind her bad memories and old life.

Tara now sat in front of her new police chief, Juan Martinez. Chief Martinez was a short but burly man. His salt and pepper hair was slicked back and pasted to his scalp. His face had too many wrinkles for a man in his late 30's. He was dressed in a nice Italian black suit that fit him well. When he spoke, his accent was thick.

"Mrs. Bancroft," he started, while looking over the transfer paperwork.

"Actually, sir," Tara interrupted. "It's Ms. Detective, if you prefer."

Chief Martinez looked up at her for the first time since she stumbled into the office. "Ms. then," he replied. "I've been told you were coming by Mayor Murray. You must have some nice strings to pull to use him in such a manner."

Tara looked baffled. She hadn't known how her old police chief got her transfer in so quickly, but she never expected it was because of the mayor. "Honestly, sir, I don't even know who that is. Phoenix police Chief Suba must have pulled the strings."

Chief Martinez nodded in understanding. "Well, Ms. Bancroft, I don't like when people go over my head like that," he informed her, flipping through her transfer file. Silence filled the room. Tara sat patiently behind his wooden desk in an uncomfortable wooden chair that was too stiff for her liking.

While he studied the paperwork, Tara looked around. His walls were filled with pictures of his achievements. Chief Martinez seemed to be shaking hands many times in different scenarios. His desk was cluttered with trinkets. On the top corner sat a small speaker monitor. A black phone was scrunched next to it. Files were spread across his desk, disheveled.

The silence was becoming even more uncomfortable than the chair, and Tara wished he would say something. When he finally did, it was 5 minutes later. "I don't know what kind of work ethics they have down in Phoenix, but here in Seattle, I do not tolerate anyone going over my head, is that clear?"

"Crystal clear, sir." She told him. He picked up a pen in a little cup and started twirling it between his fingers.

"I expect hard work and dedication on everything you are assigned, is that understood?"

"Yes sir," She nodded. "I am extremely dedicated, as you can see from my file, sir."

He sneered, causing more wrinkles to form around his mouth and eyes. "Files can be misleading, Ms. Bancroft. People always put the best things in files. I'm not interested in what files say." He stopped spinning the pen and placed it on his desk. "I will be the judge of your work. Tell me, how well are you at computers?"

Tara thought for a moment. "Pretty well, sir," she said. "I can type up to 70 words a minute and I am pretty familiar with all forms of programs."

A smile spread over his face for the first time. Tara didn't like that smile. It was cynical and made him look like a 1950's mobster. It was the first time during the conversation that she became on edge.

"Good," he told her. "Your new job here will be to type up the reports from other officers."

Tara shifted in her seat. "With all due respect, sir. I am one hell of a detective. I'm sure given the chance, you will come to see that."

He raised a hand to settle her. "All new recruits and transfers are not properly trained the way I want them to be. I don't know enough about your abilities in the field and I tend not to trust what others put in files." He went on, "Until I can physically attest to your own abilities, I can't in good conscience put you out there."

Tara had to admit that he made a good argument, but she had been a detective most of her adult life. She couldn't let it go. It was bred into her. Tara took in a deep breath and exhaled slowly. She could feel her face getting flushed with anger. She had to calm down.

"I understand you did not approve my transfer, sir. I understand that Chief Suba should have called you directly instead of going over your head." Tara got to her feet and leaned over Chief Martinez's desk. "But I have solved more crimes than any other detective in Phoenix. I have put more bad guys away than any other cop I know. Hell, I've even coordinated with the FBI on occasion. All I am asking for is a chance to prove how valuable an asset I can be to this team." Tara stared deep into his dull brown eyes. "Please, sir. Let me prove my worth. I promise you that you won't regret it."

They stared at each other for what seemed like an eternity, neither of them blinking. Martinez finally glanced down and sighed.

"Fine," he conceded in a cautious tone. "On a probationary basis. One slip up, and you will be at a desk faster than you can say Seahawks, is that clear?"

Tara grinned, "Quite clear, sir."

Martinez reached over to the small speaker and hit a couple of buttons. There was a dial tone and then it beeped a couple times. A deep husky voice arose from the speaker.

"Yes Chief?" the voice said.

"Moore, get in here," Martinez ordered.

"On my way sir," the voice replied, then the line went dead.

Chief Martinez went back to glancing at the transfer paperwork, leaving Tara to sit there in silence. A moment later, A tall slender man dressed in a gray suit and tie walked in. The man had short cropped black hair that was parted in the middle. He wore thick black rimmed glasses that seemed a little too big for his oval face.

"What can I do for you, sir," he asked?

Chief Martinez stood up, and Tara followed suit. "Jacob Moore, this is Tara Bancroft. Your new partner."

Tara held out her hand, but Jacob just looked from it to the police chief. "You joking, sir?" he asked.

Tara felt her face become flushed again. She lowered her hand and crossed her arms over her chest. "Nice to meet you too," she said sarcastically. Chief Martinez shook his head.

"No joke," he told him. "Our mayor approved her transfer. Get her up to date on protocol and show her the ropes."

Jacob looked Tara up and down, as if sizing her up. He nodded in compliance. "Yes sir."

Still red hot, Tara thanked the police Chief and followed her new partner out of his office. She had been in Seattle for a week, but she hadn't missed her old life until today. And what a day it was turning out to be.

Detective Moore led Tara through the maze of police desks toward a back hallway. The hustle and bustle of the station reminded her of rats scurrying in a sewer. Phones rang sporadically while faxes and paperwork were being completed. The policemen took no notice as they passed by, focusing on their work. Jacob finally stopped in front of a smoked glass door. A golden name plate attached to the door read 'Jacob Moore, Lead Investigator'. He opened the door and scooted Tara inside.

While the Police Chiefs office was filled with pictures and clutter, Detective Moore's office was exactly the opposite. There was a wooden corner desk with a black computer monitor on top. The same style speaker Martinez had on his desk also sat in the far-left corner. The walls were bare except for a single framed diploma from the University of Washington. At the opposite side of the room were two small wooden chairs with a round coffee table between them.

Tara frowned as she looked around, "Not much for decorations, are you?"

Jacob closed the door behind him and chuckled. It was a hearty chuckle. "I'm not much for worthless things." He went to his computer chair and sat down facing her. He gestured for her to sit in one of the wooden chairs. She did.

"I'm sorry about our first initial meeting," he informed her. "It's just surprising that Chief Martinez let you out in the field so quickly. I didn't mean anything by it if you took offense."

She nodded her head in acceptance. "No worries," she told him. "I can hold my own. I have had to deal with being a woman in a predominantly male workforce for quite some time. I've got to say," she went on, 'that compared to some of my other dealings, that was downright pleasant."

Jacob chuckled again, causing his glasses to slide down his nose. He absently pushed them back up. "I understand. It's got to be tough being a woman in the field. Most guys I know don't like women as partners. Not because they are chauvinists, but because they feel women can't defend themselves the way a man would."

"And how do you fare with having a woman partner?" Tara asked.

He smiled. "I can handle it," he said. "My last partner was a woman, and she was truly impressive in the field. I have learned a lot from her. We've had a wonderful partnership. I hope that we will have the same."

Tara studied Jacob's face. She had an uncanny ability to tell when someone was lying. She called it her spider sense. It came in handy with her line of work. Tara's old partner, Detective Spader, hated it sometimes, but that was when she caught him lying. She informed him that she didn't need her spider sense to tell him he was lying, him speaking was good enough of a lie, she joked. No lie was present in Jacob's face.

"I'm sure we will get along great," she told him. She forced herself to smile, but it didn't reach her eyes. "Did your partner transfer out?"

Detective Moore's smile faltered. He glanced toward his diploma. "No," he replied. "She passed away."

Tara saw the change in him. He went from being peppy to filled with memories he was trying to forget. Tara hated moments like this. She was trained to be a good listener and sympathetic towards the victims' families, but she wasn't very good at sympathy. "I'm sorry to hear that," she whispered softly.

Jacob shook his head, clearing away the thoughts and memories and looked back at Tara. "Thank you, but it's still difficult to discuss if you don't mind."

Tara felt grateful. "Fine by me," she replied and stood up. "So, where can I get an office of my own," she asked him.

Jacob smiled again. "There are a couple empty offices to choose from," he explained. "They are pretty close to here. I'll show you." He got up and walked to the door, but the switchboard beeped loudly. He scooted over to it and pushed the button. "Moore here," he spoke to the speaker.

A high pitch southern accent floated out of the speaker. "Jacob, darlin, we have a 419 at Gold's Gym on Broadway. Martinez wants you and the transfer in on it right away, mon cher."

"Thanks, Cynthia," Jacob replied back. "We are on our way." He pushed the button again and the speaker went dead.

"A 419?" Tara Asked. "419's in Phoenix meant car jacking's."

Jacob gave her a puzzled look. "Here in Seattle, a 419 means murder." Tara's eyes lit up. She felt a little tinge of excitement fill her over hearing the news. Her first day on the Seattle PD and she already had a murder to deal with. Not that she was happy someone had died, but at least she could be put to good use.

"We'll find you an office when we return," Jacob informed her as he fished out his keys from his pocket.

"Fine by me," Tara replied as they walked to the elevator that led to the parking garage. "I'd much rather be on a case than planning color schemes and layouts of my office anyway." As they stepped into the elevator, Tara couldn't help but grin. Maybe today wasn't going to be so bad after all, she thought to herself.

Chapter 2

The detectives arrived at Gold's Gym on Broadway just as the sun was starting to set. The brisk October air sent chills down Tara's spine as she closed the door of Jacobs midnight black BMW. She hugged herself to get warmer. Jacob seemed perfectly fine with the weather and didn't wear a jacket.

They stepped through a revolving door and was instantly greeted by a portly bald policeman with a short gray goatee. The bald man extended his hand out to Jacob, who shook it vigorously.

"How have you been, Robertson?" Jacob asked.

"You know me, Moore." the bald man said. "I'm surviving, which is more than I can say for our victim." With that, both Jacob and Robertson laughed. Tara was not amused.

"Excuse me," she interrupted, "but do you normally laugh at the deceased?"

Jacob and Robertson exchanged looks. "Austin Robertson, meet Detective Tara Bancroft. She's my new partner."

Robertson offered Tara his hand and she reluctantly accepted it. "No disrespect Detective," he admitted. "It's just, in our line of work, a little laughter eases the tension." Tara quickly dropped his hand and nodded in understanding.

"So, what do we have here?" Jacob asked, straight to business.

Robertson's demeanor changed instantly from jokester to professional. "Follow me," he said, and walked off. Robertson led the way past weight sets and elliptical machines while he spoke of the victim. "Young man, early 20's by the look. Blonde hair, Blue eyes, 5 foot 9 inches. Stabbed in the back with what appears to be a wooden table leg."

"Table leg," Tara repeated. Do gyms normally use wooden tables? Last time she was at a city gym, she hadn't seen any tables, but of course she wasn't really looking for any either. And this is Seattle. Who knows what is different here.

"Witnesses?" Jacob asked Robertson.

"None, so far," Robertson told them. "No one has come forward, anyway."

"ID?" she asked

Robertson chuckled again. "Yes, but you won't need me to tell you who it is," he replied as he led them into the girl's bathroom. It was a typical two stall bathroom with two sinks and a giant glass mirror glued to the wall. The only thing that made the bathroom abnormal was the body sprawled face down on the floor.

The victim was lying in a pool of his own blood. A large wooden table leg protruded from the middle of his back. The victim had on gym clothes that were now stained red around the back and torso. His long curly blonde hair was also stained red around the tips.

Jacob bent down and wiped the hair off the boy's face. "Jesus," he said aloud and took a step back.

"I told you," Robertson said. He laughed again, causing his belly to shake rapidly. "I'd hate to be in your shoes on this one, Moore."

Tara ignored him and looked at the face. She didn't recognize him, but she had only been in Seattle a week. The boy couldn't be more than 25. He was pasty white, reminding her of a ghost. She tried to move an arm, but it was stiff, indicating that the body had been here for hours. She found it strange that no one seemed to need to pee from the time of death to now.

"Moore, you know this man?" she asked.

It was Robertson who spoke. "Know this man?" He stared at Jacob. "Jesus, Moore, where did you find this one? Planet Mars?" He glanced over to Tara. "Everyone knows this man. His family is very influential in Seattle."

Jacob held up a hand to calm him. "She just transferred from Phoenix, Robertson. She doesn't know who the Sloan's are." He spoke while gazing at the body.

"And you're already out in the field?" Robertson's eyes filled with surprise. "Why, I do believe El Capitan is going soft." He laughed again. Tara's annoyance with Austin Robertson kept building, but she kept her mouth shut.

"Will someone please tell me who this is," she pleaded.

Jacob looked up from the victim and over to her. "This is Eric Sloan. His family comes from the early settlers of Seattle. As Robertson has said, they are very prominent in Seattle and have very deep pockets."

"The media is going to have a heyday with this one," Robertson spoke. "Very high profile. Their claws will be out and they won't hold any punches," he told her.

Tara knelt down, examining the victim. "Who found the body?"

Robertson reached into his back pocket and produced a small notebook. He flipped through the pages until he found what he was looking for. "A miss Heidi Schumacher. She wondered into the bathroom, saw the body on the floor and called 911."

"I'd like to talk to her," Tara informed him. He nodded in acceptance. She gazed at Jacob, who was still staring at the boy. A puzzled look spread over him. "What are you thinking?"

Jacob peered over at her. "The body is out for anyone to find. The skin is very pale and the pool of blood suggests that the body has been here for a while. So," he went on. "How come in the hours after his death, only one person has stumbled upon him?"

"What do you mean?" Robertson asked.

"Well, the body has been here at least four hours. No one had to use the restroom at all during that time?"

Tara smiled. "My thoughts exactly," she informed him. "Does the gym has surveillance cameras?"

"I believe so," Robertson replied. "I'll double check, and get Miss Schumacher ready for questioning." With that, he was gone.

"Nice man," Tara said sarcastically. Tara wasn't sorry to see him go.

Jacob laughed slightly. "Robertson's harmless, just tactless sometimes. You'll warm up to him"

Tara rolled her eyes. "Looking forward to it."

A knock came at the door and a young officer opened it. "The CSI's are ready whenever you are, Detectives," she said.

"Thanks, officer," Jacob replied over his shoulder. "Could you see how far out the medical examiner is as well? I'd like a plausible time of death on our victim as soon as possible."

The young officer nodded. "Will do, detective," and shut the door.

Tara stood up. "I'll go question the girl. I'll meet you at the Surveillance room."

"Roger that," Jacob replied. They walked out of the bathroom together. Tara noticed that most of the gym was now taped off. A steady stream of onlookers gawked at the tape and whispered amongst themselves. Detective Robertson was talking to a shorter lady dressed in pink spandex and a white tank top. Her straight black hair was pulled back in a ponytail, revealing a pretty face with far too much makeup on. Tara glided over to them and introduced herself.

"I'm Detective Bancroft," she whispered as to not inform any of the gawkers. "I'd like to ask you a few questions if you don't mind."

Heidi nodded, but had a blank stare, as if she was still in shock. Tara thanked Robertson and guided Heidi away from the growing crowd. They stopped at a weight bench and sat down. "I know that you have seen something horrible, Miss Schumacher, and it can be pretty traumatic. It takes a while to process everything." She did her best to try to be comforting. "But I'm going to ask you to walk me through the events of the day."

Heidi looked at Tara for the first time. "I just can't believe someone could do that. Here, in my gym." Tears threatened to flow from her eyes.

"I understand," Tara replied. No one ever expects to come across a dead body. Especially one with a table leg sticking out of them.

"It's just so awful," Heidi went on. She buried her face in her hands and let out a couple sobs. Tara patted her on her back, which, if roles were reversed, would not comfort Tara in the slightest. It was the best she could do.

"I'll do my best to make this quick," Tara told her when she stopped sobbing. "At what time did you arrive at the gym?"

Heidi was looking at Tara with renewed interest. "Around 4 o'clock, I think," she answered. "I always come here on Tuesdays and Thursdays, normally around 2 o'clock for yoga, but I had to work later than normal today." Another sob escaped her lips. Tara patted her on the shoulder and gave her a minute. People dealt with death in different ways. Heidi Schumacher was a crier.

Heidi did her best to recover quickly. She wiped tears from the corners of her eyes and shook her head, almost whipping Tara in the neck with her ponytail. "I'm sorry, I've just never seen a dead body before," she admitted.

Tara nodded. "I understand. Do you need some water or anything?"

Heidi declined the water. "I'm just ready to leave here," she spoke. "I think I'm going to cancel my membership and try a new gym."

Tara didn't blame her. She was used to seeing the dead on a regular basis. Most people aren't. If she was in Miss Schumacher's shoes, she would buy a yoga mat and practice at home. "The sooner we get through these questions, the sooner you can be on your way home." Heidi nodded. "What time did you come across the body?"

Heidi thought for a moment. "Around 5 o'clock I believe. I just finished with the yoga class and had to pee really bad. That's when I went to the restroom."

"And was anyone else in there?" Tara asked

"Not that I saw. But I really didn't stick around to find out. I walked into the bathroom, saw the body on the floor and screamed. I remember running to the front desk to Billy to call 911."

Tara saw the scenario play out in her mind. It made logical sense. "Is there anything else you can think of? Anything at all?"

"Like what?" Heidi asked her.

"Like any sounds or smells that were unusual at the time. The smallest detail can often help," Tara admitted.

Heidi's eyes lit up. "There was something. I totally forgot," she exclaimed. "There was a horrible smoke smell. Like someone was burning something or smoking."

Tara jotted it down. "Did you see any smoke in the restroom?"

"No," she replied. "But I really didn't stay in there long enough to look. As I said, I saw the body and ran to the front desk."

Tara nodded. "Thank you, Miss Schumacher. You have been most helpful." They stood up and walked back over to where Robertson stood. "Officer Robertson will take down your information in case we need to contact you again."

Heidi and Tara shook hands. "I hope you catch the bastard who did this," Heidi told her.

Tara smiled slightly. "I hope we do too." She nodded to Robertson and bent under the yellow tape to walk over to the front desk. A muscular man with a gold tank top sat behind the counter. His name tag on his left shoulder said Billy.

"I'm Detective Bancroft," she informed him. "My partner, Detective Moore is in your surveillance room." Billy nodded slyly. "Can you take me there," she asked him.

Billy got up behind the counter and escorted Tara to the surveillance room. He used a key card to unlock the door and walked her inside. Jacob sat in a chair in front of a large TV screen with four camera angles displayed on it. The bottom right corner showed a clear view of the restrooms.

"If there is anything you two need, just give me a holler," Billy told them, then walked out.

"Find anything?" Tara asked her partner.

Jacob glanced over his shoulder at her. "I've gone over the recording a couple times, but only see women walk through the bathroom. Not Eric. And no one entered between noon and when Miss Schumacher entered the bathroom." He paused a moment. "I did, however, notice something strange," he informed her.

Tara's interest was piqued. "What is that?"

Jacob pushed a button on the panel and the video in the corner rewound in a blurry haze of white static. He pushed the button again and the picture showed clear. "Watch," he said.

The video showed the bathroom door. A couple women walked through and back out a couple minutes later. The video then flashed to static for a brief moment before showing the bathroom door again. But in front of the door stood a 'closed for renovation' sign "Did you see it," he asked.

"Whoa," she exclaimed. "Well, that explains why no one used the restroom and found the victim."

"Yes, but that isn't what I'm talking about." Jacob rewound the tape again and pressed play. "Pay attention to the time stamp in the top right." She did. The woman went into the bathroom and walked out, as before. The time stamp said 11:50:23. Then static again for a brief moment. When the picture reappeared the time stamp said 2:20:48.

Tara was surprised. Whoever killed Eric Sloan had erased the tape. Two and a half hours just doesn't vanish from recordings. "Whoever is our killer knew how to cover his tracks," Jacob said.

"Yes, and someone who works here must be the killer," she told him.

"How do you figure?" he asked.

"Well, it was someone who knew about the surveillance room," She replied diligently. "Billy had to use a keycard to let us in, so it has to be someone who has a key."

"I've thought of that," he retorted. "Billy told me that there are over 30 workers here at the gym. That's a lot of suspects to go through." He took off his glasses and cleaned them with his shirt. He set them back on and looked back at Tara. "This shitstorm just keeps piling up," he informed her.

Tara thought for a moment. A high-profile case with no real witnesses and erased recordings. Shitstorm indeed.

Chapter 3

It was well into the evening when Tara and Jacob left the gym. The wind had picked up, spewing tendrils of Tara's fiery red hair in all directions. She wiped the hair off her face with her fingers. She wasn't sure she would ever get used to the weather change.

A small media group was stationed outside, trying to scrounge up any dirt on the victim and event that happened. Tara and Jacob gave them nothing. Partly because they didn't have much to go on themselves.

They spent nearly three hours interrogating staff members and still had no clear motive from any of them. The staff all said the same thing. They hadn't seen Eric that day or knew who killed him. None of them admitted to putting the closed for renovation sign outside the restroom either. Everyone was either very good at lying, or telling the truth, because her spider sense did not tingle once.

The CSI's were also stumped. They went over every inch of the restroom, and came up with nothing. No particulates on the body, no fingerprints on the murder weapon. They dusted for prints on the countertop, the doorknob, the bathroom stalls, and the sink handles. It had all been wiped clean.

The medical examiner, Yvette King, arrived on scene around 6:30, just after they had finished questioning Billy. She did a liver temp on the body, and informed them that the body had been dead for nearly 6 hours. She explained that lividity was not fixed, which she indicated when they prepped the body for transport to the medical examiner's office. Jacob told Yvette they would meet her back at her lab after they informed the family of their loss. Yvette agreed, as she wanted to do the autopsy without being interrupted.

Now in the car, Tara wondered about the victim's family. "What can you tell me about the Sloan's?"

A tinge of anger spread on Jacob's face. "The Sloan family, along with other prominent figures are what you would call Seattle's mobsters. They have their hands into everyone's cookie jar," he explained. "Boeing, Amazon, Microsoft, you name it, the Sloan's have a connection to it.

"Dominic Sloan is Eric's father, and one of the wealthiest men in the country. It is rumored that if Dominic ran for mayor, he would have beat Ed Murray hands down. But he is too criminal for such things. Instead, he serves as an advisor to Mayor Murray, most likely as puppeteer, pulling the mayor's strings."

Tara laughed a bit. "You make him sound like Al Capone," she said.

He glanced over at her. "In a way, he is. When I said they have their hands into everything, I do mean everything, including drug smuggling and murder." Jacob sat silent for a moment.

Tara waited, but he did not elaborate. "Well, go on," she ordered. "Don't stop now. I'm going to need to know what to expect when we meet him."

Jacob shook his head as if to clear away bad memories. "A couple years back, Seattle PD arrested a bunch of drug smugglers. We interrogated them for hours. One of them wanted to make a deal. He said he could provide information on who was running the smuggling operation, and indicated the Sloan's. While in the cell overnight, all of them died. There were no discernible marks. The ME said it was a mystery. He couldn't explain it. It was as if they all just stopped breathing suddenly. Quite the coincidence if you ask me."

"And you think the Sloan's had something to do with it?"

"Everyone knew the Sloan's had something to do with it, they just couldn't prove it. They are bad news. We have tried to get an undercover unit to break into Dominic's inner circle for years, but they haven't even made a dent in his operation. I'm telling you, Al Capone could have learned a thing or two from Dominic."

They arrived at 3025 Magnolia Boulevard West shortly after midnight. A huge red brick wall enclosed the house. The entranceway was only accessible through a thick iron gate with two dragons on either side. Jacob pulled up to the gate. A security camera gleamed down at him. He waved to it. It did nothing in return to acknowledge his presence.

A small silver intercom located on the brick wall sprang to life. "Can I help you?" said a silky voice that emanated from the intercom.

"Detectives Moore and Bancroft here to see Dominic Sloan."

"Regarding?" asked the voice.

"His son, Eric," Jacob answered. The line went dead. A moment later, the dragon gate parted inward. Jacob followed the smooth pathway up to the front of the house.

Tara gasped at the sight of the place. It was not a house, but a small palace. It was literally the biggest house she had ever seen, layered with stories and wings. It too was made out of brick, with large smoked glass windows sporadically spaced around the walls. The entranceway had marble columns attached to a Greek archway that covered the pavement leading to the large white front door. Two overly large stone basins with fire protruding from the inside were stationed on either side of the door.

"It pays to be rich," Tara said in wonder.

"It pays to be a thug," Jacob said absently. They got out of the car and walked under the archway to the door. Jacob pushed a small doorbell and a pleasant choir of chimes went off faintly inside the house.

An older man dressed in a suit answered the door. His hair was disheveled and gray. He was old, and his skin seemed to hang off his bones, especially around the jaw line. Wrinkles were set around his sluggish eyes and forehead. He was also stooped over, as if it hurt to stand up right.

"Detective Moore here," Jacob told him. "This is detective Bancroft." Jacob took out his badge and showed it to the old man. Tara copied Jacob. The man just looked at the badges, and then back at them. Satisfied they were who they claimed to be, he opened the door wider and ushered them inside the Foyer.

"This way," he whispered, and slowly walked toward the back of the house.

While Tara was impressed with the outside of the house, it was nothing compared to the beauty of the inside. The interior seemed to be filled with marble statues. A giant diamond chandelier hung from the ceiling, sending sparkles of light on the white walls. The floor was marble, except for the red carpet that seemed to lead to every door. Paintings from famous artists hung decoratively in large wooden frames.

Tara and Jacob followed the old man through the hallway, passing sleek white painted doors. He stopped in front of a double paneled door and opened it. Tara and Jacob stepped inside. "Mr. Sloan will be with you momentarily," he spoke softly. He bowed slightly and shut the door behind him.

Tara looked around at the room they were in. The man had led them into a huge library. The walls were covered with books that led up to the ceiling. Another chandelier hung in the center, but not quite as big as the one in the Foyer. An Iron circular stairway led up three stories to the different levels of the room. A small fire was set in the fireplace located at the back wall. In front of the fireplace stood three red arm chairs around a circular mahogany coffee table.

Tara was in awe. She felt like she had stepped into another world. It would take her half her life to read a quarter of the books. The room was cozy and she felt she could move in and live there for the rest of her life.

"This is amazing," she muttered to herself.

"The glamour gets old after a while," Jacob assured her, as if knowing something of this life himself.

"I'm sure it would, after a while, but I've never seen so many books owned by one person before." She looked around again, and smiled. She loved reading, but never really found the time anymore.

"You like it?" echoed a deep voice throughout the room. Tara jumped at the voice and looked around. Upon the second floor stood a man in a red silk robe. His hair was blonde and curly, but cut just above his ears. Even from far away, Tara could see the green of his eyes shine like emeralds. His skin was luminously pale.

"You startled me," Tara spoke up to him.

"I'm sorry for that," the man replied, moving down the stairway. "I was just doing some light reading in the stacks and lost track of time. Nice to see you again, Detective Moore."

Jacob nodded to the man. "Mr. Sloan, this is Detective Bancroft."

Mr. Sloan stopped in front of them. He held out a bony hand to Tara, who took it, ready to shake, but instead, he leaned forward and kissed her hand. "Pleasure Detective," he spoke into her hand, sending goose bumps up her arm. She withdrew her hand and halted a shudder.

"I'm afraid we have some bad news, Mr. Sloan," Jacob interrupted. Dominic moved gracefully to one of the armchairs and gestured for them to sit as well. They complied.

"I'm sorry about your old partner," Mr. Sloan said. "Natasha, wasn't it? She was a good woman, from what I am told."

Jacob turned a deep shade of red. "Yes, she was," he replied coldly. "But I didn't come here to discuss that." He took in a deep breath like Tara did in Chief Martinez's office earlier.

"Quite right," Dominic said. " You came here about Eric." He pursed his lips. "Tell me, Detective, what has he done now?"

Tara hated this part. She hated telling the families they lost a loved one. She was always the reason families cried, because she was always the one to inform them of their loss. "Mr. Sloan, I'm sorry to have to tell you this..." she started.

"Eric's dead," Jacob blurted out. Tara turned her head to him, curtly.

Dominic Sloan arched an eyebrow. "Are you sure about that?" he asked him.

"Quite sure, sir." Jacob replied. "Sorry for your loss," he told him, but his tone was harsh. Tara studied both of them. Clearly, they had some sort of history, and she guessed it had to do with his partner. If Jacob had some kind of vendetta against the Sloan's, then he wouldn't be able to think objectively. He should be removed from the case. She made a mental note to talk to him about it later.

Dominic closed his eyes and leaned back in his chair. Tears formed around the closed eyelids. "How did it happen?" he asked.

"We found his body at Gold's gym," Tara told him. "I'm sorry sir, but he, ... he was murdered." Tara watched his reaction. He stayed remarkably still and silent. She felt bad for him, even if what Jacob said about him being a crime boss was true. No one deserves to outlive their son.

A tear dripped from his eye down onto his silk robe. It quickly absorbed it and made a small dark spot on the collar. "My Eric," he whispered.

"I know this is soon, sir, but can you think of anyone who would want to hurt your son?" Tara asked. "Any personal enemies?"

Dominic composed himself. Without opening his eyes, he spoke. "We Sloan's have many enemies. I assure you, detective, the list is quite long."

Jacob leaned forward, placing his elbows on his knees. "Has anyone stood out recently above the rest?"

Dominic stayed silent for a while. His pale skin made him look like he was sleeping peacefully, or dead. "There is no one I can think of that would be brave enough to harm my family."

Tara didn't quite know how to take that statement. Was he admitting harm to someone who would hurt his family? Surely not with two detectives in the room.

"Mr. Sloan," she persisted. "Who does your son usually hang around with?"

"He has many friends," he answered vaguely. "But none of them could have done this, I assure you."

"How can you be so sure," Tara asked.

Dominic opened his eyes and a smile grew upon his sleek white face. "Trust me, Detective, I am sure." The smile made Dominic look like a plastic china doll, flawless and beautiful. It was unnerving and sent a shudder down her spine.

Jacob cleared his throat loudly, and she realized she was staring at Mr. Sloan's features. She shook her head and gazed elsewhere.

"Mr. Sloan," Jacob spoke. "Did Eric have a girlfriend?"

Dominic laughed. "If you could call it that." Dominic was still staring at Tara as he spoke.

"Please elaborate," Jacob said. He didn't like the way Mr. Sloan was fixed on Tara. A moment later, Dominic looked at Jacob.

"Her name is Kenzie. Kenzie Wright." Mr. Sloan leaned forward and spoke just above a whisper. "A vile thing if I do say so myself. I would have hoped his tastes would improve over the years, but I guess I will never know."

A knock at the door made Tara jump in her seat. She peered over her shoulder as the door opened and a beautiful young girl in a silk blue robe walked into the room. She had similar features to Eric. Long, curly blonde hair hung in rivulets around her slender shoulders. She had flawless pale skin that offset her full red lips and bright blue eyes. She too looked just like a china doll.

"Sorry to disturb you, father," she apologized. "I just wanted to wish you a good night before heading to bed." Her voice was soft and pleasant. She turned to leave but Mr. Sloan called her over.

"Bethany, please stay. This concerns you, too," he informed her. A surprised look appeared on her flawless features. She trotted over to him without glancing at the detectives. Dominic stood up and gently grabbed her hand. "Bethany, allow me to introduce Detectives Bancroft and Moore."

Bethany curtseyed slightly, "How do you do?"

"Ma'am," Jacob nodded. Tara did the same.

"Why are they here, father?" she asked him quietly. Dominic's features saddened. Another tear formed in his eye.

"They are investigating the death of.... the death of your brother," he choked out. Bethany's eyes widened. Mr. Sloan hugged his daughter tightly.

"What do you mean?" she asked. "Eric's not dead. I spoke to him this morning!"

Dominic kissed her on her forehead. "I'm sorry, sweetheart, but your brother has passed away today." Dominic held on tight to Bethany, as she began to cry. Tara felt like crying herself. She hated seeing family members cry. She looked down and felt wrong for being there. Families should be able to grieve privately without interference from complete strangers.

Bethany's muffled sobs ended the interview. Dominic told them that any questions he would surely answer in the morning, but asked that they be allowed to grieve this night. On the way out, the old man who greeted them at the door thanked them for coming and shut the door behind them.

"Well that was a bust," Tara told her partner as she climbed into his car.

"Not necessarily," he replied. "We know the name of Eric's girlfriend. Maybe she can give us more information." He started the car and drove off the property. Tara glanced at her watch. It was nearly 1:30am and she hadn't eaten anything all day. She was tired and would love to go home and sleep, but they still had to get the autopsy report from Yvette.

"Do you think the girlfriend had something to do with it?"

"I don't know," he told her honestly. "But being that we found the victim in the woman's bathroom, I'm guessing a woman had something to do with it. They go in for a little rough and tumble in the stall, they fight, she stabs him in the back."

Tara played the scene in her head. "I can see that. But the girl had to be very strong in order to jab a table leg through his back." She thought of the table leg. "At the gym, there was no table that matched the leg. That means that someone transported it there, suggesting premeditation."

"In any case," Jacob thought aloud. "Let's see what Yvette has to say."

They drove in silence the rest of the way, both lost in their own thoughts. Tara went over possibilities of how Jacob and Dominic Sloan knew each other. She wasn't sure if she should bring it up. She decided that if it comes up in conversation later, so be it. So far, the connection had not deterred Jacob from doing his job. And she had to admit, she did like him much more now than when they first met. She was a firm believer in privacy. As the saying goes, let sleeping dogs lie.

Chapter 4

By the time Tara was headed home, it was already 3:30 a.m. Yvette King didn't have anything new to report about the death of Eric Sloan. The official cause of death was a puncture wound between his 6th and 7th thoracic vertebrae, puncturing the lungs and heart. They already had the murder weapon, but what they didn't know at the gym was that the table leg had been sharpened down to a point.

Yvette X-rayed the body, but found nothing. She checked for trace elements on the clothing and skin, ran a tox screen, and washed him down thoroughly. There was nothing on the body or clothes, nothing abnormal in Eric's system, and his body was pearly white. Everything led to a dead end.

The case started to unnerve Tara greatly. Who doesn't leave any evidence behind? Professional killers and assassins, that's who. She felt she didn't know enough about the major players in Seattle to properly form an opinion on who could hire someone with that unique skill set. After a long and arduous day, Tara was so ready to crawl into bed and sleep.

"Did you find a place to stay?" Jacob asked her.

"I did," she replied. "It's not that far from here, actually. I found an apartment at The Parc in Belltown.

Jacob looked surprised. "My, my, aren't we fancy," he joked. "That place has got to be expensive."

Tara laughed. "Yes, but it's within walking distance to the precinct. All my stuff is in transit right now, including my car."

"Oh," he replied. "Gotchya." Jacob looked at his watch. "Well, it's late. Would you like a lift home?"

Tara thought about it for a moment. A ride did mean she would be home quicker, but she had to get used to the walk to and from work. Her car, along with the rest of her things, wouldn't be in Seattle for another week or so. She declined the offer.

"Thanks anyway, but I need to clear my head," she informed him. They said their goodbyes and parted ways. She stepped out the front door and into the streets of Seattle.

She went over the case in her head while passing dimly lit streets. Homeless folks, trying to stay warm, were bundled up in raggedy blankets at some of the buildings entryways. The nightlife had dwindled down like a fire burning its last embers.

Who would have enough strength to drive a table leg into Eric's back? She wondered. Whoever it was, was very strong. And smart too. Deleting the recording, leaving no evidence behind. Although she was a woman, she didn't believe a girl could have done this. We just don't possess the upper body strength to drive a table leg through someone's back.

But it had been sharpened, she argued with herself. A woman with a sharp instrument could jab another without any problem. She tried to put the pieces together. Eric was stabbed in the woman's bathroom, so it does stand to reason that a woman was the murderer. Even if the table leg hadn't been sharpened, a woman angry and on drugs could have completed the act.

Drugs had an adverse effect on the mind. She hadn't witnessed it herself, but her colleagues back in Phoenix had told her of a couple cases where they arrested coke addicts. In a fit of rage, they were as strong as oxen. Although drugs were involved, it caused them to do some insanely incredible feats. That, mixed with adrenaline, and anything was possible.

Snap!

Tara whipped around at the sound but found no one. She peered over at the other side of the street, and saw darkened buildings. The wind whirled lightly, causing goose bumps to crawl on her skin and down her back. She shivered and turned back toward home.

"Must be my imagination," she whispered to herself. She walked on, glancing at the green street sign nailed to a thin post. It read Blanchard. Just a few more blocks and I'll be home.

Faint footsteps echoed down the street behind her. She peered over her shoulder, but no one was there. Either fear or paranoia swept over her like a blanket. She picked up the pace. She left her badge and gun in Jacob's office, which she now regretted. She searched her pockets for any type of weapon, just in case. All she found was her keys and phone. She put her keys in between her fingers, making sure that each key stuck out like a claw.

The footsteps grew louder and closer. She started to run. Just a few more blocks and she would be home. The footsteps seemed to get closer, and faster. She was at a full sprint now. The wind whipped her face as she ran, but she didn't care. Her chest started to hurt as she ran through the streets. She didn't dare look behind her for fear that whoever was chasing her was right on her heals.

Someone had pushed her hard in the back. She lost her momentum and fell, hitting the concrete hard with a crack. Pain shot out from her head. She screamed in pain as someone grabbed her ankle and dragged her backward. She kicked out with her other foot, but found nothing.

Her attacker dragged her into a dark alley. Terror filled her as she was swallowed up by the darkness of the alleyway. Hands flipped her over and a dark silhouette of a man loomed over her. She lashed out with her keys, scratching the man in the face. She heard him let out a howl of pain.

She tried to get up, but the man pushed her down. He grabbed her head and knocked it into the ground. Pain burst through her entire body and she let out a scream. Her eyes filled with white spots. She could feel blood trickle out from the back of her head.

The dark shadow of her attacker punched her in the stomach. The air was instantly gone. Tara couldn't breathe. she clutched her stomach as hard as she could, willing herself to take in air. The man throttled her, grabbing her wrists with one hand and trying to unbuckle his belt with the other. She buckled in every direction, trying to push him off, but it was no use. He was strong.

"Get off her," demanded a voice from the entryway of the alley. Tara heard that voice before, but couldn't place it through the pain. The man did not obey.

"Beat it, kid, or you're next," her assailant threatened. Tara still buckled, but the man was strong.

"I'd like to see you try," the kid retorted, stepping into the alleyway.

The attacker punched Tara hard in the temple, and drowsiness threatened to take her. She had to stay awake. Her life depended on it. She couldn't move anymore; the pain was too much. Darkness beckoned her, but she forced herself to stay conscious.

The man got up and produced an object from his jacket pocket. He flipped it and a blade popped out. "You asked for it, kid," he yelled. He lunged at the girl, but she was quick, dodging the attack easily. The girl slammed her palm into his nose and Tara heard a crack. The man screamed in pain, and the girl kicked him in the groin.

The man dropped the blade and fell to his knees. One of his hands clutched his groin as the other shot to his nose. Blood flowed down the man's face and through his fingers.

"You bitch," he managed to stammer out. "You broke my nose!"

The girl laughed hysterically. "Be grateful that is all I did," she stammered back, and walked over to Tara. As she bent down, Tara noticed the whiteness of her skin and the tinge of bright blue eyes. Blonde curly hair fell forward, blocking the view of her rescuer, but there was no mistaking who it was. Tara finally recognized her savior. It was Bethany Sloan.

Bethany helped Tara to her feet and wrapped one arm around her neck for support. With her right arm, she grabbed Tara's side and ushered her slowly toward the alley entranceway. They were almost out when the man attacked them from behind. Tara fell back down, but braced herself with her right hand.

When she looked up, she saw the man strangling Bethany. Tara screamed and crawled toward her to help in any way that she could. That was when Bethany's face changed. Her flawless features contorted into something grotesque and monstrous. Her silky smooth skin turned blotchy and grey. Her bright blue eyes darkened and there was no white at all. Her lips parted, revealing sharp white teeth, like talons.

The man looked shocked and uttered an "Ugh," before Bethany sank her teeth into his neck, ripping out his throat.

Tara passed out.

Chapter 5

Tara dreamed. She was standing in a large ballroom dressed in her uniform. Bodies dressed in fancy suits and elegant ball gowns lay on the marble floor. Their faces were hidden behind masks.

She looked around and noticed Mr. Sloan sitting on a golden rimmed throne. He spoke to her, but she couldn't hear the words. A hand squeezed her shoulder and flipped her around. She screamed as she came face to face with a giant crow. It cawed loudly.

She awoke with a fright. She shot straight up and instantly felt dizzy. She laid back down and waited for the dizziness to recede. Her eyes searched her surroundings. She didn't recognize the place. She reached up and felt the back of her head. It had been bandaged.

She remembered being attacked. The man had caused her great pain. He tried to rape her, but someone intervened. Who? She couldn't remember.

She forced herself to sit up, causing her stomach to hurt. Her hands found her abdomen and rubbed lightly. That was when she noticed she was not in her own clothes. She was dressed in a silk purple robe.

She saw that she was sitting on a four post mahogany bed in a large spacious room. A nightstand stood next to the bed with the wallet, keys, and phone. A glass of water sat in the middle of the stand with a small note in front that said, "Drink."

The walls were painted a cerulean blue and held large framed artwork from Leonardo da Vinci. A replica of the Mona Lisa smirked at her, as if she was mocking Tara. It was creepy.

Tara threw off the feathered duvet and forced herself to get to her feet. As she scanned the room further, she noticed her clothes were folded neatly on a Victorian styled chair. She rushed over to them and changed as quickly as she could. It was difficult. Pain lashed out every time she moved, but she forced herself through it.

A small clock on the wall read 7:30. She must not have slept long. She remembered leaving Jacob's office around 3:30, and the attack happened shortly after. She shook her head and willed the memories away. First things first.

She stuffed her pockets with her belongings and crept to the door. She tried the handle, and to her surprise, it was not locked. She tiptoed through it as quietly as she could. She was now standing in a long hallway with a red carpet that led to many different doorways. A hint of recognition passed through her.

This is the Sloan's house, she thought. And then it all came back to her. The memories hit her like a truck and she stumbled. She remembered the attack fully. Bethany had saved her. They were almost out of the alley when the man attacked again. Her face changed into some kind of monster. She bit him!

Fear swept over her again. Her heart raced at the memories. She had to get out of there. She stumbled to the nearest door and turn the knob, but it was locked. She tried another, and another, but they were all locked. She tried the door at the end of the hallway, and alas, it opened. She burst through it into another long hallway.

She remembered thinking that the house was exquisite. Now it just seemed creepy. Who has this many hallways? She wondered. She tried more doors until she found one that wasn't locked. She stepped through and ended up on the second floor of the library where she and Jacob had first met Mr. Sloan.

Voices were echoing through the room. She couldn't make out what they were saying. She crept forward, willing herself to be as quiet as a mouse. The voices became clearer.

"I've done what I can for her," a woman's voice said. Tara didn't recognize it. "She will be fine in a day or two, if she drinks the healing salve."

"Why didn't you just force her?" a voice she did recognize asked. It was Bethany Sloan.

The woman tsked tsked. "We do not force people to do anything. It must be her choice and her choice alone."

Another voice spoke. This time, a male's voice. "You witches are so admirable. How quaint." The voice seemed to mock the woman. Tara recognized the voice as Mr. Sloan.

"You asked for my help, and I gave it to you. Now, if there is nothing else, I'll show myself out." The woman's footsteps were loud as she walked to the door.

"Thank you, Vita," Bethany told her. "I appreciate it."

The woman, Vita, spoke softly. "I hope this proves that we had nothing to do with Eric. We do not harm for our own personal gain."

Mr. Sloan spoke. "I don't believe you and your kind had anything to do with his death. But spread the word. I will find out."

The door closed behind Vita and she was gone. "You should have left her in the alley, child," Mr. Sloan said.

"But daddy, I had to bring her here," Bethany told her father. "She surely would have died!"

"Then she'd have died! That is the natural order of things in their world. How many times do I have to tell you? We do not interfere in their affairs"

"Oh please," Bethany stammered. "Don't act like you don't interfere. You have connections into everything going on in Seattle. You even control the Mayor," she argued back.

"Don't you sass me, girl," he warned her. "What I do is for the good of our family and our kind. Not for some meat stick we don't even know."

"You would have done the same if you saw what the man was trying to do!"

Mr. Sloan laughed. "I highly doubt that."

Bethany whispered lowly. "Mother would have done it."

The Sloan's stood there staring at each other. Mr. Sloan seemed lost for words. It was Bethany who broke the silence. "I'm sorry, daddy. I didn't mean to bring her up."

Mr. Sloan sighed heavily. "Listen to me, Bethany. I like that you, even with our nature, have a good heart. But I already lost a wife, and a son. I don't want to lose you too."

"You won't," she promised. "I'm not attracted to Ogres anyway." Tara was shocked. Did she say ogres? She must have misunderstood.

"We don't know that they had anything to do with it. Promise me, Bethany, that you will stay away from them."

"I can't just sit back and do nothing," she told him. "He was my brother!"

"Promise me, girl!" Sloan demanded. "You will not do anything until we know for sure who is to blame."

Bethany stayed quiet for a moment. She reluctantly promised her father. "She could help," Bethany said, changing the subject. "She has the law on her side, and she can go places we can't."

Mr. Sloan chuckled softly. "I suppose that's true, since she is listening to us right now." Mr. Sloan glanced up to where Tara stood hidden behind the stacks. "You can come down, Detective."

A tinge of fear threatened to engulf her. She pushed it aside and strolled out from her hiding place. She saw both Bethany and Dominic on their feet staring up at her. Bethany raised her hands, and in a calming voice spoke. "It's okay," she said, stepping forward. "You're safe here."

Tara followed the path to the iron stairway and stepped down slowly. "How are you feeling?" Mr. Sloan asked.

She didn't know how to answer that. So many things were going through her head. It was overwhelming. "I'm okay, considering," she replied. "Did you say Ogres?"

Bethany and her father exchanged looks. "We have much to discuss, " Mr. Sloan told her.

Tara snorted. "Yeah, like who the hell are you people!"

Bethany smiled at that. When she spoke, it was to her dad. "I think it's best if I tell her alone." Mr. Sloan rolled his eyes, which Tara thought was such a funny gesture. It made the whole situation seem ridiculous.

"Fine," he conceded. "But she will be your responsibility," he said sternly. Dominic looked at Tara with those emerald green eyes and bowed. "I shall take my leave. Good day, Detective Bancroft," and then he was just gone.

Tara gasped! "How did he do that?" she asked. She had never seen someone just disappear before. She was stunned.

Bethany let out a small laugh. "You humans," she replied. "So full of wonder. It never seizes to amaze me."

Tara wasn't sure if she was being mocked or not. "What do you mean," she asked?

Bethany explained. "You humans always have a gift for excitement. I find it one of your highest qualities. I haven't felt that in a very long time."

Tara stood mystified. She couldn't believe what she was hearing. "You mean..., you don't mean to say, ... You're not human?"

Bethany giggled. "No, Ms. Bancroft. I am not." Bethany sat down in one of the red arm chairs and leaned back. "I was once, but that was a very long time ago."

Tara backed up slowly. She didn't know how to take this news. Suddenly she wished she was back in Phoenix, dealing with Kenneth and living her life how she used to.

Bethany raised her hands in a gesture of peace. "It's okay. As I've said, you are safe here. No one will harm you, I assure you." she then gestured to one of the armchairs. "Would you like to sit?"

"I think I'm good. Over here," Tara told her. She wanted out of the room and away from the Sloan's.

Bethany smiled again, showing pearly white teeth. "Suit yourself," she said. The chair seemed to engulf her.

"What are you?" Tara blurted out.

Bethany raised her eyes to Tara and whispered softly. "I'm a vampire, Detective." Tara's eyes widened. She remembered seeing Bethany's face contort into a monstrous figure. She saw her sink her teeth into the man's neck. Fear pricked at her head, which caused it to burst with pain. She had to get out of there.

Tara bolted to the door. Bethany was suddenly there in front of her blocking the entrance. Tara screamed and ran back behind an arm chair, using it as a type of shield. Bethany sighed.

"Please, Ms. Bancroft, let me explain. I swear, afterward, you are free to go." She walked slowly toward Tara. "As I said, no harm will come to you."

Tara couldn't get past the vampire comment. They aren't real! This must be a dream. She slapped herself hard on the cheek, but she didn't wake up. She pinched the skin on her arm, but that didn't help either.

"Think for a moment, Detective," Bethany said. "If I wanted to harm you, why would I save your life? Why would I intervene when that guy attacked you? If you were in any danger, why would I put you in a spare bedroom and dress your wounds?"

She did have a point. Why go to all this trouble if the end result was just to kill her? It didn't make sense. Tara forced herself to calm down. She breathed in heavily, and exhaled slowly.

Bethany sat back down and motioned for Tara to sit as well. Tara thought about it. "So, I listen to your story, then I am free to go?"

Bethany nodded. "I promise," she swore. She placed her arms in her lap and crossed her ankles over each other. The end result made her look like a little doll again, beautiful and elegant. Tara walked around the chair at a glacial pace. She sat down and placed her hands in her lap.

Both of them sat in silence for a moment. "Well?" Tara asked. "Let's hear this story."

Bethany smiled and shook her head slightly. "My family members were born human. My father was born in London back in 1625 to a wealthy aristocratic family. He went to the finest schools, and had the finest things. He never had to work A day in his life.

"My mother grew up exactly the opposite. She was poor, wasn't able to go to school, and had to work hard. All her wages, if you could call it that, went to her family. She was a bread baker.

"One night, while my father was out getting drunk, he stumbled upon her getting raped, quite like the scene that played out earlier this morning. My father intervened of course, and although drunk, was able to fight off her assailant. He introduced himself and found out her name was Maria Behn. That same year, they got married.

"But life was different back then, especially for women. They were to be house maidens and play traditional roles. Men at the time believed women were nothing more than objects, forced to do what the man wanted. Just another piece of property. They believed that woman didn't have the brain capacity to be intelligent because of their smaller frames."

Tara interrupted. "I get that a lot in my profession even now. Chauvinists pigs still haunt the world today," she replied, pursing her lips.

Bethany grinned. "You can imagine then what my mother had to endure. It wasn't necessarily my father. He loved her dearly and couldn't deny her anything. He would have done anything to make her happy. Still would, if she was still alive today," Bethany trailed off, thinking of sadder times.

"Sorry for your loss," Tara said, and she meant it. Both her parents died when she was very young, so she knew what it was like to be without her parents. No matter how much time has passed, you never truly get over it.

Bethany continued. "My mother gave birth to my brother Eric back in 1644. I was born in 1649. We were raised properly, and were a proper family. At least in public anyway. My mother wanted more than just serving as the house maid and mother of children. She wanted equality. She wanted to be treated like a man, with all the benefits that came with it.

"Over the years that passed, my mother learned to read and write. She studied everything she could, from mathematics, to languages. She studied all about different cultures and learned of medicines and herbs, all behind closed doors, of course."

"Good for her," Tara interjected. "She learned how to fight the system."

"Yes, and no," Bethany told her. "My father let her learn these things, but warned her about telling anyone. You see, a strange paranoia seemed to sweep through the town. Rumors of witchcraft were whispered in the streets. People were frightened by anything during that time. It was much different than today.

"My father made her promise only to study and learn things behind closed doors. Out in public, she was to be the proper housewife for fear of retaliation. She agreed, and things were good for a while. " she trailed off again.

Tara heard the crackling of the fire behind her. The light from the fire cast dancing shadows over Bethany's smooth face. "So, what happened," Tara asked?

"The Black Death happened. I believe history calls it the Bubonic Plague. Living conditions were harsh in London, and people were dirty. Sewage and pollution were in the streets and in our towns water. That drew the rats to the city. But times being as they were, people were superstitious. People dying of the plague had to be because of witchcraft. No one knew anything of viruses or germs.

"People were dying in the streets. Hysteria spread like wilddfire. People pointed fingers to anyone who had crossed them in the past. All one had to do was utter witch, and they were tested. It was a horrible time.

"My family was not so superstitious as the rest. My mother taught my brother and I many things, about medicine and herbs. About different cultures. We learned more from her than in school. That was until my brother became sick."

Tara sat in rapt attention. She was enthralled with the story. "Are you saying that your brother came down with the plague?"

"I believe it was, yes," Bethany answered. "My mother went to the local apothecary, and gathered many herbs and medicines to help treat him. She saved his life with simple medicines she learned from her studies.

"But the locals knew of Eric and his sickness. When he walked out cured, the streets of London exploded with gossip. They accused my mother of witchcraft, and even went as far as saying that she started the plague herself.

"In May of 1665, men came in the middle of the night and took her away. My father and brother tried to fight them off but they threatened to kill us all. She wasn't given a trial like the rest of the accused. She was simply tried as a witch. A large spectacle was gathered around a fire pit. They tied her to a wooden post and burned her alive, all in front of the good citizens of London."

Tears threatened to break from her eyes but Bethany held them back. Tara sat there in utter shock. She couldn't believe what the Sloan's had to go through. No one should have to lose a family member in that manner, no matter who it was. "I'm so sorry," Tara whispered.

Bethany closed her eyes and leaned back in the chair again. "Thank you, Detective. But it was a long time ago."

"Still," Tara replied, "No one should lose a mother that way."

Bethany nodded and continued with the story. "My father was never the same after that. He made us promise to be normal. He wouldn't be able to live with himself if something happened to us as well. He spent most of his nights drinking in taverns and stumbling home before passing out in his own vomit. I took on the responsibilities of the house and my brother took care of me. It was a dark time for us all.

"The death of my mother didn't end the plague. It spread quicker and deadlier throughout the streets. You couldn't walk anywhere without passing a dead body back in those days. The smell was... unpleasant.

"Criminals of all sorts came out of the woodwork. Pickpockets and thieves were around every corner, waiting for someone to drop dead so they could use or sell their stuff. London was a bad place to be at the time.

"The stench of death and decay drew creatures of myths and stories as well. My father, on his way home from the neighboring tavern, ran into three such creatures. Two of them were men, and one a female. They attacked him and sucked his blood. My father didn't fight, in fact, he wished for death. He couldn't be without my mother.

"The woman vampire took pity on him and saved him. She turned him and he didn't come home that night. My brother and I searched for him, worried that he lost his way, or a vagabond got him. The townsfolk did nothing to help. They still questioned our family, remembering my mother burning on the pyre. They thought since death was still running rampant in the streets, that we too must be to blame. They shunned us.

"The next night, my father came home, to our relief. He was no longer drunk but a pasty white version of himself. He brought home three visitors. I did my best to feed them some soup we had, but they seemed uninterested.

"We questioned my father on his whereabouts, but he didn't answer. As the night went on, the men and woman changed. They were horribly disfigured. My brother and I tried to run, but they were too fast. My father intervened, and saved us. He turned us into vampires himself."

Tara blinked for the first time in what seemed like ages. "So you've been a vampire all this time?"

"Yes. That was in Autumn of 1665, just a few short months after my mother's death. I was 17 when I died, but last week I celebrated my 349th death day."

"Wow," Tara said, stunned. She took it all in. It was overwhelming to say the least. Many questions filled her head, and a small headache started to build. She didn't know where to start. "Who were the vampires?"

"They belonged to a sect out of England. Margarete was the woman's name. I believe she now is in control of the sect there. The other two, Francis and Henry, perished in the Great Fire of London. We almost perished as well in that fire, but we escaped and boarded a ship for the Americas. But I get ahead of myself," she told Tara. "I will tell it as it happened."

Tara nodded and sat straight, waiting for Bethany to continue.

"We awoke the next night with a hunger we had never felt before. The three vampires explained that the hunger was for blood. Blood is the essence of life, and since we were technically dead, we needed life to survive. Blood provided that for us. My brother hated my father for what he had done to us. I understood, he did it to save us, but my brother said he turned us into monsters. Nevertheless, he still needed to feed.

"The three used us because of our status. We were wealthy, and despite what the towns folk may have thought, my dad did hold power over other aristocrats and gentlemen. The three wanted to use that power to their own benefit. They taught us how to hunt and feed properly. They taught us how to survive, and in return, we provided them shelter and status among the citizens, claiming they were cousins who came to stay with us.

"They were ruthless on the kills. We weren't used to being so hurtful. I suspect our upbringing had something to do with it. Although we were vampires, we still felt with human emotion. It always pained us to have to take a human life. After a while, we learned to take just what we needed and erase their memories.

"The three didn't mind killing. They racked up bodies all over London. the townsfolk started to notice that it wasn't just the plague or witchcraft they had to deal with. They saw their loved one's dead with puncture wounds on their neck or wrists. They put the pieces together. They noticed how pale our skins were, how pale our cousins were. Rumors, yet again about our family, floated through the streets. We decided to leave London, and our 'cousins' and set out on our own before something happened.

"On the day we were to board a ship, the folks of London set our house ablaze. They didn't foresee that high wind later that day, and the fire spread rapidly to other buildings. We were lucky to escape. But we did hear Henry and Francis were not so lucky. Margarete fled London the night before on urgent business, or she might have been caught in the fire as well. We boarded the ship and it set sail to Virginia.

"We didn't stay in any place too long, for fear of the citizens becoming wise and history repeating itself. We spent years moving from place to place. We kept our heads down and moved with other settlers."

"So, what made you decide to stay in Seattle?" Tara asked.

"We were tired of moving. My brother and father fought all the time over this. We decided to put it to a vote. I was the deciding factor. We were to set up roots. When settlers moved to what was once called New York Alki, we traveled over the Elliot bay and met the Duwamish leader, Sealth.

"He instantly knew what we were right from the start. Instead of fear, though, he greeted us with kindness. His tribe was not all that they appeared to be either. They were what modern day legends call werewolves."

"Wait, what?" Tara asked, eyes full of excitement. "Werewolves are real as well?" Bethany nodded her head. "Any other things I should know about?"

Bethany giggled a little, "There are all forms of supernatural creatures, detective. But here in Seattle, we have a total of six."

Tara's eyes brightened again. "Six types! You've got to be shitting me."

Bethany shook her head. "Afraid not, detective. You see, we learned something from the Duwamish tribe. The land Seattle is built on holds great power, a mystical energy of sorts. Supernatural beings are attracted to it, like moths to a flame. They are wanting to use that power for their own personal gain. The Duwamish tribe used to be in charge of it, but my family has been in control of that power for decades. I believe that is why my brother was murdered."

"What do you mean?" Tara inquired.

Bethany stood up and started pacing the back and forth. "I believe someone is making a play for the energy that we control. Someone cunning and powerful. My family has been the leader of the Seattle supernatural forces for years, and not all of them are happy about that. I believe someone is trying to overthrow us."

Tara wrapped her head around the conversation. She tried to see the logic in what Bethany claimed was the reason Eric Sloan was murdered. She didn't know enough about who the players were or enough about this great power Bethany spoke of.

"So, you think that your brother was killed as a way to, what? Keep you and your family off guard while they go after this mystical energy?"

"I don't know," Bethany admitted. "All I know is that we've had a peace treaty with the neighboring factions for decades. Someone broke that treaty yesterday."

"How can you be so sure it was someone supernatural who killed him?" Tara asked.

Bethany explained. "If he had been shot, or hung, or stabbed with a knife, or hell, even ran over, he'd still be alive. We have an uncanny ability to heal. A stake through the heart, fire, or beheading are the only ways I know that can kill a vampire."

Tara remembered at the coroner's office when Yvette said that the table leg had been sharpened to a point. Someone did know who Eric was, and was strong enough to drive it through his back. Maybe she was looking for someone supernatural. She decided to get as many facts as she could.

"What about garlic," Tara asked.

"That is a ridiculous rumor. I don't know why anyone would be afraid of garlic."

"What about sunlight? Your brother was at the gym yesterday. How could he be there if he is a vampire? Don't you guys thrive at night?"

Bethany smiled, "Aw, yes. The sunlight. We do, unfortunately, have to stay in the shadows, mostly. We can, and have endured sunlight in the past, but in short bursts or it would be fatal. Yesterday was an overcast kind of day, with no direct sunlight. He was perfectly safe."

Tara made a mental note of that. "And the other factions you say are here in Seattle? Who are they?" Tara asked.

"Well, two you already know. There are the vampires and werewolves. But there are also Ogres, Witches, Shapeshifters, and Sirens."

Tara stayed silent for a while. All this information was overwhelming her. It was completely mind-boggling to think that these things were real. How is it that no one knows?

Bethany watched Tara's expressions closely. "You still seem confused, detective."

Tara shook her head, "No, it's just.... I've spent my whole career trying to put the bad guys away. I have always been an investigator and believed in science and facts, not witchcraft and vampires. I am 28 years old, and I have never come across any supernatural beings before. How is it possible that no one knows anything about this?"

Bethany gave her an encouraging smile. "We altered beings, as you will, have spent our lives hiding who we are. We like to stay hidden for fear of what the world might do. I'm sure you have met at least another supernatural being before you came to Seattle. We are everywhere."

"No way," Tara argued. "I've never seen one, and I've even coordinated with the FBI before."

"It's true," Bethany told her. "But you don't have to take my word for it. Just ask your partner, Detective Moore."

"Wait, are you saying that he knows about this?"

Bethany let out a loud cackle. "Of course he knows about this. He's a shapeshifter!"

Chapter 6

Tara left the Sloan's residence a half hour later. Bethany had talked some more about the factions of monsters and their dwellings. Bethany and her kind were ultimately in charge of all of Seattle, but their territories they controlled were Belltown, Queen Anne, and Magnolia. The wolves, she told her, were in charge of the University District as well as Laurelhurst. The witches controlled Fremont, Ballard, and Greenlake. Capitol hill, First Hill, and Madison Valley were under the control of the Shapeshifters. The Sirens had an affinity for water, and West Seattle was their territory. That left the Ogre's who chose to stay on the outskirts of Seattle near the wooden areas like Columbia City, Mt. Baker, and Rainier Valley.

Tara couldn't believe any of this was true. Her whole life, she had been taught to think rationally, which was put to good use as a detective. She had solved murders of the worst kind in the past, even worked with the FBI on a few occasions, and still never came across anything like this before. Bethany made Seattle sound like some kind of mafia hangout, but instead of gangsters, it was monsters. Some detective she had turned out to be.

The part that really got to her though, was not that monsters were real. She could accept that, given the facts and what she had witnessed with her own two eyes. What bugged her the most was that her partner, Detective Jacob Moore, was one of them. Not a vampire, but a Shapeshifter. She wasn't sure how to react toward this. Could she trust him? Out in the field, she relied on her partner to watch her back, just as her partner would rely on her. How could she trust him now knowing that he wasn't human?

Okay, she told herself, So I've only known him a day, but still. He should have told me. Now that she knew, she wasn't sure how to let him know.

Bethany drove her to her apartment in Belltown. Once inside her own place, she felt safe, secured, and in desperate need of a shower. She reached up and touched the back of her head and could feel dried blood on the bandage. She went to the bathroom and turned the shower knob to hot and pulled. Water came shooting out in long streams.

The hot water felt good on her cold skin. She watched blood and grime trickle down her body and circle the small drain. She basked in the heat of the water and went over every detail of the last 24 hours.

Tara wanted to sleep. Her eyes were heavy and her head felt murky, but it was already 10:30 and she had to work. She got dressed as quickly as she was able and left for the station at a brisk pace.

It was surprisingly warm outside. The sun was high in the cloudless sky and beamed down on her. She closed her eyes and let the sunlight wash over her. Cars zoomed by her building while Seattleites scurried along on their errands. Seattle was alive this morning, and it was thriving greatly.

As Tara walked toward work, she remembered the night's events plain as day. The assault still lingered in her mind. She decided to check out the scene where she was attacked. Five minutes later, she stood in the mouth of the alley where the man had dragged her body.

She searched the area for signs of blood, hair, anything to let her know who the man was. There were none. Bethany had ripped his throat out; there should have been tons of blood, but there was nothing to indicate an assault had even occurred. She did get a faint whiff of bleach. Someone had cleaned up, and cleaned up well.

This led Tara to ask many questions. Who cleaned up the blood? What did Bethany do with the body? Was the attack random or did someone send the man after her? Too many questions and not enough answers.

She put the thoughts out of her mind. She didn't like the idea of someone coming after her, especially if she didn't know the reason behind it. She made a mental note to ask Bethany about the body later. She walked on.

Ten minutes later, Tara arrived at the police station. As she rode the elevator up to the precinct, she realized she hadn't picked an office yet. She decided the first thing she would do would be to ask Chief Martinez for one.

The elevator doors opened with a ding and Tara was greeted by fellow police officers heading out. She smiled meekly in acknowledgment. They smiled back, but their smiles faltered when they saw how she looked. She hurried past before any questions could be asked.

The precinct had been just as busy as the day before. People moved with a sense of urgency. Phones rang off the hook, people were typing up reports and shuffling paperwork into file cabinets and drawers. It was a typical day at the station. Except it wasn't. Tara knew better. Things had changed. It was as if Tara had been let in on a joke and everyone else didn't even know the punch line. There were monsters in Seattle, and no one knew.

Without realizing it, Tara had stopped in front of Police Chief Martinez's office. She knocked hard on the wooden frame.

"Come," he said behind the closed door. She opened it and peered inside. "Detective Bancroft," he stated. "You look like hell!" She instinctively reached up to the red blotch on her forehead. She decided not to divulge the night's events.

"Fell down some stairs as I was heading to my apartment last night," She lied. Whether he believed her or not, he didn't press the issue. Point for him.

"How's the case?" he asked, changing the subject.

She filled him in on the events at the gym and the autopsy. She mentioned that according to Dominik Sloan, Eric had a girlfriend. "We will go talk to her today to see if she knows anything."

"Good, good," he said impatiently. "Keep me informed," he ordered with an almost bored like tone and went back to looking at his files. When she didn't leave, he glanced back up. "Anything else?"

"Yes, Chief. I was wondering where my office was. Detective Moore mentioned you had a few empty spaces."

He raised an arched eyebrow at her. "Talk to Cynthia. She should be able to get you settled," he replied and looked back down. "Shut the door on your way out." She took that as her queue to leave. She thanked him and walked out.

To the far right of his office was a messy desk with a young brunette sitting behind it. She wasn't dressed in a police uniform. Instead, she wore a black skirt that ended just above the knees. Her white blouse was unbuttoned a little too much for Tara's taste and revealed a little too much cleavage. A black opal necklace hung loosely over the blouse.

"Excuse me," Tara spoke to the girl. "Are you Cynthia?"

The girl stood up and extended her hand to Tara. "Why, yes, suga. You must be detective Bancroft. The whole precinct is buzzing about you!"

Tara shook her head slightly, causing her head to pound. She took in a deep breath and let it out slowly, which seemed to help. "Oh," she replied quietly. "Why is that?"

"Oh, you know how men can be," she laughed lightly. "They're surprised the Chief let you out of an office job. You know," she went on, "new hires and transfers never get out on the field right away. How'd you do it, Cherri?" Her accent was thick with southern charm.

Tara gazed at her. "I asked," she responded, emotionless.

Cynthia laughed again. "Come, come, Cherri. It's just us girls here." She leaned in closer to Tara. "You can tell me," she whispered.

Tara wasn't sure if she liked Cynthia or not, but she definitely didn't have the patience to indulge her this morning. "Listen, Cynthia. Chief Martinez told me you can hook me up with my own office."

Cynthia seemed to be caught off guard by the change in subject. She rebounded quickly. "Oh, quite right," she said. "We have a few empty offices in the back. Take your pick. I'm sure any of them would suit you just fine, Suga." She winked at Tara.

Tara thanked her and left quickly. Cynthia's over the top southern charm was getting to her and she needed to be far away. As she headed to search for an office of her own, a voice sprang out of nowhere.

"There you are," Detective Moore cried out. "I have been looking for you everywhere." Tara whipped around to face him. He was all smiles until he saw her forehead. "Jesus! What happened to you?"

She eyed him angrily. "I'll fill you in later, but first, we need to talk about some things." It unnerved Jacob to see her so blatantly serious.

"Um, okay," he replied cautiously. "My office?"

She turned around and walked to his office with him following suit. She opened the glass door and sat in the same chair she was in yesterday. Jacob closed the door behind him and inched his way to his desk. "What's up?"

Tara didn't know how to begin. Did she start with the attack? With the story about the Sloan's? With the fact that she knew he was a shapeshifter? She decided to come out right.

"I know," Tara answered finally. "What you are."

Jacob arched his right eyebrow. His glasses slid down the bridge of his nose slightly and he pushed them back in place. "Oh?" He said. "And just what am I?" He smiled his pleasant smile.

"A shapeshifter," Tara replied. Her face was completely serious when she said it, and she had to admit, it sounded crazy, even to her. The smile on Jacobs face faltered around the edges of his lips, but he quickly recovered.

"Is that code in Phoenix for something I am not aware of?"

"Oh, come off it," She yelled, standing up. "I spoke to the Sloan's. I know everything! About you; about them!" She counted on her fingers as she spoke. "About the magical energy all you beings want to harness! Bethany told me everything."

Jacobs smile was gone, replaced instead by abject horror. He closed his eyes and bent his head. "I highly doubt they told you everything," he whispered.

"Well I know enough," she retorted angrily. She wasn't sure why she was being so hostile, but she had felt betrayed, somehow. Jacob was her partner, and although she had only known him one day, she had felt he lied to her.

"Yeah?" he replied defiantly. "Well did they tell you how my old partner died? How it was Mr. Sloan himself who killed her?"

Tara flinched and recoiled. She knew there was some sort of connection between them. She had sensed it back in the library. She didn't expect that Dominik Sloan was responsible for his partner's death. Jacob continued.

"Did they tell you the rules for our kind here in Seattle?" Tara remained silent. "No?" He asked wildly. "I didn't think so!"

Both Tara and Jacob glared at each other. Tensions were high and emotions ran wild. Jacob sighed and sat down on the edge of his desk. Tara didn't know what to say. She was torn between wanting to yell and try to give him some sort of comfort.

"About a year ago," Jacob whispered, breaking the silence. "Natasha and I became romantically involved. We had worked together for a couple of years and have been there for each other through thick and thin." He looked up at his diploma before continuing.

"Around that time, we started an investigation of a body with his skin completely removed, hanging from the side of a building. As the investigation continued, it turned out to be a shifter."

"So," Tara interrupted, "you are a shapeshifter?" She meant it to be a statement of fact, but it came out more of a question. Jacob nodded his response.

"Shifter society is governed by the Royal Family, the Thompson's. They make up the rules in which all shifters must follow. Breaking the rules or committing crimes will lead to the Royal family taking your skin."

"Ouch," Tara winced. "That seems pretty harsh."

"It is," Jacob agreed. "But it's effective in keeping most of the shifters in line. Shifters can't change their appearance without their skin. It serves as a reminder to follow the rules."

"Did Natasha know? What you are, I mean?"

"No," he replied, shaking his head. "Not then anyway. Our investigation led us back to my home. We went and interviewed the Royal Family."

"That must have been tough," she interrupted. "Questioning them and knowing that they were in charge of you."

"It was, but they weren't in charge of me. You see, when I say that our investigation led back to my home, I do mean my literal home."

Realization dawned on her. "Wait. So, you're... you're some sort of supernatural royalty?"

He nodded. "Yes. The Thompson's are of royal blood. I changed my name from Thompson to Moore when I first joined the police academy."

She stood there with a gaping mouth. "How did your family take it?"

"How do you think?" he asked. "They thought when I had returned home that I was there to ultimately return to the fold, so to speak. Imagine their shock when I was accusing them of murdering one of our own."

Tara sat back down in her chair, bewildered. "But they were your family!"

He nodded again. "And the law is the law. I recognized the skinning victim as work from my family. We shifters serve our punishment, and eventually our skin grows back. I have never seen them hang someone before."

"So, what happened?" Tara asked.

"They were furious. First that someone murdered one of their shifters, then at me for accusing them of doing it. But after they saw how Natasha and I interacted, they realized that we were involved and that sent them over the edge."

"How so?"

"I am of royal blood. She wasn't even a shifter. Our law states that shifters should only be with other shifters. They may let slide a normal shifter dating a human here or there. It is 2015 after all, but Royalty had to stay within the shifter bloodlines." He got up and turned toward his diploma.

"You know she helped me finish my degree." He turned to look at Tara. "Before I was a detective. She encouraged me to keep at it, and helped me study long before we were involved. She really was a kind person, and I looked up to her."

Tara swallowed. She could see how difficult it was to bring up old memories. Should they continue? Jacob answered for her.

"My family had the power to change the law. They refused of course, thinking that Natasha was just a regular human. A plain Jane, if you will. It didn't matter to me either way. I told myself I would be with who I want to be with, whether they liked it or not."

"Good for you," Tara replied, giving him some form of encouragement.

He shook his head. "No," he said. "It was the worst mistake I have ever made." Tears swelled behind his glasses and he looked away.

Tara bit her lip. "What do you mean?" she asked.

Jacob reached up and wiped his eyes behind his glasses, then turned to look at Tara. "I should have left her alone. I shouldn't have mixed her up in any of this. If I had let her out of it, she may still be alive!"

Tara was a little confused. He blamed Dominik Sloan for her death, but it seemed to her that his family was somehow the reason they couldn't be together. "What happened?" she asked solemnly.

He closed his eyes and continued his story. "Out of all the governing factions here in Seattle, ultimately Dominik Sloan has the final say. He is, after all, the one who controls the Dradogian."

"The what?"

"The mystical energy that, how did you put it? All of us beings want to harness?" Tara nodded sheepishly. "It's called the Dradogian. You see, long ago, there was a war over the Dradogian, and, to bring peace, all the clan leaders signed a treaty, effectively ending the war. Understand so far?" Tara nodded again.

"But the Sloan family kept the Dradogian, essentially setting them apart from the rest of the clans. A council was formed to govern over the rest of the supernatural community. A member from each species sat on the council, as equals, to decide laws and affairs of the supernatural world. Each had a vote, but Dominik could overrule a verdict if a case was argued strongly enough." He scooted to his chair and sat down, elbows on his desk.

"My mother went to Dominik about my relationship with Natasha. A tribunal was called and I was kidnapped from my home in the middle of the night." Jacob looked down into his lap. Tara's eyes widened and she put her hand to her lips.

He continued. "I was brought before the council, along with Natasha." Anger filled his face. "She was locked in a cage. I tried my damnedest to reach her, but they forced me in chains. I tried to shift, but that witch, Vita, and her coven held my power at bay. My family pleaded their case, stating that I was royalty and I shouldn't be mixed up with humans, especially on a romantic level. They feared their bloodline being tainted."

Sorrow filled Tara's eyes. She couldn't believe what she was hearing. His family stood by and watched as he was chained. How could they do that? Jacob cleared his throat and continued.

"The council ruled in their favor, but I still wouldn't take no for an answer. I loved her and told them that no matter what, I was going to be with her. I told them they could skin me, but to leave Natasha out of it.

"The council deliberated quickly and came back with a verdict. Since I was royalty, it would be up to the other members of the royal family to decide what to do with me. As for Natasha, she was brought before the Council. She was stripped naked and killed before my eyes." Jacob bit his lip as the memory passed through him. He slammed his hand down on the desk, causing the speaker monitor to jump slightly.

Tara didn't know what to say. She remained silent, unsure how to proceed. What is the protocol for comforting a coworker after they watch their lover die? Sometimes there are no words.

"Mr. Sloan gave the order. I struggled as hard as I could against the chains that held me but it was in vain. I had to watch as Mr. Sloan himself sank his teeth into her neck and drain her of her blood" A sob escaped his lips and he quickly looked down to keep his face hidden.

Tara wept. She never expected this change in events. How could his family allow something so horrible to happen to the woman he loved? She didn't understand. Her parents had died when she was very young and she was the only child. She never had to deal with family issues before, but she was pretty sure her parents wouldn't have anyone she loved killed.

"After her death, I was released to my family. I was utterly sullen and angry, but my family paid me no mind. They thought I needed to be taught a lesson, so they banished me from the clan. I was told that if I ever return, that I would be skinned, royalty or not. I haven't talked to them since."

"Your family sounds like a bunch of assholes," she stated, shaking her head in disapproval.

"Yes, they are, " Jacob replied, looking up at her. "But royal assholes." They both giggled at that.

"I'm sorry for what happened to Natasha. And for how your family treated you," she said softly.

Jacob nodded and stood up. "I'm sorry that you are being dragged into all this mess. And it's only been one day since you officially started working here. I think that's a record."

"Thanks," she replied, not sure if that was a compliment or not.

Jacob shook away the bad memories. "So what happened to you, anyway?" he asked, seizing the opportunity to change the subject.

Tara explained what happened on her way home last night, and how Bethany had saved her. She told him about waking up in the spare room and Bethany's story. She recalled that Vita was there and how Bethany thinks her brother was killed over the Dradogian.

"It's entirely possible," Jacob stated. "The Dradogian is powerful, but then again, so are the Sloan's."

"If you had to guess," Tara asked, "which supernatural creature would you believe capable of doing this?" She shifted uncomfortably in her seat.

Jacob seem to think about that a moment. "I would say that the Ogres would be stupid enough to try it. They are strong but not very bright, so I don't believe they would have succeeded without help."

"What about the girlfriend?" Tara asked. "Do we know how to find her?"

Jacob smiled. "Yes," he said slyly. "She is, after all, an Ogre."

Tara recalled Bethany making some sarcastic comment about not being into ogres, but she thought at the time that she was being facetious. Guess not, she said to herself. "Do you believe she could have done this?"

"Guess we should go find out," he stated blankly. He opened the door and looked back at Tara. "You ready?"

Tara bit her lip and nodded. "Just do me a favor," she said. "Promise me that while out in the field, you will have my back. I'm still trying to get my bearings when it comes to all this supernatural bullshit. I need to be able to rely on my partner, even if he is a shapeshifter."

Jacob smiled. "Don't worry, detective. You can trust me." He winked at her and walked out. She stood there watching him go. A nagging feeling dropped in the pit of her stomach. Could she trust him? Time would tell. Even in the supernatural world, trust had to be earned.

Chapter 7

They drove south on I-5 toward Mt. Baker. They could have gone through the city, but they risked traffic lights and stop signs. Jacob told her that I-5 was the quickest option.

"So you've met the ogres before, then?" she asked him.

"Yes," he said, eyes peeled to the road. "They don't like me much."

She smiled lightly. "How could that be?" she joked.

He shot her a smile. "Actually, the ogres don't really like anyone. They are proud people who believe that ogres are the best at everything. They really only have a voice on the council because of their brute strength."

"So, they are strong?"

"Oh, hell yes," he exclaimed. "Since the war, the vampires have used them as a sort of intimidation method against the other factions. They carry out the dirty work while the vampires sit back and twiddle their thumbs."

Her eyebrows drew together as she frowned. "I thought you said that they don't like anyone."

"They don't," he replied. "But they do like money. The vamps pay them quite well for their services."

Tara pictured a green giant roaming around Seattle, terrorizing citizens and destroying buildings. The thought was ludicrous, almost laughable. But also true, she guessed. "What do they look like?"

Jacob laughed loudly. "They look just like anybody else. On the surface, at least. But that is a facade. When they get mad, that is when the facade fades and they transform into muscle bound giants with canine-like teeth."

"And they are green?" she asked in rapt attention.

Jacob peered over at her and shook his head. "No. That is Hollywood's interpretation. They are more grayish, with horribly disfigured facial features. They are definitely formidable opponents. Let's try not to upset one."

She agreed.

Ten minutes later, they got off I-5 and took the exit toward Mt. Baker.

"Do they live in houses?"

"Some do," he told her. "Most prefer the wooden areas. They like being free to eat their fill of the land animals."

"And what about humans?" she asked. "They don't eat humans?"

"Not anymore," he stated flatly. "The council outlawed that a long time ago. Seems that in order to coexist with the humans, they had to make sacrifices. Anton, that's Kenzie's father and leader of the ogres, serves on the council. He was just a boy when they made that law, so he never really got used to human flesh."

"Good," she said. "I'd hate to show up and everyone think that we are delivery." Jacob laughed. His glasses slid down his nose and he absently pushed them back up.

Tara noticed that, although the supernatural elements to the case unnerved her, she was more relaxed than ever before. It was as if it was common knowledge that vampires and ogres existed. They were just regular beings, trying to live out their lives like the rest of us. She should be freaking out, but instead, she was calm.

Jacob pulled off the main road and onto a gravel one. Houses thinned as they drove along, replaced by towering trees of Pine and Cedar. The sun beamed down on them, warming her skin through the windshield. She stared out the window. It was a beautiful sight. Tara had never seen so many trees living out in Phoenix.

The woods became increasingly thick. The sun became hidden behind the tops of the canopy and the landscape changed from beauty to gloomy within moments. Had she been in a horror movie, Tara felt that this would be the part where the car broke down and a bunch of murderers would attack. It was creepy.

"We'll be there shortly," Jacob said, stirring Tara out of her thoughts. She nodded in response and became a little nervous with anticipation. She didn't know what to expect. Hopefully, things went smoothly.

Jacob pulled up next to a large rotted tree stump beside a small walking path. Moss covered most of the stump in thick patches. It had been an old tree, at least 200 years by the size of it, yet it looked like someone had cracked it open like an egg. Trees loomed around the path with curvy branches, making a small archway. There was no house in sight.

"I thought you said that they live in houses?"

"No," he corrected her." I said some do. The Wrights prefer to live in a cave, like their ancestors before them. They have lived on this patch of land for generations now, and seem to have no interest in changing any time soon." He shut off the engine and opened his door. "Anton and his wife, Media, prefer more.... traditional settings."

"I don't like the sound of that," She told him. He smiled meekly and got out of the car. Tara did the same.

"Come on," he said. "We have to walk from here."

"The forest was considerably colder than in Seattle. Tara crossed her arms over her chest to keep from shivering as they walked. She followed Jacob through a small, winding path. The dirt became darker and the trees denser. Large ferns and weeds enclosed the path, followed by trees of Birch and Pine. Animals rustled, scurrying away as they walked on. Insects buzzed in front of them and Tara absently waved them away.

A short time later, Jacob stopped and whirled around. "Now this is very important," he told her. "When we get there, you must bow. Keep eye contact with Anton at all times when you do. "

"What?" she asked. "Why do I have to bow to question Kenzie?"

"They don't normally allow outsiders into their den, especially humans. For an ogre, it is a sign of respect and also submission. Understand?" She gave him a harsh look. "I'm bowing too, don't worry."

She didn't like the idea of bowing to anyone. This was 2015, not the 1800's. Women shouldn't have to bow to anyone. Then a thought crossed her mind.

"What would have happened if I didn't find out about all this supernatural stuff? Would I still have to bow then?"

Jacob shook his head. "No, I would have called Kenzie in for questioning."

"You mean this whole time we could be sitting in your warm office talking to her instead of out here in the freezing cold wondering around like little lost puppies?"

He raised an eyebrow. "Yeah, pretty much."

Tara's eye fixated on his. He recoiled back slightly. "Remind me to punch you in the throat later," she said between chattering teeth.

"Just remember to keep eye contact and bow." They continued on the path and came to a tiny clearing that opened into a darkened cave. The entrance had torches on each side, blazing bright and flickering against the wind. They did very little to provide light inside the cave. Jacob held up his hands. Tara followed his lead.

A shadow moved inside the cave. It became clearer as the shadow moved closer to the detectives. It stopped just behind the entranceway. Tara could make out a darkened silhouette of a man but that was all. Tara's mouth ran dry and she licked her cold lips. She was suddenly very anxious.

"We have come to seek an audience with Kenzie Wright," Jacob hollered loudly. The shadowed figure did not move. Jacob bowed but continued to stare forward. Tara felt ridiculous but followed her partner's movements.

"Enter, Shifter," the shadowed figured boomed out. It turned and faded into the darkness of the cave. Jacob got back up and peered over at Tara, who was staring into the entrance of the cave with mild fascination.

"You ready?" he asked her.

She really wasn't. She felt this was a little too bizarre. Yesterday she was doing what she loved, on a murder case collecting clues and interviewing witnesses. Today, she was heading into an Ogre's den to discuss a dead vampire.

"Ready as I'll ever be," she stammered out. Jacob walked slowly toward the entrance with Tara on his heels. They passed the flickering torches and stepped into the darkness.

Blackness was all Tara could see. She smelled a faint odor she couldn't quite place, something between stale air and rotten meat. The smell made her nostrils flare and she suppressed the urge to gag.

Her eyes adjusted gradually and she could make out the outline of Jacob's torso, but only just. A faint light appeared, small and dim, in the distance. It grew larger and brighter as they crept closer. Another light appeared. And another. More and more lights came into view until suddenly the whole cave was ablaze with torches.

The cave opened into a large cavern. Stalagmites and Stalactite grew large and stretched toward each other. People were gathered around a giant throne made of bone. They whispered excitedly amongst themselves as the visitors walked on. Tara had never seen anything like it. The air had become dense and difficult to breathe. She did her best to take in shallow breaths but it was tricky.

Drums started beating and Tara jumped at the sound. Jacob grabbed her hand quickly and gave her a look of caution. The drum beat was slow and dull at first, then gradually grew louder and faster. Tara's heart leapt into her throat as the drums speed increased. She looked around madly for signs of the drums, but didn't see them. All of a sudden, the drums stopped.

The crowd stopped whispering and bowed in unison. Jacob bowed as well. Tara took one last look around before bowing herself. She kept her eyes up like Jacob told her to. A tall, bulky man seem to appear out of nowhere and sat on the chair made of bone.

His face was scarred with lines but the most prominent was a thick scar running from his left eye to his right cheek. His hair was mangy and brown, as if he hadn't seen a barber in weeks. He had a full brown beard that, judging from the length told her that it had to be a couple months old. He wore a loose black shirt and baggy shorts, that under different circumstances, would have made him seem comical.

His dark eyes glared at the visitors with hostility. Tara did as she was told and didn't look away. He sneered at them before speaking. "Rise, shifter," he said. His voice was deep and husky. "You too, human." They obeyed.

"It's not every day that a shifter would risk his own life, or the life of a humans, by entering our dwelling," he said.

"I meant no disrespect, sir," Jacob nodded to him. "We are here investigating the murder of Eric Sloan."

The crowd whispered frantically amongst themselves. "Silence!" Anton screamed. The crowd stopped immediately.

"And you came here to accuse one of us?" he asked. His face deepened with hostility.

"On the contrary, sir. We were told that Eric and Kenzie were involved." The crowd exploded into chatter. Anton raised his hand and the crowd again became quiet. Jacob continued. "We came here to ask her a few questions."

Anton began stroking his shabby beard. "Interesting that you think my daughter would have anything to do with the blood suckers," he said with an almost bored tone. He looked from Jacob to Tara. "Do you know what else is interesting, shifter?" Jacob shook his head. "That you bring a human here. In this sacred space."

The crowd murmured their dissatisfaction. Tara cringed. She didn't like where this conversation was heading. She gave Jacob a heated glance. Anton continued.

"Tell me, human. Who are you?"

Tara took in a deep breath of the stale air and almost choked, but suppressed it. She forced her heart to slow down. "My name is Tara, sir. Tara Bancroft. I am a detective for the Seattle Police Department."

Anton studied Tara with a look of curiosity. He had started rubbing his beard again slowly, barely aware that he was doing so. "You are a brave one," he said to her. "Coming here to talk to us. Tell me, human. What do you know of our kind?"

Tara's face turned red. She always hated being put on the spot. She hadn't expected to be interrogated. She was used to being the one who interrogated others. "I'm afraid I don't know much, sir," she admitted. "Only that you work for the vampires."

The crowd roared! Anton straightened in his seat, becoming rigid and stiff. He put both hands on the arm rests and leaned in toward the detectives. "We do not work for the blood suckers!" he bellowed. Tara's heart began to race again. Jacob shot her a look of concern. She felt like she had put her foot in her mouth. So much for not upsetting an ogre.

Anton rose to his feet. The crowd stopped their chatter and bowed once more. Tara took that as her queue to do the same. Jacob, however did not bow.

"I apologize for my partner," he said loudly. "She has only recently learned of our world and cannot be to blame for her ignorance."

Anton stepped closer to them, each step echoing throughout the cavern. Chills were sent shooting down Tara's spine. She wanted to shrug them off but remained still. As Anton inched his way over, Jacob continued.

"Please, sir, let us question Kenzie so we can report to the Sloan's of your clan's innocence."

"Are you their errand boy, exile?" he asked. He let out a giant roar of laughter and the crowd laughed along with him. "How is it that you can serve them, when Mr. Sloan is the reason your beloved is dead?"

This caught Jacob off guard. Tara noticed Jacob shift uncomfortably. It was subtle, but there nonetheless. Jacob recomposed himself quickly. "I serve the law, sir. It is true that I have no love for the vampires, especially for what they did to my partner, but I have been assigned with finding out who killed Eric Sloan. Not by the vampires, but by the human justice system!"

Anton laughed again. "Tell me, shifter," he replied, still moving closer. "Do you think that the human justice system has any barring here? In this place?" Anton raised his hands upward.

"Maybe not, sir," Jacob said defiantly. "But as a member of the council, and in recognition of the ogres on the treaty, you are bound by our law to comply."

Anton sneered. "That is true," he admitted, "But you are banished from your people, are you not? You are not here as a member of your tribe, nor are you a member of the court. You come here as a nobody. An exile." Anton stepped forward again until he was inches away from Jacob. "What makes you think that you have any sway here?"

Jacob began to speak, but Anton was suddenly there in his true form. Tara let out a gasp as she saw Anton grow well over 8 feet tall. His body turned a pale shade of gray and he doubled in body mass. His face twisted and bulged, becoming rigid and bumpy. Even with his mouth closed, Tara saw his canines grow and protrude through his lips.

Anton moved quickly. His hairy hand clasped around Jacob's throat. He lifted her partner off the ground, his feet barely scraping the damp floor. Jacob's hands shot to his throat. He struggled to break free, but it was no use. Anton held him tight.

Tara filled with dread. The situation took a deadly turn, and she knew she had to do something fast. She had to find a way to smooth things over and make Anton comply. But what?

"Excuse me," she yelled. Anton gleamed over at her, snarling. Jacob's eyes were wide. She tried to remain calm as she spoke. "I am new to all this supernatural stuff, but I am a pretty good detective. It seems to me, with how you have a seat on the council, you would welcome an opportunity to clear your clans name."

"Explain, human," he ordered. His jaw opened and saliva slid from his mouth in a steady strand, like an hourglass that had just been turned upside down.

"Well," she told him, getting to her feet. "You and your clan are formidable, whether friend or foe. Feared by all. It's no wonder with all the supernatural elements in this city, we came here first."

Chatter began again from the crowd. Anton glanced over to the mass and the murmurs died off. "My patience is wearing thin, human. If you have a point, then make it."

Tara really didn't have a point. She was stalling but if he was talking, then he wasn't killing either of them. If she could convince him it was in his best interest of his people, then maybe they could all walk out of there alive.

"By allowing us to interview Kenzie, it will show the other creatures how powerful you really are."

Anton seemed to think for a moment. "Explain," he said. Tara took in a deep breath and let it out slowly.

"Think about it, sir. You are feared by all the other clans. They know of your power and strength. By allowing us to talk to Kenzie, you show them just how unafraid you truly are."

Anton seemed lost in the conversation. Tara continued, making it clearer. "Whomever killed Eric knew of your greatness and wanted us to believe one of your people could have done this. With Kenzie's testimony, you show them, not only your physical strength, but your willingness to keep the peace. You show them your true power as a leader of your people. Allow us to question Kenzie, sir."

Anton stood still for a few moments. The only sound heard was that of Jacob struggling for breath. Tara wasn't sure if her argument made sense to Anton. Hell, it barely made sense to her. But Jacob was turning blue and if Anton didn't release him soon, Tara would have to shoot him. She doubted they would have made it out of the cave alive.

Suddenly, a smile spread on Anton's disfigured face. He let out a hearty laugh that echoed throughout the cavern. "I like you, human," he said. He released Jacob who landed with a thud gasping for air. Jacobs hands rubbed his neck gently as he sat on the ground. Anton turned toward two guards near the back of the cavern. "Escort them to my daughter," he ordered them. they bowed in submission and beckoned Tara and Jacob forward.

Tara helped her partner to his feet. His neck was deep red and bruised, but at least he was alive. As they passed by, Anton spoke again. "I will give you twenty minutes," he said. "No more, no less." He walked back to his throne. "Be sure to tell the other monsters that we Ogres aren't afraid of anything. We are powerful and are not to be trifled with!"

Tara nodded. "I will, sir," she replied, then turned toward the guards. They passed by without looking back. As they followed the two guards, Jacob stopped her.

"Thanks for the save," he said. She smiled in reply. Whatever faults she had, no one could say she couldn't lie her way out of a situation.

"Give it up for good old fashioned bullshitting," she smirked.

Jacob smiled.

Chapter 8

The guards led them through a winding tunnel. The air had changed, becoming denser and mustier. It became increasingly colder as they descended further into the cave. Tara's hands were numb and she stuffed them into her jacket pockets, but that provided little warmth. Her body shivered as she walked. She hoped they would make it there soon, wherever there happened to be.

Jacob didn't seem to notice the cold. She wondered if that was because he was used to Seattle's weather, or if it was some sort of shapeshifting side effect. She made a mental note to ask later.

The guards carried torches that offered little to no light at all. Tara was surprised that they could navigate the tunnel as well as they did. She figured they probably knew the cave like the back of their hands. She stayed close to them for fear of losing her way and being lost inside the darkness.

They continued for another five minutes in silence before the guards finally stopped. They stood in front of an even darker hollowed hole in the cavern wall. They turned toward the detectives and gestured for them to enter.

"Kenzie is in there?" Tara asked, her teeth chattering as she spoke. They didn't acknowledge that they even heard her. Jacob and Tara exchanged glances.

"Hello?" She said. "I'm talking to you. Is Kenzie in there?"

The guard on the right nodded and pointed into the darkness. The other guard stood there, like a statue at the Sloan's house.

"Come on, let's go," Jacob said, grabbing Tara by the hand. Tara wasn't sure she wanted to go in there. Sensing her hesitation, Jacob squeezed her hand slightly. It offered no comfort. Jacob stepped forward and guided Tara inside.

They were swallowed by the darkness. Tara couldn't make out anything and her instincts told her to flee back toward the light. Her heart beat quickened and she became very alert.

"Can you see?" she asked, whispering to her partner.

"A little," he replied back. "I'll guide us through. Watch your step."

"I wish I could," she grumbled, trying to sooth her building fear with humor. All she could see was blackness. Jacob guided her ahead.

Her eyes adjusted slightly and soon she could make out a shape; the silhouette of her partner was scarcely visible. Their footsteps echoed down the corridor. The walls of the tunnel were damp and slimy as she scraped the side of it with an outstretched hand.

"I see a light up ahead," Jacob informed her. She couldn't, but she trusted him. They crept forward, inching their way along the wall. Suddenly she could make out a faint blur up ahead. It grew larger and brighter as they waded through the darkness. Relief washed over Tara like a blanket.

The light came from a torch posted to the cavern wall. It blazed bright, illuminating a small room. She couldn't make out much, but was grateful for the light and it seemed to ease her fear. Jacob, on the other hand, changed her mind.

"Oh my god," he exclaimed, dropping Tara's hand. He booked it into the room at full speed.

"Wait," Tara yelled after him, but it was too late. He disappeared inside the room, leaving her in the darkness. She ran after him. The light was bright enough now that she could make out objects clearly. The room was filled with metal cages. At least seven of them sat together against the right wall. Three circular cages hung loosely from stalactites up above. Chains were drilled into the far side wall.

A large metal table with straps at the corners sat smack dab in the middle of the room. Blood stained the top of the table and the floor beneath it. Bits of flesh and bone were sprawled out in odd places; against walls, on the legs of the table, hanging off the cages. The stench of death and decayed flesh permeated the room, causing Tara to cough madly as she inhaled a big whiff. She covered her nose to keep the smell away.

Jacob was bent down near the far right corner of the room. She hurried over to him.

"What are you...," She stopped. A leg was barely visible, blocked mostly by Jacob's torso. She moved closer and could make out a body chained against the wall. She ran to Jacob, who was checking for a pulse. Tara let out a small squeal.

The body was that of a young woman. She lay motionless against the cold, dank floor. Her hands were chained at the wrists and there were deep cuts along her arm where she tried to break through the chains. Her hair was long and greasy brown. Dirt covered her face and neck

"Is she...," Tara started to ask.

"She's alive," Jacob whispered. "Barely," he added. He gently shook her thin shoulder. She didn't respond.

Tara stooped down next to him and wiped her greasy hair off her face. The girl whimpered softly. Jacob shook her again, this time with a little more force. The woman stirred.

She opened her eyes and recoiled against the wall at the sight of the detectives. Jacob held up his hands. "It's alright," he said soothingly. "We're not here to hurt you."

The girl leaned heavily against the wall, clawing wildly at it as she tried to get away from them. "It's alright," Tara assured her. "We're police officers. We are here to help you."

The girl didn't seem to believe her. She clawed the wall hysterically, chipping away dirty fingernails in the process. Tara fished out her badge and offered it to her. "See," she said. "I'm detective Bancroft. This is detective Moore. You're safe now."

The girl saw the badge and relaxed a little. She looked at Tara, then at Jacob. "Shifter," she managed to say in a shaky voice.

"That's right, I am," Jacob nodded. "But I am a detective with the Seattle P.D. I'm not here to hurt you."

The girl's eyes grew wide and backed away from him. She pulled and yanked against her chains in a panicked haste. Jacob tried to comfort her, but she was like a wild horse who didn't want to be tamed.

"Jacob," Tara said. "Go wait by the entrance." He looked at her with a questioning stare. Tara grabbed his arm and dragged him away from the girl. When they were far enough away, she spoke again. "The girl is obviously frightened of you."

"Yeah, I've noticed," he replied.

"So, let me calm her down. We aren't going to get anywhere if she is frantic." Tara noticed the redness of his neck was fading. "Go wait by the entrance and let me talk to her."

Jacob started to say something but the girl caught his attention. She was still pulling wildly against the chains, and with a determined nod, he turned and walked to the entranceway.

Tara went back to the girl who was picking at the chains with her bloody fingertips. She jumped against the wall as Tara approached her. "It's alright," Tara said in a quiet, gentle voice. "I'm not going to hurt you." She knelt down and scooted closer.

The woman huddled against the wall and stayed there, covering her knees in her arms. She whispered quietly, "My father..."

"Your father?" Tara asked. Recognition hit her like a slap in the face. "You mean, you're Kenzie Wright?" The girl nodded and sobbed loudly.

Tara couldn't believe it. Her own father had her chained up like an animal. She had seen some pretty horrible child abuse cases in her time, but none had compared to this. None of the parents had ever chained up their own children. This was a new one.

"Why?" she asked quietly, mostly to herself. "Why would he do this?"

Kenzie looked deep into Tara's eyes. "I disobeyed."

Anger seeped through her. She shook her head and wished she did shoot him when she had the chance. "What did you do that warrants such a punishment?" she asked in disbelief.

Kenzie licked her cracked lips. She moved closer to Tara, and the chains scraped against the floor. The sound was like nails on a chalkboard and Tara suppressed the urge to cover her ears. "He found out I was dating Eric Sloan," she told her. "He hates the vamps."

Tara shifted to her other knee. "He chained you up for that?" Kenzie nodded between sobs. "How long have you been here?"

"I don't know," she admitted. "A few days." She pointed to the bottom of the wall. Four lines were edged into the wall with a diagonal line dissecting them. Five days, Tara thought. She couldn't believe this was happening. How could he do such a horrible thing?

"It's alright now," Tara said. "I'm going to get you out of here." Tara stood and went to where the chains met the slimy rock wall. She grabbed them with both hands and gave them a hard yank.

"That won't help," Kenzie assured her. Tara peered over at her. "It's been spelled by the witches. A gift for my father's birthday. Only my father can release me."

Tara dropped the chains with a shrill thud and dusted off her hands. "Well that's just great," she mused. Tara sat back down near Kenzie. She hadn't met the witches yet, but if they gave gifts like that for torture, she didn't want to meet any.

"How did you get past my father?" Kenzie asked, stirring Tara out of her thoughts.

"We came here to talk to you. Your father allowed us access."

Kenzie raised an eyebrow, showing specks of skin beneath the dirt on her face. "You must have impressed him for you to get all the way back here. For a human, that is no easy feat."

"That I did," she responded. She hesitated in telling her the rest. "Do you know? About Eric?"

Tears welled up in Kenzie's eyes and she began to sob again. "My father told me this morning." She buried her face in her palms and cried. Tara patted her on the back, unsure what else she could do. She sat staring out into the chamber feeling helpless.

Footsteps echoed as she saw Jacob running toward them. Kenzie stopped crying long enough to see Jacobs approach and she became mad with fear. Tara was suddenly on her feet and met Jacob half way across the room.

"Our time is almost up," he said. "The guards are coming."

Shit, she thought. Time was flying by and she hadn't had any real time to ask Kenzie anything important. She was too distracted by Anton's abuse.

"You have to stall them," she told him. He gave her a puzzling look.

"Easier said than done," he retorted. "How do you suggest I do that?"

"You'll think of something," she replied. "Go, while I talk to her." Jacob straightened up and gave her a salute, like a private addressing his commander. He turned on his heels and ran back to the entranceway.

Tara ran over to Kenzie. Under normal circumstances, she would bide her time, gaining her trust before asking her intimate questions, but she didn't have the time. Instead, she thought she'd just dive right into it.

"I'm sorry Kenzie, about your father, but I need to know if Eric had any enemies."

Kenzie shook her head. "He was a likable guy. Everyone that knew him thought he was great."

"No arguments or strange phone calls, or visitors you can think of?"

Kenzie started to shake her head, but then her eyes widened once more. "He did end up in a fight about a week ago," she confessed.

"What happened?" Tara asked, looking over her shoulder.

"We were at Heiligtum that night," Kenzie told her. Tara didn't know what that was and it must have shown on her face. Kenzie elaborated. "It's a night club in Belltown. Exclusively for our kind."

"Just ogres, or all supernatural beings?" she asked.

"All altered beings. We had a drink when one of the wolves bumped into Eric. He pushed Eric hard and Eric pushed back. They caused a bar fight, but the bouncers kicked all of us out. The wolf threatened to kill him if he ever saw him again."

There was a deafening crash behind her that caused Tara to jump. She whipped around in time to see Jacob roll off the bloody table and onto the floor. The two guards were calmly walking toward her.

"Quick, Kenzie," she pleaded. "Did you happen to catch his name?"

Kenzie wasn't listening. At the sight of the guards, she became like a feral tiger, thrashing against her chains. She changed into her true form, becoming equally as formidable as her father. Tara recoiled backward away from Kenzie and the guards seized her arms, pulling her toward the entrance.

"What was his name?" Tara yelled over the commotion. "Kenzie! What was his name?"

Kenzie thrashed more, snapping her jaws like a rabid dog. She ran toward the ogres, but the chains held her out of reach. Just as they pulled Tara into the darkness of the tunnel, Kenzie screamed, "Michael Beagan!"

Chapter 9

The car ride back to the station was an awkward one. Tara sat behind the wheel unsure what to say to Jacob. They drove in silence for most of the ride, until Jacob turned the knob on the radio. "This is Jubal from Brooke and Jubal in the Morning bringing you all the hits." A song Tara had never heard sprang through the car speakers.

She glanced at her partner who was still bleeding from his nose. Not a full stream of blood; that did happen about 20 minutes ago. The blood trickled out slowly now. When they had gotten back to the car, Tara found some tissues in the glove compartment. He now had them stuffed up his nostrils, and under different circumstances, it might have been comical seeing her partner like that. The blood seeped through the tissues but it was slowly drying.

His glasses were gone as well. When he rolled off the table, the left eye glass shattered on the floor. He had the pieces in his suit pocket, along with the frames.

"I'm sorry," she told him. "I wasn't thinking."

Jacob didn't respond. He was still upset with her for making him stall the guards. She drove on, eyes glued to the road, passing small houses and large trees before turning onto I-5.

After the guards had escorted them back to the main chamber, things became increasingly deadly. The crowd had disappeared. Anton sat in his chair, alone in the empty hollow. Tara was furious with him. She had half a mind to arrest him for child abuse but thought better of it. All she needed was for him to transform into his true self while behind bars. How would they cover that up? Instead, she played nice. Jacob, on the other hand, did not.

"You're own daughter!" Jacob screamed, stomping toward Anton. "How could you chain her up?" The guards blocked his advance, holding him back. He struggled to get past them, but it was in vain. Anton watched the spectacle with mild amusement.

"The exile has guts," he said to the guards. The guards laughed back in response. Jacob struggled to break free, but they held him tight.

"Please, sir," Tara said. "Why keep Kenzie locked up?"

Anton shifted his attention to her. "She is being punished for her own good," he told her plainly. His voice held no emotion. It was as if he was bored with the conversation.

"But Eric is dead now," Tara argued. "Surely that is punishment enough."

"I will decide what is punishment enough," He roared. "I am Anton Wright! King of the ogres, human. Our ways may seem strange to a frail sack of bones like yourself, but she will be stronger for it."

"She will hate you for it," Jacob yelled back.

"Enough!" he screamed. "You came to question her, and you have. Now leave my sight before I change my mind." He nodded to the guards who instantly reacted and dragged Jacob toward the entrance of the clearing. Tara shook her head and gave Anton one last disapproving look before following the guards out.

She made it to the entrance in time to see them throw Jacob onto the soft, patchy grass. He landed on his face and skidded about a foot. Tara ran to help him up, but he shook her off. Jacob got to his feet and ran back to the cave, but it was no use. The guards blocked the entrance.

Now in the car, the radio filled the silence that passed between them. "At least we know Eric had an altercation with one of the werewolves," she said, offering him a small condolence.

"Yay," he replied glumly, staring out the window.

"Kenzie said the werewolf threatened to kill him." Jacob looked at her, then back out the window. "Come on, Jacob. Talk to me," she pleaded. "I've already apologized. What more can I do?"

He shook his head. "It's not you I'm mad at. It's me," he confessed. "I shouldn't have lost my temper like that. I knew the type of man Anton was and what he was capable of doing. I just can't get over the fact he had his own daughter chained up."

"Trust me," she replied. "Neither can I."

Yeah," he said. "The last person I saw chained up was Natasha. Seeing Kenzie like that just brought up some bad memories."

Tara hadn't thought of that. Having a lover chained and murdered right before your eyes would drive anyone insane with anger. Seeing anyone chained up after such a horrific act would make anyone lose their minds.

"I'm so sorry," she whispered. She understood why he tried to attack Anton. It wasn't just for Kenzie. It was for Natasha.

Jacob continued staring out the window. They were northbound on I-5, cruising at 65 miles an hour. Traffic was heavy and she thanked god that Washington had carpool lanes.

"Did Kenzie give you a name?" he asked suddenly.

"She did," Tara nodded. "Michael Beagan."

"That's...unfortunate," he told her.

Tara raised an eyebrow at him. "You know him?"

He shook his head. "I know of him. He is second in command of the wolves. Pack society is highly structured with the most dominant one as the leader. Michael Beagan, from what I am told, fought through the ranks until he became second. Rumor has it he has made plays toward pack leader, but failed."

"Who is the pack leader?" she asked with renewed interest.

"His name is Troy Lynch. He became leader many years ago. Turned Michael himself, from what I've been told. But Michael has never been content with being second. Rumors also say that he won't rest until he finds a way to overthrow Troy."

"And Troy knows this?" Tara asked.

"From what I've been told, yes."

"So why doesn't Troy do something about it?" she asked. If she was the leader of a group of people and was challenged, she would make sure that person would never challenge her again.

Jacob shrugged his shoulders. "Wolf politics isn't my strong suit. And as I have been exiled, most of my connections have dried up." He stared out the window, then turned to look at her. "Probably because it hadn't worked in the past." Tara could see that. If Michael wasn't strong enough to overthrow Troy, why bother trying to stop him?

Tara yawned. She was tired. It was only 2:30, yet so much had happened in the past 24 hours. It was exhausting. She hadn't slept much and her head still hurt from last night's attack. She went over everything in her mind. She still couldn't believe that Kenzie was chained up. Then a strange realization hit her. Kenzie had been afraid of Jacob. Why?

"Why do you think Kenzie was afraid of you?" she asked him.

Jacob glanced over at her. "I don't think she was afraid of me specifically. It has more to do with what I am than who I am."

"How so?" she asked.

A small smile spread over his face. It was the first smile she had seen since they got back into the car. "The shifter society has its upsides," he told her. "We are able to transform into anyone we touch." She gave him a disbelieving glance. "It's true," he stated.

"Why touch? Can't you just look at someone and take on their appearance?"

Jacob shook his head. "It doesn't work that way. We have to touch them first. We sort of absorb part of their DNA when we touch them. The DNA gives us the ability to shift, but it burns up after a while."

"What's a while?" she asked him.

He shrugged. "Depends on the amount of contact. A short handshake, for instance, would give me the ability to become them for about 20 minutes. The longer the contact, the longer I could stay in the guise. It's quite useful if I ever needed to do undercover work."

Tara shook her head. "I still don't get why Kenzie would be afraid of you." Jacob sighed softly before continuing.

"You know the rumor of how cameras can take part of your soul after capturing a picture?" Tara nodded. "Some cultures believe it. It's superstitious and stupid, but nonetheless, some people believe it strongly enough to never be photographed. It's kind of like that. Some of the ogres believe that when we take on the form of someone else, we take part of their soul."

Tara's eyes widened and her jaw dropped. Jacob continued.

"It's utter nonsense of course, but useful in certain situations. Especially if you want to excite fear."

"What do you mean?"

"Well, my family has used shifting to gain the amount of power and wealth they have for centuries. They can be great allies and terrifying enemies. They use the superstition to their advantage. It makes the ogres compliant in certain scenarios."

Tara smirked. "So essentially, your family has bluffed their way when dealing with the ogres?" Jacob shrugged again.

"It's not just the ogres who believe it. All manner of supernatural creatures believe it. We just happen to use the superstition against them. Here in Seattle, the vampires seem to be the only ones truly not afraid."

Tara recalled how Bethany changed when she attacked the man's neck in the alley. She became grayish and bumpy. She was ferocious and scary. Kind of hard to incite fear into someone who was already dead.

"Yeah, well, if I looked as scary as Bethany did when she changed into her vampire form, I don't think I'd be afraid of a rumor either."

"Point taken," he said. "But the vampires have their own fears. Even more so now that one of their own has been killed."

That brought them back to the case at hand. Although Tara was a good detective, she felt like an amateur cadet, just learning the ropes of the supernatural world. "Well, we know one thing for certain," she stated. "Kenzie had nothing to do with Eric Sloan's death."

"I don't think the wolf did either," Jacob confessed.

"Oh? Why is that?"

"Well from what I understand of pack society, they are more concerned with their own affairs. Truth be told, they would rather not be part of the council, but because of the treaty, Sloan makes them participate."

"How does he do that?" she asked him.

"I'm not sure, actually. Probably through manipulation and fear, like the corrupt vampire he is," Jacob said grudgingly. Tara noticed he gripped the passenger side handle tightly at the mention of Dominik's name. He really didn't like Mr. Sloan. She waved the thought away and focused back on the case.

"I'd still like to question him about his alibi," she said.

"Fair enough. I'll have Cynthia look into his number when we get back to the station."

They arrived at the police garage 10 minutes later. Once up the elevator, they headed straight to Cynthia's desk.

"Oh suga, what happened?" Cynthia asked, eyes full of pity after seeing Jacob.

"Got into a fight," he told her.

"My god," she said, placing her hand on her black opal necklace. "What can I do, Cherri? Need anything? Come, let's get you cleaned up," she said sympathetically.

"It's alright," Jacob replied. He leaned in and cupped his hand around his mouth. "You should see the other guy," he whispered. Both laughed shrilly. This seemed to ease Cynthia's worry. Tara rolled her eyes. She wasn't sure she was going to like Cynthia. There was just something fake about her that unnerved her.

"Anyway, Cynthia," Tara interrupted. "We need a number to a Michael Beagan when you have a moment."

Cynthia looked at Tara as if noticing her for the first time. She snapped out of the giggly school girl act and back to work. "Okay, suga," she replied. Cynthia started typing away on her computer, the keyboard a blaze of finger strokes. "Did you pick out an office you like?"

Tara had completely forgotten all about getting an office. She had been too distracted with ogres, and shapeshifters, and werewolves. Ogres, and shapeshifters, and werewolves, oh my!

"Not yet," she answered solemnly. "I'll get around to it sometime today."

Cynthia nodded. "Well I hope you'll be happy with the choices available. I wish I could have an office, but the chief needs me here." Tara wondered if it was more for her spying skills than her filing skills.

"Okay," she said. "I have three Michael Beagan's in our database. One in Queen Anne, one in Wallingford, and one in Laurelhurst. Which number do you need?"

Tara honestly didn't know, but Jacob seemed to. "The one in Laurelhurst, please," he replied.

Cynthia grabbed a pink post-it note off her desk and jotted down the number. When she finished, she handed it to Tara. "Here you go, honey," she said.

Tara thanked her. They hurried into Jacob's office. It was time to call the wolf man.

Chapter 10

They went to CJ's Eatery for lunch. Tara left three messages for Michael, but he hadn't call back yet. Neither of them had eaten anything in the last 24 hours, and hunger was becoming an issue. Jacob told Tara of an amazing breakfast joint on 1st avenue close by. The words 'breakfast' and 'close by' won her over.

Now, as she chewed on her biscuits and gravy, she began to wonder what the rest of the supernatural world was like. Bethany had told her there were many different types of creatures, but only six of them lived in Seattle. She had met vampires and ogres, and they were scary enough. Jacob, although a shapeshifter, did not appear to be scary. What he told her of his family made her believe that they were more ruthless than frightening. What were the other monsters like?

Jacob took a bite of his French toast and saw the wheels turning in her head. "What are you thinking about?" he asked, taking a sip of his black, no sugar coffee.

She swallowed her food and gulped down her orange juice. "Honestly? I feel like I'm out of my depth. Finding out everything this morning and seeing what I've already seen. I know it shouldn't be possible, and yet, it is."

He gave her a sympathetic look. "I imagine it will take some getting used to," he replied. He took another slurp of his coffee.

"Bethany said there are other," she leaned in closer as to not be overheard, "creatures that aren't in Seattle." Jacob nodded in agreement. "How many more?"

He shrugged. "Lots," he said while cutting up his hash browns. "Some nice, some not so nice, and then some a hell of a lot worse than what lives here in Seattle."

"How do you know they aren't here in Seattle?" she asked him intently.

She waited for him to swallow what he had in his mouth. "The witches took care of that a long time ago. From what I've been told, after the treaty had been signed, everyone wanted to make sure that no other creature could come and try to provoke another war. The witches put up a sort of barrier around Seattle that wards off creatures who get too close to the city."

Tara's eyes grew wide as she sat there staring at him. He took a sip of his coffee before continuing. "If a creature passes a certain perimeter, they suddenly feel the need to head into the opposite direction. The more persistent ones who continue to push on get disoriented and lose their way. The barrier eats away at them until they have no choice but to turn back."

Tara thought about that for a moment. She couldn't believe they were actually having a conversation about witches and spells. It all just seemed too unreal. The witches must be very powerful to be able to make a spell like that. Then a thought occurred to her.

"What happens if you decide to leave Seattle? Can you come back? If that barrier keeps supernatural creatures away, how does it not affect you?"

Jacob chuckled, spewing bits of hash browns down his chin. He wiped it with his napkin and swallowed. "I'm sorry," he said. "It's just that your curiosity amuses me." He laughed again, and the whole dining room turned to stare at him. Tara felt her cheeks go red. She kicked him under the table and turned toward the crowd.

"Sorry, everyone. I'm just a funny gal," she told them. Most went back to their food without a second thought, but some gave her a look of annoyance. She bent closer to Jacob. "Look, I'm doing my best to understand you and your kind," she whispered. "Don't laugh at me for asking questions. Seems I have the right to know them."

He raised his hands to calm her anger. "All right, all right. Sorry," he told her. "I just never had to explain everything to anyone before. It's still new to me too." He took a bite of hash brown before continuing. "To answer your question, the barrier only works if you're outside it. Everyone inside is fine."

"And if one of you leaves?" She asked, cupping her orange juice with both hands.

"We are able to get back in, but you have to wear a talisman that the witches provide."

"You're joking," she said.

He shook his head. "Afraid not. It's just another way for the Sloan's to exert their control over Seattle."

She didn't understand. "What do the Sloan's have to do with it?"

"Well think about it for a moment," he said. "You must run to the witches if you want to leave and come back. The witches hold power over the rest of the clans. Mr. Sloan runs the witches. He is like a king, sitting in his high castle, watching over the rest of the peons who live below him." He shook his head again and anger flashed in his eyes.

"Well he certainly built quite the regime, hasn't he?" she asked him. He shrugged in response. She felt a buzz go off in her pocket that caused her to jump slightly. She grabbed at it and realized it was her phone.

"This is detective Bancroft," she spoke into it.

"You called me?" a deep male voice said in reply.

"Is this Michael Beagan?" she asked. Jacob was suddenly very attentive.

"Yes," he said, "But whatever it is, I don't know nothin about nothin."

"Well, Mr. Beagan, I would like you to come to the station and answer some questions in regards to Eric Sloan."

"Ah," he said. "Is that what this is about? That little pompous ass told you I threatened him, didn't he? Well, you can relax, detective. It was a bar fight. Just two guys blowing off steam. Nothing more."

"I'd love to relax, Mr. Beagan, but you see, Eric was murdered last night."

Silence filled the phone. She waited patiently for his reaction. "And you think I killed him?"

"I don't know," she confessed. "But by your own admission, you did threaten him, did you not?"

"It was a bar fight," he repeated. "Things get said in fights. It doesn't mean that once the dust settles, you plan on following through."

"Look, Mr. Beagan. I've been informed by my partner, Detective Moore, that you are second in command of the pack." She paused to give him time to understand that she wasn't just a human. She was a human who knew what he truly was.

"Is that how that shifter gets his rocks off? By telling humans of our kind?"

"Oh, he didn't tell me, Mr. Beagan. The Sloan's told me, but that is not the point," she replied, switching the phone to her other ear.

"Yeah, so what is your point, de-tect-ive?" he annunciated every syllable. She rolled her eyes. She had been up against tough guys before and none of them have ever succeeded in intimidating her.

"Maybe I should have a talk with Troy and see if he can make you a little bit more cooperative," she said sweetly.

"You do what you have to do," he replied, then the line went dead.

"Charming man," she told Jacob as she put her phone away.

"So, didn't get anywhere?" he asked as he took the last bite of his French toast.

"Not really, no. He claims he didn't do it." she began drumming her fingers on the table.

"Do you believe him?"

She thought for a moment. "I don't know," she admitted. "He comes across as arrogant and hostile. But that doesn't make him a killer."

Jacob took a swig of his coffee. "Guess it's off to meet the wolf pack then."

"Why is that?" she asked him.

"Well, I doubt we will get anywhere if he's lying. Troy, on the other hand, will make him tell us the truth."

She squinted at him. "I don't see how Troy can be of much help. Even if he is the pack leader, it doesn't mean he can force Michael to be honest."

Jacob smiled slowly. "You have much to learn, young padawan."

Tara hated Star Wars. It was Kenneth's favorite movie and they must have watched it at least one hundred times within the first year of them dating. She shook the memory away as the checks arrived.

Tara finished her orange juice before she fished out $20.00 from her wallet. Jacob paid his tab with a credit card. Their waitress, an older lady with a gray perm and a small limp in her step, graciously accepted the $5.00 tip Tara left inside the book. She nodded to them as they headed out the door.

The brisk air hit Tara like a smack in the face. Although it was still sunny out, it had gotten colder and the wind had kicked up hard. Tara was reminded of an old wild west movie she had seen once, where the wind sent tumbleweeds and dust clouds across the dirt walkways. People were busy heading in all directions. Colorful coats passed her by. She noticed people wearing hats and gloves. She envied them. She should probably buy some herself when she found the time.

An object on the concrete reflected the sunlight into her eyes. It was a shiny penny. See a penny, pick it up, all day long you'll have good luck, Tara thought. On a day like today, she could use some luck. The more, the merrier, right? "Couldn't hurt," she whispered to herself and bent down to grab it.

Something whizzed past her head and into the glass door of CJ's, shattering it. Tara had a moment to glance back before her partner pulled her to the ground. She heard gunshots echo through the street as bullets collided with the building behind them. People exploded with panic, running frantically in every direction. One girl wearing headphones didn't hear the shots and got hit in the neck. Her body slammed into the brick wall with a thump before falling to the ground, dead.

Screams echoed over the gun blasts. Car windows exploded, sending shards of glass raining down on the detectives. People lay bleeding on the chilly sidewalk and all Tara could do was watch. She wanted to help them, but the bullets kept coming.

Then as quickly as the shooting began, it had stopped. Tires burned the asphalt as the shooters sped away. Jacob got up, gun in hand, and chased after the van. Tara bolted to the injured.

An older man was bent over a lady who had been shot in the shoulder. Tara grabbed his hands and forced them on the wound, telling him to keep pressure on it. She told a woman in a trench coat to call an ambulance. The woman nodded to her and pulled out her phone.

Tara ran to the girl with the headphones. Music blared out of the tiny speakers as she lay in a puddle of her own blood. Her lifeless eyes were staring straight at Tara. There was nothing she could do for her.

Jacob came rushing back. He whipped Tara around and checked her over. "Are you hit?"

"No," she said, shaking her head. "You?"

"No." He dropped his hands and checked the scene. "Jesus fucking Christ!" he screamed.

"Did you get a license plate?" She asked him, looking around at the wounded.

"No, it was blacked out," he replied.

She bent down to help a man who got shot in the stomach. "Go check inside. I'll help out here." Jacob did. In the distance, Tara could hear the faint sound of sirens. "You're going to be okay," she told the man. "The ambulance is on its way." Blood was spilling out of his abdomen in spurts. He screamed loudly as she pushed hard on it to stop the blood flow. He passed out from the pain. The sirens grew closer.

People were crying and yelling out in pain. Pedestrians were helping the other injured and Tara felt grateful. She couldn't get to them all. Cars stopped on the road and some got out to help as well. Who says people don't help when tragedy hits?

If it hadn't been for that penny, she thought as she kept applying pressure to his wound. Lucky penny indeed.

Chapter 11

The street was closed off, blocked by yards of yellow tape. Traffic had been redirected up to 2nd Ave and policemen tried to keep the crowd of thirsty onlookers behind the line. The wounded were strapped to gurneys and being led into flashing ambulances. Tara overheard one of the EMT's say they were going to Virginia Mason, but she wasn't sure what that was.

There was an abundance of cops on the scene. Some were inside checking out the bullet holes and interviewing witnesses. The same was happening outside CJ's as well. Officer Robertson was asking both Jacob and Tara questions about the shooting.

"And you didn't see anything unusual before the shooting began?" he asked.

Tara shook her head. "No," Jacob told him. "I've already told you. There was nothing abnormal going on. One minute we were walking out of the diner, the next, gunshots were fired." Jacob was livid. They had been sitting against the back of an ambulance for almost an hour getting checked over while Robertson conducted his line of questions.

"Hey, don't bite my head off," Robertson told him. "You know how this game is played."

"This isn't a game," Tara interrupted. She was annoyed that he kept asking the same questions over and over. It was cold outside and her hands had gone numb. She should be out helping the injured, but Robertson delayed her.

The only upside, if you could call any of this an upside, was that CJ's Eatery gave the officers working the scene free coffee and tea. She respected them a lot more now than when she had left.

The same waitress that waited on them was out on the street refilling cups with a large pot of coffee. She deserves more than a $5.00 tip, Tara thought to herself.

Robertson pressed on. "Then what happened?"

Jacob sighed and shook his head. "We ducked behind that car," Jacob said, pointing to the green Nissan near the curb, "and waited for the gunfire to stop. The van sped away and I chased after it."

"Did you get the make and model of the vehicle?"

"It was a gray van with tinted windows. Four doors, as far as I can tell. Blacked out license plate."

Robertson jotted down some notes on his little notebook. "What did you do while he chased the vehicle?" he asked Tara.

"I checked the scene and began helping the injured." She was clutching the penny in her right palm with renewed force.

"That's when I came back and made sure she wasn't hurt. Then I went inside to help while she stayed and helped out here." Jacob glanced at his watch impatiently.

"Well, it seems to me, you did all that you could, given the circumstances. I'll Inform the Chief," Robertson told them. Tara nodded.

The girl with the headphones was being moved and a white sheet was dredged over her body. Tara stared at it while the EMT's lifted her into an ambulance. Robertson noticed and whispered. "You did all that you could."

"That doesn't make me feel any better," Tara replied, watching the ambulance drive away. The sun was beginning to set, casting hues of red and purple throughout the night's sky. It illuminated the Space Needle which appeared above the tops of the buildings nearby. Under different circumstances, it would have been beautiful.

Flashes of light caught her attention. She turned to see newscasters and bystanders taking shots of the crime scene. She could tell Facebook was going to be filled with the images in less than an hour. She shook her head.

Chief Martinez strolled over to them. "How are they?" he asked Robertson.

"Fine, as far as I can tell, sir. The EMT examined them, found injuries, but both claim they are not from this incident."

"They're not," Jacob replied. "Trust us."

"Then you want to explain the injuries?" Robertson asked. Chief Martinez waited for a response. Tara and Jacob exchanged glances. How do you tell your boss that you were beaten by ogres? Or that a vampire saved your life after almost being raped?

"Captain, do you trust me?" Jacob asked him. The chief stared into Jacob's eyes. He arched an eyebrow, causing more wrinkles to appear over his face. After studying Jacob for a while, he finally nodded. "Then trust that these injuries have no merit here."

Robertson grunted.

The captain studied the detectives. He then bowed his head, defeated. "Cut them loose," he ordered Robertson.

"But....but sir," Robertson started, but the chief raised his hand to silence him.

"It's been a long day and they are exhausted. Let them rest and recuperate. I'm sure whatever they will have to tell us will be equally as interesting tomorrow morning."

Robertson looked like he would explode. His face became the color of deep crimson and he bit his lip to keep from speaking. "Yes, sir," he said grudgingly.

Tara stood and gave Robertson a pleasant smile as Chief Martinez waltzed over to the nightly newscasters. Robertson was infuriated.

"You know I think you are a good cop, Moore," he said behind clenched teeth. "But you are keeping secrets, and for all we know, those secrets are why that girl is dead in the ambulance."

Jacob recoiled. It was like a slap in the face. "You think this is my fault?"

"For all we know, this could be," Robertson cried out sharply.

Jacob moved right up to his face. They stood so close that their noses touched. Neither of them backed down. Tara squeezed between them and pushed both backward.

"Walk away," she screamed at Jacob, then turned to Robertson. "The bad guys are out there! Not here."

"You'll want to move now," he replied angrily. He balled his hands into fists and made to move toward Jacob again.

"That'll be perfect," Tara stated. "Let's fight in front of the news crew. The media will see that instead of trying to help the victims and catch the perpetrators, we are too busy fighting amongst ourselves."

He stopped midstride. He glanced from Jacob to Tara. He turned toward the media who was already pointing cameras in their direction. He backed off and composed himself. "Good boy," Tara said playfully. She turned and grabbed her partner by the arm, leading him away.

"I should have punched him," Jacob huffed.

"Yeah, maybe, but not with all the cameras around." She led him to the side of the diner. "Besides, he did have a point."

Jacob gave her a sharp look. "What? You can't possibly believe that this shooting had anything to do with me?"

She shook her head in response. "No, I think it has to do with our case." He scrunched his face in disbelief, then she noticed the wheels turning in his head. Realization hit him and his eyes went wide.

"When I got attacked last night, I thought that it had been a random mugging. But when I checked the alley this morning, there was no evidence that an attack had even taken place. Someone had cleaned up. It got me thinking, 'who would do that?' Then after we stepped outside CJ's, someone shot at us. Not the diner, or the pedestrians that were walking by. Us."

Jacob took in a deep breath and exhaled slowly. "Still, the two events could be unrelated."

"Call it an educated guess," she responded. "But I don't think so. I literally felt the bullet whiz past my face. If I hadn't bend down to pick this up," she held the penny up for Jacob to see, "I'd probably be lying side by side with the girl in the ambulance."

"And you think that they have to do with our case?" He asked, still unsure. "The shootings, I mean?"

"I do," she said solemnly. "Someone doesn't want us on this case. Someone doesn't want us to know who killed Eric Sloan."

Jacob turned and kicked the brick wall. He winced in pain after realizing that the wall did more damage to him than he to it. "Sorry," he said softly as the anger leeched away. "This case is turning out to be worse than I originally thought."

"I understand your frustration," she said soothingly. "but I need you focused, got it?" He nodded.

"Psst," came a soft whisper in the shadows. Both detectives jumped at the sound and turned to look down the road. It was Bethany. She waved them over and then disappeared into an alleyway. Jacob glanced at the other officers still on the scene. No one had even noticed they weren't there. No one was paying attention. They were too busy handling the news crew and keeping the crowd at bay.

They crept quietly down the road and into the alley. "Are you guys okay?" she asked. Her pale face was full of worry.

"We're fine," Jacob huffed. "But not everyone was so lucky."

"What are you doing here?" Tara asked her.

"I saw the news on TV and came as soon as I could."

"Why?" Jacob asked tensely. This seemed to startle Bethany.

"Because I told you, no harm will come to you," she spoke to Tara. Tara looked at her, then at her partner. Tara began a giggle that grew into a full chortle of laughter. She glanced at Bethany again and doubled over, laughing as loud as she could. Both Bethany and Jacob exchanged worried glances.

"I'm sorry," Tara managed to choke out, "It's just, someone didn't seem to get the memo." This sent her into overdrive, and tears rolled down her cheeks as she laughed. She clutched her side as pain began to build from the laughter. Jacob joined in, and soon, both were laughing madly. Bethany stared at them in wonderment.

"I'm sorry," Tara uttered again as the laughter dissipated. "It's just comical with everything that has happened in the last two days." Jacob nodded in agreement.

"I can imagine," Bethany replied. "I sometimes laugh at inappropriate times as well." She was standing there completely still and her face was utterly blank of expression. Tara wondered if that was actually true considering how much lack of emotion she had.

Jacob looked back up the street to check on the cops. No one was coming. "Well, thanks for checking on us," he said, "but as you can see, we're fine. You can go now."

Bethany crossed her arms over her chest. "I think not. Someone has just tried to kill you both. I think, for the time being, it's best you two stay at my place tonight."

Jacob was taken aback. "What?" he asked in disbelief. "Uh, no thanks. There is no way I am staying at the house of the man who murdered my lover."

"But with the shooting and the attack in the alley last night, clearly you are being targeted." Tara gave him a smug look. She secretly applauded Bethany for making the same connection.

"Yeah, well I'll take my chances," he said heatedly. "Besides, I don't think your father would like that anymore than I would."

Bethany shrugged. "Suit yourself, exile. But Tara is a big girl and can make her own decisions."

"I'm with Detective Moore on this one," she stated calmly. "I haven't slept in my own bed in close to 40 hours. After what happened, it would be nice to go home and not think of anything."

"I understand, but I don't think your places are safe anymore."

"Why is that?" Jacob asked, rolling his eyes at Bethany.

Bethany gave him a harsh look. "And you call yourself a detective. Think for a moment. How did the gunmen find you?"

That was a thought Tara didn't think about. How had they found them? If the shooting had to do with the case, how did they know where they were? They didn't tell anyone they were going to CJ's for lunch. The gunmen had to either follow them from the police station or they tracked them through some other means, probably through GPS on their phones. Either thought was disturbing. If they could find them at a diner, most likely they could find them at their homes as well.

"Ah, there you go," Bethany said softly as she watched Tara make the connections. "Your places aren't safe. Not until you find whoever killed my brother."

"I'm not completely convinced that the shooting had anything to do with your brother's death," Jacob stammered out. He had put his hands on his waist in a defiant stance.

"Tell me, exile," Bethany said in a sweet voice. "Is it pride as a man that holds you back from accepting my help, or shifter arrogance?"

Jacob balled his hands into fists. His face turned red and he took a step toward Bethany. She didn't even flinch.

"Enough!" Tara ordered. "Jacob? Go get the car."

"Why?" he asked, staring at Bethany. He didn't move.

Tara grabbed his arm and pulled him away. "Excuse us a moment," she said. She led him to the mouth of the alley. "Look. I don't like it anymore than you do. But right now we have people after us. The best course of action is to stay at a safe place. If Bethany can provide us with a safe house for the night, then so be it."

Jacob took in a deep breath and shook his head. "Fine," he conceded. "But for the record, I hate this idea."

"Noted," she said, giving him a soft smile. "Now please. Go get the car."

Chapter 12

A half hour later, Bethany escorted the detectives into her home. They passed the foyer and walked down the hallway toward the giant library. Once inside, Bethany turned on the fireplace with a push of a button. Sparks exploded over the wood, and an instant later, fire was raging inside the hearth. They crowded around it, facing each other as they sat around the oval coffee table.

Getting away from the crime scene had been no easy feat. Cops were everywhere and traffic had been diverted. The car had been trapped behind the yellow tape and Jacob had to order two younger officers to let him pass. Robertson had seen Jacob trying to flee and ran over, holding up his hand.

"Where do you think you're going?" he asked sternly.

"Look, Austin," Jacob started but Chief Martinez waltzed over.

"Let him through," he barked at the officers. They nodded quickly and sprang into action.

"Chief, I really don't think he ought...," Robertson said, but Martinez held up a hand again.

"I told you to let them rest. We can all talk tomorrow morning. Now do your job, Robertson, and help the EMT's."

Robertson took in a deep breath. "Yes, sir," he said behind a clenched jaw. He stomped off toward an ambulance.

Jacob thanked him, but Martinez shook his head.

"Don't thank me. I know you know more than you're letting on. You have that look on you. But whatever it is, it had better be good. Get some rest, and fill me in tomorrow morning." Jacob nodded and pulled onto the street.

He had to double back in order to pick up the girls. Tara got into the front seat and Bethany sat behind her.

"Any trouble?" Tara asked.

"None that I couldn't handle," he replied as he backed out of the alley.

Now that they were safely inside the Sloan's home, Tara didn't know what to do next. She supposed they should all put their heads together and figure out who tried to kill them, but she was physically and mentally exhausted.

"I can show you to your rooms if you'd like. We can talk more in the morning." Tara nodded in agreement but Jacob would have none of it.

"I'd like to get something straight, vampire," he said, leaning on his elbows. "Just because my partner may trust you, doesn't mean I do." Bethany stared at him stoically. "Just because you helped us out with a place to stay doesn't mean we are friends."

"I understand your trepidation, detective," she replied calmly. "But this is for your protection. I can sympathize with the loss of a loved one, seeing as how my brother is now dead, but I do suggest you suck it up, or it's going to be a long night."

Jacob opened his mouth to say something, but Tara leaned forward. "Thank you, Bethany. We," she made the word firm, "appreciate your kindness."

The door opened behind her and Dominic Sloan glided through. He took in the scene and his face furrowed instantly. "Bethany, what did you do?"

"Father," she said in a surprising voice. "We have house guests tonight."

He continued without acknowledging them. "You silly girl! How could you bring them here? Do you know what has happened tonight? They," he pointed to the detectives, "are bad omens, and you bring them here? Now?"

Bethany stood and crept over to her father. "Someone is trying to kill them, dad." She wiped a stray strand of blonde hair out of her face and continued. "They are our best chance at finding out what has happened to Eric. We have the strength to protect them."

"Oh, do we now?" he asked mockingly. He shook his head disdainfully at her, then turned toward the detectives for the first time. Tara shuffled uncomfortably as Dominic's gaze locked in with hers. "How do you two feel about staying here?"

Tara's mouth went dry and she wet her lips with her tongue before speaking. "If it keeps us alive," she started, but Jacob interrupted.

"I was against it from the start," he admitted. Tara shot him a sideways glance before continuing her original statement.

"If it keeps us alive, then we are grateful for your hospitality." She smiled up at him, but it didn't meet her eyes.

Dominic stood remarkably still as he stared at Tara. If she hadn't known better, she would have thought he was a statue or one of those street performers that only move after you tip them. He finally stirred and looked back at his daughter.

"Just the one night," he conceded, shaking his head again. Bethany smiled brightly, flashing nothing but white teeth. She leaned in to hug him, but he held up his hand to stop her. "Whether they get killed or not, they will not be staying here another night. Do I make myself clear?" Bethany frowned but nodded in agreement.

"What do you mean, 'whether we get killed or not'?" Jacob asked, but Dominic was already gone. Tara hadn't seen him leave. Man, he was quick.

"Don't worry about him," Bethany told them as she sat back down in her chair. "He's just nervous because the ball is in a couple days." She was staring at Jacob as she spoke. Jacob made a slight jerk and Tara caught it.

"That time a year already?"

Bethany laughed lightly. "You've been out of the loop now that you've been exiled." Bethany meant it as jest but Jacob balled his hands into fists. He started to shake with anger. Bethany looked amused.

Tara wasn't sure what was going on. She put her palm on his arm and he tensed slightly. He whipped his head toward her as if startled. He relaxed a little when he saw her confused expression and nodded his appreciation.

"What's the ball?" Tara asked aloud.

"It's an annual dance my father hosts with the Royal families," Bethany told her.

"It's more than just a dance," Jacob whispered.

"What do you mean?"

"Well, all the royal families are required to be there," Bethany explained. "Every supernatural creature here in Seattle can attend, and most do. They pay homage to all the families, and in return, the Royals offer them protection and prosperity throughout the year."

"You mean become the Royals slaves for the year or they leave them to fend for themselves," Jacob shot at her.

Bethany sneered back. "I would hardly call it slavery. We just remind them that it's in everyone's best interest to be a part of the family rather than to be alone." Jacob rolled his eyes but did not try to correct her.

Tara was still confused. "Protection from what?"

Bethany turned to her. "Pardon?"

"You said the Royals offer protection to their subjects. Protection from what?" Tara asked again.

"From humans, of course." She said it like it was plain as day. Tara shook her head. Jacob elaborated.

"You see," he started. "Once humans find out about something different, they tend to freak. Instead of learning more about it, they would rather harm or kill what they don't understand."

"That can't be true for all humans," Tara stated in disbelief. "I don't want to harm any of you. I'm more worried about getting harmed from you." She meant that last part as a joke, but the look on both Bethany and Jacob's faces told her they didn't take it that way.

"You did freak out when you found out I was a vampire," Bethany reminded her. "Just imagine what a group of humans would do. First, they would panic. Then a mob mentality would form and they would try to destroy us."

Bethany had a point. People were always fearful of the unknown. That was one of the reasons why most people are afraid of the dark as a child. Who knows what kind of monsters could be waiting for them in the dark. As you grow up, you realize the only type of monsters are the human kind. You lock your doors at night and sleep tight. What would people do if they found out monsters were real? Would they want to kill them just for existing? Probably. But it seems that the monsters are equally as fearful of humans. Strange coincidence.

"Anyway," Jacob continued, "the ball unifies the community and shows the clan members that the Royals have the power to protect them. In theory, anyway. It's ultimately for the Royals to gain more power."

"Jealous, exile, now that you won't be able to attend?" Bethany asked.

"Not in the slightest," he retorted.

"Are you two going to quibble back and forth all night or can you two stop long enough for us to figure out who tried to kill us?" Tara said harshly.

They looked at her, and for the first time, Tara saw Bethany look embarrassed. It was as if Tara caught her with her hand in a cookie jar. Jacob nodded his head and bit his lower lip.

"Alright," she said. "Now, do you think the ball has anything to do with how your brother was killed?"

Bethany thought for a while. "It's possible," she stated. "Or that whomever killed him would certainly be there."

"It definitely doesn't look good that a royal died right before the ball," Jacob told her.

"How so?"

"Well think about it. If the subjects are supposed to be protected by the royal families, yet they can't even protect themselves, it does not bode well for the future." Jacob sighed. "I wouldn't be surprised if some of the supernatural creatures left Seattle by now."

Tara could see how someone looking for protection would leave and try for a safer area. But if it was her, she would stay and stick it out. Trust the devil you know. Then a thought hit her and she was surprised she hadn't thought of it before.

"Maybe it's someone's intention to make the royals appear weak," she told them.

"What do you mean?" Bethany asked.

"You said that the royal families gain power from their subjects and a royal was murdered right before this ball. The rest of the subjects have got to be frightened a little. Might drive some of them off, causing the Royal's to lose some of their power."

Jacob shook his head. "I don't think whoever the killer is targeted all the royals. Seems to me that they just focused on one family in particular."

Bethany arched an eyebrow at him. She scooted closer to the edge of her seat. "We have always been a targeted family, detective. We hold the Dradogian."

"True," he said, agreeing with her. "But no one has ever succeeded in killing one of you before yesterday. It has to make the subjects a little frightened. Whether you hold the Dradogian or not, someone is powerful enough to come after your family."

Bethany squinted slightly, then she was back to her straight face. She gave Jacob an icy glare. Jacob seemed not to notice.

"Of course, this is all speculative until we can find the evidence to support this theory," Tara interrupted, trying to smooth things over.

"Quite right," Jacob nodded. "We really need to talk to Troy tomorrow."

"And, alas," Bethany told them. "I believe it's time to show you to your rooms for the evening. I must go and feed soon." Bethany stood up so suddenly that Tara let out a gasp of surprise. "You've both had a long day, you have got to be exhausted." No one argued with her.

She led them up the spiral staircase and out into a corridor. Tara recognized the doors they passed. It was the same locked doors she had tried earlier that morning.

"Why do you have so many rooms?" she asked Bethany.

"Where else are the other vampires going to sleep?"

Tara stopped walking. Other vampires? "I thought it was just your family here in Seattle."

Bethany smiled at her. "It was, for a time. But all royals need subjects and you can't expect the master of the city to rule the size of Seattle without some backup, can you?" She laughed as if the idea was ludicrous.

"Great," Jacob whispered. "Your own personal vampire army. So glad paranoia doesn't run in this family."

"Well ever since the fire, we've had to make some...adjustments to keep what is ours."

Tara wasn't sure what fire she was talking about, but Jacob seemed to. He stiffened faintly as he followed. Tara made a mental note to ask him about it later. Right now, she wanted to shut everything out. She had had enough with dealing with the supernatural world for one night. All she wanted to do was sleep.

Bethany led them to the same room Tara woke up in. Jacob got the room across the hall from her. "Sleep well, detectives," Bethany called from the hallway. "I'll make sure food will be brought up in the morning." she nodded to them, then was suddenly gone.

Tara shut the door behind her and lurched toward the bed. She fell face first into the soft duvet. Within minutes, she was sound asleep.

Chapter 13

She dreamed. Tara was standing in the middle of a large room. Hundreds of people were dancing in fancy suits and gowns all around her. She tried to wade through the dancers, but they seem to cut her off at every turn. The dancers sang and waltzed cheerfully behind masquerade masks.

All of a sudden, they stopped in unison. The entire room turned and stared at her. Tara yelled at them, but they didn't move. A large caw echoed throughout the room and Tara had to cover her ears. The caw vibrated inside her head.

All at once, the crowd advanced toward her. She tried to back away but couldn't move. She was glued to the floor. The crowd lifted their masks and she screamed. Their faces were gone, replaced by skulls. Maggots and worms crawled through the eye sockets and out their noses. They opened their jaws and laughed, spewing maggots onto the floor. They reached for her. She screamed again.

The dream changed. Tara was now in a graveyard leaning against a hollowed out tree. Mist swirled around her feet and she shivered in the moonlight. She glanced around and saw a group of people dressed in funeral attire. They were huddled around a single gravestone.

She recognized one of them. It was Anton Wright. He held a single red rose that flashed bright in the moonlight. He placed the rose gently on the coffin in front of him, and it began to inch itself into the ground. She walked up to the crowd and read the name on the Tombstone. It said, Dominic Sloan.

She gasped loudly. The group turned and stared at her. A caw echoed off in the distance. She looked up and saw crow eyes peering down at her. Her heart began to race as the crow leaped from its branch and flew toward her. Tara began to run. The crow cawed after her. She screamed as the crow swooped down upon her.

"Wake up, Tara!" Jacob yelled. Tara shot up out of bed so quickly that she knocked him to the floor.

"What happened," she asked groggily.

Jacob rose slowly, bracing himself on the bed. "You were dreaming," he replied. "Loudly." Tara sat back down on the bed and took in a deep breath. Her heart was still beating incredibly fast and she could feel it against her chest, like a caged animal trying to break out. Sweat dripped down her matted hair. She wiped her forehead with the back of her hand.

"Must have been some dream," he stated. "You're covered in sweat."

"It was," she replied. Her breath was heavy in her throat and she was thirsty.

"Care to tell me about it?"

She shook her head. "It was just a dream," she told him. "I normally don't have bad dreams, but lately it's been nothing but."

Jacob smirked. "Yeah, well, you found out monsters are real. That has got to be messing with your psyche somehow."

"You're probably right," she admitted. "But these dreams are crazy." she looked around for a clock but didn't see one. "What time is it?"

Jacob glanced at his watch. "4 A.M."

Damn, Tara thought. It was still too early. "Sorry I woke you up. And for knocking you on the floor."

"Well, it's been a crazy couple of days. Getting knocked on the floor is the least of my worries." He gave her a comforting smile. She smiled back.

"Still, I wouldn't be surprised if you request a new partner," she jibed. "One that isn't abusive."

Jacob shook his head. "Oh don't think the thought hadn't crossed my mind. Since you became my partner, I've been choked by an ogre king, thrown out by guards, broke my glasses, and, oh yeah, shot at." He smiled again, winking at her. "Have I forgotten anything?"

"Staying at your immortal enemy's house?"

"Quite right," he replied. "I think that one hurts the worst. Still, you're doing remarkably well, considering."

"At least you weren't mugged," she said, giving him some sort of condolence.

He laughed. "Yes, there is that. Although, technically, neither were you." He had a point. Bethany had saved her before she was mugged, or worse. That seemed so long ago, yet it was only a night before. Much has happened since then.

Jacob stood slowly. "Well, I'm going to try to sleep some more. I hope you can get back to sleep as well." They nodded their goodbyes and he turned to leave, but Bethany was suddenly there.

"Jesus!" Jacob shrieked. "You don't just sneak up on people like that. You make noise when you walk."

"Quiet, shifter," she ordered. "Time to go. Grab your things."

Tara was suddenly alert. Bethany's face was a blank canvas but she thought she saw worry in her eyes. "What's happened?" she asked quietly.

"Later," she replied. "Right now we have to get you two someplace safe."

"We? Who's we?" Jacob asked as Bethany left the doorway. Jacob followed her out with Tara on his heels.

"Us," a deep voice said in front of Jacob. Tara sidestepped her partner and came face to face with three men. The one on the right was shorter than the other two, maybe 5'5, but his broad shoulders and arms were the size of elephant legs. His hair was shaved close to his scalp. His slanted eyes were bright blue, with specks of green flakes. He was beautiful, almost feminine looking, if not for his huge body mass.

Next to him stood a taller, slender man. He was almost a foot taller than elephant arms. He had his long red hair braided into a single braid that hung over his right shoulder. He wore a black tank top and sweats. He wasn't nearly as built as the shorter one, but he was definitely toned.

The last guy was a bald black man. Tara noticed he wasn't just dark, he was the color of night himself. He was thinner than the other two but taller than both. He towered over everyone in the hallway. His clothes seemed to hang off him as if he bought them too big.

"What's going on?" Tara asked urgently. Maybe it was the tone in her voice or the entourage, but Jacob answered for Bethany.

"They're here, aren't they?"

As if on cue, gunshots rang out somewhere inside the house. Tara's heart began to beat fast again. "Shit!" she stammered.

"You know what to do," Bethany spoke to the three men. They nodded in unison. Then she was gone.

"Follow us," the redhead ordered and ran down the hallway. The other two waited for the detectives to move. Tara and Jacob exchanged worried glances, unsure if they should follow him or go help Bethany. Tara's instinct was to face the bad guys, not run from them.

"Please," the shorter man said. The bald guy held out a hand as if to say lady's first. Jacob seemed to be waiting for Tara to make a decision.

She conceded and headed toward the redhead. The other men followed closely behind her. More shots rang out inside the house and Tara wished she had ran to help Bethany instead. The shorter man sensed her concern

"Don't worry, detective. The Sloan's are able to protect themselves."

"Tell that to Eric," Jacob replied. Tara agreed with him but pressed on. The red head was quick but not supernatural quick. He either wasn't a vampire or he was moving slower for their sakes. She was betting it was for them.

He led them into a bedroom. This one was completely different than the room she had slept in. It was covered in tapestries. A small twin bed was positioned at the far right corner. An old musty carpet smell filled the room and Tara couldn't help but cover her nose. The men seemed to not have noticed. The redhead ran to the bed while the other two guarded the doorway.

"What are you doing?" Jacob asked the man, who was examining the bed. Tara heard a click and watched in awe as the bed lurched forward, revealing a set of stairs leading downward.

"Saving your lives," The redhead replied. He held out a hand to Tara. "Come," he motioned to her.

She hesitated, looking at her partner. Jacob shrugged in response. "I'll be right behind you," he assured her. She took in a deep breath and grabbed the man's hand. They descended the staircase into the unknown.

Chapter 14

The redhead led Tara down flight after flight into darkness. She could barely make out his silhouette let alone anything else. Their steps echoed as they pressed on. Tara almost lost her footing but the man caught her.

She was still holding his hand and it was beginning to get clammy. She tried to let go, but the man had a firm grip. "Trust me, detective," he spoke to her, "you'll want to keep holding. I can see where we're going. Can you?"

She couldn't. She wanted to argue, but what good would that do? He led her down for what seemed like an eternity. then suddenly, he stopped. Tara had almost walked right into him.

"What's wrong?" she asked him.

"We're here," he whispered back, and let go of her hand. She still couldn't make out where 'here' was, but she took his word for it. Footsteps drew closer as Jacob and the others met them at the bottom of the stairs.

"What now?" she asked.

"Now we go through the tunnels," the shorter man answered.

"You mean the sewers?" Jacob asked him.

"No," he replied. "The tunnels from the old city."

"Old city? What are you talking about?" she asked aloud. She heard a guy snicker and was betting it was the bald man. She shot him a glance, and in the darkness, was not completely sure he saw it.

Jacob's voice trailed through the darkness. "Seattle has a rich and colorful past. Much of the old city was destroyed in a fire back in 1889."

"Yeah, thanks to you lot," the redhead interrupted.

Jacob pressed on. "Anyway, because of the fire, the streets of the old city were just built over. The streets today sit about 22 feet above the wreckage. But the old city is still there. Guessing the vamps have been using it to move around in the daytime?" he asked.

"Sometimes," the shorter man said. "But it wouldn't be possible if it hadn't been for you and your kind." Tara thought she heard a mixture of pleasure and remorse in his voice. Tara was feeling a headache coming on.

"What do you mean?"

"Later," the redhead said. "Let's get these two to safety first. We can discuss the past at a later time." She heard a series of clicks and felt the floor vibrate beneath her. She heard something heavy sliding on the ground and it stopped with a bang.

"What was that?" she asked.

"A hidden wall," the shorter man answered.

A spark flashed in her eyes and she instinctively shielded her eyes from the blinding light. The redhead lit a torch and the room blazed to life. She squinted, waiting for her eyes to adjust. She peered through the opening.

They were standing in an arched brick entranceway that led to wooden streets. The ceiling had wood panels every ten feet or so, blocking the dirt and rubble from crashing down. There were a series of bricked up arches along the walls that led through the passageway.

"Impressive," Tara whispered, as she stared out into the passageway.

"Let's get moving," the redhead told them.

"Aye-aye captain," the shorter man replied saluting him. The bald man hit him on the arm in protest.

"That's enough, Harper," the redhead said. His voice held a tinge of threat in it. Harper nodded and kept silent.

"What's your name?" Tara asked him.

"Russell," he told her. She turned to look at the bald man.

"And yours?"

"Oh, he can't speak," Harper explained. She looked shocked. She had never met a mute before. "His names Andre."

"Why can't he speak?" Jacob asked rudely. Tara shook her head at his lack of tact.

"No tongue," Russell responded. Andre crossed his arms over his chest and looked away. Tara could tell he was uncomfortable with this conversation. She chose to change the subject.

"Now that we all know each other, someone want to tell me where we're going?"

"Our orders are to see you safely through the tunnels until we get to the police station," Russell said.

"Well then, after you," she held out a hand toward the tunnel. Harper smiled, exposing straight white teeth. It was a dazzling smile. One you see on a model. She hadn't noticed any fangs. Maybe he was just hired muscle and not a vampire. He stepped through the passageway and the group followed in after him.

They walked in silence, each lost in their own thoughts. Tara had never seen underground tunnels before. She felt like she was walking through the catacombs of Paris, except they haven't come across any bones.

Had Seattle really just built over the old city? Lots of history here, preserved in time. She was sure it happened all over the world. Conquering nations would capture a city and just rebuild over the rubble. But Seattle had never been conquered by anyone, at least not that she knew of.

"I didn't realize the tunnels extended this far into magnolia," Jacob spoke.

"There is a lot of the city you may not be aware of, detective," Harper said serenely.

"Harper," Russell said, and that was enough. Harper fell silent. Tara could tell he was afraid of Russell. She was betting Harper was the youngest in the crowd.

Russell stopped and held his arms out. He sniffed the air and growled low.

"What is it?" Tara whispered.

"We're not alone," he said. Tara's heart began to beat faster. The bodyguards circled around the detectives. Jacob drew his gun, clasping it in both hands. Tara forgot she had a gun and withdrew hers as well. Her police training kicked in and she felt calmer. More relaxed, somehow.

"Russell," Harper whispered.

"I hear them," he replied, his voice barely audible. "Dre, go!"

Andre tilted his head to one side and Tara heard his neck crack. She cringed at the sound. He was suddenly gone.

Shots rang out further down the tunnel and Tara saw faint flashes of light, followed by screams. More flashes echoed down the passageway but stopped abruptly.

"Harper," Russell whispered. Harper nodded and then he too had disappeared inside the tunnel.

Tara felt stupid just standing there. She wanted to know what was happening. Jacob had the same idea. He started for the tunnel, but Russell held up a fist to stop him. Harper and Andre appeared. "All clear."

"How many?" Russell asked.

"Four, for now," Harper explained. "But there are more further up ahead. And I'm betting they heard the gunshots."

Russell turned to the detectives. "Alright, we will take care of them. You two wait here."

"I don't think so," Jacob said angrily. "We can help." Tara nodded in agreement.

"Listen, detectives," Russell told them. "It's our job to make sure you two are safe. We don't know how many we're up against and we can't be worried about your safety and eliminate the threat at the same time."

"We're officers of the law," Jacob retorted. "We're trained to handle situations like this. We can take care of ourselves."

Harper let out a laugh. Tara shot him a stern look. "We appreciate your enthusiasm," he said mockingly, "but best leave it to the professionals, exile."

Jacob's face turned a deep red. His eyes narrowed and fixed on Harper. He took a step forward him and Harper seemed even more amused. Tara touched his arm lightly and tugged him back softly.

"Look, Harper," Tara stated. "It's been a long couple of nights. We can either stand here debating over how to get us through the tunnels safely, or we can all press on together. Seems to me we all have a long way to go and the longer we stand here, the faster the bad guys can find us." Harper's grin faltered.

Tara continued. "Now, as we are officers of the law, we choose to defend ourselves. You can either join us or get out of our way. Either way, we're going."

Russell's eyes brightened and Andre's lips spread to a grin. Harper stared at her for a moment before chuckling to himself. He turned toward Russell. "I like her."

"So glad you approve," Tara sneered back and turned to Jacob. "Ready?"

"Always," he replied. They continued down the darkened path with the three guards trailing at their heels.

The tunnel turned left and they followed it in silence. The torch had gone from blazing fire to small kindling, flashing in and out of existence. The air had gotten colder and heavier. Tara found it hard to breathe but tried to focus on the flashing darkness, checking for signs of life.

Up ahead, the tunnel turned into a large room with three entrances to other passageways. On the floor were three bodies sprawled out in odd positions. Another body was pinned to the far wall with a rifle sticking out of his right shoulder.

"Jesus," Tara whispered and turned to Andre. He stiffened but stared back. Jacob checked the bodies on the ground.

They were dressed in military uniforms. BDU's. All three had semi-automatic rifles. One's head was twisted a complete 180. Another lay in a pool of his own blood. Jacob turned him over and saw that his left arm was completely missing. Tara looked around and saw the arm a little up the middle tunnel. The third was bent in half, back broken and throat ripped out.

Tara felt woozy. She wasn't sure if it was the heavy air or seeing the bodies the way they were. Probably a combination of both. She felt like she was going to puke. She had seen some awfully bad things in her time, but this took the cake. She took a wobbly step forward and felt herself fall. Russell caught her.

"Are you alright?" he asked sincerely.

She steadied herself and closed her eyes. "No, I'm not alright," she whispered. "This is what vampires do?"

"If we have to," Harper answered defensively. Tara turned to him with disgust in her eyes. He held up his hands. "Hey, it's either us or them, and I don't plan on dying here tonight. Do you, detective?"

He had a point. Still, she didn't like it. This wasn't just defending themselves. This was torturous.

"We can discuss their brutality later," Jacob chimed in. "Right now, we need to get moving." Tara turned toward her partner and nodded.

"Which way," she asked Russell.

"This way," he said and headed into the far left tunnel. Tara was grateful. She didn't want to pass the man pinned to the wall. She followed quickly, trying to put as much distance between her and that room as fast as possible.

Jacob caught up to her but didn't say anything. She appreciated that. Anger still fumed in her head and she didn't feel much like talking. What was there to say, anyway?

They walked in silence, passing several corridors and entranceways to shabby burnt buildings. Tara was tense, alert, and jumpy. The slightest noise made her skin crawl and raise her gun.

Russell stopped abruptly and sniffed the air again.

"What is it?" Jacob asked. Russell held up a hand to silence him. He took another sniff and straightened. He was like a statue and his stillness unnerved Tara. All of a sudden, he whipped around and screamed.

"RUN!"

It was too late. Shots sped through the darkness and into his back. His body jerked wildly with each bullet and Tara screamed. Harper and Andre were already on the move. Jacob threw himself on her, forcing her to the ground. Screams and bullets sprang out through the air. More screams echoed up ahead as Russell hit the ground in front of her; his eyes lifeless, cold, and dead.

Chapter 15

Tara's heart felt like it would burst from her chest. Adrenaline kicked in and she raised her gun firing into the darkness. She heard her bullets collide with something in the distance, but couldn't make out what.

Jacob was also firing back. Bullets whipped past them. One was dangerously close to hitting Tara in the face. She felt it zoom by her cheek. She rolled to her side and fired again.

More screams shot out of the darkness and the firing stopped. Both detectives lay on the ground, guns raised ready to fire. The only sound was the beating of their own hearts. Tara held her breath waiting for someone to move.

Footsteps echoed down from the corridor and Jacob fired again. Tara followed. A hand grabbed her shoulder from behind. Tara jerked around, gun raised, ready to fire at her attacker, but it was Andre. He was shaking his head and ushering them to lower their weapons. Tara slowly lowered her gun. Harper appeared next to Jacob, bending down to check on Russell. He cursed under his breath.

Tara got to her knees and peered over at Russell. His sweats were now stained with blood and a puddle expanded outward like a glass of spilled milk. There were a dozen bullet wounds in his back. Harper clawed one out with his fingers and cursed again. He held the bullet up to Andre, who took it and crushed it in one fist.

"What is it?" Jacob asked.

Harper was shaking his head. "Wooden bullets," he said aloud, still looking down at his friend. "Whoever they are, they knew to bring wooden bullets." He cursed for the third time. Andre bent over and rolled Russell onto his back. He made a series of hand motions and Harper nodded.

"What's he saying?" Tara asked him.

Harper looked at the detectives and pursed his lips. "He said there still might be a chance to save him."

Tara stared down at Russell. Blood was still spilling out of his wounds. She had never seen so much blood from one person before. It was unnatural. He appeared dead. She felt a tinge of sadness and fear. Sadness over Russell, although she had barely known him. No one deserves to die this way. Fear that whoever sent these mercenaries had not been fooling around. They knew about the vampires and even brought wooden bullets. Who could want them dead that badly? Had they stumbled upon a clue to Eric's death that made the attackers nervous? Did this have anything to do with Eric's death, or was this unrelated? So many questions, not enough answers.

"What's the chance?" Jacob asked.

Harper looked down at Russell in admiration. Tara noticed a hint of skepticism behind his eyes as well. "We have to feed him."

Tara took a step back. She hadn't realized she did it until she felt Jacob behind her. "What do you mean feed him?"

"We have to give him blood."

Shit.

Tara shook her head in defiance. There is no way I'm feeding someone my blood, she screamed in her head. Jacob peered over at her and saw the hesitation. He closed his eyes and nodded to himself. "I'll do it," he said aloud. He stepped forward but Andre held up a hand and pointed to Tara.

"It can't be you," Harper told them.

"Why not?" Jacob asked, crossing his arms over his chest.

"You're a shifter. Vampires can't sustain themselves off shifter blood. We need human blood to live. Your blood is no good to us," he explained.

Double shit.

All three men turned to look at Tara. She shook her head defiantly. "No fucking way," she told them.

"He'll die if you don't," Harper whispered, his eyes pleading brightly. He bit his lip and fear spread over his face. She sympathized with him, but still stuck to her resolve. She was not going to give her blood to anyone, least of all a vampire.

"He looks dead already," she replied quietly.

"Your blood can save him," Harper argued.

"I don't care," she retorted. She took another step back.

Jacob stepped toward her. "He got shot saving our lives," he said calmly. "We owe it to him to save his." Tara shook her head again. "I'd do it myself if I could." He was staring at her.

Guilt made her look away. He had a point, and she was beginning to think she was the bad guy for not wanting to share her blood. She knew it was selfish, but she couldn't bring herself to do it.

"Please," Harper pleaded. She glanced up at him and saw real concern out of his bright blue eyes. She was glad Andre couldn't speak. He was blank-faced but knew he too wished for her to save Russell's life.

She looked at each of them, then down at Russell. She shook her head one last time. "Fine," she said, "I'll do it, but I still don't want to."

Harper beamed at her, and for the first time, she noticed a hint of fangs. It made her regret her decision. Was it too late to back out?

"What do I have to do?" she asked somberly.

Harper reached a hand into his back pocket and produced a small silver knife. "Let me see your wrist," he ordered.

"Forget that," she yelled and took another step back.

"It's either this, or you can let him bite you. With your hesitation, I'm betting this is the lesser of two evils."

He had a point. She did not want bite marks. If it came down to being bitten or having a cut, she would slit her wrist herself.

Harper continued. "I promise to only cut deep enough to draw blood. You'll barely feel it."

"I doubt that," she whispered to herself and held out her wrist. With a quick swipe, the blade collided with her flesh and she winced as a small red line of blood trickled down her arm. Her instinct was to grab her wrist to cover it, but she let it bleed.

"Now what?"

Harper moved closer to her. "Lower it to his mouth," he told her. She got to her knees, careful not to kneel in the blood on the ground. She placed her wrist against Russell's lips. Nothing happened. Her blood smeared his lips but he didn't respond. Was he truly dead?

"Open his mouth," Harper whispered. She did. Blood dripped down his throat. At first, nothing happened. Then she saw his tongue twitch. Light returned to his eyes, dim at first, then brighter as her blood nourished him. Harper let out a sigh of relief. Jacob uttered a gasp of surprise. Andre stood remarkably still, his face a mask of emotion.

Russell's hand clasped Tara's wrist quickly. She let out a surprised wheeze and tried to jerk her arm away. It was no use. Russell's grip was firm, holding it in place. He drank her with loud slurping sounds. She could feel her blood rushing out of her faster than she expected and was beginning to get woozy.

All of a sudden, she cried out in pain as she felt his fangs sink into her wrist. "No," she yelled and turned toward her partner. Russell grabbed her wrist with both hands and held her tight. Blood oozed out her arm and panic set in. Her vision became blurry and she swayed on her knees. She almost fell, but Jacob was suddenly beside her.

Jacob tried to pull her arm away and Tara screamed as pain rushed through her with each attempt. Russell was too strong. Darkness swirled around her, and for the first time in her life, she felt the fear of dying.

The last thing she heard before the darkness consumed her completely was a gunshot. Then she was no more.

Chapter 16

She awoke on a small green cot attached to tubes. An IV was connected to her left forearm and small circular disks were attached to her chest and upper shoulders. She heard rhythmic beeping as some machine blinked a small red light at her. Tara tried to sit up but instantly regretted it. Her head swooned as nausea crept up inside her. Her head collapsed back onto the soft pillow behind her. She closed her eyes as she waited for her nausea to subside.

Once the dizziness dissipated, Tara opened her eyes slowly, looking around at her surroundings. She was in a small wooden room. Deer heads of various sizes peered down at her from the tops of the walls and Tara let out a surprised gasp. She willed her heart to slow when she realized the deer were hung up as trophies instead of some form of monster. Was there such a thing as a Deer monster? Who knew, but with the way things had gone in the last 24 hours, she wouldn't have been surprised.

Moving slowly, Tara unplugged the IV along with the suction cups. The rhythmic beeping stopped. She managed to sit up without getting dizzy. She glanced at the IV bag. It was almost empty. How long have I been here?

She noticed two small puncture wounds at her wrist and a tiny slit bisecting the holes. The memory of what happened in the tunnels hit her like a brick to the face and her head swooned once more. She stretched out her arms and steadied herself, breathing in deeply and releasing the breath slowly. The breathing helped but only slightly. "Bastard," she managed to choke out as her head calmed itself.

She was dressed in the same outfit she wore when she woke up at the Sloan's house. Where was she? Where was Jacob? What happened to the Sloan's? What happened after she passed out? You won't get any answers waiting in bed, she thought to herself.

Moving at a snail's pace, she managed to stand but had to brace herself as she fell back down onto the cot. She tried once more, this time with arms stretched out for balance. She was a little wobbly but was able to stay up. A Point for me, she thought.

Now that she was up, she could see more of the room. There was a curtain behind the bed, as if it was the only thing separating the room from the rest of wherever she was. A small nightstand stood next to the beeping machine. Her gun, badge, wallet and keys sat neatly on top. She grabbed them and stuffed the wallet and badge into her back pockets. Her keys were placed in her front pocket, but she left the gun out.

Tara checked the magazine and noticed she was almost empty. She remembered firing into the tunnels but couldn't be sure if she hit anyone or not. She never got the chance to find out. Russell had almost died in front of them, and to save him, she had to feed him. "Bastard," she whispered once more. She wasn't sure if she was in danger now, but instinct told her to be cautious. She had her gun at the ready, just in case. Better safe than sorry.

Tara took a deep breath and pulled back the curtain, gun raised toward the unknown. The room opened up into a large living room. A small gray sofa sat in the middle of it. A wooden coffee table holding a pile of books and coasters was positioned in front of the couch. Toward the back wall was a brick fireplace with a mantel on top. The hearth looked out of place in the wooden room. More animal heads were attached to the walls and Tara felt like she had stepped into a home from Field and Stream. It was eerie.

She hobbled cautiously toward the fireplace. Framed pictures sat on top of the mantel. One was a picture of three children sitting on a log surrounded by forest. Another had an older version of two of the children holding up swords. The next picture had Jacob in it with an elderly couple. The man in the picture was much older, with graying hair. Jacob had much of his features, except for his chin and eyebrows. Those were clearly visible on the elegant woman standing next to them. Jacob's parents? If so, then these must be his brothers, she thought, picking up the frame with the three sitting on the log.

Had Jacob brought her to his place? No, she thought. He wouldn't do that. Not after being shot at. If their perpetrators could find them at the Sloan's house, they surely could find them at Jacob's place. Where was she?

A rustle of keys outside startled her and she whipped around as fast as she could, raising her gun toward a wooden door. She heard a key fill into the lock and she moved quickly behind the door. She heard a click as the door unlocked and creaked opened. Someone walked in, a lady with red hair. She couldn't make out the face, but Tara held the gun up to the back of the lady's head.

"Don't move," Tara yelled. The woman stopped instantly.

Tara shut the door with a swing of her leg, keeping the barrel of the gun glued to the woman's head. The lady stood frozen in place. She was the same size as Tara, which worked in her favor. "Walk," Tara ordered, and the woman complied.

"This is a great way to thank me for saving your life, detective," the woman said. Tara knew that voice. She heard it all her life. It was her voice!

Tara grabbed the lady around the shoulder and whipped her around. She let out a startled scream as she stood there staring at herself! It was a perfect likeness, from the hair to the frame, to the small dimpled chin.

"What the hell is going on?" Tara screamed. The other Tara smiled slyly. Tara's head started to swoon once more.

The door opened again and Tara whipped around, gun raised toward the door. Jacob came in holding a paper bag in one hand. He stopped mid stride when he saw the gun pointing at him.

Tara didn't lower the gun. She was freaking out, and she wasn't sure what the hell was going on. Jacob glanced from one Tara to the other. His eyes widened as recognition set in. "Shit," he said softly.

Shit was right. What the hell was happening? "Someone better explain what the hell is going on," Tara managed to choke out.

Jacob raised his free hand slowly to caution her. "I can explain, Tara. Just lower the gun."

The other Tara crossed her arms with a look of amusement. "She doesn't know?"

Tara shot herself a harsh look.

"She knows," Jacob answered quietly, "but has never seen it before." Jacob sighed. "Least of all on herself."

"What are you talking about?" Tara stammered out. "Someone better explain to me what is going on before I start shooting."

"Tara, I'd like you to meet my brother, Adam." Tara's mouth dropped open. Brother?

"Hi," the other Tara said, extending a hand out toward her. She stared at it without moving an inch. The other Tara's eyes brightened and she smiled widely. She was enjoying this.

"Someone better explain," she said sternly. Her hand was starting to wobble as the weight of the gun began to creep in. She had to either shoot or lower the weapon soon.

"Are you going to shoot me?" Jacob asked. Honestly, she didn't know.

"I haven't decided," she admitted. "But I need answers. Now. What the hell is going on?"

Jacob huffed slightly. "I'll explain everything, just lower the gun."

"Now, now, detective," the other Tara cautioned, "let's not be too hasty. Can you trust him?" she mused with an evil grin on her face. Tara hated seeing that grin on herself.

"Adam, go change," Jacob ordered. "I'm coming in. You can either shoot me or not, but these groceries are getting heavy and I'd like to set them down."

Tara considered this for a moment. She decided to trust him, if only to get what was going on. She lowered the gun and Jacob let out a sigh of relief. The other Tara's smile faltered. "Damn," she said. "I was hoping to tell mother you've been shot. I'm sure she would have loved the news."

"Go change," Jacob ordered again, this time there was a hint of threat in his voice.

"Fine," Tara, or rather, Adam said. But the smile returned on his face and spread like wildfire. "Watch this, detective."

"Don't," Jacob yelled, but it was too late. The other Tara started to change. Tara watched in awe, and disgust, as the skin, her skin, cracked open into wide fissures. Her face was no longer her face. It was now splitting open like an egg. The old skin fell off her face in large puddles. The skin hit the floor and evaporated instantly, revealing the muscle and bones underneath it. The flowing red hair shriveled up, and new strands of black began to sprout upward.

The other Tara's skinny arms split open and pulled away. The muscles expanded and new skin began to grow over them. The other Tara's skeletal system began to grow taller and Tara almost puked as a foul stench filled the room; smoky and decayed. Tara covered her nose and suppressed the urge to vomit.

The whole scene lasted no more than a minute, but Tara would remember it forever. Where the other Tara stood, now stood a man a little smaller than Jacob, but with much of Jacob's features. He stood about 5'9, was slender like Jacob, with short cropped, wavy black hair. He beamed at Tara. She had come face to face with the real Adam.

Tara fainted.

Chapter 17

She felt light taps against her cheek. She opened her eyes and saw Jacob peering down at her. He had moved her to the small sofa. "What happened?" she asked, eyes wide.

He gave Tara a sympathetic smile. "You fainted," he whispered. "Can you sit up?"

She didn't know, but she would try. It took effort, but she managed to sit halfway up on the couch, leaning against the soft cushions.

"You sure seem to faint a lot, detective," She heard Adam call out. From her position, she couldn't see him. His voice was a little deeper than Jacobs, but it was good to finally know what his voice sounded like. At least it wasn't her voice she heard.

"It's been a rough week," she admitted. She looked around the room, searching for Adam, but still, couldn't see him. "Where are we?"

"This is Adam's 'Retreat,'" Jacob air quoted. "It's mostly used for hunting, but every now and then, it has other uses." Jacob rose to his feet and walked around the wooden table toward the kitchen. The grocery bag he previously carried was now sitting on a countertop, and he reached inside it, withdrawing a 16oz water bottle. He tossed it to her, and Tara caught it in midair. "Drink," he told her. "It'll help replenish your fluids."

Tara obeyed, not realizing how thirsty she had been. She drank the entire bottle without taking a breath.

Adam appeared beside the couch. He looked so normal, considering what had just happened. He looked completely human. But she knew better. She had seen him change. The thought made her want to puke, but she resisted the urge. Instead, she focused on the memories of the tunnel and the attack that had taken place.

"What happened?" she asked again.

"You fainted on my floor," Adam replied, smiling. "It was quite a comical sight, detective."

"Adam," Jacob said calmly, but the name was enough. Adam made a twisting motion at his lips and acted like he threw a key away. Tara was betting she was not going to like Adam. If this is how Jacobs brother was like, she could only imagine how the other members of his family were. Growing up with them must have been something special. "What's the last thing you remember?" Jacob asked her as he walked back toward the couch.

She thought for a moment. "Feeding Russell, and struggling to get him off me." After that, she couldn't remember anything until she woke up on the cot.

"Well, he wouldn't let you go, so I did the only thing I could think of. I shot him."

Tara's eyes widened. "What?" Jacob nodded.

"It was a through and through, in the arm. Your blood did the trick. He healed, but I had to get him off you somehow. That was the only thing I could think of." He looked down guiltily. "It worked, but you had already passed out from blood loss."

She understood, but the whole thing sounded insane. "What about Harper and Andre?"

Jacob smiled for the first time. "They weren't too pleased. Andre tried to put me in a headlock, but Russell actually stopped him. He apologized for drinking too much from you. He couldn't explain why he lost control like that. My guess is that being so close to death took a lot out of him and he needed the nourishment."

Tara didn't like hearing that her blood was nourishment in any regard, but she waved the thought away. "He did appear dead."

"Imagine that," Adam interrupted. "A vampire appearing like a dead man. What are the odds?" Tara shot him a look, and he just stared back behind innocent brown eyes.

"Anyway," Jacob continued, "Russell carried you out of the tunnels. Needless to say, we couldn't go to the police station in your condition, and hospitals were out of the question. The Vamps had no idea what to do next."

"And that's when my exiled brother thought to call little ol' me," Adam chimed in, finishing the story.

Jacob nodded. "Reluctantly, but yes."

"I thought you didn't talk to your family anymore?" Tara stated.

"Oh, he doesn't," Adam replied. "And we do our best to keep it that way. But I can't resist making our mother upset. That loony old bat drives me insane."

"Adam!"

Adam peered over at Jacob with an innocent look, one that a child would give if caught with his hands inside a cookie jar. "That's our mother, Adam. Be respectful."

Adam's eyes narrowed into small slits, but he kept his mouth shut. Tara was intrigued to see the brothers interact. She was an only child and didn't really have any family besides an aunt. It would have been nice to have a sibling to grow up with, play with, or even argue with, but oh well.

"Can someone explain to me why you were walking around as me?"

"Ah," Adam stepped forward with a look of satisfaction. "That was my idea. And it worked brilliantly if I do say so myself." He beamed his million-dollar smile at her.

Jacob raised his hand to quiet him. Adam looked annoyed but quit talking. "We were supposed to debrief the Captain about the shooting, if you recall." Tara nodded. "Since you were out of commission, Adam offered to go in your stead."

"And it was awesome!" Adam said loudly. "No one could tell the difference. Silly humans," Adam laughed heartily. Jacob rolled his eyes at his brother's amusement.

Tara couldn't believe it. Had Adam really gone as her? Her body language, her mannerisms, and demeanor? Had no one really noticed it wasn't her? Granted she had only been on the Seattle PD for two days, but it still seems unlikely that no one would be able to tell it wasn't her.

Jacob seemed to have read her mind. "Along with absorbing someone's DNA, we also get memories and attributes of the host's body." Tara's eyes widened again.

"You mean you can literally become the other person if you wanted to?"

"Yes and no," Adam replied. "To be the other person, you would have to absorb a tremendous amount of the hosts DNA. Body contact is required for longer periods of time. But let's say I had your hair I could stuff in my pocket, then I could pass for you as long as the hair strands held."

"This is insane," Tara whispered, closing her eyes. Her head pounded with this new information. "Please don't tell me you have my hair on you."

An evil grin spread on Adam's face. "Wouldn't you like to know."

"He doesn't," Jacob interrupted. "I wouldn't let him."

Adam shot Jacob an annoyed glance. "Spoil my fun, big brother." Adam stomped his foot lightly, and for the first time, Tara noticed how young he was. Maybe young wasn't the right word. He was royalty, so perhaps the word she was searching for was spoiled. Jacob continued without missing a beat.

"He held your hand for a while in order to pass as you for the day."

"For the day," she repeated. "How long have I been out?"

"How long have you been up?" Jacob asked.

She thought for a moment. "Maybe 15 minutes before you two came in."

Jacob nodded as he glanced at his watch on his wrist. "Then about 10 hours or so."

Tara's eyes widened as the news caught her off guard. Wow, she thought. Russell must have done a real number on me. She had never been a heavy sleeper. The slightest noise would always wake her up. She couldn't remember the last time she had slept more than 5 or 6 hours in one night. It was unusual if she slept longer than that. Of course, this was an unusual cause.

"How did the debriefing go?" she asked, desperately wishing for a change in subject.

"Oh, it went great," Adam replied cheerily, giving her an okay symbol with his right hand. "You both talk bullshit like pro's."

"What he means to say," Jacob started, giving his brother a harsh look, "is that we had to come up with a cover story as to why we had all those bruises. I told the Captain that I had joined a boxing gym."

"And I," Adam said in Tara's voice, "told him I was into S&M."

Tara coughed loudly. "You didn't!" She made it a statement.

Adam's evil grin grew back wider than the last time. "Didn't I?"

Tara was in shock. She glanced from Adam to Jacob. Jacob's face held a hint of concern through his neutral expression. The concern was not for her health or well-being, but for her reputation on the police force. His look told her it was true. Shit. She would be labeled the kinky sex slut now.

"Fuck! How could you let him do that?" she yelled, slapping Jacob on his arm. Jacob instinctively reached over and rubbed where she hit, although it hadn't hurt.

"What lie was I supposed to use? Should I have told Martinez the truth? He'd have thought we were completely insane."

"I don't know," she replied heatedly. "You could have told him anything, other than that. The best thing you could think of was to tell him I'm into S&M? Seriously?" Anger rose inside her.

"It was my idea," Adam admitted. "And considering the alternative, I think it was a great idea."

"Well you don't have to work with these people every day," she snarled at him.

His eyes narrowed, fixed on her. "Geez, try to do a human a favor and she bites your head off." He shook his head in disappointment. "Let's not forget that I just saved your ass. The least you could do is show some appreciation."

"You want appreciation for telling my captain that I'm into some kinky sex shit? Really? That I like it when men beat on me and control me through S&M! Fuck you!" Her anger had reached a boiling point. She could feel her face turning red with anger and she balled her hands into fists.

Adam smiled sweetly at her. "Who said it was men?"

Tara's eyes widened so large that it seemed they would have popped out of their sockets. That was the tipping point. She was going to explode. She turned to Jacob. "Where's my gun?"

Jacob raised his hands in caution, trying to calm her down. "Listen, Tara," he stole a sideways glance at Adam. "Although he might have been a little hasty in telling the captain this, he did sell it pretty well. Martinez believed it, and it's much easier to explain your sexual habits than to tell him you almost got mugged and raped and saved by a vampire."

Tara glared at her partner. "They are not my sexual habits!"

Jacob nodded, "Yes, but Martinez doesn't need to know that."

Tara pressed her lips together. Her face was the color of a ripe tomato. "Fuck, now no one will respect me. They will just see me as a sexual plaything. Do you know how hard it is for a woman to be on the police force? You have to work twice as hard as the men to gain any sense of respect." Tara slammed her fist onto the table. Pain shot up her arm but she was too upset to notice. "I've worked my ass off to be recognized as a serious detective. And with this S&M bullshit, all of that, the accomplishments I've made, were just thrown out the window!"

Adam smiled slyly. "So you like kinky sex. Who doesn't these days?. Honestly, it's not the end of the world."

"I do not like kinky sex!" Tara yelled. Heat filled her face and her heart was in her throat. Adam's smile widened again, exposing pearly white teeth.

"Who cares, honestly?" Adam replied with an almost bored tone. "If anything, What I did for you makes you more interesting."

Tara's eye's narrowed and she glared at him with such hatred, but Adam didn't seem to notice.

"Anyway," Jacob interrupted. "We are in the clear to go talk to the wolves, once you feel up to it." Tara noticed his attempt to change the subject, and she was even angrier. She had had enough of the shapeshifters, enough of the politics with the vampires, enough of everything. At that moment, she really missed Phoenix and being ignorant to the supernatural.

She glanced between the two brothers. Tara sighed loudly and shook her head. She had to let it go. If she didn't, she would be no good on this case and Eric's killer would get away. Whatever the Captain thought of her sexual habits didn't matter. She would do her best to solve this case. Tara closed her eyes and took in a deep breath, willing herself to calm down. She felt her heart slow and the blood drain from her face.

"Anyone know if the Sloan's are okay?" She asked.

Jacob's eyes flashed with appreciation, and let out a breath. "I've called over there and Walter said they were fine."

"Walter?"

"You know, the old man who answered the door when we first arrived at their house."

"Ah," she nodded. It seemed so long ago, but she recalled that he never introduced himself. She hadn't asked him his name either, which was odd, considering the circumstances. "Did he say anything else?"

Jacob shook his head. "Not much. He implied that they were interrogating one of the intruders, but guessing because I'm a cop, he didn't want to tell me too much."

Adam started laughing. Tara and Jacob both glared at him. "And you call yourselves detectives," he said when the laughter subsided.

"What's that supposed to mean?" Jacob asked harshly, flaring his nostrils.

"It's not because you're a cop, big brother. It's because you might have had a hand in the home invasion." Jacob looked as if he had been slapped in the face. His expression was hard to read. He stared at his brother with a hint of hurt behind his eyes.

"Okay, I'll bite," Tara said. "What do you mean, 'he might have had a hand in the home invasion? You can't seriously think your brother had anything to do with it?"

"No," Adam replied. "But think for a moment. There are only five kinds of 'monsters' here in Seattle besides the Vamps." He counted them on his fingers. "The Ogres, the Wolves, Sirens, Shifters, and Witches."

"We know that already," Jacob started, but Adam held a hand up to quiet him.

"The Witches are out because they are in Sloan's back pocket. The two go hand in hand like two peas in a pod. The Ogres are tough and stupid enough to try a home invasion but lack the brains to pull it off. That leaves the Sirens, Wolves, and Shifters."

Both detectives sat quietly as Adam spoke. So far, what Adam said made sense to Tara. "Go on," she said, wanting to see where his train of thought was leading.

"The Sirens are mostly a peaceful race. They care more for solving problems than starting them. The Wolves are smart enough, but I doubt Troy would be bold enough to make a move against Dominik. Besides, the wolves care for nothing but pack business. That leaves us Shifters."

"You can't possibly believe that one of us had anything to do with it?" Jacob's voice rose with anger, but Tara also caught a faint whiff of doubt.

Adam smiled. "Of course not, big brother. We aren't stupid enough to try to attack the Sloan's, especially in their own home. At least, not all of us." Both brothers exchanged quick glances, but Tara noticed there was something behind that exchange.

"What do you mean not all of you?" Tara asked.

Adam swallowed, shaking his head before speaking again. "Given the history between my dear brother and Dominik, it is plausible that the Sloan's might think that he had something to do with last night's excursion."

Tara laughed heartily. "You can't be serious?"

"Why not?" Adam questioned. "Since you are new here in Seattle, I would doubt you had anything to do with it. But Jacob on the other hand...:" he stared at his brother for a moment and Jacob nodded, realization dawning in his eyes.

"They might think it was me."

Tara remained skeptical. "How is that? You and I both had to flee the house. They were trying to protect us both last night."

"Yeah, well, if you knew the history between Jacob and the Sloan's," Adam stated.

"She knows," Jacob interrupted quietly. Adam's eye sparkled with sympathy for a second but he quickly recovered.

"Well then," he said. "You can see why they might jump to that conclusion."

"What conclusion?" Tara argued, shaking her head. "Last night, Bethany approached us. It was by chance that we ended up staying at the Sloan's house, and your brother was against it from the start."

Adam smiled slyly once more. "Exactly! How did anyone know that you two were there? If the intrusion happened and you guys hadn't been there, I would think that it was a coincidence. But since the only ones who knew you two were staying are the Sloan's, I'm betting they aren't ruling Jacob out, especially since he has such a personal history with them."

Tara remembered Jacob telling her about his old partner, Natasha. How Mr. Sloan had personally drained her of blood. She knew Jacob had hated Dominik because of it. It did make sense to think he might have had something to do with the intrusion, to an extent. But what about the shooting at the Cafe? And if Jacob just happened to be behind the home invasion, why had he fled along with the group? Why not stay and exact his own revenge? Dominik had to have known that if Jacob had anything to do with the attack, he would have gone after Mr. Sloan himself.

Of course, the shooting and the invasion might have had nothing to do with each other. Coincidence? She was betting no. The attackers were persistent. Whomever was behind the attacks didn't mind going up against the head honcho of Seattle. Their mistake.

Tara turned her attention to Jacob, whose neutral face revealed nothing. His eyes seemed lost in his own thoughts. Adam brought him out of his haze. "Fess up, big brother. Come clean and promise to never do it again. I'm sure they will forgive you." Adam smiled brightly, amused at his own joke.

"You know I didn't do it," Jacob answered solemnly.

Adam shrugged. "I don't care if you did. After what happened, Dominik and his lot can go suck it for all I care."

"You don't like the Sloan's?" Tara asked.

"Adam doesn't like anything outside of our own species," Jacob answered for him. Adam just smiled and shrugged once more.

"Great," Tara rolled her eyes. "A shapeshifting racist. Why did you bring me here again?"

"Hey!" Adam stammered out. He looked shocked, possibly hurt by the question.

"He did help save your life, Tara," Jacob replied.

"That's right, I did. Is it too much to ask for a little appreciation?" Adam's stare bore into Tara. He had helped keep her alive. And between his arrogance and jokes, she could tell there was intelligence behind it all.

"Thank you," She said to him in her best and honest tone she could muster up. "Thank you for helping to save my life."

He beamed his perfect smile once more. "I accept $50's and $100's. Tip up front." He winked at her, and for the first time, she smiled at him. "So she can smile. There is a god after all." Tara shook her head.

"Moving on," Jacob said, looking at her. "Are you up for meeting the wolves?"

Tara thought about it. She wasn't certain if she wanted to continue with the investigation. Already she had been mugged, shot at, drained of her blood, and unconscious more times than she cared to admit. What would happen once she met the werewolves? She really didn't want to find out, yet she couldn't let Jacob go alone. What if whoever was after them caught up to him and she could have done something to help? She had asked him to have her back out in the field. She would do the same. She closed her eyes and nodded, and at the same time, her stomach grumbled loudly.

"Seems we need to feed your human," Adam said. All respect he had gained was now thrown out the window.

"I'm not his human!"

Adam shrugged indifferently. "But you are hungry." She couldn't argue with that.

Jacob walked back to the kitchen and reached his left hand inside the bag. He pulled out a loaf of bread and a package of turkey slices. "I'll make us some sandwiches while you get ready." She nodded her appreciation.

"Do you have a shower around here?" she asked Adam.

"But of course, detective," he replied. Then an evil grin donned on his face. "If I can watch." Tara choked and coughed loudly.

"Adam!" Jacob yelled behind shocked eyes.

"Only joking," Adam said, hands raised. "Besides, I've been her, remember? I've seen it all." Tara coughed once more and turned a deep purple. She didn't realize she could be so embarrassed this easily.

"You two really should lighten up more," he said. "Life is a hell of a good time when nothing really matters."

Jacob shook his head in disappointment. "Just show her where the bathroom is, Adam." Adam stood straight up and saluted his brother. Tara took a minute to get to her feet. She was still slightly light headed from the blood loss, but the water she drank helped.

Adam helped her to the bathroom while she leaned into him for support. She expected some witty comment or sexual innuendo, but none came. Point for him.

The room was small and cold, filled with just a small shower stall, a toilet, a round hand sink, and an oval mirror hanging above it. "I'll get you a towel," Adam told her and left her on the closed toilet seat. A moment later, he appeared with a fuzzy pink towel.

Tara eyed the towel. "Pink? You don't strike me as a pink kind of guy."

His eyes narrowed slightly. "You're not the first girl I've brought up here," he stated.

"Gotcha," she replied, nodding her head. "And gross" He chuckled.

"You're alright, for a human," he said, winking at her.

"Glad you approve," she said glumly. "I'm showering now." With that, Adam was gone, leaving Tara to her own thoughts.

Chapter 18

The detectives sat in Jacob's car waiting for the traffic to move. Neither of them spoke, but both wished they weren't in the middle of I-5 during rush hour. The car inched its way forward at sporadic intervals. Traffic was so heavy that Jacob barely missed hitting the back of a blue Toyota Camry as it made its way onto the interstate. Cursing under his breath, he slammed on the horn. The Camry seemed not to notice.

Leaving Adam's cabin had been a feat unto itself. After Tara's shower, she crept slowly back to the living room. She had felt better and more energized by the shower. She wasn't 100%, but food would fix that. On the wooden table sat a small plate topped with sandwiches. She made her way over to the couch and scarfed them down, barely noticing the taste before swallowing.

Jacob and Adam were convened in the kitchen arguing. "But I can help," Adam protested.

"It's too dangerous," Jacob responded flatly.

"Oh, please. I've come across far more dangerous foes than the pups and you know it," Adam retorted.

Tara cleared her throat loudly as she walked steadily to the kitchen entrance. Both men turned to look at her. "What are we arguing about?"

Both of them turned to look at each other. "Nothing," They said in unison.

She eyed them suspiciously. "Uh-huh," she said. "Come on, dish."

Jacob pressed his lips together. "He wants to come with us."

"To interview the wolves?" Tara asked. Both men nodded.

"I said no," Jacob told her. Adam looked back at his brother, crossing his arms over his chest. Jacob stared back as he spoke. "I told him it was too dangerous."

"You know I can take care of myself."

"No one said you couldn't, but people are shooting at us," Jacob pleaded with him. "I don't want you to get hurt. I would never forgive myself is something happened to you because of me."

"How touching," Adam said, rolling his eyes. He turned to look back at Tara. "What do you think?"

"I think your brother is right," Tara replied quickly.

Adam huffed loudly. "Figures."

"This is a police investigation for one," she continued. "Bringing a civilian along reflects badly on us as well as the department. Not to mention that this case has gotten us into some pretty deep shit."

Adam stared at her blankly. Jacob nodded his head in agreement. "Besides, it's illegal," she added.

"Oh, whatever," Adam retorted heatedly.

"Why do you want to go?" Jacob asked.

Adam whirled around to face his brother. He put his right hand on his chest. "Why, to help out my dear old brother, of course," he said a little too innocently.

Jacob arched his right eyebrow. "Uh-huh. What's the real reason? You said less than an hour ago that the vamps can go suck it," he air quoted. "You could care less if we solve this case or not, so what's the real reason you want to tag along?"

Adam looked shocked at his brother's bluntness. "Why, don't you trust me, big brother?" Jacob just stared back. Adam shrugged in response. "Call it mild curiosity. Or maybe I've just missed you and want to spend more time with you."

Tara didn't need her spider sense to know that was a lie. She snorted at the comment and Adam shot her a deadly glance.

"Try again," Jacob said suspiciously.

"Alright, alright," Adam said, taking in a deep breath. "I'm bored and I think confronting the wolves with you could be exciting."

Jacob's eyes widened. "You want to antagonize the wolves? That could start a war between us."

"What do you mean us?" Adam replied harshly. "You haven't been one of us in a while, exile!" Adam put heavy emphasis on the last word. Jacob recoiled as if a snake had bit him. His face turned crimson and his expression went from anger to hurtful. Tara felt sorry for him.

"You know that's not fair," Jacob said softly.

"Fair or not, it's the truth. Besides, it's only a matter of time before this truce of ours is broken. Why not help it along?"

Jacob shook his head in disbelief. "You're unbelievable! You would start a war, one that could kill many on all sides, out of boredom? You can't be serious?"

Adam shrugged then crossed his arms over his chest again. "What's wrong with ruffling some wolf pelts?" He asked innocently.

"Is your brother insane?" Tara asked Jacob.

"Quite possibly."

"There is a fine line between insanity and boredom, detective," Adam answered back.

"Not from where I'm standing," she replied.

"Yeah, well, humans don't see much."

Tara was about to reply, but Jacob spoke up first. "You're not going, and that's final."

Adam laughed at his brother. "Oh, is it now? You know I don't need your permission to go."

"You do if you expect a ride out there," Tara told him.

"I'll drive myself!"

Jacob looked angry for the first time since she awoke that day. His face became flushed and his eyebrows merged closer together, wrinkling his forehead. "Look, Adam. If you go and mess with the wolves, I will go to the council and demand that they skin you."

True shock spread on Adam's face. Jacob continued without skipping a beat. "Exile or not, I'm sure they would want to know you are trying to break the treaty that our family signed so many years ago!"

"You wouldn't?"

"Try me, Adam," Jacob threatened. "If I even get an inkling of you stepping foot in the University District, Royalty or not, the council will deal with you." Adam's anger flared. The two brothers stared at each other and silence filled the cabin. Tara stood utterly still as the tension between them grew. She waited for one of the brothers to react, but they both just stood their ground, sizing each other up.

Finally, for what seemed like minutes, but had only been a few moments, Adam slunk down and the tension eased out of him. His childish grin was back, playful and cheery once again. "Geeze, big brother. You know, for an exile, you sure haven't forgotten how to play the game."

Jacob inhaled slowly, then released it. "I've had a good teacher," he replied, relaxing a bit. Adam nodded. "Promise me you won't get involved any more than you already are."

Adam crossed his arms over his chest and nodded. "Fine. I'll stay out of it, but if you need any more help," he inched his head toward Tara, "I won't be around to provide it."

Tara wasn't sure if she should speak. She didn't want to be in the middle of sibling rivalry, even if it did involve her. She decided to keep quiet.

"Deal," Jacob replied, holding out a hand to Adam. Adam shook it and a strange tinge emanated from their clasped hands. A moment later, it was gone. Tara gasped, but it happened so fast that she wasn't sure if she truly saw anything. Maybe her mind was playing a trick on her.

Now in the car, Tara remembered the glow from the handshake. "Jacob?"

"Yeah," he replied sullenly.

"When you and Adam shook hands earlier, I thought I saw something. A kind of light or something. What was that?"

Jacob gave her a side glance quickly then his eyes were back on the road. "Well, when two shapeshifters touch, our body contact reacts to one another."

"What do you mean?" She inquired.

"Remember when I told you that we absorb others DNA?" She nodded. "Well, that really can't be helped. Our bodies absorb it whether we want to or not. There is no off switch."

"Um, okay?" She said, still not getting what that had to do with the glow she saw.

"Well, when two shapeshifters touch, our ability to absorb DNA clash with each other." He glanced at her and noticed her confused expression. He reiterated. "Think of it like two separate currents rushing toward each other. What happens when they meet?"

"They crash into each other." Jacob nodded in agreement.

"There is nowhere to go, so the currents collide and spark. That spark is what you saw."

"I get it!" she said. "So, you can't absorb another shifters DNA?"

Jacob shook his head. "There have been tales of powerful shifters that could, but those are myths passed down from generations before. Kind of like the legends of the Greek gods or other myths."

"Gods aren't real?" She asked eagerly.

Jacob let out a hearty chuckle. "Not that I've seen. There are many creatures out there, but to my understanding, gods are just beings that people met with strange abilities that they didn't understand."

"I can see that," she agreed with him. Is that how some of the legends started? Superstitious folk with no real knowledge of the world meeting creatures they didn't understand? It was certainly possible.

Jacob mentioned that there had been many creatures out there. Tara had met vampires, ogres, and shapeshifters. She was about to meet the werewolves for the first time. Those creatures had been scary enough. She would hate to meet other creatures outside of Seattle. The world was complicated enough without supernatural beings coming into the mix. Now it's gotten scarier.

Although it had only been a couple days since she learned about the Sloan's and the monsters in Seattle, she longed for a more normal case. One that didn't include the words vampire or werewolf.

Fingers crossed.

Chapter 19

They arrived at the Blue Moon Tavern 20 minutes later. Glancing out the window, Tara noticed a scantily clad woman sitting on a crescent moon between the words 'Blue Moon' written out of neon lights hanging above the entranceway. On the side of the brick tavern was the same Blue Moon logo, but in a psychedelic orange paint.

"This is an interesting place to meet with Troy," Tara commented.

Jacob nodded. "He owns it. This, and a couple other bars around the University District."

Tara had never really been a bar type of girl. She preferred going to the movies or to a good concert over a bar where you can buy the same amount of alcohol much cheaper at a store. It was a waste of money, in her opinion. C'est la vie.

The Blue Moon Tavern was kind of poetic, if you got the connection. She was guessing most of the patrons didn't. It's not like Troy would bring a 'Hello, I'm your local werewolf leader, nice to meet you,' t-shirt to work every day.

They got out of the car and walked to the doorway. "Anything I should know before I go in?" Tara asked Jacob.

Jacob thought for a bit. "Troy is usually accommodating. It's the other ones you should watch out for. Not all of them are as tolerant as he is. But don't worry. Troy won't let anything happen in his establishment." Jacob put a hand on the doorknob, then halted. "If you can, try to tell the truth. They can smell a lie."

Tara wasn't sure why she would need to lie, but she nodded in compliance.

"Ready?" he asked her. She nodded. Jacob opened the door and led the way inside.

The room was substantially darker inside than out. Hanging lamps were dimly lit from the ceiling and illuminated the tables and bar. The smell of beer and stale nachos filled her nostrils. Overall, the place was relatively clean, except for the peanut shells covering the floor. The bar was surprisingly filled with customers laughing and playing pool. Old 80's rock music blared out of the speakers near the stage and toward the back tables.

Jacob led the way to the bar, crunching shells as he walked. The bartender was a toned Hispanic woman wearing a black tank top. It fit her perfectly and made her breast look robust. Tattoos decorated her muscular arms. Her long black hair was pulled back into a ponytail she let flip over her right shoulder. As Jacob moved closer, she glanced up from filling a glass of beer from the tap. A smile spread over her face.

"Jacob! Long time no see, stranger," she said in a sweet accented voice.

"Good to see you too, Gina," he said. She leaned over the counter and gave him a hug and a kiss on the cheek. He smiled politely back at her.

"What brings you to our neck of the woods?" she asked.

"We're here to see Troy, if he is around," he answered. She nodded, then looked at Tara. "Gina, this is my partner, Tara. She just transferred from Phoenix a couple days ago."

Gina extended a well-manicured hand toward Tara, who shook it. For a toned woman, her handshake was surprisingly elegant. Tara also noticed that her hand was soft as silk. "Nice to meet you, Tara," she said.

"Likewise," Tara replied. She wasn't sure if Gina was a werewolf or not, but if she was, she liked her regardless.

"So, Troy? Is he around?" Jacob asked her.

"Of course he is," she said sweetly. "He's in the back office. Would you like me to get him?"

"Well, I think it's best if we speak away from the crowd," he said, looking around.

Her brow arched slightly, then she nodded. "You know the way," she said, then turned to help an older man with an order.

Jacob walked to the left side of the bar and into a small corridor. Tara followed suit. The hallway led to two doors, one labeled 'closet' and the door adjacent read 'office'. Jacob knocked on the office door.

"Enter," a deep masculine voice said behind the door. Jacob obeyed.

The office was tiny and cluttered. A short desk sat in between two gray filing cabinets against the back wall. Pictures of people laughing and posing inside the bar filled most of the space on the walls. Behind the desk sat a bulky man in a gray dress shirt with his back turned to the detectives.

"What is it?" he asked without looking up.

"Your office smells like wet dog," Jacob jibed. Tara's eyes widened at the remark.

"What can I say," the man retorted. "Your mom loves it here!" The man turned and looked at Jacob, then a grin spread from ear to ear. Both Jacob and the man chuckled as the man stood up and embraced him.

The man was just a hair shorter than Jacob, who stood about 5'10. His face was pleasant and muscular with a chiseled jaw line and perfectly arched eyebrows. His oval brown eyes matched his short cropped hair and two-day stubble on his chin. A black tie hung underneath the collar of his shirt.

"Good to see you, man," he said to Jacob.

"Same here," Jacob replied cheerily. "I just wish it was under different circumstances." Tara cleared her throat and both men turned to look at her. "Oh, I'm sorry, this is my new partner, Tara Bancroft. Tara, this is Troy Lynch."

Tara held out her hand, but instead of shaking it, Troy raised her hand to his lips and kissed it gently. "It's a pleasure to meet you, detective." She jerked her hand away but blushed at the gesture.

"Still think you're a ladies' man?" Jacob asked

Troy laughed heartily and his face lit up, causing him to look younger than he probably was. "Better than you'll ever be."

Jacob shrugged at that.

"So, I take it you two know each other pretty well?" Tara asked Jacob.

"Oh, we go way back," he replied.

"Unfortunately," Troy said jokingly. "Although it has been a while. You should come over more often."

Jacob shrugged. "Well, being exiled tends to ruin friendly reunions," he said flatly. Troy quickly glanced at Tara, then back at Jacob. A shocked expression was quickly masked behind his pleasant smile, but Tara managed to notice. "Don't worry," Jacob assured him. "She knows."

This time, Troy didn't try to hide his surprise. "You told another human?" Jacob shook his head.

"It wasn't him," Tara told Troy. He looked at Tara with mild curiosity.

"Who told you?"

"The Sloan daughter, Bethany," Jacob replied with a hint of disdain in his voice. Troy shook his head vigorously.

"Where does she get off exposing all our secrets to humans?" Troy asked, anger filling his voice. "It's shameful."

"Hey!" Tara stammered out. "As one of the humans you are referring to, I think that the case we are working on requires me to know. It's better I know ahead of time than find out later and freak the hell out."

Troy considered this for a moment, then nodded slightly. "Still, it would have been nice to be consulted on this matter. I'm...particular in who I tell about my wolves."

"Well, don't worry," Tara replied. "I don't know anyone else in this city, so your secrets are safe with me." This seemed to ease Troy's mind slightly. Tara noticed his tense shoulders go slack and his face became naturally pleasant once more.

"Well," Jacob said. "Not that it's not great catching up, Troy, but this is kind of official police business."

"You mentioned that," he replied, becoming serious. "How can I help?"

"We need to talk to Michael Beagan," Tara stated. Her voice was as neutral as she could make it.

Troy glanced around his small office, and then looked back at the detectives. "He's not here."

"Gathered that," Jacob said flatly. "But I know you can summon him."

"Ah, I could, yes," Troy said. "But tell me why I should."

Tara and Jacob exchanged glances. Jacob sighed a little. "You know what happened to Eric Sloan?"

Troy nodded solemnly. "My condolences to the Sloan's."

"Well, believe it or not," Jacob continued, "We are the ones with the distinct pleasure of finding his killer."

Troy was quiet for a moment, then he let out a booming laugh. "Surely you're kidding me?" Jacob just shook his head. Tara crossed her arms over her chest.

"How's that for irony," he choked out behind his laughter. He quit when he saw Jacobs angry face. "Sorry," he shrugged and shook his head. "So what's this have to do with Michael?"

"Michael was seen having an altercation with Eric the week before he was murdered," Jacob told him.

"So?"

Tara couldn't help but look shocked at his lack of interest. "So, he threatened to kill Eric that night. Quite the coincidence Eric just happened to die the next week."

"If Michael was going to kill him, he would have ripped him to shreds or at least bit him. Did Eric have any signs that a wolf was even involved?"

Jacob shook his head. "No. No signs that a wolf was present during the attack, but still, we do need to follow up on it."

"And I ask again. Why?" Troy crossed his arms over his chest and stood on the balls of his feet staring at the detectives. His demeanor changed from friendly to defensive.

"Even if he had nothing to do with Eric's death," Tara added, "he might have seen something that night that might lead to catching the killer."

"If that night had anything to do with Eric's death," Troy shot back. "Forgive me if I'm wrong, but the Sloan's have many enemies, correct? Seems to me you guys are grasping at straws."

"It's a lead, Troy," Jacob said calmly. "I'm sure the Sloan's would like to know that everyone was cooperative in the investigation. I'm guessing Dominik wouldn't take too kindly to knowing the leader of the werewolves was not being very helpful."

Troy's eyes grew wide and his face turned a deep red. "Are you seriously threatening me right now?"

Jacob held his hands up in submission. "I'm not threatening anyone, just stating a fact." Troy eyed Jacob. Tension built between them and Tara could feel it like a static charge. One wrong move and the room would ignite into flames. "Please," Jacob said in a comical voice.

Troy let out a huff, then shook his head. "Fine," he said. "But I'm telling you, no wolf of mine would have harmed that vamp." Troy walked to his desk, then turned back to the detectives. He closed his eyes and stood completely still.

"What's he doing?" Tara whispered to Jacob, who held a hand up to silence her. She was mildly offended but remained silent.

The air in the office changed. Instead of regular air, the room filled with a thickness Tara had never experienced before. The thickness grew and became heavier. Tara found it difficult to breathe. It was as if her lungs couldn't process the heaviness of the air. Her breath caught in her throat and she tried to cough, but couldn't. She was suffocating.

Troy opened his eyes and Tara tried to scream. His eyes weren't human anymore. They were pure amber. The pupils were completely gone, replaced by solid golden brown, sap-like eyes. Energy flowed up her arm and down her spine, causing her to shiver and quake. It was as if the room had suddenly been hit by lightning and her body was feeling the charge. She tried to speak, but only managed to grunt.

As soon as it had come, the energy was suddenly gone. The air returned to its natural state, as if nothing had happened. Tara coughed madly and sucked in as much air as she could muster. Her heart had leaped into her throat and she found it difficult to speak. She was shaking all over.

"What...the..hell was...that?" she huffed out in between breaths. She caught Troy's eye and noticed they had returned to normal.

He shrugged indifferently, as if what happened was an everyday occurrence. "I did what you wanted and summoned Michael," he said in a bored-like tone.

"You mean to tell me you can call any of your wolves with whatever the hell you just did?"

"Since Troy is the pack leader," Jacob answered for Troy. "He has the power to summon any wolf to his aid, yes." Troy shrugged again.

Tara blinked as her heart finally started to slow. "That's some phone call," she stated in disbelief.

"It comes in handy in certain…. situations," Troy answered cautiously.

"I bet," she said. "And none of your wolves can deny your call?" Troy shook his head.

"Only another master wolf could. Seattle currently doesn't have anyone nearly as powerful as Troy to become a master, although some do try." Jacob told her. Tara was betting he was referring to Michael. Troy nodded in agreement.

"Is Michael coming here to the office?" she asked, looking at the cramped space. "Seems four would definitely be a crowd."

"No," Troy answered her. "We will meet him in the basement."

"Oh god," Jacob let out. "Seriously?"

"Why'd you have to say it like that?" Tara asked. "What's the basement?"

"You'll see," Troy said. A sly smile spread slowly over his face. It made Tara think of Chucky, the doll that ran around killing people. It was unnerving. "If you two will follow me," Troy ordered. He opened his office door and walked past Gina without a glance. Gina seemed preoccupied with a group of younger men ordering a round of drinks.

Troy led the detectives to the left of the stage and past a red curtain hanging from the ceiling. Behind the curtain was a staircase leading down. Troy started downward and Jacob followed, but Tara held back. Realizing Tara was still at the top of the steps, Jacob looked up at her.

"Coming?" he said, holding a hand out to her.

"I don't think so," she replied. "Last time I went down some staircases, I nearly died."

"That won't happen here. The basement's more of a meeting hall. Only one way in and one way out. You'll be safe," he assured her.

She eyed him suspiciously. He moved his hand closer to her, and with a deep breath, she took it. He led her down into the basement where werewolves and god knew what else was waiting for them. 'You'll be safe' Jacob had said. Sure, she thought. One way in and one way out with a room full of werewolves. Safe as houses.

Chapter 20

It was a short walk down the steps before they reached the basement. Troy stood in front of a red wooden door with a tiny peephole in the upper center. Troy extended his arm and knocked three times. Tara heard a combination of clicks before the door opened inward. Troy walked in and the detectives followed.

The basement wasn't a basement Tara had ever seen before. The room wasn't a room at all. It was a huge cavern. The floor was paved marble and the walls were slick and appeared to be chiseled with art. It was the most extensive relief artwork Tara had ever seen, with depictions of wolves spreading throughout the cave. Stalactites hung like chandeliers from the ceiling. The air was that from the underground tunnels: stale and cold. It sent goosebumps up Tara's arm and she shivered at the memory of the tunnels.

Tara felt movement behind her. She tensed and whirled around, noticing for the first time that others were in the room. A tall, thinnish woman with red dreadlocks stood leaning against the red door. A slightly short but muscular man with a Mariners cap stood with arms crossed over his chest next to her. He wore a black muscle tee, which made his arms look like thick branches.

"Detectives, these are two of my newest members, Sara and KJ," Troy told them. Sara smiled softly and KJ nodded. Both remained silent at the door.

"Newest members?" Tara asked.

Troy nodded to her. "They came under my protection about a month ago."

Tara looked at her partner. "I thought you said Seattle has that barrier around it to ward off other creatures?"

"Oh, it does," Troy confirmed. "These two," he nodded toward his wolves, "were bitten here at Seattle University."

Tara's eyes widened at the news. She turned toward the two at the door and gave them a sympathetic smile. Sara's eyes glared back at her in protest and KJ looked away, as if he had been distracted by a more interesting conversation somewhere else.

"Bitten at the University?" Jacob asked. "I thought the council limited the amount of recruitment you're able to do."

"They did," Troy answered with an annoyed look. "These two weren't recruited by choice. One of my wolves got a little anxious." Tara whipped her head back toward Troy. "A problem I've corrected," Troy said confidently. Tara noticed his hand twitched slightly and she doubt his last statement had been completely true.

Jacob huffed and walked closer to Troy, causing the two newest werewolves to stiffen alertly. "You're telling me that one of your wolves accidently let loose on civilians?"

The annoyance of Troy's face remained present as he replied. "It happens from time to time. Not often," he assured the detectives. "But, when it does, we take them into our pack and teach them the ropes."

"How humanitarian of you," Jacob replied curtly. Troy glared at him in protest but remained silent. Tara noticed the new wolves had moved closer to the detectives, as if waiting for instructions to attack. The pleasant visit could turn deadly at the drop of a dime. Troy held up a hand to ease them back. It was like telling a dog to heel, and they obeyed.

"What happened to the one who turned them?" Tara asked.

"He's being...reconditioned," Troy said. Tara didn't like the sound of that but didn't press the issue. They didn't come here to confront the leader of the werewolves on how he handles his pack. They came because someone was murdered and they needed answers.

As if reading her mind, Jacob moved further into the room. "Where are we going to question Michael?"

Troy smiled slyly and gestured toward the back of the cavern. "This way," he said, nodding to the two wolves. They nodded back and locked the bolts on the door. Tara tensed at the action, not feeling comfortable being locked in with at least three werewolves, but reminded herself that the door was locked in the first place. Was it to keep people out, or to keep something in? She shuttered at the thought.

Sensing her nervousness, Troy spoke. "Relax, detective. The locked door is for everyone's protection. We wouldn't want a customer to accidentally stumble upon us during our meeting. Most humans don't know about us, and we'd like to keep it that way." He winked at her comfortingly, trying to ease her distress. It helped, but only just.

Troy led them to the back of the cavern where there was an assortment of wooden chairs situated sporadically. Stalagmites sprang from the floor at different intervals near the chairs. Tara thought how difficult it would be to sit in one of them while being so close to the growing mound. There were torches lit on placards on the walls, casting shadows that swayed back and forth to the dancing flames.

Tara noticed how surprisingly warm the basement was. When they first walked in, the room had been cold, but the back of the cavern had a sort of dry heat that permeated the space. She glanced around but saw no heater or vent of any sort and wasn't sure where the heat was coming from.

Troy gestured for them to sit in one of the chairs. Jacob sat immediately. Tara stood next to one.

"You might as well sit, detective," Troy told her. "We could be waiting for a while, depending on where Michael was when I summoned him. If he was across town, traffic would definitely slow him down."

She nodded and reluctantly sat in one of the chairs. It was surprisingly comfortable for wood, but she scooted the chair away from a pair of identical stalagmites. Once she was comfortable, she crossed her legs and put her hands in her lap, waiting patiently.

"How long do you think it will take him?" Jacob asked Troy eagerly.

Troy shrugged. "Not too much longer, hopefully. I'm guessing he was down by the marina, so he should be here soon."

"Why the marina?" Tara asked.

"That's where he works, most days." Troy reached up and undid his tie. It reminded Tara of someone loosening a noose. "He helps the fisherman bring in the fish, and in turn, brings some of the fish to the pack."

"Ah," Jacob replied. Tara wasn't sure why he needed to bring fish to the pack. She decided to ask.

"Well, think about it," Troy answered. "My older wolves have learned self-control, but when you're new at shifting, you become like a wild animal and instinct kicks in. To counteract the urge to primally hunt prey, we tend to lock up our newer members until they learn to control themselves. But we still need to feed them. The fish help to nourish our young ones while we protect them from harming others."

"That's pretty awesome, actually," Tara told him. "I'm impressed that you go to the trouble."

"Thanks," replied Troy. "We've learned a few tricks to go undetected."

"So how long does it normally take before they gain self-control?" she asked him.

Troy thought about it for a moment. "Depends," said Troy. "Each wolf is different, just like each person is different. Each come with different temperaments and abilities. Some take no time at all. Others can take up to 8 months or so."

"Wow, that's a pretty long time," Jacob said. "How do some of your wolves feel about babysitting the young pups?"

Troy chuckled and shook his head. "Most are agreeable, remembering how it was for them the first couple transitions. Others…," he glanced around making sure no one was listening, "aren't as cooperative."

Tara was betting he was talking about Michael, but wasn't completely sure. He did say Michael brought fish to feed the new wolves, so maybe Troy was talking about other wolves she hadn't met yet. That did bring up another point. "How many wolves are in Seattle?"

Troy and Jacob exchanged glances. Tara caught the look and eyed them. Had she asked something wrong? "What?" asked Tara. "Did I ask something I shouldn't have?"

The men remained silent for a moment. Jacob spoke first. "Most of the altered beings aren't used to being asked such a personal question, especially by a human."

"Well, we've been talking for a while now, and none of the questions seemed to have bothered either of you." Both nodded in agreement. "So why this one?"

"I'm sorry detective," Troy answered her. "Our numbers aren't usually brought up in conversation. One thing that keeps us formidable against the other factions here in Seattle is our size. To discuss it would put us at a disadvantage."

Tara raised an eyebrow at Troy. "So let me get this straight," she said. "The other races have no idea how many wolves are in your pack?"

"No, they don't," replied Troy. "And no offense, but I'd like to keep it that way," he said while staring at Jacob, who looked back sheepishly.

"I understand," Jacob replied. "But as an outcast, I doubt I would have an opportunity to discuss it. Besides, who would believe an exile like myself?"

Troy nodded. "Still," he told him. "I'd like to keep our numbers quiet, if it's all the same to you."

Tara was still confused. It didn't make sense to her. Why would the council limit the number of wolves Troy could recruit if they had no idea how many existed in his pack in the first place? That seemed rather stupid.

"So, without knowing your true numbers, the council limits the number of wolves you can make? Forgive me if I find this hard to believe, but how does the council know that you don't have millions of wolves in your pack?"

Troy smiled at her politely. "The council doesn't know how many wolves are in my pack because it was part of the treaty we signed. Each race can make up to a certain number, but not beyond it. I don't know how many vampires Dominik controls or how many Sirens there are, and they have no idea about my wolves. Each race must abide by the rules of the treaty. Make sense?"

"Yes, and no," she said truthfully. "How does the council know that you are abiding by the rules? You just told us that one of your wolves turned two others without your permission. It seems to me that a signed treaty does little to stop the recruitment process."

Troy's face became annoyed once more. "It's very easy for someone to get the wolf gene. Just one scratch and it could make you one of us. Because of how easy it is to transfer from person to person, the council felt it appropriate to limit the amount we are able to create."

"I still don't see why they would limit the number without knowing how many are in the city in the first place," Tara said honestly.

Troy shrugged and pursed his lips. "I think they might worry that we would eventually outnumber the other races over time. If we ever ended up in another confrontation, they would want to make sure we don't have a sizable advantage over the rest. Vampires and Werewolves are the only ones who can make more of their kind so easily. The others would be at a serious disadvantage."

"I guess that makes sense, but as you said earlier, accidents happen. How do the other families know you aren't recruiting anyway?"

"Trust me," Jacob interrupted. "The council eventually finds out everything. They have ways of knowing things, spies everywhere, to tell them all they need to know."

"Except who killed Eric," Tara mentioned. Both men stared at her.

"Touché," Jacob replied quietly.

"In any event, the politics of the city keep the laws enforced, and we obey to keep the peace. No one wants another war on our hands. Frankly, I'm surprised you two haven't thought to question any human subjects. Anyone of our kind knows what it would mean to have another war on our hands."

"Another war?" Tara asked, looking at Jacob for an explanation.

"We've touched base on it slightly down in the tunnels. Years back, all the factions were at war with each other. After years of fighting..."

"And years of bloodshed," Troy interrupted.

"After years of fighting," Jacob repeated, "the races formed a truce. The council was formed and laws were established to keep the peace."

Tara remembered Harper thanking Jacob and his kind for the tunnels of the old city. He had mentioned a fire but didn't elaborate on the subject. Was the fire somehow related to the war Troy and Jacob were talking about? Tara tried to imagine what a war between the monsters would have been like. She imagined ogres and vampires fighting werewolves and god knows who else in the streets of Seattle with human bystanders caught in the middle. The thought was terrifying.

"It seems to me that the peace is a bit shaky," she admitted. Troy snickered and Jacob bashfully nodded his head.

"It is," Troy replied, straightening his tie a little. "But for the most part, we have learned to coexist relatively easy. We wolves stick to our own business and rarely venture out to talk to the other races. The council seems to respect our decision to be left alone."

"As long as you follow the rules," Jacob mentioned. Troy shrugged his shoulders once more.

A faint banging echoed throughout the cavern and all three turned toward the door. Tara barely made out KJ opening the door before a broad man pushed him aside and stomped his way toward the detectives. She saw Sara and KJ exchange words, but couldn't make them out. As the man drew closer, she noticed he was dressed in leather chaps, a black biker shirt and a blue bandana covering most of his red hair. His face was dark tanned, as if he fell asleep at the beach too long. His tannish face caused his facial hair to lavishly stand out against his skin.

He walked with a kind of limp but seemed to concentrate hard on walking normally. He had his hands balled into fists and a look of anger swept over him as he saw Troy stand up to greet him.

"What have I told you about summoning me like a dog?" He yelled at Troy, who seemed not to have noticed his anger. Troy spoke calmly and collectively back at him.

"It couldn't be helped, I'm afraid." Troy motioned to the two detectives. "The police need to ask you a few questions."

"I don't give a damn who needs to talk to me! I am not a servant you call like some stray mutt whenever you want." Michaels tanned face flushed a deeper shade of red and Tara could literally feel his anger sweeping through the room.

Troy smiled softly and bowed. "My apologies, Michael. Next time, I'll try your phone, but this was the only guarantee that you would meet with us." Michael let out a long huff and crossed his arms defensively. He glanced at the detectives for the first time. His brown eyes sized them up quickly before glancing back at Troy. "Please, sit," Troy said pleasantly.

"I'm fine standing," Michael retorted, reeling back on his left leg.

"Suit yourself," Troy said, smiling. Tara got the distinct impression that he was enjoying Michael's discomfort.

"I'm detective Moore, and this is my partner, detective Bancroft," Jacob stated.

"I know who you two are," Michael replied hastily. "You're the ones who called me yesterday."

Tara nodded. "And what a pleasant conversation we had," she said sarcastically. Michael nodded.

"Well, as I told you then, I had nothing to do with the vamp's death."

"Yes, you did say that," she retorted. "But nonetheless, here we are." Anger seeped further into the room as Michael's face turned purple. He bit his lower lip and shook his head at her.

"Then what am I doing here?" He asked Troy.

"Mr. Beagan, maybe there was something from that night that could lead us to who really killed Eric," Jacob said diplomatically. "Since you happen to be at Heiligtum at the time, and so far, as we can tell, the only person who last saw Eric alive, maybe you can answer some questions to help us in the right direction."

"As I said on the phone, detectives, I don't know nothing about nothing." He turned back to Troy. "I'm leaving now," he said and turned to walk away.

"I don't think so," Troy replied, and suddenly Michael was still. He seemed to try to move but couldn't. Troy circled Michael as he spoke. "I'll let you leave once all the questions are answered, Understood? Nod if you do."

Michael struggled against whatever power Troy had him under, but couldn't break free. Tara stared in awe at Troy's control of him. No wonder Michael had never succeeded in overthrowing Troy. If Troy could literally control a member of his pack, how could anyone think to go up against power like that? Michael managed to nod his head, but only just. Suddenly, whatever power held him in place was gone, and Michael fell to his knees.

Troy bent down to speak to him. "That's a good pup," he said, patting him on the head.

"Fuck you," Michael said softly. Troy laughed and extended his hand out to help him up. Michael swatted it away and stood up on his own accord. Troy laughed once more. It was a sick cackle, and it unnerved Tara.

She shifted in her seat. For the first time, she noticed that Troy had a vindictive side. Did he treat all of his wolves like this or was Michael special? Maybe it was some sort of payback for trying to take his place in the past. Either way, she wasn't comfortable with it. She glanced at Jacob, whose face was suddenly a mask of emotions. If he didn't like the abuse, he did his best to hide it.

Michael turned back toward the detectives. "What do you want to know?" he asked through a clenched jaw. Troy winked at Tara and sat back down. Jacob asked the first question.

"What time did the fight start at?"

Michael eyed him. "Around 7:30, I think."

"You sure?" Tara asked.

"I don't know exactly, I wasn't wearing a watch, but the sun had just set."

"Walk us through what happened," Jacob ordered. Michael turned to Troy, who nodded back at him. He took in a deep breath and released it slowly. He started his version of events.

"I was with some friends at Heiligtum. I walked toward the bar to grab a drink when that vamp bumped into me on purpose."

"Did you know who he was?" Tara asked him.

"Everyone knows who he is," he replied heatedly. "The ass makes it a point to go out of his way to make sure everyone knows who he is and who his father is."

"Made," Troy corrected him.

"What?" Michael asked.

"Made," Troy said again. "He's dead now, so the correct term would be made, not make." The two exchanged glances. Michael bit his lip again, holding back his anger at Troy.

"Back on topic," Jacob said. "What happened next?"

"I pushed him. He pushed back. I threw a punch, then he threw one back. We brawled for a moment before getting thrown out. We exchanged words and went our separate ways. The end."

"But you threatened to kill him if you ever saw him again?" Tara asked, leaning forward, elbows on her knees.

"I was upset, detective," Michael assured her. "It was just tough guy talk. No way was I going to look like a pansy in front of my friends."

"And would you have?" Jacob asked. "Killed him, I mean. If you ever saw him again?" Troy straightened slightly in his chair.

"If I would have seen him again, I might have considered it, but I didn't. He left with that Ogre bitch, and I went to Hot Mama's for pizza."

"And where were you two nights ago when Eric was murdered?" Tara asked him, staring straight into his eyes.

"I was working at the harbor on a fishing boat," he replied without blinking. "Lots of witnesses on the boat to confirm my whereabouts, if you'd like to check." He eyed her with a smug look on his face.

"I'd like to check," she responded. Her tone oozed with disdain for him. Michael huffed, reached into his pocket and produced his cell phone. He tossed the phone to Tara.

"Call the captain if you don't believe me. But I'm pretty sure that they will remember me being there. I happened to save a man's life that day. Besides," he continued. "Rumor has it that the vamp died at a gym. My gym is in the U-district. Nowhere near his. I'm sure staff and cameras can confirm I wasn't there."

Jacob smiled brightly at him. "It's funny you should mention camera's, isn't it, detective Bancroft?"

"Oh yes, it is," she said, keeping her eyes glued to Michael's. "Hilarious, actually."

"Do you know why it's funny, Mr. Beagan?" Jacob asked playfully. Michael shook his head slightly. Jacob's smile grew wider. He leaned in closer to Michael as if he was going to tell him a secret. "Because the cameras at the gym had been erased. A good 30 minutes of footage was wiped out."

"Well I sure as hell didn't do it," Michael roared. "I swear I was out on the boat when he was killed!"

Jacob held his hands up. "I believe you," he said quickly. "But a hot head like you can't let go of a grudge so easily. You have connections here, am I right? What a coincidence that you just happened to be out on a boat when a guy you threatened just happens to turn up dead."

"What's that supposed to mean?" Michael drew closer to Jacob, almost knocking a chair over as he passed by. "You think I put someone up to it?"

Jacob shrugged. "You could get your revenge for making you look bad in front of your friends and still be in the clear, with many witnesses nearby to vouch for you."

"You're not going to pin this on me!" Michael screamed. "I didn't do it!"

"I agree with him," said Troy. "Seems to me that you two are fishing, detectives." He shook a finger at them and tsked a couple times. "Michael may be a hot head, as you say, and he should learn to control his temper, but a bar fight is a long leap to murder, Jacob."

Michael turned to look at his leader. For the first time since his arrival, Tara noticed a gleam of respect from his eyes. He nodded to Troy in appreciation.

"There is one way to make absolutely sure you had nothing to do with Eric's death," Jacob told them, ignoring Troy's statement.

"And what is that?" Michael asked.

"Come with me to see Vita."

Both wolves looked at Jacob with a crazed expression. "You can't be serious?" Michael yelled. "That's suicide for a wolf, and I believe you know that."

Tara wasn't sure what was going on. She heard the name Vita before. Jacob and Bethany had both mentioned her. She was at Bethany's house the night Tara got attacked. Why would the wolves be afraid of her? Should she ask in front of everyone or wait until Jacob and she were alone? She decided to wait.

"I agree with him," Troy said disapprovingly. "Questioning him is one thing. Delivering him into the heart of the witch's territory would be condemning him to certain death."

"You know Vita can extract memories from people," Jacob stated. "If she searches his mind and finds nothing, then we know he is telling the truth."

"No fucking way," Michael screamed. Troy held his hand up to silence his wolf, then scooted closer to the edge of his seat.

"When you asked to speak to Michael, I allowed it for no other reason than to prove his innocence, but I will not allow one of my wolves to commit suicide by willingly face off against the Coven of Rain. Especially Vita!"

"You know I didn't mean it like that," Jacob said softly.

"Regardless, detective. Unless you have evidence that implicates my second beyond a simple bar fight, then I see no reason to subject him to torturous means." Troy clasped his hands together and licked his lips. "Do you have any further evidence, or is this simply a wolf hunt?"

Both Tara and Jacob glanced at each other. Tara could tell Jacob was searching for a way to keep the questioning going, but the air had changed drastically. Instead of warmth, Tara felt the air shift to cold and stuffy. She shrugged at Jacob, conceding to defeat. Jacob turned back to Troy.

"No other evidence at this time," he whispered.

"Then this meeting is over," said Troy, standing up. "You may go," he told Michael.

Michael smiled brightly and turned to leave. Before he got too far, Troy spoke again. "Oh, and Michael?" He stopped and turned toward his pack leader. "Make good choices," Troy said, winking at him. He nodded his response and fled the cavern.

Both detectives stood at once. "If he did do it, you know that Dominik won't rest until he is brought to justice," Jacob said in a hushed voice. "Something tells me that the repercussions would reach far beyond your second."

"If the Sloan's believed that any of my wolves could have done this, I don't think you would be here asking questions. It would be the king himself at my door." Troy stretched his arms before speaking again. "In any case, until you can produce concrete evidence that Michael had anything to do with Eric's death, he is innocent." Sara and KJ were suddenly at his side. "These two will show you out."

Chapter 21

The detectives stopped at the top of the stairs before Tara broke the silence. "What just happened?"

"We were kicked out," Jacob replied quietly.

"I got that. I'm trying to figure out why. Why are they afraid of Vita?"

He looked at her and held a finger to his lips. "Not here," he replied. "Too many prying ears." He walked past the curtain back into the main bar. Fewer people were there, but a couple sat near Gina giggling and eating peanuts. Gina looked up from wiping the counter and nodded pleasantly at the detectives. Jacob half waved and walked out of the bar. Tara smiled meekly and followed her partner.

The sun was beginning to set, casting shades of purple and red throughout the cloudy sky. The wind was fierce, scraping against her face like an icy slap. She shivered as she walked to the car.

Once inside, the questions started. "Whose Vita?"

"She is the leader of the Coven of Rain," Jacob stated.

"And that is what exactly?"

"The witches everyone keeps mentioning? It's their coven. Most witches here belong to the coven, and Vita is the leader of it." Jacob started the car and cool air blew through the vents. He bent toward the heater and turned up the knob.

"And the reason Michael and Troy didn't want to go see her is...why?" Tara asked.

"She is one scary woman," Jacob said simply. "She has more power than most in the coven, and although there is a truce going on between all the supernatural creatures, the witches will not hesitate to exact revenge on a wandering wolf."

"So Vita can extract memories?"

Jacob nodded. "Among other things."

"So why wouldn't Michael want to prove his innocence? If this Vita can tell us whether or not he did it, then seems to me you came up with a logical solution."

Jacob sighed. "The witches aren't exactly careful when it comes to the wolves. Remember the war I mentioned?" Tara nodded her head. "Well, many of the witches were slaughtered by werewolves. It's hard to explain how deep hatred can go for anyone who doesn't understand the whole history of events, but the witches signed the treaty on one condition."

"And what was that?" Tara asked, still trying to understand the whole situation.

"That no wolf be allowed back into their territory."

Tara eyed her partner. "So what happens if a wolf does enter?"

Jacob's eyes grew wide. "Then the witches can handle the situation as they see fit," he said ominously.

Tara thought about that for a moment. "So if there is a ban on the wolves, then why would you suggest it to Michael?"

Jacob shrugged slightly. "A couple reasons, actually. The first one being that Vita would know exactly if he was innocent or not. The second was to see if the scare tactic would somehow force his hand. I didn't expect Troy to disagree."

"So what, if he entered the witch's territory, he would be captured? Killed?" Tara couldn't believe how normal she felt talking like this. She was a cop, and she felt fine discussing a wolf's murder like she was bringing up the weather. What was wrong with her?

"I don't think Vita would have an issue, as long as we suggested it to her first. But there are many witches in Ballard and Fremont. If just one saw the wolf, his life would be forfeit."

Tara shook her head in disdain. She frowned at the thought of the witches hurting the wolves over an old grudge. "So now we have no leads, no other suspect, and nothing to go on."

"We can always re-examine the body. Maybe we missed something the first time," Jacob offered encouragingly. It was worth a shot.

Tara's cell phone rang, causing her to jump in her seat. She stared at the number but it had been blocked. She pushed the small green phone symbol and spoke into it. "Detective Bancroft."

"It's me, detective," Bethany Sloan said.

Relief washed over Tara at hearing Bethany's voice. "I'm glad you're alright," Tara said honestly. The attack at the mansion had caused her to worry, even though she had only known the Sloan's for a couple days. Tara had many questions but didn't know exactly how to start. "Is your dad alright?"

"He's fine, detective," Bethany answered. "I'm glad to hear you're alright as well. After Russell told me what happened, you can imagine how upset I was that you had been hurt."

"Don't blame him," Tara pleaded. "If it hadn't been for those three, we might not be alive."

"In any case, you also saved one of us, so for that, I thank you." Tara didn't know what to say. She had never been good at taking credit. She changed the subject quickly.

"I heard you captured one of the intruders," said Tara. "Find anything out?"

"Yes," Bethany said into the phone but didn't elaborate. "I was wondering if you could meet me outside of Heiligtum tonight."

"Why there?" asked Tara.

"Whereas I'm sure your investigation into my brother's death is going well, I think people might be more inclined to answer questions if I'm with you."

Silence filled the phone for a moment. "...Okay," Tara responded. She had thought to head there and see what the bartender remembered about the fight, but never thought to bring Bethany along.

"Besides," Bethany added. "After everything that has happened, I could really use a drink."

"I understand. What time?"

"Thirty minutes, give or take." Tara glanced at the clock on her phone. It was now 6:45. Depending on traffic, she could be back in Belltown in 20 minutes.

"I'll be there by 7:30," Tara told her.

"Perfect," Bethany said cheerily. "See you then." Tara was about to hang up when Bethany spoke again. "Oh, and leave your partner out of this."

That caught Tara by surprise. She remembered Adam mentioning that the Sloan's might have thought Jacob had something to do with the home invasion. Surely, after questioning their captor, they couldn't really believe that.

"Why?" Tara asked.

"Well, given his hostility toward my family, I don't think it would be a good idea for him to come along. Plus, since he is an exile, things would not bode well for him if any other shifter happened to be present tonight. If we want people to answer our questions, he will need to stay away."

Tara nodded, then realized that Bethany couldn't see her. "Okay, but he isn't going to like it." She glanced at Jacob, whose eyes bulged madly. She quickly looked away.

"Trust me, detective. It's in everyone's best interest, especially his."

"I understand," Tara lied. "See you soon." They hung up and silence filled the car. Tara faced her partner, who was shaking his head.

"No," he stated.

"Why not?" asked Tara.

"I'm not going to leave you there by yourself. You have no idea what danger you might be walking into." Jacob's voice rose as he spoke.

"I've been wanting to question the bartenders about that night. Now would be the perfect time to do it." Tara said confidently. "Besides, I won't be alone. Bethany will be with me."

"No," he stated again. "It's too risky. You won't just be walking into one type of monster; you'd be walking into a sea of them. Who knows what could happen to you there."

"You said it yourself that Heiligtum was a neutral spot between all the races. And I'm sure humans have wondered in from time to time. So what's the big deal?" she argued.

"Are you forgetting that we still don't know who tried to kill us?" Jacob asked. "What if they, whoever they are, happen to be there? Are you 100 percent certain that Bethany will keep you safe?"

Jacob did have a valid point. Was she so certain that she would be safe? Maybe not 100 percent, but it was the best lead to go on. They had gotten nowhere. All the leads had led to dead ends. If she could find out anything to help in the investigation, then she owed it to Eric to find out what happened. Jacob knew it as well.

"I'm going, Jacob. You suggested taking a look at the body. That sounds like the perfect thing for you to do while I'm there. I'll call you to come pick me up when I'm done."

Jacob shook his head again. "I still don't think this is a good idea." This time Tara shook her head.

"Look," she said pointedly. "You're an exile, right? What would happen if you ended up going?" Jacob kept quiet while Tara waited expectantly. "Well?"

"I'd probably be strung up and skinned if I was caught."

"Well, there you go," Tara said, slapping her palm on her knee. "You can't go, but I can. I'll find out what I can and we can report back to each other later."

"I can always shift into someone else," he told her.

"Do you think that is a good idea?"

He shook his head. "No, but you shouldn't go without someone to watch your back," he said. "Someone alive."

She sighed loudly, mostly for his benefit. "This is happening, Jacob. I understand you want to protect me, but the training wheels have to come off. If I'm going to be working on cases that involve the supernatural, then I have to be able to handle myself. And so far, I think I've been coping pretty damn well."

"Yeah, well you haven't been to Heiligtum yet," he shot at her.

"Either way, you can drop me off or I can get Bethany to pick me up. But I'm going. What's it going to be?" Jacob stared at her in disbelief. She stared back, not backing down. After a good five minutes, Jacob turned toward the steering wheel and put the gear into drive.

"Where are we going?" she asked him.

"To Heiligtum," he muttered. "Buckle up." Tara smiled as they drove off into the fading light.

Chapter 22

Jacob dropped Tara off around the corner of El Gaucho on 1st and Wall. On the way to Belltown, Bethany sent Tara a message to meet her around back. Jacob was reluctant but held his tongue.

As she got out of the car, she hugged herself tightly as the cold sent shivers down her spine. The night's breeze had diminished slightly, but it was considerably colder now that the sun had set. She checked her phone for the time. 7:25 pm. Five minutes to spare, she thought to herself. She said goodbye to Jacob and walked down the alleyway.

Bethany appeared almost at once. Tara jumped at the unexpected materialization, but she quickly regained her composure. She was getting used to vamps sneaking up on her.

"I'm sorry if I frightened you, detective," Bethany admitted. "I didn't know how long you'd be. I trust detective Moore was more than reluctant to let you come alone."

"Oh, he put up a good fight, but I told him I could trust you to protect me if anything should go wrong," Tara replied. "I can trust you, right?"

Bethany looked hurt by the question but answered without any real emotion. "Of course. I told you no harm shall come to you while under my protection, and I meant that."

Tara nodded. She noticed Bethany's attire for the first time. She wore a strapless white dress that ended just above the knees. The dress accentuated all her curves flawlessly. Her open toed white heels strapped up her ankles. Bethany's doll-like hair was pulled back into a ponytail with just a few curly strands hanging over the side of her forehead. Her normally white skin seemed a bit darker, with auburn cheeks and dark blue eyeshadow that highlighted her eyes. Her lips wore a maroon shade of lipstick that seemed to blend effortlessly with her complexion. She was beautiful.

"Just what kind of place are we going to?" Tara asked looking down at her own clothes, "Because I don't think I'm going to fit in."

Bethany smiled. "Not to worry, detective. I have a dress for you." Bethany held out her hand toward Tara, who stared at it as if it was a snake that would bite her if she got too close. "Don't worry," Bethany said calmly. "I just figured you'd like some privacy in order to change, but if you prefer to change out here in the alley, I can go get the dress."

The thought snapped Tara back to reality. Changing in an alley where anyone could walk by and see was definitely not on her top 10 things to do in her lifetime. She shook her head and slid her hand into Bethany's. Bethany gave her a weak smile and led her further into the alleyway. She stopped at a back door of a building and knocked twice. The door slid open a notch and Tara noticed a pair of dark eyes staring down at them.

"Password?" A high-pitched voice echoed down the alley.

"Leben ist fur die lebenden," Bethany uttered. The door slid shut and a series of clicks rang out from the other side. The door sprang open and Tara was guided inside a darkened hallway.

Her eyes hadn't adjusted to the dimly lit lights hanging above her, but she could see a long corridor with a couple rooms throughout the hall. Tara was reminded of being in the ogre cave. How many caves do monsters need, she wondered? And what was their obsession with dark ominous hallways?

Bethany led her to the first door on the right. "You can change in here," she said. "Once done, I'll come in and finish the final touches." Bethany opened the door and reached inside. Suddenly the room was illuminated with a bright overhanging light. Tara peered inside to see a small bathroom with a double paned mirror. A black gown was hanging near the sink and a pair of black strapless shoes sat on top of the counter.

"By the looks of you, I'd say you were a four. The dress should fit you perfectly," Bethany told her. Tara nodded, stunned at how elegant and beautiful the dress truly was. "I'll leave you to it," Bethany said cheerfully and shut the door behind her.

Tara changed into the gown and it did indeed fit perfectly. She noticed that it also gave her some breathing room that most dresses don't give. It seemed to flow and sway when she moved. Even the shoes fit completely well, yet were comfortable enough to walk in. Bethany returned a short time later to do her hair and makeup. In less than 15 minutes, Tara was transformed into a beautiful and elegant woman.

Tara hated going out, even dressing up, but she felt in awe as she stared at herself in the mirror.

"Perfect," Bethany said aloud. "Now we're ready."

"For what, exactly?" Tara asked, still staring at herself in the mirror. Tara's wavy red hair was held up in a small fishtail braid, and her bangs were parted, showing more of her forehead than she normally liked, but she had to admit that Bethany did an amazing job.

"To talk to Brandon."

Tara turned to look at Bethany. "Who's Brandon?"

Bethany smiled back at her. "I keep forgetting that you are new here. Brandon Brooks is the owner of Heiligtum. He is one of the few humans who is allowed to know about us. And in order to talk to him, you must make a great impression."

"I could always just show him my badge," Tara said.

Bethany shook her head. "That won't work. He would allow you to question him, but probably wouldn't answer so freely."

"So you want me to what? Flirt with him and hope he likes me?"

Bethany's smile grew wider. "Something like that," she said honestly. "Brandon is a ladies' man. He most certainly will have an entourage of women by his side. What I want you to do is find a way to join them. You certainly have the looks."

Tara blushed slightly. She wasn't used to people giving her compliments on her beauty. The last guy who did that was Kenneth, and that had ended badly. She shook the memories away. "And then what?"

"And then talk to him. Find some way to bring up my brother. Judge his reactions, see if you can jog his memory about Eric." Bethany put her hands on her hips.

"To what end?" Tara asked. She eyed Bethany slightly and her lip curled. "Do you believe Brandon had anything to do with Eric's death?"

"No, but he knows everything that goes on in his club. It's his sanctuary. A rat couldn't get in without him knowing about it."

"Speaking of rats," Tara mentioned. "Are you going to tell me what you found out about the men who tried to kill us?"

Bethany nodded. "Later. After we talk to Brandon. Ready?"

Tara gave her a questionable look. She didn't like flirting to get information, but if it worked and they were closer to solving the case, she would play ball. She turned and gave herself one last look in the mirror and nodded. After putting her belongings in a purse, Bethany held her hand out and waited for Tara to take it. "Shall we?"

"We shall," Tara replied, taking her hand again. Bethany led her back through the darkened corridor where another bouncer stood guarding a black sliding door. He gave Bethany a queer look before speaking.

"We don't normally see you here anymore," he said in a raspy voice. "To what do we owe this pleasure?"

Bethany replied in an innocent voice. "Just showing my friend around. She's not from around here."

The bouncer sniffed the air while glancing at Tara, who stood there silently. She felt awkward just standing there while the bouncer eyed her like a hungry kid eyeing a slice of chocolate cake.

"You going to let us in or are we gonna stand here all night?" Bethany asked in a childlike voice.

"You brought a human here?" the bouncer asked. "Tonight, of all nights?" He added, eyes wide in shock.

Bethany shrugged her shoulders indifferently. "Tried to talk her out of it, but she wouldn't take no for an answer." Bethany looked at Tara for backup.

"What can I say," Tara replied. "It sounded fun." She tried to make her voice sound as bimbo as possible but wasn't sure she was convincing.

"Now be a good boy and let us in," Bethany said playfully. The bouncer eyed both of them with mild amusement but opened the door. Music sprang out of the opened space, loud and booming, which caught Tara by surprise. It must have shown on her face because the bouncer let out a soft laugh.

"You haven't experienced anything yet," he whispered to her, barely audible over the thumping bass. "Have fun," he chided, winking at the two women. Bethany nodded to the bouncer and walked into the club. Tara smiled weakly, then followed awkwardly.

At first glance, Heiligtum was just like any other nightclub Tara had been to in Phoenix. Loud music blared through overly large speakers mounted high above on the walls. The dance floor was flooded with people swaying and moving to the beat and there were crowded lines leading to the bars. Strobe and disco lights flashed throughout the club, temporarily blinding the detective.

Once her eyes became acclimated to the party scene, she quickly realized how wrong she had been about Heiligtum. Through the strobe lights, Tara noticed cages hanging in odd variables with frightened looking people staring down at the crowd. A few were bleeding in various spots and the blood trickled out and down onto a couple darkly dressed folk. She suppressed the notion to gag when she saw them raise their head to the ceiling and open their mouths wide to catch the dripping blood.

Tara's heart leaped into her throat and she moved with a quickened pace to help the caged people. Bethany caught her arm and forced her to stop.

"Don't worry, detective," Bethany whispered into her ear. "It's all part of the show."

"We have to help them," Tara replied, ripping her arm away from Bethany's grip.

"They are here on their own accord," Bethany said calmly. "No one dies here and no one comes to any harm." Bethany raised her eyes to the nearest cage. "They are paid quite handsomely for a few hours of being locked in a cage."

"Then why are they bleeding?" Tara asked doubtfully.

"Again, by their own choice. They get paid extra if they allow the clientele to take a few drops of blood."

Tara's eyes grew wide. "That's sick!" she screamed.

"And having a lady take her clothes off for horny men and get paid for it isn't?" Bethany asked. Tara saw her point. Humans had a different set of standards. From the perspective of the monsters, she suspected lots of things probably didn't make sense. Still, she didn't have to like it.

Bethany continued. "Rest assured, detective. They get paid more than you can imagine and nothing ever happens to them. They are quite safe here." Tara shook her head in disbelief but ultimately conceded to defeat. At the present moment, there was nothing she could do about it.

"Let's go," Bethany said, taking Tara's arm once more. She led her to a small table near the back of a large, candlelit room filled with couches. From their viewpoint, they could see mostly all of the club and its inhabitants.

"So which one is Brandon?" asked Tara, scanning the crowd. It was hard to distinguish anyone in a crowd this large.

"On the second floor peering down on us," Bethany replied nonchalantly. "If you must look, do so casually, as if you are just taking in the sights." Tara understood. She couldn't just look up without letting Brandon know they were intentionally looking for him. She had to play it cool.

Tara scanned the crowd once more, then stared at the caged men. She noticed a second level that was mostly deserted. A handsome man with thick brown hair dressed in a black suit sat with four overly dressed women crowded around him. They were laughing and flashing their beautiful smiles, as if they had just won the lottery. She quickly glanced away.

"So that's him," Tara stated.

"Yes," Bethany confirmed. "Must be a slow night. Normally his entourage is much more extensive."

"What's the plan?" asked Tara.

"We wait for an opportunity to present itself," She replied flatly. "Don't worry, my guess is one will happen soon." Bethany scanned the room. A sly smile crept on her face as her eyes settled on the crowd.

"What?" Tara asked. "You see something?"

"Let's get a drink," she replied and headed toward the bar near the entrance. Tara followed her quickly, making sure not to lose her in the crowded room. As they weaved their way toward the bar, Tara noticed some of the people didn't look all too human. A couple of people seemed to glow a pale shade of blue between the strobes flashing lights. Was that a trick of the light?

As they continued, Tara saw a giant wolf dressed in a gray suit standing on two legs. Was that a werewolf, she wondered? She just came from seeing Troy, but none of the people transformed into a wolf. Is that what they look like when they transform? And if so, why was he in wolf form? It wasn't a full moon tonight. She made a mental note to ask Bethany later.

She turned to follow Bethany deeper into the crowd, but Bethany had bumped into a young woman, spilling her drink down her red strapless dress. The girl looked up with anger filled eyes that intensified when she saw who caused the accident.

"Watch where you're going," the woman shrieked.

Bethany smiled sweetly at the young woman. "Tina Malcolm, aren't you a vision tonight," she said in a mocking sort of way. "Nice dress. I hope it's not ruined."

Tina gave Bethany an angry huff. "It'll be fine. What are you doing here?"

Bethany turned toward Tara. "Oh, I'm just showing my friend a night on the town." Tara nodded to Tina who seemed not to notice.

"Yeah, well, have fun," Tina replied and turned to leave. Bethany was suddenly in front of her. Tara hadn't seen her move.

"Now, now. What's your hurry, witch? The night's still young and it's been awhile since we were able to catch up." A grin that Tara hadn't seen on Bethany before had spread thinly on her darkened face.

Tina took a step back. The crowd of people seemed to have ignored the music and began to enclose them like sharks smelling blood. All eyes were on the two girls.

Tina spoke calmly. "Get out of my way, Bethany."

"What's your hurry?" Bethany asked again.

"Not that it's any of your business, but I'm on a date." Tina responded. "Now are you going to move, or am I going to have to force you?" Tina's arms outstretched and her palms turned toward the ceiling. Bethany found this amusing and began to laugh.

"Oh, I've missed you, my little witch. You can put your arms down. This is just a friendly little chat." Bethany stopped laughing almost at once. She reached up and wiped a strand of hair off her forehead. "Besides, your mother would hate it if you came home with bite marks on your neck." Bethany winked at Tara, then looked deadly serious at Tina. "If you came home at all."

"Was that a threat, vampire?" Tina began moving closer to Bethany, who stood her ground. The crowd inched closer, whispering their excitement at the possibility of a fight.

"You should know by now that I don't make threats. At least not ones I can't back up." Bethany retorted. She raised an eyebrow at Tina who drew closer. She stood about two inches shorter than Bethany but seemed to have no fear of her whatsoever.

Tara didn't know what to do. Should she try to break them up? Clearly, they had some history she wasn't aware of. Tara decided to intervene if they started coming to blows.

"You wouldn't start anything tonight," Tina stated. "Not with the ball tomorrow night." Tina smiled mockingly at Bethany. "But I'm kind of hoping you do, because I really think someone should put you Sloan's in your place."

Bethany's lip curled and she hissed at the witch. "As you wish, dear," she said. Moving with incredible speed, she picked Tina up and threw her into the crowd, knocking a group of people to the floor. Her face changed from beautiful to horrific in a blink of an eye. Her fangs were completely visible and dripped saliva as she hissed madly at Tina.

Tina got up slowly and whispered a word Tara had never heard before. A green orb of fire the size of a tennis ball materialized above her right hand. It seemed to hover there for a moment before Tina hurled the ball at Bethany. Bethany dodged the ball with ease as she moved quickly through the crowd. The fireball stopped in midair and, like a homing beacon, zoomed toward Bethany once more. Bethany dove out of the way just in time as the fireball smashed into the floor where she stood not moments before.

The crowd erupted into screams and chaos ensued. It was like a bomb had gone off inside a theater. People began to run in all directions, knocking over some and trampling others. Tara tried to make her way through the oncoming stampede but wasn't making any headway. With each step forward, the crowd pushed her further and further away.

Tina began chanting in Latin and her hands began to glow soft and dim. With each passing word, her hands became brighter. Bethany seized the opportunity to attack. She grabbed Tina around the neck and leaned in to bite her, but Tina grabbed her arm. Bethany screamed in agony as her arm sizzled and smoked. She let go of Tina's neck and coddled her burnt arm. Tina kicked Bethany in the stomach, causing her to double over in pain.

Tina's white glowing hands descended toward Bethany's face, but Bethany suddenly held Tina's wrists. Tina struggled to break her grip, but it was no use. Bethany was strong and held her captive with ease. As she leaned in to bite her once more, Tara saw real fear in Tina's eyes. Tara screamed as loud as she could, trying anything she could to distract Bethany.

Suddenly, the bouncers were there, pulling the girls away from each other. "ENOUGH!" boomed a deep voice that echoed throughout the club. Brandon descended the stairs onto the first floor.

Both Tina and Bethany struggled against the bouncers, but couldn't break free. Brandon waltzed over and stopped between them. "This is a safe haven for your kind," he spoke angrily. "No one is allowed to fight here. You have a vendetta against each other, then settle it outside my club!"

Bethany continued to struggle but her bouncer, a tall black man built like a brick building, held her with ease.

"Didn't seem to stop my brother from being attacked by that wolf," Bethany blurted out. Brandon flashed her a heated glance.

"You Sloan's seem to think that all of Seattle belongs to you. And maybe it does, to a certain extent." He turned to look her dead in the eyes. "But not here. Not Heiligtum." He scanned the remaining crowd. "This is a safe place. I allow you to come here at your leisure to enjoy being who you are, without fear of reprisal." He turned to Bethany again. "And no one, and I mean no one is above the rules here. Understood?"

Bethany tried once more to break free, but the bouncer's arm tightened around her throat.

"Am I understood?" Brandon yelled. Bethany nodded as much as she was able. Brandon turned toward Tina, waiting for a reply. Tina nodded once.

"She started it," Tina said, but Brandon raised a hand to silence her. He walked to where the green fireball landed on the floor. Scorch marks singed the marble.

"You'll be paying to replace the floor," he said to Tina. She eyed him with a disbelieving glance, but nodded her head. "Now, you two can either leave and continue to kill each other outside of my sanctuary, or you two can stay, provided there is no more fighting. And considering tomorrow is the Annual Ball, I would suggest you two stay away from each other."

Both girls nodded in response. Brandon gave both bouncers a look and they released the girls. Tina eyed Bethany as if she was going to say something, but thought better of it and walked away into the crowd.

Tara ran to Bethany. "Are you alright?" she asked, carefully taking hold of her arm. The burn was healing, but it was still swollen and black.

"Magic is a bitch to heal," Bethany confided. "It'll be gone by the end of the night."

Brandon walked over to them. "I'm sorry for what happened to your brother, but I meant what I said. No more fighting here." Bethany stared at him with a peculiar expression. "Who's your friend," he asked, changing the subject.

Bethany introduced them. "This is Tara Bancroft. Tara, this is Brandon Brooks, the owner of Heiligtum."

"Yeah, gathered that," Tara replied, holding out her hand. He took it and kissed the back of it.

"A Pleasure," he said softly. Tara blushed.

"I was just showing Tara around and we thought we'd get a drink," Bethany told him.

"Oh?" he replied. "New to Seattle?" Tara nodded intently. "Well, welcome. Despite recent events, what do you think of Heiligtum?"

Tara turned her head to the bleeding men in the cages. "The decor leaves much to be desired. Other than that, it's nice."

Brandon let out a laugh. It was a nice, hearty laugh that echoed throughout the club. "And what kind of monster are you?" he asked, eyeing her up and down. Tara didn't like the look, nor did she like being referred to as a monster, but chose not to say anything.

"She's human," Bethany answered for her. Brandon's eyes grew wide with shock.

"You brought a human here?"

"Relax," Bethany said coolly. "She knew what she was getting into." Tara turned a deep shade of red. She felt awkward with the two talking about her like she wasn't there.

"I highly doubt that," he replied. "In any case, welcome. I have a bottle of champagne upstairs. What do you say to a toast, to celebrate your first time here?" Bethany turned to Tara and gave her a long, knowing look. They had originally come to question him about Eric. Bethany said she was waiting for the right opportunity to present itself. With the ending of the fight, it seems one did.

"I'd like that," Tara replied as sweetly as she could. Bethany smiled slightly.

Brandon turned and offered Tara his arm. "Then shall we?" Tara let her hand settle lightly inside his outturned arm and nodded. He grinned as he led her up the stairs. Bethany followed close behind them.

Chapter 23

The upstairs was darker and quieter than Tara expected. Except for a few stragglers, the three of them were completely alone. Brandon escorted them to his VIP couch.

The second level was faintly lit by tea light candles and one fluorescent purple light in a round fixture that hung low from the ceiling. Tara could still make out the small wooden table with the top of a bottle of champagne sitting in a small tub of ice. Three long stemmed champagne flutes sat on white square coasters.

Once seated, Brandon uncorked the bottle, which the cork flew off with a pop. Fizz slowly dribbled down the neck of the bottle as he poured the champagne into each glass. He handed the girls each a glass, then raised his own.

"A toast," he said. "To new beginnings." Both Tara and Bethany raised their glass and the three clinked together before each took a sip. "Now then, what brings you to Seattle?"

"Work, originally," Tara replied. "But I really just wanted a fresh start."

He smiled sympathetically. "Bad breakup?"

Tara blushed. "That obvious, huh?"

"Not at all," he assured her. "But I think fresh starts are great. They help with the healing process."

Tara took another sip of her champagne. "Speaking from experience?"

He smiled back at her, flashing pearly white teeth. "Yes, but not from any relationship standpoint. My fresh start has more to do with family issues."

Bethany winced as she crossed her arms over her lap. Both Tara and Brandon turned to look at her. "How's the arm?" Tara asked her.

"Hurts, but it will heal," she replied flatly before taking a long gulp of her champagne.

"Yeah, well, serves you right for picking a fight with such a powerful witch," Brandon said grimly. "You of all people know how powerful the Malcolm's are."

Bethany shrugged indifferently. "She needed to be taken down a peg. I would have succeeded if your henchmen hadn't stopped me."

Brandon's lip curled and he sneered at her. "Maybe, but not before Tina burnt my place to the ground." Bethany shrugged again. Brandon continued. "Why are you Sloan's always picking fights? First, it was your brother who I had to stop from hurting that wolf, then you from a witch."

Tara turned back to Brandon. "You mean Eric started the fight with Michael?"

Brandon's eyes lit up and surprise filled his voice. "You know of the fight between them?" She nodded her head.

"Everyone knows of the fight they had," Bethany replied. "I'm wondering if something that happened that night had anything to do with why he was murdered."

Brandon laughed, and it was cold and calculated. "Don't be silly, Bethany. Bar fights, although rare here in Heiligtum, scarcely turn deadly. Your brother and that wolf were broken up long before any real violence could happen."

"Doesn't mean the wolf didn't do it," she replied coldly.

"Maybe not, but if you ever met Michael, you'd know that his bark is worse than his bite." He leaned back into the couch and crossed his legs.

Tara took another sip from her glass. She felt oddly comfortable on the couch and knew she shouldn't. She had just witnessed a fight between a vampire and witch. That alone should have freaked her out, yet she was calm. *What the hell is wrong with me?* She thought.

"If I had to guess," Brandon continued. "I'd say that no one who steps foot inside Heiligtum would have had the guts or skill to kill your brother."

"Why do you think that?" Tara asked.

"I know my clientele," he replied. "They are monsters, yes, but none of them chose to be. They come here to be themselves, around others like themselves, free from the guises they have to wear during their normal lives. This is a safe haven for them. You're human, so you may not understand, but imagine you had to live in a world that would hunt you down and kill you just for being who you are. The pressure to be a normal person can be overwhelming, constantly worrying about being found out." He took a long gulp of his champagne before continuing. "Here, they don't have to hide. They are free from persecution. Free to be themselves."

Tara was impressed at his speech. It made complete sense to her. She never truly thought what it would be like to be one of the monsters. Where could you go to be you? "Is that why you opened Heiligtum?" she asked him. "To give them a place to be who they are?"

"Yes, and no." He stated. "A huge part of it was to say fuck you to my family, but that is a deeper story than I care to get into at this current juncture." He smiled and Tara couldn't help but smile back.

Bethany cleared her throat, which caused both of them to break their gaze. "I hate to burst your bubble," she said, leaning in closer to Brandon, "but as one of the monsters, I can tell you that you can't fight your nature. You're right that we wear masks to keep us safe in the human world, but against each other, we will fight tooth and claw. Just because they come here for a little release doesn't mean they won't seize an opportunity when one arises."

"Good point," Brandon replied, "but with the treaty signed and the council formed, isn't it in everyone's best interest to keep the peace? No one wants another war. From what I've been told, it was brutal back then."

Bethany nodded her head once. She let her eyes drift away as if recalling memories long since buried. Tara chose to change the subject.

"How long has this place been open?"

"Oh, about 10 years now. At first, it was just a few stragglers, but soon every monster seemed to find some sort of relief here. Business has been booming ever since." He poured himself more champagne and offered Tara some. She shook her head no, remembering that technically, she was still on duty. Better to have a clear head.

"What about you?" he asked her. "What do you do for work?"

Tara glanced at Bethany for any indication as to what to tell him. Bethany shrugged as if to say tell him at your leisure. She decided honesty was the best policy. "I'm a detective for the Seattle P.D."

Brandon stared at her for a moment with his mouth slightly opened, then he erupted in laughter. Tara wasn't sure if she should be offended or pleased that he found her secret amusing. "You're just full of surprises," he chided playfully. "Is that how you got mixed up with this girl?" Bethany shot him an icy glare.

"Detective Bancroft is one of the officers assigned to my brother's case, yes," Bethany stated.

"So this whole meeting is to what? Question me about what I know?"

Tara felt shame creep through her. "Sorry for the misdirection. But if you had something to hide, asking as a cop probably wouldn't bring it out of you."

He laughed again. "We all have something to hide," he told her. "But I applaud you for coming to me as a beautiful woman instead of as a stuffy old cop." He winked at her and she blushed. "Honestly, I stand by what I said. No one here would have harmed Eric, especially with the ball being so close."

"That's not actually helpful at all," Tara admitted. "Thanks for your honesty." He laughed again and Tara laughed along with him.

"What do you do when you're not working?" he asked her quickly.

"What?"

"I was thinking dinner. I know a great Italian Restaurant that makes excellent authentic food." He leaned in closer to Tara. "It's in a great location with an exceptional view of the Space Needle."

"Are you asking me out on a date?" She asked. She was shocked at this change in events.

"Only if you say yes," he replied, giving her a sly smile. "If you say no, then it was just a suggestion."

She blushed and looked over at Bethany. She seemed to have found something particularly interesting about her champagne glass as she was staring deeply inside it.

"I'm on a case at the moment," Tara responded shyly. "I don't have time for a date." It was the truth.

"Maybe later, when you've caught the bad guy and everyone lives happily ever after." His stare bore into Tara and she turned a deep shade of crimson. She thought about it. Was she ready to move on completely from Kenneth? Time heals all wounds, or so they say, yet she felt sufficient time hadn't passed yet for her to jump back on the bandwagon.

"I just moved to Seattle. I need to catch my bearings a bit before I allow myself to date. I haven't even unpacked yet."

He nodded then shrugged his shoulders. "I understand. Still, a girl's gotta eat, right?" He reached inside his suit pocket and produced a sleek black pen. He jotted down something on a coaster and handed it to Tara. "Here's my number. Feel free to call or text anytime."

She stared at the coaster, then opened her purse to put it away. Her phone was blinking red, indicating she had a message. She picked up the phone and clicked it on. Her eyes widened slightly as she saw she had five missed calls and three text messages, all from Jacob. Had he found out something new with the body? She glanced up to see both Bethany and Brandon staring intently at her. "Excuse me for a moment," She told them and walked toward the stairway. She dialed Jacobs number.

"Are you okay?" he asked desperately as he answered on the first ring.

"I'm fine, Jacob," She replied softly. "What's up?" She glanced over her shoulder to see Brandon and Bethany talking politely.

"I'm going to need you to come take a look at this," he responded.

"A look at what, exactly?" She asked.

"It's better to see it in person," he said. "But trust me when I say that our case just got a hell of a lot more complicated." Shit! What could be more complicated than a 350-year-old dead vampire and having no viable suspects? "How soon can you get here?"

"Give me 20 minutes. I'm on my way," she told him. They hung up and she walked back to the couch. "I have to go," She told them both. "It was…"

"Comforting?" Brandon suggested. He was right. She nodded as she held out her hand to him. He took it gently and kissed the back of it. "I'll be expecting a call; in case you ever get hungry."

She blushed yet again and quickly turned toward Bethany, who was already on her feet. "I'll come as well."

"Sorry, Bethany, but I can't allow that," Tara said. "It's official police business, and you know I can't allow you to get involved."

Bethany put her hands on her hips and her lip curled slightly. "You can try to stop me, detective. But it is my brother. I'm going, so deal with it."

Tara rolled her eyes. "Fine, whatever. I don't have time to argue." She turned and walked down the steps.

The crowd was back and lively once more. It was as if the fight between a vampire and a witch never happened. Tara and Bethany had to weave their way through inch by inch until they reached the entrance.

The bouncer at the door smiled politely as they exited. "Had a good time?"

"It was...interesting," Tara admitted to him. He laughed as they walked to the restroom for her to change back into her clothes.

Chapter 24

The police department was only 15 minutes away from Heiligtum. Tara told Bethany they could walk since the night hadn't been too cold. Once into the alley, the girls headed off toward the police station. They made it to the edge of the street before Tara noticed Tina walking toward them. Shit, she thought. Just what they needed.

Tara expected Tina and Bethany to start fighting again and she unconsciously drew her hand to her gun. Shock spread on her face as Bethany embraced Tina and gave her a deep long kiss.

"What the hell is going on?" Tara asked with a sense of confusion.

The two girls broke apart and Tina stepped closer to Tara. "We haven't been properly introduced," she said, holding out her hand. "I'm Tina Malcolm, Bethany's girlfriend."

Tara's jaw dropped. "What the hell?" she said out loud.

"I hate the word girlfriend," Bethany explained. "It sounds so kiddish. I prefer the term life partner."

Tara stood there staring at them. Her head began to hurt from the confusion. Bethany waved her hand in front of Tara's face, drawing her attention. "Hello, detective? You with us?"

Tara snapped out of her haze. "But you two nearly killed each other tonight!"

Bethany laughed cynically. "All part of the plan," she said.

"What? What plan?" Tara asked.

"You didn't tell her?" Tina asked, looking at Bethany. It was her turn to looked shocked.

"I thought it would be more convincing if she didn't know," Bethany replied. Tina shook her head in disdain. Bethany shrugged it off. "It worked, didn't it?"

"Tell me what?" Tara demanded. "Someone better explain to me what the hell is going on!"

Tina took a step forward. "Bethany called me tonight and asked me to put on a show."

"What do you mean?" Tara asked, still confused.

"Remember when I said I was waiting for the right opportunity for us to get Brandon's attention?" Bethany asked. Tara nodded slightly. "Well, I knew starting a fight would be one way of getting that attention, so I recruited Tina for help."

Realization dawned on Tara's face. "So the whole fight was just an act?"

Bethany beamed at her. "And it worked like a charm. You humans are so predictable."

"Hey!" Tina said defensively, but Bethany leaned in and kissed her passionately. Tara's head was reeling.

"So let me get this straight," Tara said. "You two just pretended to fight to get Brandon down on the first level?" Both Bethany and Tina nodded in unison. "And you didn't think it relevant to inform me?"

Bethany shrugged once more. "I needed your reactions to be genuine. I didn't know how you would react otherwise."

Anger started to seep through Tara. "So I was bait in your little scheme?"

"Unfortunately, yes," Bethany answered honestly. "And it worked. I'm sorry for the deception, detective, but I needed a good show, and you provided one. Besides, no one was seriously hurt and we were able to talk to Brandon alone." A small smile spread on her face. "Plus, you got his number, in case you," she air-quoted, "ever get hungry." She chuckled loudly.

"He gave her his number?" Tina asked, shocked by the news.

"Yes," Bethany answered quickly. "Seems Brandon is smitten with the detective here." Both girls beamed at Tara. Tara didn't know if she wanted to blush or smack both of them across the face. Her headache came back with a vengeance and pounded hard across her temples.

"Fine," Tara said, "your plan worked, and I'll forgive you for not telling me. Later. Right now, I have more important things to worry about."

Bethany straightened up. "Right," she said, remembering they had business at the morgue. She turned to Tina. "We have to go." She leaned in and kissed Tina once more. "I'll stop by later on after we're done."

Tina gave her a sympathetic look. "Yeah, that's actually why I'm still here."

"What?" Bethany asked.

"My mom wants to see her," Tina said plainly.

Bethany and Tara exchanged glances. "What? Now?" Tina nodded. Bethany continued. "Why?"

"I'm not sure, but she said it was important."

"And Vita is your mother?" Tara asked her. Tina nodded. "So, you're part of this Coven of Rain I've heard about?"

Tina's eyes grew wide. "For someone who just got to Seattle, you sure are well informed."

"She's partners with the exile shifter," Bethany told her.

"Ah," Tina said as if that explained everything. "Anyway, my mother said it was urgent. Can you come with me now?"

Tara shook her head. "Sorry, I have something that needs my attention. Give me the address and I can make it over after," she said, fishing in her purse for her phone. When she looked up, she saw Tina with a saddened expression.

"What?" Bethany asked. Tina bit her lower lip.

"My mother said not to take no for an answer."

"And that means what?" Tara asked. Bethany stepped a little closer to Tara.

"Don't," Bethany whispered. Tara turned to Bethany and for a brief moment thought she saw fear in the girl's eyes. It quickly dissipated.

"I'm sorry, my love," Tina whispered back. "You know what will happen if I refuse."

"What's going on?" Tara asked, confused. Things happened quickly. Bethany moved fast, managing to tackle Tina in a blink of an eye. Tara barely had time to register the attack before Tina uttered a word she had never heard before. Suddenly, Bethany was howling in pain and collapsed on the cold concrete.

Tara let out a shrill shriek and knelt beside Bethany, trying to help. Tina managed to get to her knees and leaned toward Bethany, kissing her forehead gently. "I'm sorry," she whispered before looking at Tara.

Tara instinctively grabbed for her gun, but Tina moved faster than she anticipated. She held out her palm and blew a pink powder into Tara's face. Tara blinked as the powder collided with her eyes. She sneezed once, and then she felt woozy. She tried to stand but every bone in her body wouldn't cooperate. It was as if her body was filling up with lead and the weight pulled her to the floor. She felt tired and her eyes became heavy. The last thing she knew before passing out was Tina whispering something into Bethany's ear.

She dreamed she was locked inside an iron cage. Tara pushed and pulled on the bars, trying to will them away but it was no use. She screamed as fear and anger filled her. She heard footsteps approaching, creeping closer to her. She shook the bars harder, trying to escape before whoever came into view. She knew if she saw whomever, or whatever it was, it would be the end of her.

She shoved her whole weight against the cold iron, but still the bars held. The footsteps drew closer. Her heart leaped into her throat and she thrashed like a wild animal trying to break free.

A figure stepped closer to her. She couldn't make it out at first. The figure drew nearer and the shape became clearer. The body was that of a man, dressed in a gray suit. He took another step closer and stretched out his hand toward her. It was taloned and covered in gray, cracked skin. She looked up and screamed in fear. In place of his head was a crow's head. Its beak was unusually long and its black obsidian eyes stared at her, looking past the flesh and into her soul.

The crow opened its beak and let out a piercing caw that echoed throughout the darkened room. The caw became deafening and shook the cage with such force that the iron bars vibrated. Tara covered her ears but it was no use. The caw was inside her head and it grew louder. She screamed in pain and writhed on the floor.

She felt a slap against her cheek and Tara woke gasping for breath. A sharp burn tingled her cheek and she cupped it with her palm. Looming over her was Tina.

"Finally," she said. "I had to slap you three times before you finally woke."

Tara felt herself sitting in a chair. She looked passed Tina and noticed she was sitting in a dining room. Pictures of women and families were evenly placed against the walls. The chair she was in was more elegant than comfortable and positioned around a large table topped with dishes of food. The smell filled her nostrils and her stomach grumbled in response. She hadn't eaten anything since she and Jacob left Adam's cabin, and she was famished.

She tried to stand, but she was groggy and her legs wouldn't cooperate.

"Easy," Tina told her, bending over her, helping her to stand. "The powder that knocked you out may take a minute to subside. You'll be alright in a few minutes."

Anger filled her eyes. "You didn't have to knock me out," she responded. "I would have come on my own accord." Bethany gave her a sympathetic look but remained silent. Tara turned around to see the room fully. She noticed it was just the two of them inside the room. "Where's Bethany?

"I had to leave her behind," She said guiltily. "Mother wouldn't want her here."

Tara whipped around and stared at her in awe. "You knocked your girlfriend out and left her in the street?"

Tina's eyes grew wide. "She's a 350-year-old vampire, detective. I think she will be able to handle herself." Tara shook her head in disapproval. If she was ever left on the street by anyone she dated, she would be pissed.

"Why am I here?" she asked, changing the subject.

"Mother wanted to talk to you. She'll be along shortly." Tina turned and gestured to the table. "You must be hungry by now. Eat. When you're done, my mother will come see you."

"Am I a prisoner here?" Tara asked.

Tina laughed. "No, detective. You are free to go as soon as mother meets you. Please, eat." she said calmly. "It'll help counteract the effects of the powder." Tara wanted to argue but she was hungry. She knew nothing about witchcraft, and if eating would help her get her strength back, then she could knock out two birds with one stone.

"I'll leave you alone so you can eat in peace," Tina told her. "Mother will be along shortly." Tina disappeared down a long corridor and Tara was left alone.

Upon the table sat a plate of roasted chicken, a medley of vegetables, a small salad, a couple apple slices, and a glass of what looked like tea. Tara's stomach lurched in hunger and she dove into the chicken. Tara barely had time to taste anything before all the food was devoured. The tea had been chamomile, and it went well with the food.

Tara noticed that Tina had been right. Her strength had returned and she was able to stand without getting dizzy. She braced herself on the table and walked slowly to the pictures on the wall. Most of the frames seemed to have the same people in them just at different ages. The one that stood out the most was an older woman, probably around 50 years of age. She didn't seem to age at all in the pictures.

One picture showed her carrying a small baby. Another showed her with three children, probably around 7 or 8 years old. As the children grew in age, the woman appeared to stop aging.

"Like them?" A voice asked, startling Tara. She whipped around to see the older woman from the pictures smiling at her. She had curly gray hair that was cut short just above her shoulders. She wore a black nightgown that swayed as she moved closer. As she approached, Tara noticed her skin was a light almond color and her face was practically wrinkle free except for the crow's feet around her brown eyes.

"You startled me," Tara admitted.

"Sorry about that," The woman replied. "You seemed lost in thought when I arrived." The lady held out her hand. "My names Vita. Vita Malcolm."

Tara shook her hand lightly. "So you're the reason I was kidnapped."

Vita chuckled lightly, causing lines to form around her mouth and eyes. "I'm sorry for how my daughter brought you here. I assure you, you are perfectly free to leave at any time." Vita turned to stare at the pictures.

"These are your family members?" Tara asked. Vita nodded.

"Most of them are grown up and have families of their own now," Vita told her. "This picture," she pointed to the last frame on the wall, "is a picture of all the grandkids." The picture had seven kids all smiling and laughing at the camera.

"So you're, what, the head of Coven of Rain?" Tara eyed her suspiciously. Vita nodded again, not noticing Tara at all. Her eyes were fixated on the last picture and Tara noticed a sense of triumph fill her expression.

"Why was I brought here?" Tara asked, snapping Vita out of her haze. It had been a long couple of days and Tara was tired and cranky. She didn't have time to wait around for Vita to get to the point of her visit. Better to get it over with so she could leave as quickly as possible.

Vita turned to her at last and gestured for her to sit. Tara complied and waited for an explanation. "How is the case coming along?"

Tara crossed her arms over her chest. "I can't discuss an open investigation with civilians. If that is why I was brought here…"

Vita held her hand up to silence her. "I wish it were, detective." Vita took the chair next to her and crossed her ankles. The nightgown was loose enough that it hung off the sides of the chair. "I'm not sure how familiar you are with witchcraft," Vita started.

"Besides what I've seen tonight, not familiar at all," Tara admitted truthfully. "And quite frankly, I'm not sure I want to know anymore."

"I understand," Vita said calmly. "It can be a... finicky thing at times. Each one of my progeny has an affinity for certain talents. Tina, for instance, is very good with powders and potions." Vita turned to point at a picture on the wall. It showed Vita with Tina and two other people. One a male, and the other a female. Both had similar features to Vita. "Stephanie, Tina's twin sister is very good at elemental magic. Brody, my eldest, communes with the dead."

Tara took it all in. Vita's family was powerful and frightening. These are the people who the wolves are afraid of. The ones who put a boundary spell around Seattle warding other creatures away. So why was she here?

"I happen to enjoy reading palms and tarot cards, as I have more of an intuitive nature." Vita cleared her throat. "Which brings me to you."

Tara was bewildered slightly. "What's any of that have to do with me?"

"You may or may not recall this, but we have met before. Briefly, at Dominik's house." Tara shook her head. "Understandable," Vita continued, "as you were pretty out of it. I left a potion for you to drink on the bedside table. I see you didn't drink it."

Tara blushed, and she wasn't sure why. "No offense intended, but I was just attacked and woke up in a strange room. For all I knew, that drink could have been poisoned."

Vita smiled softly. "I understand. Still, that potion would have healed your injuries instantly."

Tara's eyes widened. "You can do that?"

"Oh yes, detective," Vita replied. "That, and so much more."

"I still don't understand why I needed to be brought here, against my will I might add, in the middle of the night." Tara studied Vita. So far, it seemed like Vita was avoiding telling her exactly why she was there. "Tina said it was urgent."

"Since our brief encounter, I felt a sort of connection I couldn't quite put my finger on. I dismissed it at the time, thinking only of helping out Dominik during this troubling time. But as time went on, I've been feeling it more and more."

Tara felt confusion once more. A connection? What connection? She had only been in Seattle less than a week. How could there be a connection between the two of them? She had never really met this woman.

"I'm not making this very clear, am I?" Vita asked. Tara shook her head silently. "Then let me clear it up. I've mentioned that I am an intuitive person. One of my hobbies is casting of Runes. It's an ancient form of fortune telling, but has unclear results at times, as do most methods of fortune telling. The signs are there, but it takes skill and knowledge to interpret them correctly. Understand?"

Tara thought she did, which was kind of weird since she didn't believe in fortune telling. She figured it was a way for con artists to sucker people out of a few bucks. In a way, the conmen were great observers of human behavior, just like a profiler. They see a notch in a man's belt and tell him he has lost weight recently. It wasn't magic, it was simply reading the observations. "Go on," she told Vita.

"Well, since meeting you, I have cast the runes repeatedly, and have ended up with the same results. I even did a tarot reading to see what would happen, and the reading backed up the results from the runes." Vita cleared her throat and stared deeply into Tara's eyes. "All the signs are there, detective. Trouble is on the horizon."

Tara tried to follow, but Vita still hadn't said anything that would make her daughter kidnap her in the street. "And this has to do with me, how?"

"You're the key," Vita stated plainly. "The piece that is missing. Something about you brings all this together."

Tara's eyes brightened wide. How could she be the key to anything? She was just a human trying to do her job. It didn't make sense to her. "This is ridiculous," Tara snorted, then got up to leave. She made it halfway to the door before Vita spoke again.

"Tell me, detective. Have you been having bad dreams?" Tara stopped in mid-stride. Vita continued. "Dreams that have only occurred since your recent move to Seattle?" Tara turned to face Vita. She had turned pale and she felt a little clammy. How did Vita know about her dreams? She stood there, feeling awkward, staring into Vita's brown eyes.

Vita gave her a concerned look, which seemed to confirm Vita's suspicions. "Please, detective. Sit back down."

Tara walked slowly back to her chair. When she sat, she asked, "How could you know that?"

Vita leaned in closer to Tara. "Because I too have had bad dreams." Vita looked frightened by her revelation. "And I believe our dreams are connected somehow."

"Explain," Tara demanded.

"I've been dreaming of a ballroom and of a graveyard. The last dream I've had consisted of me being locked in a cage." Vita's eyes were fixed on Tara as she shifted uncomfortably in her seat. Tara's eyes brightened widely. It had been the same dreams she had experienced. How was that possible? "I can tell by the look on your face that you've had similar dreams." Tara nodded silently.

"As I've said," Vita continued, "I believe you and I are connected. After the first dream, I thought maybe it was my psyche trying to work out my feelings over recent events. But as the dreams continued, I realized that they aren't my dreams I'm dreaming. They are yours."

"That's not possible!" Tara stated. "I just had the dream about being locked in a cage tonight. How could they be my dreams you're dreaming if you've had that dream first?"

"Anything is possible where magic is concerned," Vita explained. "Two nights ago, you never thought vampires were possible, yet you were saved by one."

She did have a point. Two nights ago, Tara had no clue there was anything that truly went bump in the night. None of it seemed possible, yet here she was, talking to Seattle's head witch about dreams they both had shared. She longed to be back in Phoenix, to be naive about it all.

"So, you think you've somehow piggybacked on my dreams?" Tara asked.

Vita smiled at her choice of words. "Something to that effect. I've been around a long time. Some might say too long, but throughout that time, I've mastered many skills of magic. Dreamwalking or dream sharing has never been one of them." Vita stared straight into Tara's eyes. "Not before you arrived in Seattle."

Tara nodded slightly as she took it all in. "So, what are you saying?"

"I'm not sure, to be honest," Vita responded, shaking her head. "That's why I had Tina bring you here. I would like to do a reading on you if you would allow it. I believe this might help clear things up."

"A reading?" Tara asked.

"Tarot reading," Vita clarified. "The cards will indicate our connection and where to go from there." Vita pointed to a wooden box on the opposite side of the table. "Would you allow me to find out what the reason is for this connection?"

Tara wasn't sure how to respond. A pack of cards is going to tell why Tara was having bad dreams? Sure, she thought, and pigs really can fly. "What do I have to do?"

"Just touch the cards and let them do the rest," Vita replied confidently as if this request was something that happened all the time.

Tara took a minute to think about it. She could always say no. She did have a partner who was probably worried sick about her and a vampire who would probably be ready to rip out some throats to save her. But she was curious. She had to know if the tarot reading would work. One drawback to being a detective was that she needed to find all the pieces to the puzzle.

"Alright, I'll do it," Tara sighed. "On one condition."

Vita pursed her lips together, which made her look older. "What's that?"

"You let me call my partner and explain things to him."

"Agreed," Vita said a little too eagerly. "Your stuff is next to the door." Tara turned and saw her purse lying against the wooden frame of the door. She got up, snatched out her phone, and hit redial.

Chapter 25

Five minutes later, Tara was crowded around the wooden table. Everything had been cleared away except for the small box. Vita brought out a few thin white candles and was busy lighting them when Tara finished on the phone.

The call to Jacob went as well as could be expected. He answered on the first ring.

"Are you okay?" Jacob asked quickly. "I've been worried that they might have done something horrible. Please tell me you're fine."

"Relax, Jacob. Breathe," Tara replied calmly. She heard him take in a deep breath and exhale slowly. "Feel better?"

"No," he admitted. "Seems my partner got herself kidnapped tonight. I knew I shouldn't have let you go alone." Tara could practically see him shake his head disdainfully through the phone. "Where are you?"

"At Vita's house."

The phone was silent for a brief moment. "As in Vita Malcolm?" She heard him sigh harshly.

"The one and only," she said.

"What does she want?" Jacob asked her. Tara debated on whether to tell him over the phone. She thought that it might be better to tell him in person. Whether he believed her or not was the real question. Hell, she barely believed it herself.

"It's a long story, and I'll explain everything later. I just wanted to give you a call so you wouldn't worry."

"Too late for that," he said truthfully. He sounded tired. When was the last time he had any sleep? Tara wondered.

"I'm coming to get you," he stated. Tara glanced at Vita who was busy clearing the table.

"Give me about half an hour," she told him. "Vita and I have some things to discuss first." Jacob remained silent for a while and she wondered if the connection was lost. "Jacob? You there?"

"I'm here," he answered. "It'll take me about 15 minutes to get there. You have until then. If you're not outside by the time I get there, then I am breaking down the door and rescuing you."

"Don't be so dramatic, Jacob. I'm fine," she repeated. "But I'm not sure if Bethany is. Can you do me a favor and check on her?"

"She's fine," he told her. "She's here with me, actually. Seems she has some choice words for Tina when she sees her again." Tara shuddered. She could only imagine what Bethany would say.

"I'm glad to see you two can get along. It only takes me getting kidnapped for that miracle."

"You have 15 minutes, Tara," he told her. "Don't waste it on bad jokes."

"Right," she sighed. "See you soon." They hung up.

Now as she waited for Vita to do the reading, she wondered if Jacob would really break down the door to rescue her. For his sake, she hoped not. Seems the witches could outmatch him in every way.

Vita reached into the wooden box and withdrew a hefty stack of green cards. She knocked on them three times. "To wake them up," Vita said. Tara thought how absurd that was, but kept her opinion to herself. Vita shuffled the cards over and over. At last, she asked Tara to clear her mind and place her hand on the deck.

Tara had a little trouble clearing her mind but managed to think of nothing as she reached for the cards. A slight vibration emanated from the deck as she laid her hand upon it. It tingled slightly and the sensation traveled slowly from her fingertips and up her palm to her wrist. The shock of the vibration forced her to withdraw her hand quickly.

Vita shuffled the cards one last time before speaking. "I'm not sure how familiar you are with tarot readings, but there are a couple spreads we can choose from. The most basic is a three-card spread, but that won't work for our goal here tonight."

Tara nodded in understanding. "Which spread are we going to do?"

"Well, seeing as you are the one in question, I would choose either the Celtic Cross spread or the Tree of Life. Both are a 10-card spread that will help in understanding the current situation. The choice is yours."

Tara thought for a moment. She had never had a reading before, so either would be fine but the Celtic Cross sounded more interesting. "The Celtic Cross," Tara said confidently and Vita nodded.

"Now I can do the whole reading and tell you what it means after, or I can lay down the cards one at a time and explain the meanings as we go." Vita waited patiently for Tara to decide.

"I think telling me as you go will help me understand a little better," Tara admitted.

"Alright," Vita replied and laid down the first card. The card showed a man and a woman inside a building. Above them stood three stars, each with a circle around them. "The first position in the spread has to do with the influences surrounding you. Here," she pointed to the card, "is the three of pentacles. It has to do with teamwork and cooperation."

Tara could see how that could be connected to her. She had her partner Jacob who was trying to solve a murder. Vita laid down the next card horizontally right on top of the first. This card showed an elegant woman with a crown of stars on her head. She was sitting on what appeared to be a throne of pillows outside in the forest.

"The position in the spread," Vita claimed, "represents the obstacles blocking you." She pointed to the lady on the card. "This is the Empress. She represents femininity and fertility, but it's in reverse."

"Is that bad?" Tara asked.

"No, not necessarily," Vita shook her head. "It just means that you have a creative block at the moment."

Vita laid the next card down below the first two. This card had a man and a woman holding two chalices in front of each other. "This is the two of cups, but in reverse. It represents a break-up or an imbalance in a relationship."

"And the position?" Tara asked.

"This position represents the recent past which leads to the current situation," Vita told her.

Tara's mouth dropped open. She only moved to Seattle because of what happened with Kenneth. So far, the cards were right on track. Vita laid the next card down to the left of the first two.

"This placement represents the distant past. One that was not fully dealt with," Vita warned. The card had an older man on it in old robes holding a lantern in the dead of night. "The Hermit," Vita continued. "It represents being alone and inner guidance." Vita stared at Tara and bit her lip.

"What?" Tara asked.

"I just realized how personal this might get for you," she replied. Tara looked down at the cards. Four had been placed. There were 6 left. "I can stop if you'd like," Vita whispered.

Tara shook her head. "No, I don't think you should. If this helps clear up what is happening, then I think it's best we continue."

Vita gave her a sympathetic smile and quickly laid the next card down above the first two. "This position is your wish or goal you'd like to achieve." The card had a man with a crown sitting on a throne. He had a sword in one hand and a weight scale in the other.

"This is the Justice card. It represents the law and fairness; of justice and truth." Tara nodded while Vita continued. "I don't think I need to tell you how this relates to you, being a detective and all."

The next card she laid down was to the right of the first two. "This position represents the future." The card showed an angel playing a trumpet high in the sky while bodies of women and children reached out for her. "This is Judgment. It represents your inner calling and rebirth."

Rebirth? What did that mean? Tara didn't have time to ask as Vita laid the next card to the right of the third position.

"The 7th placement indicates your own personal attitude or position on this matter." The card had a man with a sword in his left arm and two in his right. Two swords lay at his feet. Men seemed to be walking away from him. "This is the five of swords. It represents conflict and tension."

Tara didn't know what she felt about that. The placement was to be her own attitude about the situation. Did that mean she was fighting something? Or did it mean she will be fighting something later on?

Vita seemed to sense her confusion. "The card has many interpretations, detective. It can represent your ambition, but negatively so, or it can simply be a conflict between coworkers. It can be as small as not seeing eye to eye on a matter. The important thing to remember here is resolution by staying true to yourself and your beliefs. Understand?"

Tara thought she did. She nodded. "Can I continue?" Vita asked. Tara nodded again quietly.

Vita put the next card above the 7th placement. "This position represents how others see you." The card had a lady sitting on a silver throne outside. She had a golden crown on her head and a long sword in her hand. "The queen of swords represents independence and organization. You are seen as a quick thinker and a perceptive one at that." Vita smiled lightly at Tara.

Tara blushed slightly. She strived to be a good person, and if that is how others see her, she was happy about that. Vita laid the next card above the last.

"This position represents your hopes or fears." The card had a woman in a white robe petting a lion. An infinity symbol that always reminded Tara of the number 8 sat above her head. "This card is strength reversed," Vita said. "Reversed means self-doubt or weakness."

Tara understood immediately. She had always feared she would make a wrong decision. One that would cost someone their life. It wasn't easy being a cop somedays. You wake up hoping that whatever case you are on, you find the bad guys and put them away. Sometimes doubt sinks in and you second guess yourself. It's inevitable. You just hope that you follow your instincts and things work out in the end.

"One card to go," Vita stated.

"What does the position represent?" Tara asked, scooting closer to look at the cards.

"It represents the outcome of the situation." Tara nodded her head and swallowed. Her mouth was slightly dry and she was nervous. Did she really want to know? One last card couldn't possibly explain everything going on, could it? Only one way to find out.

"Lay it down," Tara ordered. Vita nodded and placed the last card down. Tara gasped and darted backward away from the table. The card had a skeletal figure riding a white horse. It's bony hand carried a black banner with a white flower in the middle. Right below the horse laid a man, pale and dead. A lady with two children pleaded with the skeleton to leave him be. Tara didn't need Vita to tell her what the card meant. She already knew. It was death.

Confirming her belief, Vita spoke. "Death represents all sorts of things. It could mean the end of a situation and the beginning of another. Or it could mean transformation. It may seem ominous, but death doesn't necessarily mean the death of a person."

Tara nodded slightly but had the nagging feeling Vita was thinking the same thing. Despite Vita's words of comfort, Tara still felt that the card represented someone dying.

"Did any of that help figure out why these dreams are happening?" Tara asked Vita, still staring at the Death card. She glanced up into Vita's face and saw a hint of frustration.

Vita sighed. "Truthfully? No. But it did give me an insight into who…" Vita stopped short. She was staring at the cards and a gasp escaped her lips.

"What?" Tara asked, looking down at the cards. Something moved in the Hermit card. A black bird, faint and small at first, flew in the background. Tara's eyes bulged and her heart began to race. The bird soared closer, circling the backdrop. It rose higher and swooped lower. Tara could hear a faint cawing from its beak.

She wanted to look away but was mesmerized by the sight. The bird drew ever closer to the Hermit until it was right above his head. It opened its beak and let out another caw, this time louder and more profound, before swooping down in an arch and out of the card. It appeared in the Five of Swords. It cawed madly and Tara's heart leaped into her throat.

Tara let out a small scream as she recognized the bird. It was the crow from her dream! She tried to jump up from the table, to back as far away as possible, but was held captive by her own fascination. The bird swooped down and out of the card and into the Strength card. It cawed yet again, circling around the woman petting the lion before disappearing out of the card and finding its way into the Death card.

It finally landed on the skeleton's shoulder. It turned its attention toward Tara and cawed. Suddenly, the skeleton came to life. An awful cracking sound echoed out of the card as the skeleton turned its head toward the two women. The horse buckled as death opened its jaws and cackled wildly. The crow cawed once more before leaping from where it perched and flew straight toward the women.

Tara let out a blood-curdling scream as the crow smashed through the card, sending the remaining cards flying in all directions. The bird broke through with such force that Tara and Vita were sent flying backward off their chairs and onto the cold tile.

The crow hovered a moment, turning its attention from Tara to Vita, then back again, as if debating on a target. It then descended on Vita. The bird pecked forcefully at Vita's face and managed to tangle its claws in her hair. Vita screamed in pain, covering her face to keep the bird away. Tara got up as quickly as she could and kicked the bird in its midsection. She heard a hard thud as it smashed into the wall and slid down to the floor in a haze of feathers.

Dazed, the crow stood up and still for a moment before ruffling its black feathers and cawed yet again. It jumped toward Tara and was headed straight for her face. Tara grabbed the nearest chair and used it as a shield. The bird tried to soar around it, but the chair was thrust toward it, blocking its way. Suddenly, the bird burst into green flames. It let out a horrifying shriek before being engulfed completely and disappeared. Singed feathers floated slowly to the floor before burning up. Tara dropped the chair with a clang before seeing Tina with an outstretched hand in the air. She nodded to her, heart still racing as she bent over Vita.

The woman laid on her side panting. Blood seeped out of the beak marks the crow had left. Tina ran to her mother and knelt beside her. "Are you alright?" She asked frantically.

"I'll be alright, child," Vita managed to choke out. "Thanks to detective Bancroft." She turned her head toward Tara. "You saved my life."

"You can repay me by telling me what the hell was that?"

Chapter 26

Tara sat quietly in the car while Jacob drove. Bethany was in the back seat apparently lost in her own thoughts, as she too was eerily silent. The only sound that could be heard was the steady drumming of the engine.

Jacob and Bethany arrived at Vita's house a couple minutes after the bird attack. They stormed into the house ready to pick a fight, but lost all will to carry out their plan after seeing Vita covered in blood.

"What happened?" Jacob asked with real concern on his face.

"We got attacked by a bird," Tara told him. She left out the part about the bird magically soaring through the tarot deck and into reality. Bethany was still fuming with anger over Tina's betrayal, but kept her mouth shut after seeing how worried she was over her mother. Sometimes you have to pick your battles.

Tina helped Vita upstairs and told them it was probably best if they left. "Will she be alright?" Tara asked.

"I can whip up a healing potion. She'll be right as rain soon enough," she replied shakily. Tara gave her a concerned look. "Really. She'll be fine."

"Care to tell me what that was?" Tara asked her.

"I'd like to know that as well," Jacob chimed in.

"Honestly, I'm not sure," she said shaking her head. "All I know is that I felt its energy." She grabbed Tara's arm. "It was dark. And powerful. Whatever it was, it was strong."

"Have you ever come across something like that before?" Tara asked. Tina shook her head in response, wiping a stray hair away from her face. She glanced up toward the stairway.

"You guys better go. It's been a long night and certainly, everyone can use some rest," she said softly. There was no argument there. As Jacob and Tara turned to leave, Bethany stepped toward Tina with a longing look; one between admiration and sorrow. Tina smiled weakly in response. "I love you," she whispered, "but my mother needs me."

Bethany swallowed loud enough that Tara could hear and nodded her head toward her lover. Without saying a word, she turned toward the door and walked out of the house.

Once in the car, Tara put her seatbelt on while Jacob started the engine. Tina appeared on the passenger side window and knocked three times. Tara cracked her window just enough to hear what Tina had to say.

"My mother wants you to have this," she said, offering her a gold chain with a metal infinity symbol attached to it. "She said it will protect you from any magical means of attack." Tara took the necklace and thanked her. Tina nodded curtly, gave one last look at Bethany in the backseat, turned, then strutted back inside the house.

Tara put on the necklace and tucked it behind her shirt. The infinity symbol was surprisingly warm against her cool skin and sent a shiver of heat throughout her body. A moment later, it was gone.

"You going to explain what happened?" Jacob asked as he drove away.

"Yes," Tara replied faintly, 'but not now. I need time to process things myself before I tell you." She glanced at her partner. "I hope you understand."

He gave her a quick look then his eyes diverted back to the road. Tara could tell he desperately wanted to know what happened, but he didn't press the issue.

"I'm glad you're alright," he admitted. She shot him a gentle smile. So much had happened in the last couple of days that by definition was not alright. Point of fact, she was anything but alright, but choosing not to upset her partner, she kept her mouth shut.

"So you found something about my brother?" Bethany asked from the backseat, changing the subject. Jacob glanced in the rearview mirror and nodded.

"Yes," he said, "but I'm afraid I can't tell you anything, seeing as it's an active investigation."

"But it's about my brother," she stated flatly. "Whatever you found, I should know." She scooted closer to Jacob. "Besides, if we're on our way to the morgue, then I am going to find out anyway."

"We, as in detective Bancroft and I, are on our way to the morgue," Jacob rebutted. "First, we are dropping you off at home."

"Why?" Asked Bethany with anger in her voice.

"Because Tara and I have more work to do. You, being a civilian, are not allowed to be a part of the investigation."

"Well that's stupid," she replied heatedly. "And as far as plans go, I've heard better ones."

"Oh really?" He asked sarcastically.

"Really," she responded. "Think about it for a moment. My home was broken into because of you two. Someone is after you, and you think driving up to my house, the only place for certain they knew you went to before, is the best course of action?" She shook her head vigorously. "No, I think not. Not after my guys risked their lives to protect you."

"She has a point," Tara whispered and cringed as Jacob gave her a disturbing glance.

"Thank you," Bethany said.

"Let's not forget that my partner almost lost her life because of your guys."

"That was by her choice, detective," Bethany responded calmly. "She chose to save Russell's life. And none of it would have happened if you two hadn't been there."

"She is sitting right here," Tara told both of them. "And let's not forget that you invited us to your place, remember?" Her annoyance over their constant arguing was heightening. "Matter of fact, a lot of things that have happened to me in the last couple of days is because I was with you."

"Hey!" Bethany shouted angrily. "I didn't twist your arm, detective. Everything was by your own volition. Your choices led to another, and the consequences aren't my fault."

"Do you feel the same way towards your brother?" Jacob asked cynically. Bethany recoiled slightly as if she had been punched in the eye. She started to say something, but her words were caught in her throat.

"Let's not lose perspective," Tara added soothingly. "All my partner is saying is that it is a conflict of interest for you to be at the morgue while we are examining the evidence."

Bethany turned her head toward Tara. "You were allowing me to tag along before Tina intervened."

Jacob shot another troubling look at Tara. "She was persistent," Tara said in response. "Besides, she could easily break in herself. I just figured if she's with us, at least no one would be getting hurt."

Jacob shook his head disdainfully at her and sighed. "You know it's illegal."

"This whole city is filled with supernatural beings. Some of the things I have seen in the last couple of days are illegal. Hell, you had your brother pose as me for the day. That's not exactly legal."

"Wait," Bethany interrupted. "Your brother posed as Tara?" Bethany snorted loudly. "Which one?"

"Adam," Tara replied, which sent Bethany into convulsions of laughter.

"That must have been an interesting experience," Bethany said, then laughed again. Tara noticed she had tears streaming down her cheeks.

Ignoring Bethany's behavior, Jacob spoke again. "Fine, she can come, but I'm telling you, she will not like what I have found out."

That stopped Bethany from laughing. "Why is that?"

"You'll see," he said cryptically, ending the conversation. Tara sat back in her seat staring out the window. She was tired, irritable, and really just wanted to go home to shower. She bet Jacob was feeling the same, and was wondering how much strength she had for Jacob's surprise.

Sleep weighed heavy on her eyelids as she thought about the day's events. Waking up at Adam's retreat, meeting the werewolves, being at Heiligtum. It had definitely been a long day. The cherry on top of the cake was coming face to face with a creature from her nightmares. Thinking about everything did bring up a question she had been wanting to know.

"What did you find out about the men who invaded your home?" She turned to Bethany and asked.

"What?" Bethany replied as if she hadn't heard the question.

"Well, you said you would tell me what you found out from one of the men who tried to kill us."

"I'd like to know that as well," Jacob cut in. "Who are they?"

"Hired mercenaries," Bethany told them. "The one man we 'interrogated' was more than willing to spill everything he knew once he saw what became of the other men."

"Who hired them?" Jacob asked.

"Don't know," she replied with a shrug of her shoulders. "He bled out before we could find out who was behind it."

"Did you find out anything worthwhile from him?" Tara asked, a little concerned about how he bled out but didn't ask.

Bethany nodded. "Yes, but considering one of the suspects of who hired him is driving the car..."

"Wait, wait, wait." Jacob interrupted. "You can't possibly believe I had anything to do with it."

"Why not?" She asked him. "You do have a grudge against my family. What better way to exact revenge than to hire people to break in and kill my father."

"First of all," Jacob said angrily. "If I was going to exact revenge, I wouldn't hire someone to do it for me. I would do it myself. I would love to see your dad get what's coming to him, and I would literally piss on his grave after he was dead, but I am a member of the law and if you knew anything about me, you would know that I respect the law more than anything."

"Seriously, Bethany. You don't really believe Jacob had anything to do with it, do you?" Tara asked her softly.

"No, not really, but as far as we can tell, whoever did hire them had money and resources. Not many people we know have the means to hire them. The cost alone means it has to be someone with some serious moolah."

Tara smirked quietly. She had never heard anyone use the word moolah before, and hearing a vampire say it was definitely comical. She shook off the urge to laugh aloud.

"Then you know for sure it wasn't me," Jacob stated. Both women turned to look at him. "I'm exiled, remember? All of my assets were seized when my family banished me. There's no way I could've hired them, not on a policeman's salary."

"In any case," Bethany said, "We didn't find anything relevant about who hired them or why they want you both."

"Assuming they were there because of us," Jacob sneered. "Let's not forget that your father has enemies. It could be a coincidence that we were there last night."

"Maybe," Bethany considered. "But my father has had enemies for years, as you well know. No one has made such a bold move against him in decades. Not since the war." Bethany shook her head. "No, I don't believe it had anything to do with him. The only other variable is you two."

The detectives contemplated this, giving each other a side glance as Jacob pulled into the parking lot of the police station. Jacob drove for a minute before finally deciding on a spot near the elevators. As they got out of the car, Tara wondered who would want them badly enough to hire trained mercenaries? And why?

The Morgue was located in the basement of the police station. Jacob walked to the elevator and pushed the B button on a small panel. The doors opened with a ding and the three walked in silently. Once the door shut, the elevator let out a small hum as it started downward.

"Is Yvette still here?" Tara asked Jacob.

"She was when I left to come find you," he replied blankly.

"Yvette?" Bethany asked. "Why does that name sound so familiar?"

"She's Lilith's daughter," Jacob told her.

"Ah," Bethany nodded as if that explained everything. "I hadn't realized that so many royals worked at the station." Tara didn't know what they were talking about.

"Who's Lilith?" Tara asked her partner.

"The queen of the Siren's," Bethany answered her, matter of factly. "I can't imagine that she is happy with Yvette working at such a job. It's unbecoming of a princess."

Tara's jaw dropped open. "Wait, Yvette's a Siren?" she asked. Jacob and Bethany nodded in unison. She had met Yvette briefly when first discovering Eric's body at the gym. Yvette was young and beautiful, and seemed completely normal. "How many supernatural creatures work here?"

Bethany laughed, causing Jacob to give her a scolding glance. "Just the two of us, as far as I know," he told her. "Most want nothing to do with humans. But some of us feel it is our duty to protect and serve."

Bethany let out a snicker yet again. "I wouldn't expect you to understand," Jacob chided. "After all, you feed on humans."

"Which is why no vampires work for the police department," Bethany shot back. "Besides, there are human laws, and then there are our laws. We as a species have been following our laws to the letter. My father makes sure of that."

This time Jacob let out a laugh. "That's ironic, considering how your father has a lot of shady dealings with organized crime."

"Really?" Bethany asked sarcastically. "Prove it, detective."

"Now, now, children," Tara interrupted with a roll of her eyes. "We aren't here to debate Mr. Sloan and his business deals. We are here because of Eric. Put aside the bickering and let's get this done."

Bethany opened her mouth to say something but the elevator doors slid open. Jacob walked first into a long corridor, leading the way to the morgue. Tara and Bethany walked closely behind him. They walked passed a couple of offices before coming to two swinging doors. Jacob pushed through them and they followed one by one.

The morgue was spacious enough to fit three long metal tables in the middle of the room. Retractable lights hung directly over each table. Morgue cabinets filled the back and right side wall. The left side wall held a work desk with various filing cabinets. Yvette sat at the desk writing down paperwork. She looked up when they walked in.

"You're back," she stated quietly and Jacob nodded. She glanced from Jacob to Tara, and raised an eyebrow at seeing Bethany. "She can't be in here," she said.

Bethany crossed her arms over her chest and took a defensive stance. "Trust us," Tara said. "We have tried to tell her that, but she wouldn't take no for an answer." Yvette bit her lip and looked back at Jacob with sorrowful eyes.

"Did you tell them?" she asked.

"I didn't know how," he replied honestly. "I think showing them will make it clearer."

"Tell us what?" Tara asked with a little uncertainty in her voice. Jacob nodded once more to Yvette who let out a slight sigh.

"Follow me," she ordered and led them to one of the meat lockers. She opened a metal door with the number 207 on it and slid out a body covered in a white blue sheet. Before uncovering the body, Yvette took one more look at Jacob. "You sure about this?"

"It's a good a time as any," he replied softly. She nodded to herself and pulled back the sheet. A man with curly black hair cut just a little past his ears lay lifeless on the slab. He was very pale with a muscular body and good looking features. If he had walked past Tara when he had been alive, she probably would have found comfort in staring at him. Staring at him now made her feel a little queasy.

"Who's this?" Bethany asked.

"Look," Yvette replied, lowering the sheet a little more. The cause of death was pretty clear. The man had a hole in his chest as if someone had stabbed him with something heavy.

"Someone was killed like my brother was?" Bethany asked.

"Not exactly," Jacob whispered.

"Then what?" Bethany asked. "Where is Eric?"

"That is what we are trying to figure out," Yvette replied. "Earlier tonight, detective Moore came to re-examine the body..."

"You mean my brother, Eric," Bethany corrected. "He's more than just a body." Yvette nodded and apologized for her lack of tact and continued without missing a beat.

"He came to re-examine Eric who was put in this locker. We were in the middle of looking him over when he...changed."

"What do you mean he changed?" Tara asked.

"Into this man," Yvette replied. She held out her hands toward the body on the slab. "Right before our eyes." Tara let out a gasp while Bethany stood there looking confused.

"What?" Bethany asked. She couldn't contain the shock in her voice. "What do you mean he changed into this man? How is that even possible?"

"Well the only beings in Seattle that have the ability to take the shape of someone else, as far as I know, are us shapeshifters," Jacob told them.

"So you're telling me that this is a shapeshifter?" Bethany's eyes darkened and her body tensed. "Then where the hell is my brother?"

"That is what I would like to know," Jacob responded a little harshly.

Tara took in a deep breath after hearing this new information. "I didn't know you could take on the appearance of the dead," she confessed to her partner.

"Theoretically, we shouldn't be able to," he told her. "Their DNA's dead. We can't absorb DNA from the dead, though I've never tried."

"Well that changes the game quite a bit," Tara said shaking her head. Jacob nodded silently.

"How so?" Bethany asked.

"All this time, we've been searching for your brother's killer. We've interrogated people based on your brother's recent experiences. This could have nothing to do with you or your family at all."

"Except for the fact that this shapeshifter was using the face of Eric Sloan," Yvette butted in. Everyone in the room turned to look at her. "All I'm saying is that I wouldn't count it out that this has to do with the Sloan's." She did have a point.

"Are you sure it's a shapeshifter?" Bethany asked?

"I extracted blood from the body and ran it through the centrifuge. The DNA has the same properties as shifter DNA, so I'm pretty sure," Yvette told them. She reached up and brushed a stray hair out of her face.

"How did you not catch it from the original autopsy?" Tara asked, still reeling from the change of events.

"It wouldn't have shown up in the original autopsy," Yvette responded softly.

"She's right," Jacob agreed. "We absorb DNA, which means our DNA is virtually identical to the original host. Only after we switch back would it be detectable."

"So, my brothers alive?" Bethany asked. A smile spread on her face from ear to ear. She beamed at Tara, and Tara couldn't help but feel a small sense of relief for her.

"Don't get too happy," Jacob said. "We still don't know where your brother is or why this shifter had on his face."

"It doesn't matter," Bethany responded. "He's alive."

"We don't know that for sure," Yvette said quietly. "With this being such a high profile case, the newscasters have been blasting nothing but your brothers face all over the news. Which begs the question…"

"Why he hasn't come forward," Tara finished her train of thought. "If he is alive, then he would have tried to contact someone, one would assume."

"Unless…," Jacob started but stopped. He glanced at Bethany with a small grimace.

"What?" Bethany asked.

"Unless he is responsible for the killing." The silence was deafening. The only sound Tara could hear was that of her own heartbeat as everyone contemplated Jacob's response. Bethany broke the silence with a loud laugh.

"Or he is in a position where he can't call for help," Bethany said, doing her best to be supportive.

"So you think now he has been kidnapped?" It was Jacob's turn to laugh.

"I don't know, detective," Bethany sneered. "I just found out that my brother may still be alive, and you go and shit on that moment by suggesting that he is now the murderer."

"In any case," Tara interrupted, "We don't know enough about this to form any solid conclusion." She glanced between the two. Jacob lowered his head in a form of shame and submission. Bethany's stance was harsh, but she kept her mouth shut. "Now," Tara said, turning toward Yvette. "How do we explain this to Chief Martinez?"

"Oh, I've got that covered," Yvette assured her. Tara raised an eyebrow waiting for her to explain. Realizing she needed more of an explanation, Yvette elaborated. "I'll say someone came in and switched out the body when I was out."

"You'll get in trouble for sure," Jacob said sympathetically.

"Maybe, but it's better than the alternative." She had a point. If he found out that Eric was still alive, it would bring up too many questions that none of them were ready to answer without giving the supernatural world away.

"And what do we do if Eric does turn up?" Tara asked.

No one spoke. None of them had thought that far ahead. They were just winging it. They would have to play it by ear. If Eric did happen to show up, they would have to come up with one hell of a convincing story to cover everyone's asses.

"In any case, Bethany, I think it's best if you keep this between the four of us," Jacob told her.

"What!" she stammered out. "No way. My father deserves to know that his son is still alive."

"Might still be alive," Jacob corrected. "Besides, we don't know enough about this murder to form a clear picture yet."

"So?" She replied curtly. "Who cares! He might still be alive. You don't think my father should know?"

"And what if it turns out Eric isn't alive?" Tara asked her. "What if the shifter was forced to take Eric's DNA in some way and pose as Eric because something bad has happened to him?"

"You're grasping at straws, detective," Bethany said defensively.

"But she does have a point," Yvette said. "We don't know where your brother is, and until that is a definite, do you really want to give your father false hope?"

Bethany eyed Yvette suspiciously. Yvette stood her ground, seemingly clueless to Bethany's demeanor. "Just wait a little while longer for us to find out what is really going on," Tara told her. "After we find evidence of what really happened to Eric, alive or not, you can tell Mr. Sloan whatever you would like."

Bethany thought about that, then nodded. "You have until after the Ball. Then, if you still don't know anything about my brother's whereabouts, I'm going to tell my father what I know."

"Agreed," Tara said, holding out her hand. Bethany stared at it for a moment, then smiled. She reached her hand out and shook it.

"I have to go feed," Bethany told them. "Tomorrow is a big day and I have lots to get ready." Before anyone could say anything, Bethany was gone.

It was late and Tara was exhausted. Yvette pushed the shifter back inside the locker and closed him in. She turned and stared at the two detectives.

"What?" Tara asked.

"I heard what happened at CJ's," She confessed. "If I was a detective, I would say that it was not a random shooting." Both detectives remained as still and as silent as the dead inside the lockers. Yvette continued. "Furthermore, I would deduce, given your lack of clothing options, that you two haven't been to your homes in a couple days. Which means you two need a place to crash until you find out who is after you."

She was good, Tara had to admit, and a place to stay for the evening did sound appealing.

"No," Jacob stated flatly. "Thank you for the offer, but it's too risky. I'd hate myself if you were harmed because you helped us."

"Nonsense," Yvette replied, swishing her hand as if swatting a fly away. "Where would you go otherwise?"

"We can rent a hotel room or even sleep upstairs," Tara chimed in.

"A hotel is the first place I would look if I was after you both. You're staying with me and that's the end of it. Besides," Yvette continued. "I have a warm shower and comfy beds."

Tara and Jacob exchanged worried glances. Tara shrugged and Jacob conceded. "It could be dangerous," he warned.

"I'm a Siren. I can take care of myself," She said, and blinked. Another set of eyelids blinked sideways, and that caught Tara off guard. Yvette really wasn't human. "Just give me a minute to close up, then I'll meet you two upstairs."

Jacob and Tara walked out together. Tara's buzz over the night's events was starting to wane and she was physically and mentally exhausted. Today had been a long day and she thought that tomorrow would be even longer.

"So where do we start tomorrow?" She asked Jacob.

"I have a place in mind, but it's probably the most dangerous place I know," he said with a little fear in his voice.

"Oh?" She asked. "Why is that?"

"Because I'm banned from ever returning," he replied with a sigh.

"Wait. You don't mean...?" She started and he nodded.

"Yup. Time to go see Mommy Dearest."

Chapter 27

The next morning, Tara and Jacob were on their way to Capitol Hill by 7:15 a.m. Despite having little sleep from the night before. Tara felt invigorated. The sunrise had been a beautiful one against the misty fog-filled streets of West Seattle. Tara could see why people would want to live in the Pacific Northwest, despite the rain and cold.

Jacob was unusually quiet and Tara felt it best to let him gather his thoughts. After all, it wasn't her family that forced her into exile. She tried to imagine what it must have been like on both sides of the coin, though her morality didn't match up with what Jacob considered "shifter society". She would feel betrayed and extremely hurt by her family if they happened to put her in the same situation.

One of Yvette's houses was located near Alki Beach in West Seattle and it took them a little over 15 minutes to drive there from the morgue. Because she was a Siren princess, she told them, she had more than one property to choose from, which given the situation, would come in handy should anything arise. Like people hunting down her house guests.

She chose the smallest of her properties that faced Seattle's Industrial District. The house itself was unremarkably white and average on the outside. Had you been driving by, you may not have given it a second glance. The inside, however, was extremely different.

Artwork decorated almost every inch of the walls. She told Tara that every single piece belonged to local artists. Digital clocks and fancy lamps illuminated the hallway that led into the living room. The Room was filled with modern furniture and high-tech gadgets.

Yvette showed them each to a separate bedroom and gave Tara a change of clothes for the morning. She said she would also make breakfast in the morning but Jacob declined.

"We will be gone by 7," he told her. "Tomorrow is the annual ball, as you know. Everyone will be busy getting ready, so the earlier we catch my mother, the better."

Yvette understood. She hung out two towels for them in case they wanted to shower before she got up. They gave their thanks and departed ways. Tara was very grateful for Yvette's generosity. They may be tired and cranky leaving as early as they planned, but at least they would be clean.

The moment Tara hit the bed, she was out cold. She had a dreamless night and wanted to sleep longer, but Jacob got her up at 5:30 a.m. Traffic into Seattle wasn't too bad at that time, but the lanes were filling up quickly. They made it past the police station at 7:15 and headed on their way to Capitol Hill.

"Hungry?" he asked her. "I know a pretty good breakfast spot."

"Coffee will suffice," Tara answered bleakly, staring out at the traffic. It always amazed her at how busy a big city was so early in the morning. It reminded her of ants scurrying away after a foot lands on their hill.

"Right," he mumbled back and pulled into the nearest Starbucks he could find. Jacob ordered an Americano. Tara got a Venti Mocha.

"So you grew up in this neighborhood?" she asked him after taking a sip of her coffee.

"Yes," he blushed slightly. "But things have gotten progressively worse in some areas."

"Oh? What do you mean?"

"The cost of living has skyrocketed over the last 10 years. It's hard to find a decent yet affordable place to live. Plus, we've seen an increase of homeless migration happening on the hill."

Tara looked around at large apartment buildings and small businesses. She tried to imagine what the neighborhood could have looked like when Jacob had been a child. Things couldn't have changed too much.

"So where is your house?" she asked him.

"My mother's house," he corrected her, "Is located on 19th Ave. When you're ready, we will head that way." He straightened his tie, black with purple accents, and fidgeted with his suit sleeves. He wore a black suit with a purple dress shirt. Had he not been her partner, she would have found him very handsome. She wondered if he wore the suit because of work or to impress his family. She was guessing the latter.

He drove in silence the rest of the way to 19th Ave. They passed many residential homes before stopping at a gated off section of the street. Jacob wiped his forehead with the back of his hand before looking at her.

"Ready for this?" he asked. Tara was betting it was more to himself than to her, but she answered anyway.

"I'm here with you," she said softly. He nodded and gave her a small comforting smile. They got out of the car and walked to the gate.

The gate was made of solid black iron with an ivy pattern growing up the bars. A number pad mechanism was attached to the side of the fence. Jacob punched in a code but the gate remained closed.

"They must have changed the code," he said and grimaced. He tried again but the gate remained locked. "Hmm," he mumbled.

"It won't open," A male voice floated out to them from behind the gate. Tara looked up to see a tall man, around 6 foot, with much of Jacob's features. His wavy brown hair was parted down the middle and cut just above his ears. He was muscular, perhaps even more than Jacob, and seemed to relish in that fact. He wore a blue muscle tee with form fitting jogging pants.

"Curtis," Jacob said. "Nice to see you again."

"What are you doing here, Jacob?" He responded quickly. His gaze fell from Jacob to Tara. "Come to show us your new girlfriend?"

Tara became instantly defensive, but Jacob smiled politely. "Actually, big brother, this is Tara Bancroft. Detective Tara Bancroft. We are partners. Nothing more."

"Remind me again about your last work partner?" Curtis said harshly then sneered at Tara. Jacob's eyes focused on his brother with intense heat.

"Are you going to let us in?" he asked, shaking the gate with both hands.

"You are exiled from this family, or have you forgotten?" Curtis took a step closer to the gate. "Tell me, why would you risk mother's wrath by coming back here?"

"Believe me," Jacob stated, "I wouldn't be here if I didn't have to be. But the case we are working on requires it."

"Leave," Curtis responded. "Go, before mother sees you and skins you alive." He meant to sound intimidating, but Tara caught the fear in his voice. Was Jacob's mother really that scary?

"Excuse me," Tara intervened. Curtis turned to look at her. "Yeah, hi. We have a murder investigation going on. Perhaps you've heard. Eric Sloan was killed the other night.

"I don't see how that has to do with us in any way," Curtis said defiantly.

"Be that as it may, our investigation led us here. So, unless you want to be hauled in for impeding an active investigation, I would suggest you put the family drama aside and let us do our job."

Curtis eyed her up and down. Tara crossed her arms over her chest and eyed him back. Jacob stood eerily still, waiting for the next play to go down. Curtis let out a breath then turned to his brother. "At least this one has sass," he said, unlocking the gate.

"Thank you," Tara replied while walking past. Jacob and Curtis stared at each other for a brief moment, as if they had never seen each other before. Jacob raised his arms and embraced Curtis quickly before he could protest. Curtis, caught off guard, held back a moment longer before he returned the embrace.

"Good to see you," Curtis finally said, "but mother will have a fit. You know this already."

Jacob nodded. "Couldn't be helped, I'm afraid. Can we talk inside?"

Curtis bit his lower lip but nodded slightly. He turned and guided the detectives up to the white front door of the house. The house was enormous, not as enormous as the Sloan mansion, but still impressive in size. Tara glanced around and noticed that every house on the block had to be worth at least a million each, but this house had to be worth at least 5 million. Curtis opened the front door and ushered them inside.

Tara gasped as she entered the dwelling. The outside was impressive, but the inside took her breath away. The foyer was colossal with a golden chandelier hanging from the ceiling over a circular blue mink rug. The foyer had two double staircases made completely out of dark oak with a dark blue carpet ascending both sides. Family pictures were painted on large canvasses that were neatly placed all the way up each side of the steps. A large china cabinet held trinkets of small statues and glass animals at the far end of the room.

"Wow," Tara managed to utter. "You grew up here?"

"I told you it loses its appeal after a while," Jacob whispered back. He looked around at what used to be his home, then shrugged at her.

"Yeah, but you didn't say you lived like this!" Tara said, stunned that people actually lived like this. She grew up in a small house and couldn't imagine living in such an exquisite place.

"Jakey!" said a small girlish voice. A girl about four feet tall ran to Jacob and Jacob instinctively scooped her into his arms.

"Oh my god, Rhea! You've gotten so big already," Jacob said playfully. "Soon, I won't be able to pick you up anymore."

"I've missed you too," she said, clamping her arms around his neck. "Are you home for good?"

"No," he told her quietly. "But I've missed you more than you know." He hugged her tightly. "I have someone I want you to meet." He turned to Tara. "Rhea, this is my work partner, detective Bancroft."

Tara held a hand out to Rhea and the girl shook it. "It's so nice to meet you," Tara said.

"You're pretty," Rhea said. "When I grow up, I think I will want to have red hair." Tara smiled sweetly at her. At least someone in this family appeared to be normal, Tara thought to herself.

"Put her down!" yelled a stern voice from the top of the stairs. Tara whirled around to see a slender woman wearing a teal dress staring down at them. Jacob did as he was ordered. "Rhea, go to your room and clean up your toys."

"But I want to stay with Jakey," she argued defiantly.

"Don't sass me, girl," the woman warned. "Now do as you're told before you get punished and miss the ball tonight."

Rhea crossed her arms and stomped her feet out of the room. Tara smiled at Rhea's small tantrum. She was a cutie.

"Nice to see you too, mother," Jacob said coldly. He automatically took a defensive stance and crossed his arms like Rhea did. Tara could see the family resemblance.

"Just what do you think you are doing back in this house?" she asked, descending the stairway. She walked elegantly toward them when she reached the bottom. "I believe my position was quite clear last time we spoke."

"They said it was a matter of a police investigation," Curtis chimed in. The woman turned to Curtis and smacked him in the face.

"You let him into this house without my permission?" She screamed at him. "How dare you." Her face went from beautiful to crazed in a fraction of a second.

"Hey!" Tara screamed. "Do that again and I'll haul your ass in for assault." Jacob's mother turned to her as if noticing her for the first time. A small sneer appeared on her face.

"And just who do we have here?" she asked, waltzing around Tara.

"Isis Thompson, meet my partner, Tara Bancroft," Jacob answered flatly.

Isis looked Tara up and down. Her sneer stayed firm. "Charmed, I'm sure," she said before turning toward her son. "No offense, girly, but this is a family matter. How dare you tell me how to discipline my son."

"I don't care what kind of matter it is," Tara shot back. "What kind of mother hits her own son because another one returns home?"

Isis recoiled slightly as if she had been the one to get slapped. Curtis's eyes widened in shock. Jacob remained neutral, but there was a hint of a smile at the corners of his lips.

"How dare you speak to me with such an insolent tone! Do you know who I am?" Isis shrieked.

"Yes, I do, and frankly, I don't give a damn. We came here because one of your shapeshifters is dead and to ask you some questions about it. But it seems all you care about is whether your son can be allowed back inside your house," Tara said.

"A shapeshifter is dead?" Curtis asked with renewed interest.

Jacob nodded. "That's why we're here."

Isis huffed loudly and shook her head. "You told another one of your partners about us?"

"I didn't tell her," Jacob responded defensively. "Mr. Sloan did." Isis's eye flashed brightly at the news then sneered once more.

Tara rolled her eyes at the display. "Yes, I'm a human who knows about shapeshifters. Let's move past that and focus on why we're here, shall we?"

Isis huffed loudly once again. "Fine," she said, shaking her head, then turned to Jacob. "You will be forgiven for coming back home. This time. But make no mistake, you step foot in here again and I will have your skin decorating the dining room wall. Understood?"

Jacob nodded, clearing his throat. Tara balled her hands into fists and it took effort not to punch Isis in the face. "Follow me," Isis said and walked out of the room. Curtis gave Tara a slight smile, as if to say thank you for sticking up to his mother but turned quickly to follow.

"Nice mother," Tara said sarcastically. "Can I shoot her?" Jacob raised an eyebrow at her. "Just in the leg?" she added. Jacob laughed quietly.

"She just takes some getting used to," he told her. "Come on, let's get this over with." He led her into a room where Isis sat on a small throne. Curtis sat near her on the floor while Jacob and Tara took the loveseat.

"Tea?" she offered them, raising her hand to the tiny table next to her with a pewter teapot and four pewter cups.

"No, thank you," Jacob declined politely. Tara shook her head. "Where's father?"

"Not that it's any of your business, but he has matters to attend to in Europe." Isis poured herself a cup of tea and sipped it loudly before turning her attention to Tara. "Tell me, detective Bancroft. Are you familiar with what happened to Jacob's last partner?"

Jacob suddenly became very still, like a stone statue at a graveyard. "Yes, I am," Tara replied harshly. Isis smiled brightly.

"And do you think it wise to threaten the queen of the shapeshifters after knowing that little tidbit?" Her voice echoed off the walls of the room. "After finding out what happened to, what was her name again?"

"Natasha," Jacob whispered painfully. Tara looked at her partner and saw tears threatening to come out. She turned back to Isis with renewed hatred.

"Honestly, I don't care if you are the queen of the shapeshifters. You lay a finger on your son again, and I will cuff you so fast you won't be able to shape into someone else."

Isis's smile spread widely on her face. They stared at each other with different emotions. Tara stared with hatred in her eyes, but Isis stared with amusement. It was as if she was watching a mouse trying to stand up for itself against a hungry cat.

"You are either very brave, detective, or very stupid. I'm not sure which one yet, but either way, I think I like you. You've got fire in your soul."

Jacob seemed to relax a bit. He let his shoulders go slack and Tara noticed the tension ease away.

"Great," Tara retorted sarcastically. "Now that we've gotten that settled, can we get back to business?"

"Quite right," Isis agreed. "Tell me, Jacob. Who is this shifter?"

"No one I've seen before, but there are many I don't know about," He told them. He reached into his inside coat pocket and produced a photo of the man. He offered it to his mother. She took it and glanced at it briefly before handing it to Curtis. He let out a small gasp and covered his mouth with his left hand.

"Recognize him?" Tara asked

"Yes," she replied. "His name is David something or other."

"David Marx," Curtis confessed. "He goes to my gym." He handed the picture back to his brother.

"Gold's Gym? On Broadway?" Tara asked. He nodded.

"How did he die?" Curtis asked.

"He was murdered," Jacob admitted. Curtis let out another gasp. Anger flashed in his mother's eyes.

"Someone killed one of my shifters?" She stood up quickly and let out a shriek. She ran to a cabinet with an assortment of trinkets on it. She picked up a vase and threw it out of anger at the wall. It shattered, spilling water and glass in every direction. Tara had to duck behind the cushions to avoid ricocheting glass. She turned to Jacob who had the same worried expression on his face.

"Who did this?" Isis screamed at the detectives. "Who killed one of my subjects?"

"That's what we are going to find out," Jacob said as calmly as he could. "We just need to know more about him if we are going to catch this killer."

"When you find him, you bring him to me!" she ordered. "I will deal with him."

"If it is indeed a him," Tara mentioned. "We will do our job and let the law do its job." Isis picked up another vase and threw it at the wall. It smashed against the far wall, sending flowers all over the paintings.

"Calm down, mother," Jacob demanded. "We will catch this bastard. We just need to know where to look."

Isis fumed with anger as she walked back to her throne. She sat down, straightened her hair, then crossed her legs. She looked completely normal as if nothing had happened. Tara's mouth gaped open as she watched this transformation.

"Curtis, you've seen to recognize him more than mother has. What can you tell me about him?"

"Well, for starters, he was a good guy," Curtis told them. "Always friendly and willing to be your spotter." Curtis leaned closer to the detectives. "He always seemed to be at the gym whenever I was there."

"And what days were that?" Tara asked.

"I work out about five days a week," he answered. "I take a break Wednesdays and Sundays."

Curiously, Tara asked. "Were you there when Eric Sloan was killed?" Jacob gave her a stern look of surprise.

"I was there in the morning, yes. But I didn't see Eric there," he added quickly.

"How about David?" Jacob asked his brother.

"He wasn't there either," Curtis replied. Tara felt a tingling sensation wash over her. It was the same sensation she got every time someone lied to her. He was lying, she was sure of it. The question was why?

"You sure?" She asked.

"Not that I recall," he replied. The same sensation passed over her and she trembled slightly. He was lying. Did she confront him and potentially set Isis off on another vase throwing rampage or wait to tell Jacob later? She chose to wait. It was the lesser of two evils.

"Did David have any enemies that you are aware of?" Jacob asked him.

"None that he spoke of, to me at least. Like I said, he was a good guy. I can't imagine anyone wanting to hurt him."

"You knew him that well?" Tara asked.

"Not really," he said. "Just from the conversations in the gym." She tingled again. Why was he lying? Then a thought crossed her mind.

"Was David gay?" she asked him

Curtis jumped slightly. "I fail to see how that is any use to you, detective," Isis told her.

"Any detail about his personal life could lead us to who killed him," she told them. Jacob nodded in agreement. "Besides, my understanding of the gym goers is one of two things. Either you are really into fitness and want to stay healthy, or you are a gay man who wants others to look at you. Sometimes, those facts aren't mutually exclusive."

"Well, I'm not sure about his status," Curtis said. "We really weren't that close. As I've said, I've talked to him a few times, but only when he spots for me."

"Did he mention in your conversations anyone he might be dating?" Jacob asked his brother. Curtis shook his head. "How about friends he might hang out with or things he liked to do when he wasn't at the gym?"

"I'm sorry, brother. I wish I could offer more, but as I've mentioned..."

"You weren't that close," Tara finished for him. He turned to her and gave her a weak smile. She smiled back. "Well, thank you for your time." She stood up quickly. Jacob looked as if he still had questions, but he stood up with her.

"You find the bastard who did this to one of our own," Isis said again. "And make him pay with his life."

"I'm going to pretend I didn't hear that last part," Tara said aloud.

"Don't worry mother. Whoever is behind this will pay." Jacob offered his certainty. That seemed to satisfy her enough to offer a grimacing smile.

Curtis stood up. "I'll walk you out." He escorted them to the entranceway.

"Please give my love to Rhea," Jacob told his mother. She raised an eyebrow at him then nodded meekly.

"Goodbye, exile," she said softly, then turned to Tara. "Next time we meet girly, I may not be so accommodating."

"I can hardly wait," Tara threw back. Isis smiled widely again.

"She really is fearless of me, isn't she?" she asked Jacob. He shrugged and walked out of the house. Tara and Curtis walked behind him, leaving Isis in the doorway. Once to the gate, Tara had to ask.

"Wanna tell me why you were lying in there?" She turned her attention to Curtis.

"What?" Jacob wondered. "What are you talking about?"

"I can't explain it, but I could tell your brother was lying the whole time. I'm wondering why?"

Curtis looked at her with a mixture of surprise and guilt. "Was it that obvious?" He looked back to see if his mother was still standing in the doorway. She was not.

"You lied on a police investigation?" Jacob asked with surprise in his voice.

"I'll tell you in the car," he responded and opened the gate. Jacob and Tara exchanged glances and followed Curtis to Jacobs SUV. Once inside, Curtis started immediately.

"I'm sorry I lied to you, brother." he admitted. "I just didn't want mother to find out."

"About what?" Jacob asked uneasily.

"I lied about David being away from the gym when I was there. He was there," he confessed and sighed.

"Why lie about that?" Jacob asked him.

"Because he wasn't there to work out, per say."

"Go on," Tara told him. "Why was he there?"

Curtis took in a deep breath and let it out slowly. "You asked me if he was gay, and I told you I didn't know."

"To which was another lie," Tara interrupted. Curtis nodded.

"We were close," Curtis whispered.

"Wait," Jacob said. "How close?"

Curtis eyed his brother. "Close," he told him. Jacob didn't understand right away, but Tara did. Realization spread on Jacob's face once he understood what Curtis meant by 'close'. Tara was betting that it never occurred to him that anyone of his family could ever be gay.

"Oh," Jacob whispered. Curtis nodded again.

"We had just started seeing each other about a month ago. It was a casual thing at first. Things progressed pretty quickly."

"Any relationship issues?" Tara asked.

"What do you mean?" He replied back.

"My understanding of the gay culture is that gay men are more promiscuous than others. He was a good looking guy. Did you have any other competition?" Jacob gave her a look. She shrugged back at him as if to say sorry, but gotta ask.

"No," Curtis told them. "No real competition, as you put it." He thought for a moment. "Well, besides Eric Sloan."

"Wait," Jacob interrupted. "Eric Sloan? I thought he was dating Kenzie Wright?"

"Oh, he was, 'officially'," Curtis air quoted. "Unofficially, he would cruise both David and I all the time at the gym. It was harmless flirting, and we both brushed off his advances."

"Did anything ever happen between you and Eric?" Jacob asked quickly. "Unofficially, that is?"

Curtis blushed a bright pink. "Once," he admitted. "A day before he had been killed."

Jacob's jaw dropped. "And you didn't think to inform the police once Eric was found murdered?"

"Why would I?" Curtis asked desperately. "I had nothing to do with his death!" Jacob's eyes grew bright and he shook his head at his brother.

"Was David the jealous type?" Tara asked him.

"What? No," He answered quickly. "Besides, he had nothing to be jealous about."

"And why is that?" Jacob asked. "You just told us that you cheated on him with Eric Sloan."

"No, I didn't," Curtis clarified. "He was there with us when we did it." Jacob's jaw hit the floor. He closed his mouth, then opened it to say something, but shut his mouth again. He was speechless.

Tara changed the subject. "What time did you leave the gym that day?"

"I had an appointment at 10:30, so around 10."

"And David was still there?" She inquired. He nodded.

"He told me he wanted to get in a few reps before lunch. That was the last time I heard from him."

Jacob was still boggled by his brother's confession. "So, someone that you slept with is murdered, and you haven't heard from your boyfriend in a couple days. And you still didn't think to inform the police?" He sighed loudly.

"Again, why would I?" he asked. "He told me he was heading to New York for a work conference in the afternoon. I assumed that is where he was before you came here."

"It never occurred to you to text him?" Tara asked.

He shrugged at her. "Honestly, I didn't want him to think I was needy. I thought I'd play it cool and wait for him to get back. I assumed he was doing the same."

Tara thanked him for his honesty. He nodded to her and then looked at his brother. "Are we okay?"

Jacob nodded. "You're my brother, and I love you. Your choices are your own, as well as your life. As long as you are happy, then I am happy for you."

Curtis nodded, then opened the car door to leave. "You will find whoever did this, won't you?"

"We will do our very best," Jacob assured him. "I'll deliver the news personally."

"I hope not, or mother really will have you skinned," Curtis added. Jacob shrugged as if to say fuck it. Curtis got out of the car.

"Curtis?" Jacob called to him. He turned and looked at his brother.

"Thanks for telling me," Jacob said. Curtis nodded and shut the door behind him.

Chapter 28

Jacob took Tara to Coastal Kitchen for Breakfast. They decided to eat for a couple of reasons. For one, they were hungry, but they also needed a place to sit and discuss everything that had happened the last couple of days.

Jacob listened intently as Tara told him what happened at Heiligtum and how she ended up at Vita's house. He was shocked to learn that the bird came through the tarot cards and attacked them. She listened intently as he divulged his feeling about Curtis being gay.

"It doesn't really bother me," he admitted. "It's just surprising, is all."

"Surprising that he's gay or that he happened to mess around with our dead body?" she asked.

"Both, I think," he confessed. "But he thinks both Eric and David are dead. I still don't fully understand why he didn't make a connection between both of them when he found out Eric was murdered. I mean, come on. His boyfriend just happened to be traveling to New York on the same day that Eric was killed in the gym they both attended earlier that day?"

"Well, sometimes people jump to conclusions. Maybe he thought he would wait to hear from David before forming any opinion." She took a sip of her coffee before continuing. "No one wants to see their significant other in a bad light."

Jacob took a bite of his pancake. "Maybe, but I'll tell you one thing. If I saw on the news that a girl I had been with was murdered the day after we had sex and my girlfriend hadn't contacted me in a couple days, I would go to the police."

Tara nodded silently. "Maybe, but after meeting your mother, I can completely sympathize with Curtis. Seems to me she would probably skin him alive if she found out. She did hit him just for letting you inside the house."

Jacob chuckled, spewing bits of pancake out of his mouth. He wiped his mouth with a napkin and apologized. "You're right on that. I think mommy dearest would probably have a heart attack." Tara took another sip of her coffee. "How did you know he was lying?"

She shrugged. "It's a gift. I'm pretty good at telling when people lie. My last partner called it my spider sense. It drove him nuts at times because he would purposely try to lie to me. It never worked."

A human lie detector," Jacob joked. "You must be a big hit at parties."

She mimicked him sarcastically and they both laughed loudly. Once the laughter subsided, Jacob spoke. "So, back to the gym? I want to take another look on the cameras now that we know who to look for."

"Sounds good," she said, finishing up her oatmeal. David had transformed into Eric when he died. Had a night of passion given him enough of Eric's DNA to keep him in that form even after death? She didn't know how long the effects lasted before the DNA burnt up, but she was betting not that long.

She remembered Adam looking like her all day. That had been possible with a simple holding of her hand. Sex, if passionate enough would last much longer. Was it possible? Maybe it was.

They paid the check and headed out the door. "So, what exactly are we hoping to find on the tapes?" She asked.

"Not sure, exactly. But maybe by following David on the cameras, we can get a glimpse of who the killer is."

"Alright," she said. "While you're watching the tape, I'll have a chat with the staff and see if they recognize David. Maybe that will jog their memory about something."

They arrived at the gym at 11:15. The gym was bursting with guests but the staff were accommodating enough. Billy, the same man Tara had interviewed previously, sat behind the reception desk and greeted them with a fake smile.

Jacob headed off to watch the tapes while she questioned Billy. She handed him a picture of David.

"Oh him? He hasn't been in here in a couple days," Billy told her.

"He wouldn't, considering he's dead," Tara stated flatly.

Billy covered his mouth with his palm to hide his oh-my-god expression. "What happened?"

"That is what we're here to determine," she replied. "I have it from a reliable source that David was here on the same day of Eric Sloan's murder."

"Was he?" He asked as he started typing on his computer. "Ah, yes, our records show he checked in, but didn't check out."

"You didn't see him that day?" She asked as she leaned on the desk.

He thought about it for a minute. "Honestly, I can't recall, but we get many people in here and it's hard to keep track of everybody."

"Don't they have to come to you to check in?"

"Yes, but I could have been on break or he could have come in before I started working," he told her.

"I understand," she said. "What can you tell me about him?"

"Not much, I'm afraid," he said while leaning back in his seat. "He was a good client. Always paid his membership on time. A real healthy guy. He was practically here every day."

"Friendly?" she asked. He nodded.

"Ever notice any confrontations or arguments here?" She asked him.

"Yes, all the time, but not any with him. He was a pretty likable guy," Billy responded.

"Did he have anyone, in particular, he hung out with here?"

Billy thought a moment, then nodded. "There were a number of men he hung around with here, but he always seemed to follow that Sloan guy around."

"Eric Sloan? As in, the victim we found in the bathroom?" She asked him. He nodded.

"And you didn't think it relevant to tell me last time we talked about Eric being followed around?" Her eyes bore into him and he winced slightly at her expression.

He held up his hands, "Whoa," he said, "It was never stalking or anything like that. It was mostly friendly spotting and working out together. Besides, Eric had a number of followers here. He was quite the player."

Tara arched an eyebrow. "How so?" She asked him.

Billy cleared his throat. "He would leave here with all sorts of women, and some men as well. He was very friendly and good looking if you catch my drift."

"You sound envious," she said.

He chuckled lightly. "Maybe I am, but only because he had a natural gift of making you want him just by the looks he would give you."

"Hmm," she mumbled. "Did you ever go home with him?"

Billy turned a deep shade of red. "No," he told her, "but I might have wanted to awhile back. Before I found out how much of a player he was."

She took in a deep breath and exhaled slowly. "Well, thanks for your time. If I have any more questions..."

"You know where to find me," he said. They shook hands and she headed off towards the surveillance room. She knocked on the door and Jacob opened it without hesitation.

"So here we are again," she said.

"Yes, but this time, the cameras do show David here," he assured her.

"What did you find?" she asked him, taking the seat next to him while looking at the video screens.

"Well, he came in around 9:00 that morning. The cameras show him interacting with Curtis and they were each other's' spotters."

"Okay, so that part is true," Tara stated. "Did you find anything else?"

"Curtis left, like he said. David stayed, but it doesn't show him heading to the woman's restroom."

"Does it show Eric arriving at all?"

"No," he replied.

"Okay, so Curtis said they had a thing with Eric the night before David died. He was found taking Eric's form. Could a one-night stand keep him in Eric's form long after he was dead?"

Jacob seemed to think about it. "Honestly? I'm not sure." He turned back to the video screen. "It might be possible, considering that during sexual intercourse, there is a lot of body contact and bodily fluids. As a shapeshifter, we physically can't stop the DNA Transfer."

"Yeah, but would it be possible to keep his form a couple days after death?" She asked him.

"Before last night, I would have said no. I didn't even know we could take the form of vampires, though I've never tried before."

"So, if you die looking like the other person, you don't automatically revert to your natural state?" She asked him. "I would assume that you would just switch back. I mean, isn't that how it's done in the movies?"

"You watch too much TV," he told her. "Honestly, all this is news to me as well. Theoretically, we should just switch back, but maybe because it was vampire DNA, it took longer than expected."

Tara looked troubled. Something was nagging her and she couldn't quite place it. It was like she lost her keys and was searching for them all over, even though the keys were right in front of her. In this instance, the clues were there, she just couldn't see it properly.

Sensing her disturbance, Jacob spoke. "What are you thinking?"

"This case is just baffling," she told him honestly. "Maybe it's because it's about supernatural creatures, but I can't seem to see everything clearly. I don't understand why David would turn into Eric. According to Billy, the receptionist, Eric was a player. He would leave with both men and woman, but according to his family and the ogres, Kenzie and he were lovers. Something is off with that."

"I see your point, but let's say you were going to cheat, would you announce it to your family?" He asked her.

"No, I guess I wouldn't," she responded quickly. "Still, where is Eric? Since the body turned out to be David, you would assume Eric would show up to clear the air, unless…"

"Unless what?" He asked her.

"Unless he is the reason David is dead."

They sat there in silence for a moment, both thinking about that conclusion. "Well, that's one theory," Jacob said, breaking the silence. "Let's elaborate on that."

"Well there are a couple plausible possibilities," Tara said. "The first one is that David was forced to turn into Eric to either protect him, giving Eric time to escape from whoever is after him. In which case, Eric is hiding to avoid detection."

"Okay," Jacob said uneasily. "I don't really buy that but go on? Second possibility?"

"The second is that Eric met David here, convinced him somehow to turn into him and killed him. If that's the case, he wanted to fake his own death. To what end, I'm not sure, but it would explain why he hasn't come forth."

Jacob nodded. "Any other possibilities you see?"

"One more," she nodded. "If someone was after Eric, then back to scenario one, where David turned into Eric to protect him, ended up dead, and Eric is hurt or kidnapped and can't do anything about it."

"Maybe Eric knew someone was after him and convinced David to turn into him without David knowing anything about being pursued," Jacob offered.

"Also a possibility," Tara responded.

"There is one more possibility I see," Jacob said.

"What's that?"

"That Kenzie found out about Eric and David and disposed of them both," he said flatly. "I wouldn't put it past the Ogre to do something about it."

"The jealous girlfriend does seem like an obvious scenario, but I don't think that happened," she said shaking her head.

"Oh? Why not?"

"Well, if you remember, Kenzie had been locked up for at least five days when we saw her. Those chains were magically imbued by some witchy woo, and unbreakable. There is no way she could have done it." Tara started drumming her fingers on the surveillance stand.

"Maybe not directly," Jacob retorted. "But she is still an ogre princess. She could easily get someone to expose of Eric if she wanted." Tara gave him a skeptical glance. He continued. "Think about it. You said that he was a player. He would come and go with both men and women, right?"

Tara nodded.

"So, if Kenzie found out about Eric cheating, what better motive than to have him killed while she is locked up? No one would suspect her because she was chained up."

It made sense, but it still didn't explain where Eric was now. Sensing her thoughts, Jacob continued.

"So, whoever killed David thought they killed Eric, then saw Eric out somewhere and panicked, thinking they didn't do a good enough job, so took Eric and disposed of him."

"Maybe, but I still doubt it," Tara replied. "Bethany said it was nearly impossible to kill a vampire. Hell, sunlight doesn't kill immediately. So besides a stake in the heart and a beheading, Eric would still be alive. And I've seen Bethany in action. She is a tough son of a bitch. Eric would be the same. Do you believe anyone could just take Eric down?"

"All we know for sure is that Eric's missing," Jacob said, drumming his fingers on the control panel.

"So where do we go from here?" Tara asked her partner.

"We need to talk to Dominik again," Jacob said. "Maybe his shady dealings had something to do with it."

"Do you really believe so?" Tara asked skeptically. He shrugged.

"If anything, we need more information. If Eric is alive and hiding, we need to know where he would go, and if he is hurt, it's probably Dominik's dealings that caused him to get hurt. The more we know, the better off we will be."

"And if he's dead?" She asked.

"Then we definitely need to know who the enemies are," he said flatly.

"And if we get attacked again?"

"Let's take it one step at a time," Jacob told her. "I doubt someone will attack during the day. Seems like they would lose an advantage under the cover of night."

"We could always see if he would meet us at the station," Tara suggested.

"I think given the ball tonight, he wouldn't show until tomorrow. Being the boss of Seattle, he must have a lot on his plate today."

"Even if he knew his son was alive?" She asked.

"We don't know for sure he is alive," Jacob retorted. "We have to stay objective." Tara nodded and smirked slightly. The thought of Jacob staying objective was comical to her. This whole investigation, Jacob hadn't been objective when it came to Dominik Sloan. It was ironic to hear him lecture on objectivity. But he did have a point. Why give false hope if there was none?

She conceded to going back to the Sloan's mansion, but was still feeling ambivalent about it. There was still the matter of their own pursuers and because of this case, they barely had time to find out anything about them. That was another matter altogether. Jacob was right about one thing, though. One step at a time.

Chapter 29

The detectives left the gym a little after 1 pm. They needed to hurry to the Sloan's house if they were going to catch Dominik before the Ball. Jacob mentioned that the Ball started at 6pm, but as the head of Seattle, Dominik might leave earlier to oversee the festivities. To make sure he was at home, Tara called Bethany.

"Now's not really a good time to talk, detective," Bethany said after answering. "We have a lot to do and not much time to do it."

"I understand, but we need to figure out where your brother is," Tara replied. "Is your dad around?"

"Of course, he is," she stated, "but I don't think he will want to talk right now. He's getting fitted for his tux at the moment."

"It'll just take a minute," Tara argued. "We will be out of your hair in no time." Silence filled the receiver. "You there, Bethany?"

"I'm here," she responded. "You do know that it might not be safe for you to come here."

"We know," Tara replied. "But we are willing to take the risk."

"My father will be livid if another shooting happens, especially today," Bethany stated. "The Ball is in just a few hours."

Tara shook her head. Seriously, Tara thought. It seems the vampires care more for a stupid dance than finding out what really happened to Eric. Are all supernatural families this way?

"Look," Tara started, "Your brother may be alive, and your father may be able to help locate him. All we are asking is for a little help. Surely, finding your brother is more important than a stupid ball?"

"I thought you didn't want to tell my father about Eric yet?"

"We don't," Tara replied, getting irritated. "But your father may have information that could be helpful in locating him. We won't tell him what we've found. All we want to do is ask him a few questions."

Bethany sighed through the phone. "Fine," she whispered, "but you have to be gone by three. We will be setting up around that time, understand?"

"Thanks, Bethany," Tara said, and hung up the phone.

"I take it the vamp had an issue?" Jacob said grudgingly.

"Of course, but we have the okay to go question him." She looked down at her watch, "If we hurry." Jacob gave her a playful salute, then turned onto Denny towards Magnolia.

"So where is this ball going to take place, anyway?" Tara asked. She couldn't imagine a space large enough to house every supernatural creature in Seattle.

"At the Paramount Theater," he told her. "Everyone dresses for the event and, considering the guest list, there aren't many venues to host the party."

"And this is an annual event?" Tara asked. Jacob nodded.

"It started shortly after the treaty was signed. All the Royals thought it would boost cooperation and friendship between the clans and set aside differences."

"Did it work?" she asked.

"Not at first," he told her. "It's hard to let go of old grudges, but as time went on, most of the members forgot the war and new members, never experiencing the bloodshed, learned to coexist." Tara understood. It's hard to be prejudice against others when you don't know why.

Jacob continued. "There are still biases and such, but those are mostly harmless. The witches are like elephants, though. They will never forget what the wolves have done. Hence the banishment from their territory. But most get along when they can."

"I see," Tara said. "Seems to me that each clan we've talked to so far holds grudges. Sounds like the truce is a bit shaky," Tara said.

"Oh, it is," Jacob replied. "Has been that way for years now, yet most fear the reactions of the council, should anyone truly step out of line."

Tara could see why. They had Jacob's old partner killed just for dating him. What would they do if someone lashed out at a different clan? She didn't want to find out. She changed the subject. "So, every Royal family will be there?"

Jacob nodded his response. "And most of their subjects, though I'm not sure how many. I haven't attended in years, actually."

"Why not?" She asked, turning in her seat to look at him better.

"Well, like I said at Sloan's house, I believe that it's a form of slavery."

Tara did remember him saying that. "You said that they can either pay homage to the royals or get cast out on the street." Jacob nodded. "They wouldn't really throw one of their own away, would they?"

Jacob shrugged. "I'm not sure. You see...," he said, but didn't get a chance to finish. A black SUV smashed into the driver side door, rocking the car sideways and causing the detectives to whiplash around in their seats. Tara hit her head hard on the passenger side window, cracking it.

She was barely conscious but aware that she was bleeding from her head. Pain erupted and spasmed from her wound and her eyes filled with a bright light before slowly fading to black. The last thing she saw before the darkness took her was Jacob's body bleeding from the neck as a large shard of glass protruded out of it. She reached out a wobbly hand toward Jacob before passing out.

Chapter 30

Tara woke to a particularly strong smell of vinegar and fish, causing her to gag. Her head was woozy and she could barely see. Her body ached all over and it was hard for her to move her head. Out of the darkness, a figure walked toward her.

"Finally," the figure spoke. "I was worried you had lost too much blood to wake." The voice was high pitched and sweet. As Tara's eyes focused more, so did the figure in front of her. It was a beautiful woman in a red dress. Her black hair was tied in a bow while the front hung in wavy curls. She was thin and couldn't have weighed more than 120 lbs. She looked like someone Tara knew, but couldn't place her.

"How are you feeling?" The woman asked her innocently. Tara tried to speak but her mouth was numb and dry. She licked her lips as best she could and found that she was drooling.

"Oh, the numbness should subside any minute now," the woman explained, pacing back and forth. "I had to give you a strong sedative or you'd have bled to death."

Tara tried to move, but found her arms and legs were bound to a wooden chair. Suddenly, she was more alert. She mustered up as much strength as she could and managed to speak.
"Whe...whe...re...am... I?"

"At my place," the woman answered. Tara lifted her head as best she could and tried to look around. She managed to move her eyes back and forth. She saw she was in a darkened room filled with fishing crates and boxes. Wooden posts protruded from the ground high into the ceiling. That was all she could make out.

"Who…are…you?" Tara whispered as her lips began to have life in them again.

"Oh, how rude of me," the woman said. "Where are my manners. My name is Lilith. Lilith King."

Tara's eyes flashed wide with shock. That is where she recognized her. It was Yvette's mother. The resemblance was striking and she looked like an older version of her daughter.

Tara tried to move but the ropes held strong. The more she moved, the tighter they seemed to get. She felt a tingling sensation in her hands and feet as the ropes continued to cut off her circulation. "What do you want?"

"Me?" Lilith answered, raising a hand to her chest. "Nothing. From you anyway. But a promise is a promise, dear."

Promise? What Promise? She had no idea what Lilith was talking about. She remembered being in the car talking to Jacob, then someone crashed into them. She remembered Jacob bleeding. Suddenly she became very alert. "Jacob! Where's my partner?"

"The exile? He's fine, dear. Sleeping if you will," Lilith said, waltzing over to Tara. She grabbed the back of the chair and turned it around with ease to show a large metal cage covering half the room. Inside was her partner hanging limply from his wrists, bleeding and broken against the wall.

"Jacob!" Tara screamed, twisting against the itchy ropes trying to break free. It was no use. The ropes held.

"You should just kill her and get it over with," a deep male voice echoed from behind her. She turned her head to the side, but couldn't see who it was.

"That might have been the plan," Lilith replied, "but now she is promised to someone else. Understand?"

"Fine," the male said. "But I don't have to like it."

"You'll have to forgive my colleague here," Lilith told Tara while staring deep into her eyes. "Death gives him much more pleasure than I can stand. He just doesn't understand the big picture."

Tara wondered what she was talking about. Big picture? Promised to someone else? What the hell was going on?

Lilith turned the chair around once again and Tara saw the man that spoke. She gasped as she recognized him immediately. He was young looking, about 20 years old or so, with curly blonde hair, like his father's. He was pale, like the rest of his family, with bright sapphire eyes and full red lips. He too bore a striking resemblance to a china doll. It was Eric Sloan.

"Surprised to see me, detective?" he asked, smiling cynically. She was scared and wasn't sure what was going to happen, but she needed time to stall. She tried for witty banter.

"Alive, no, not really," she admitted. "Here, with Lilith? Yes"

He frowned slightly. "Not surprised to see me alive?"

"Not at all," she told him. "Considering the dead body we uncovered was actually David Marx." She gave him a sly smile. He seemed to falter a little but quickly recovered.

"How do you know that?" he asked, walking towards her.

"Well here's a tip. Next time you want to fake your own death, maybe you shouldn't use a shapeshifter. They have a bad habit of transforming back into their original state after a while."

Lilith gave him a harsh look. "I told you that you killed him too quickly! If this causes my plans to be delayed…"

He raised his hands to calm her. "It won't, I assure you. The ball is happening just as we've planned and nothing will stop what's to come."

"For your sake, you better hope that's true," she threatened. Tara noticed real fear on the boy's face, but he quickly shook it off.

"Is that what this is about?" Tara asked. "A stupid dance?"

Lilith laughed maniacally. "Silly girl, heavens no!" she walked over to Tara and leaned in close enough to feel her hot breath on her skin. "I don't care about the ball. I care that Dominik will be there. And the Dradogian."

Tara started putting the pieces together. Bethany told her that the Dradogian imbues them with more power. Whoever controls the Dradogian also controls Seattle. "So, you want to be in charge of Seattle?"

Lilith laughed again. "I don't care to be worshiped or feared like Dominik is. My motives have nothing to do with power." Tara didn't understand. If she didn't want the Dradogian for power, then why did she want it?

Lilith continued. "Now, as a detective, let's see how good you are," she said sweetly. "Tell me why I would want the Dradogian?"

"I know Dominik and Bethany won't go down without a fight, and considering how they hold the Dradogian, I'm guessing it's gonna hurt." Tara glared at Lilith with anger in her eyes. "A lot."

Lilith stared at her for a moment, her smile never swaying. She blinked her eyelids, then another set of eyelids blinked from the sides of her eyes. Tara saw the same thing happen on Yvette last night and it was equally as creepy then as it was now.

Lilith reached into her bosom and produced a small dagger. She turned Tara around again, walked lightly to the cage and opened it. She knelt over Jacob's unconscious body and held the dagger to his throat. Tara screamed loudly.

"Answer my question, girly, or your partner dies, right here!" Lilith explained. She smiled sweetly as if she was a teacher greeting her student in the morning.

"What do you want to know?" Tara asked desperately.

"Tell me what you have figured out so far? Why would I want the Dradogian?" She demanded with a crazed look in her eye.

"I know Eric faked his own death," she said gasping at the knife. "I'm guessing he got close to David in order to use him as a cover."

"It could have gone either way," Eric told her. "It was either David or that Curtis guy. And since Curtis had already left for the day, I chose David." Tara turned her head towards him. "It worked, but I didn't expect him to turn back into himself."

"You slept with them in order to gain their trust. How did you convince David to become you?" Tara asked.

"Ah, that was pretty tricky," Eric said laughing slightly. "Curtis told me one time that he had a thing for twins. Since the two of them were dating, I convinced David to turn into me so we could surprise Curtis and fulfill one of his fantasies. David loved the idea, since we already had a 3-way. It turned out perfect for me."

Tara felt like she was going to be sick. "You are a twisted son of a bitch." Eric walked up to Tara and slapped her with an open palm. Pain shot up her face and she felt blood on the inside of her mouth. She managed to spit some of it out on the ground.

"None of that, love," Lilith ordered. "She is already injured from the accident. My beloved wants her with as few bruises as possible." Eric bowed to Lilith, then stepped back out of view. "He certainly has a temper, doesn't he?" she tsked at Tara. "If I were you, I would try not to insult the undead."

"If I'm promised to someone, why send people to try to kill us at the Cafe? Why send people into Dominik's house?" Tara asked.

"Ah, yes, about that," Lilith started. "Originally the plan was to kill you. We couldn't have you gallivanting around actually solving the murder before the ball happened, now could we? What happened if you actually succeeded and warned Dominik of what's to come?"

Lilith traced the tip of the blade along Jacobs skin. "But then, my master saw something in you and decided against it. My master wants you, and look! Here you are?"

"I still don't understand why we can't kill the exile," Eric stated. "He is of no value at all, and I am getting bored."

"Patience, love," Lilith cooed. "He is leverage over the girl." She looked back at Tara. "Vampires are so impatient, don't you think? I mean, they have all eternity, yet they want things right away."

Tara glared at her, causing Lilith to switch her tone. She made a small slit of the knife along Jacob's arm. He let out a moan as blood dripped down his forearm and onto the ground. Tara screamed at her to stop.

"Don't you think?" Lilith asked louder, wiping the blood off her blade with the side of her dress.

"Yes!" Tara screamed at her. "Stop, please!"

Lilith lowered the knife by her side. "Continue, dear," She ordered Tara. "Why would I want the Dradogian?"

"Honestly, I don't know! I didn't even know you were involved until I woke up here!" Tara thrashed against the chair, trying to break free of the ropes, but it was no use. Lilith laughed at her as she glided over to her.

"That is such a pity," Lilith said dramatically. "She told me you were good. Hmm. Oh well, let me fill in the blanks then, shall I?" She bent down so she was eye level with Tara. She slid the blade back between her breasts and placed her hands on Tara's thighs.

"Here's a little bedtime story for you," Lilith said. "Once upon a time, there were a very peaceful people called Sirens who loved the water and all of its beauty. They traveled the oceans and seas for centuries exploring the creatures and different lands.

"During one of their explorations, they came upon a land that was quite beautiful and filled with other peaceful creatures. They became friends with the land and its people, and for a time, it was bliss."

Lilith drew closer to Tara's face, and she had to turn her head away. "Then the monsters came to the peaceful land. One's that drank the blood of the land dwellers, and stole a rare and powerful object from them. Can you guess what that object was, dear?" She looked deep into Tara's eyes, willing her to guess.

"The Dradogian," Tara muttered softly. Lilith smiled.

"Oh, you are good, aren't you?" She said sarcastically. "Other monsters came to the land as well, and sensing its power, began to fight amongst themselves for decades. Blood rained down from the skies as vampires fought against ogres, werewolves against witches, shapeshifters against sirens." Lilith swallowed hard.

"Now stop me if you've heard this part," she said standing up quickly. "Some of the monsters formed an alliance to put an end to the bloodshed peacefully. Others joined forces to eradicate their enemies.

"One particular day, as the peaceful Sirens met with the vampires to discuss how to put a stop to the war, the shapeshifters and the werewolves saw an opportunity and seized it. While the meeting took place, the treacherous monsters lit the building on fire, trapping the vampires and sirens inside. But the fire spread quickly throughout the city, and soon, most of Seattle was ablaze."

"You're talking about the Great Fire of Seattle? Back in 1889?" Tara asked. Lilith leaned on Tara and dug her claws into her legs. Tara let out a painful gasp.

"It's rude to interrupt," Lilith told her. "Can I tell the story, hmm?" Tara nodded as her eyes welled up tears.

"The vampires, tricky as they are, fled quickly from the burning building. The sirens couldn't move as fast, and though they came to end the war peacefully, the vampires left them there to die!" Lilith's face changed from beautiful to monstrous. She dug her nails deeper into Tara's leg and Tara screamed louder. Lilith stood up and started pacing again.

"Now, the queen of the sirens couldn't attend the meeting with the vamps that day, as she was busy giving birth to a beautiful baby girl. Her loving husband and her devoted daughter went in her stead. And do you know what happened?"

Tara shook her head quickly. Lilith frowned. "Oh I think you do, dear," Lilith said. Take a guess."

Tara licked her cracked lips and swallowed. "They died in the fire."

Lilith nodded. She stood still for a moment staring down at Tara, then started pacing once more. "By the time word got back to the queen, it had been too late. The fire destroyed much of Seattle. The monsters, seeing the destruction they had caused over their own desires, vowed to end the war. A treaty was signed and a council was formed, ending the bloodshed between all of them for good.

"But the queen of the sirens ached in her heart for her lost family. That heartache turned to hatred, and soon, she began to scheme against the vampires, shapeshifters, and werewolves for their betrayal. She vowed her revenge, and soon, found another who felt the pangs of loss," Lilith raised a hand toward Eric.

"You see, dear, the queen had no idea that her daughter had fallen in love with a vampire boy, and he with her. They grieved together, then soon, plotted together. A plan was made, and they bided their time until all the pieces came together."

Lilith stopped pacing and looked down at Tara once more. "And then you came along. You see, dear, the siren queen had a goddess on her side. One that she prayed to for centuries. The goddess talked to her, nurtured her, and guided her and her people. Although stuck in a metaphysical realm, the queen promised to give her goddess a body, and in return, the goddess would bring her family back."

Lilith's face turned menacing once more. "But before she could put her goddess in a body, the witches closed off Seattle around a barrier! They stopped my family from returning to me! So she waited, and waited, and then finally, the opportunity came. All that is about to change, now that you're here!"

Me? Tara thought. "What do I have to do with any of this?"

Lilith smiled, and Tara wished she could smack it off her face. "You're the key, my dear. Your blood can set my goddess free. It's your body she wants as her vessel." Lilith leaned in and whispered into Tara's ear. "And tonight, she will be reborn in you."

Tara struggled against the ropes as Lilith cackled madly. "I have one thing left to do, and that requires the Dradogian," she said.

"They'll never give it up," Tara yelled. "And you're a fool to think you could win against them."

Lilith smiled again. "Perhaps not, my dear. But the vamps have poisoned this world long enough. It's time to see how they like it," she said, blinking both sets of eyelids before turning toward Eric. "Get her ready," she ordered. "I want her freshened up for when I get back."

"I don't see why I can't go with you," he complained. "I want to see the look on my father's face when you kill him."

Lilith walked over to Eric and cupped his cheeks with her hands. "My sweet boy," she said soothingly. "We've been over this. You need to prepare the vessel while I take the Dradogian." He looked skeptical. "Don't worry, love," She assured him. "You will soon be back with Yasmine."

He stared at her as a child staring at his mother, then kissed her palm before nodding. Lilith took one last look at Tara. "If she resists, kill the shifter," she said, then walked upstairs out of the room. Eric smiled as Tara screamed.

Chapter 31

Eric walked slowly toward Tara and stopped just before her. "Cheer up, love," he whispered. "Just think of it as an initiation ceremony. One where you get the ultimate prize." He bent down and smiled widely.

"Why are you helping her?" Tara asked. Eric's smile turned into a sneer.

"Because Yasmine died thanks to my father. He turned his back on me when he chose to let her die. As far as I'm concerned, he can rot in hell," Eric screamed, spewing dribble onto Tara's face.

She cringed at his anger. She understood the pangs of love, but couldn't understand his logic. "That was over a hundred years ago. You can't possibly believe that this goddess will bring her back. Besides, aren't you dating Kenzie Wright?"

He huffed deeply. "Misdirection," he stated. "I needed my father to believe that I had moved on in order for him not to suspect."

"And what about Bethany?" Tara asked him. "Do you know how determined she was in finding your killer? She loves you. Are you going to let her die?"

He knelt down and grabbed her chin. His fingers dug sharply into her skin. "I love my sister," he said truthfully. "But she stood idly by while the love of my life screamed in pain as she burned!" He let go of her face and quickly turned away. "She deserves her fate."

Tara shook her head. She couldn't comprehend being in love so much that you would sacrifice your family in order to be with your love. She understood mourning the loss of a loved one, even being angry at his family, but this was taking it a bit far.

"Even if this goddess does bring back Yasmine, the council won't let you be with her. Look at what happened to my partner. He loved a human, and for that, they killed her. Do you really believe that they will let you two be together?"

He turned to her. "All of that won't matter after tonight. The Dradogian will be with Lilith, and whoever controls the Dradogian, controls Seattle." He looked down at the thin black watch on his wrist. "I think that's enough chit chat. It's time to get you ready."

He moved fast, faster than Tara had expected. Suddenly Tara was lifted off the ground, chair and all, and was being brought up the stairs. She twisted and thrashed frantically against the ropes that held her, but it was no use. She tried to roll forward to slow his momentum, but it was as if she was weightless and he held her with ease. She screamed at the top of her lungs, but only managed to make him squint.

"Scream all you like, love. There is no one else here," he told her. She continued to struggle against the ropes as he brought her into a small darkened room lit only by candlelight. He set her down gently in the middle of the floor. "That should do it."

Her eyes took a minute to adjust to the change in lighting. Once acclimated, she saw she was in the middle of a pentagram. At each point of the star stood a blazing candle enclosed with salt.

"So what?" Tara asked. "We just sit here and wait until Lilith brings back the Dradogian?"

Eric sneered at her. "She doesn't need to come back with it. Once the barrier is down, the goddess will fill you and you will be reborn."

"What's the Dradogian have to do with the witch's barrier?" She asked him.

He rolled his eyes. "You really know nothing of magic, do you?" He frowned at her, crossing his arms over his chest. "Those witches needed a powerful object in order to create and maintain the barrier. The only thing powerful enough and not burn up in the process is the Dradogian." He smiled again.

"But once that's gone, other creatures could come to Seattle," Tara explained.

"True," he agreed. "But the goddess is strong enough to protect us all." He laughed heartily. "Let them come. It will be a fatal mistake."

Tara shook her head. "Lilith will never get close enough to destroy the Dradogian! The ball will be filled with supernatural creatures. Do you really think that they will allow her to destroy it?"

Eric smiled cynically. "Unless she somehow took everyone out at once."

Tara's eyes went wide. Could Lilith do that? How could she? Would she risk killing everyone just to have her husband and daughter return? It was maddening. "But that's insane!" Tara screamed. "You're talking mass genocide! All just to bring back someone you loved over a hundred years ago?"

"Sacrifices have to be made," he retorted calmly. "Besides, every type of monster had a hand in Yasmine's death. They all deserve their fate." His look became maniacal and crazed. He truly was insane with love.

A door closed somewhere inside the house, causing both Eric and Tara to jump. "Hello?" a voice cried out. Tara started to scream, but Eric was suddenly there with a hand over her mouth. "Mother?"

Tara's eyes grew wide as she recognized the voice. It was Yvette.

"Shit," Eric whispered. "Just what I need." He ripped off part of his shirt with ease and stuffed it inside Tara's mouth. "Not one sound or your partner dies," he said, waving a plump finger in her face. Then he was suddenly gone.

"Hello?" Yvette called out, closer this time. Tara could hear the faintest of footsteps drawing nearer. "Anyone home?"

Tara had to do something quick. Would Eric risk killing Yvette? Probably not if he wanted to keep Lilith as a partner. But he could certainly knock her out. Tara twisted frantically against the ropes again. The chair budged forward slightly. If only she could break it somehow.

She used her body weight to try to shimmy the chair lose. It lifted a hair off the ground before crashing back down. She tried again, this time gaining more momentum. The chair moved higher off the ground but again, landed back neatly in its place. She tried one more time, this time with every ounce of her being. The chair hobbled on its side and balanced for a brief moment on two legs before her body weight forced her sideways. She hit the floor with a hard thud and moaned as the pain soared through her body.

Yvette must have heard the commotion. "Who's there?" she asked. The voice was right outside the door! Tara tried to scream, but only managed a few muffled sobs. The door handle jiggled. Tara tried to spit the gag out of her mouth, but it was lodged tightly in place.

The door opened just a crack and Yvette's head peered inside. "Oh my goodness!" she called out and burst through the door. "Tara! What's going on?"

Eric suddenly had Yvette in a headlock. Yvette was so stunned that she just stood there for a moment before she realized what was happening. Her eyes bulged and she grabbed at the arm around her neck.

"I'm sorry about this," Eric whispered in her ear as Yvette continued to flail about. "But Lilith would be upset if you helped the vessel escape."

Yvette's eyes were wide with panic, then turned a deep onyx black. She stopped convulsing and grabbed Eric's arm. She started to change. She was no longer Yvette. Her skin became a pale aquamarine and her hand grew long and grotesque. Her nails became black talons. Her face transformed, becoming overly smooth and her nose disappeared, revealing two tiny slits. Her teeth turned sharp like a shark. She bent down and bit Eric in the arm.

Eric screamed in pain as blood rushed out of his wound. He tried to shake the creature off him but she held on tight. Suddenly his body began to convulse and sway. He seemed to lose feeling in his body as his arm fell away from her neck. His eyes glazed over and his face became droopy.

Yvette let go of Eric as he swayed in place. He opened his mouth to speak but only drool came spilling down his chin. His legs began to quiver and he fell to his knees, swaying from side to side before finally falling over.

Tara's eyes grew wide with shock at the sight. The creature that was Yvette turned to her and came closer. Tara tried to scream but it was muffled behind the gag. The creature held up its talons. "It's alright, detective," the creature said behind Yvette's voice. 'It's me."

Tara stared in awe as the creature transformed back into Yvette. She bent down and took the gag out of Tara's mouth. Tara took in a huge gasping breath and coughed a couple times.

Yvette was kneeling down trying to untie the ropes at Tara's ankles. "Are you alright?" She asked anxiously.

Tara was staring at Eric's body as it spasmed against the floor. "What did you do to him?" she asked Yvette in a shaky voice. Yvette turned to look at Eric.

"Our saliva is a powerful paralytic," she answered. "He'll be alright in a couple hours. Bastard."

"How did you find me?" Tara asked as Yvette worked frantically at the ropes.

"Bethany called me," She explained. "Seems you and Detective Moore were supposed to meet at her place. She got worried when you didn't show." She almost had Tara's right wrist free. "Where is detective Moore?"

"Chained up in the basement," Tara told her. Yvette shook her head.

"When you didn't show up at the precinct, I called Tina Malcolm and asked her to do a locator spell. I was shocked when she told me you were here." Yvette finished with the knot on her wrists and helped Tara stand up.

"Not as shocked as you're going to be," Tara answered as Yvette helped to walked toward Eric. His eyes followed them as they drew closer.

"What do you mean?" Yvette asked.

"Your mother is going to kill everyone at the Ball tonight!" Tara told Yvette what happened with the car crash and what transpired downstairs in the basement. Yvette listened with utter horror on her face. The horror changed to sorrow and Yvette closed her eyes as tears ran down her cheeks.

Tara couldn't possibly understand all the emotions that were running through her. It's not every day that you find out your mother wants to commit mass genocide. Tara gave her a moment to grieve before she remembered her partner was hurt.

"Come on," she said. "Help me with Jacob." Yvette still had her eyes shut but nodded silently.

"How could she do that?" Yvette asked behind her palms.

"I'm sorry I had to be the one to tell you," Tara said gloomily.

"Not how, detective." Yvette lowered her hands. "But how. How will she kill everyone at the ball?"

Tara thought for a moment. "She said that the vamps have poisoned the world long enough." Yvette's eye's widened as a thought crossed her mind. "What?"

"She is very good at poison's," Yvette confided. "She even made a couple that have no detection properties. She could poison everyone and no one would ever suspect. I'm so sorry, Tara," Yvette said.

"You had nothing to do with it," Tara assured her. "It's not your fault. But we have to hurry before your mother succeeds."

"What do we do with him?" Yvette asked. Tara looked down at Eric and rage filled her. She wanted to stake him out of spite, but she wasn't a killer. She was a cop and swore to protect people, whether they deserved it or not.

"We'll chain him in the basement. Dominik can deal with him later."

The two women dragged his limping body down the stairs. When they reached the bottom, they dropped him hard against the floor as Tara ran to the cage. She tore it open and knelt beside Jacob. He was still unconscious. She checked his pulse and found a steady heartbeat. She breathed a sigh of relief as she fiddled with the cuffs. They wouldn't budge.

"Jacob," she said shaking him lightly. He groaned but didn't wake.

"He looks bad," Yvette told her. "He'll need to see a doctor quickly." Tara nodded and patted his face.

"Jacob, wake up. Please, Jacob. You have to wake up." He groaned again and this time managed to open his eyes. Upon seeing Tara, he mustered up a small smile. Tara let go of the breath she didn't realize she was holding.

"What...happened?" he choked out raspily.

"Later," Tara said "Right now we have to get you to a hospital. Do you think you can move?" Jacob didn't seem to have the strength. He tried to stand, but his legs gave way. Yvette caught him and helped him up. He became more aware after noticing he was chained up.

Tara studied the chains. Jacob's wrists were too large to slide through. She could probably slip through them with ease. An Idea came to her. "Jacob, I know you're tired and hurting, but we have to get you out of here. In order to do that, I'm going to need you to shift into me."

"What?" he asked her.

"Shift into me," Tara repeated. "It's so you can slip through the chains."

"Are you sure that is a good idea?" Yvette asked her. "Shifting takes energy, and right now it doesn't seem he has much. It could kill him."

"So what's the alternative?" Tara shot back. "Let him stay here and bleed to death? Do you have a better idea?" Yvette turned red and shook her head.

Tara took his hand. "Jacob, shift into me," she said, locking eyes with him. He stared blankly at her for a moment before nodding.

Jacob's face and body began to crack open. Yvette let out a startled gasp of disgust as Jacob's skin melted away. Jacob screamed in pain as new skin began to grow in patches over the exposed muscle and his hair turned red. Tara held his hand as he transformed into her. When it was complete, Jacob collapsed into unconsciousness.

Tara quickly slipped the chains off his wrists and pulled him away from the wall. With Yvette's help, they managed to carry him to the foot of the stairs. They dragged Eric inside the cage and did their best to bind him with the chains.

"That won't hold him," Yvette told her.

"Doesn't matter," Tara replied. "All we have to do is stop Lilith and their plan will fail."

They carried Jacob quickly but carefully up the steps and out of the basement. As they got closer to the front door, Tara noticed a massive painting of a cloaked woman with three crows circling her.

"Who's this?" Tara asked as she stared at the painting.

"That's the goddess Morrighan. My mother prays to her often," Yvette told her.

Realization hit her like a ton of bricks. This is the goddess that she was meant to be the vessel for. It was all connected. The dreams of the crows. The attack at Vita's house. It was all because of Morrighan.

"Come on," Yvette said, breaking Tara out of her daze. "We have to hurry." As they passed the painting, Tara could have sworn she notice the goddess wink at her.

They got Jacob into Yvette's car. "Get him to the hospital," Tara ordered. "I'll go after your mother."

"You'll need backup," Yvette warned. "My mother is a queen, and she is quite powerful. I can help you."

"Right now I need you to look after Jacob," Tara pleaded with her. "Please, Yvette." Yvette bit her lower lip and nodded.

"You'll still need help," Yvette said again.

"I got that covered." Tara whipped out her phone and searched for a contact she had put in last night. The lady answered on the third ring. "I need your help!"

Chapter 32

Yvette let Tara use her car after they got to the hospital. Tara wanted to stay with Jacob and make sure he would be okay but she didn't have time. The Ball had already started and she wasn't sure when Lilith would put her plan in motion. After helping Yvette bring Jacob to the emergency entrance, she sped away.

Traffic had slowed her down and she wished Yvette's car had a police siren. As it was, she was weaving in and out of traffic as fast as she could. She drove in silence, having nothing but her own thoughts for company.

How could Eric betray his family like that? Over a hundred years is a long time to hold a grudge. She understood Lilith's pain and her desire to have her family back. That made sense to her. But not Eric.

As she drove, she thought about her own parents. Would she be desperate enough to harm another if it meant she could have them back in her life? No, she told herself. She couldn't do it. She would hate herself forever.

Besides Jacob, she felt Bethany had become an actual friend. She knew that Bethany was only trying to get to the bottom of her brother's disappearance, but she felt they had connected beyond the standard police - victim aspect. Tara knew she shouldn't get too attached. Becoming attached could lead to mistakes, but she couldn't help worry about her.

Her heart started to race as the theater came into view. The sun was just setting and the sky started to crackle as storm clouds swept into the night's sky. Raindrops lightly pelted the windshield as she parked in front of the entrance. Two police officers ran to her, waving their hands and shaking their heads.

"I'm sorry, miss, but you can't park here," the taller, more muscular guard told her as she got out of the car. "There is street parking further down."

Tara whipped out her badge and raised it to his face. "Seattle P.D. I need inside asap."

The two guards exchanged glances. "Sorry officer, but this is a private event. Unless you have a warrant, I'm afraid I can't let you inside," the shorter, skinnier guard explained.

Tara got angry. Were these guards supernatural? She was betting so. She doubted that Dominik would have real police officers stand guard over such an important event. If she had to guess, she would bet they were werewolves.

"Look," she told them. "One of the guests is planning to kill everyone inside. You can stand here and argue with me or you can help stop it. I'm guessing Troy would reward you for helping prevent his death." The two guards exchanged glances again. "Either way, I'm going inside." She swept past them, bursting through the doors of the theater. The two guards came in right behind her. "Where's the ball?" She asked, turning to them.

"Third floor, second door to your left," the shorter guard told her. She nodded and started heading up the stairs. "What can we do to help?"

"Do you have a fire alarm here? We need to get everyone out as quickly as possible!"

Both guards nodded. "Yes, there's one near the maintenance desk," the taller guard answered.

"Pull the alarm. Help anyone who comes down. I'm going up." They moved quickly as she bolted up the stairs two at a time. The alarm blared loudly as she reached the third floor. She waited expectantly for people to head in her direction, but none came. Had she been too late?

She made her way to the second door and burst through it with her gun at the ready. Her heart was racing so fast that she could feel it in her throat. A look of shocked horror spread on her face as she saw hundreds of bodies lying on the floor, dead. Broken glasses of wine lay all around them.

In the heart of the crowd stood Lilith with a stake in her right hand. She bent over a body and raised the stake high into the air. Tara raised her gun and cried out, "Freeze, Lilith. Or I'll shoot."

Lilith looked over, startled, then smiled brightly. "You're too late, detective. I have the Dradogian now." Lilith raised her left hand out to Tara. In it was a small object attached to a chain. It looked like a crystal, but it wasn't exactly solid. It glowed a bright green and pulsated wildly.

Tara walked slowly toward Lilith, avoiding the bodies on the floor. "How could you do this to everyone? You would perform mass genocide just to get your family back?"

"The deed is done, detective," Lilith answered as the body on the floor let out a horrible groan. It was Dominik Sloan! "Take one more step and I'll plunge this stake into his heart!"

"You do that and I'll shoot you in the head," Tara warned. Lilith's eyes flickered to the gun in Tara's hands.

"Seems we are at a standstill then," Lilith replied sweetly. She blinked both sets of eyelids before looking down at Dominik.

Keep her talking, Tara told herself. If she destroys the Dradogian, then the barrier comes down and Morrighan is free to come. Keep her talking. "Tell me, Lilith, you said your family were peaceful beings. Is this what they would want? To be brought back by so many deaths?"

Lilith's smile faltered. She seemed to think about that for a moment, then she shook her head. "At least they'd be alive."

"But they'd hate you knowing they were the cause of wiping out most of Seattle's supernatural world. Think about it."

"They'd forgive me. In time," she screamed. "Now dear, it's time to end this." She raised the stake high above her head. Tara aimed and concentrated. Please, god. Don't let me miss, Tara thought to herself as she was about to pull the trigger. Lilith plunged the stake down but Dominik's hand caught her wrist. Lilith let out a surprised gasp as Dominik held her wrist tight. She tried to lower it but he was strong.

Tara bolted toward them as they struggled. Dominik was still weak and was losing the battle as Lilith leaned her body weight into her thrust. The stake inched it's way closer to his heart. Just as the tip of the stake pierced his chest, Tara slammed into Lilith and they went sprawling over. Lilith lost the grip on the stake and Tara lost her gun, flinging both high into the air.

Tara rolled over and braced herself on her palms. Lilith was already getting to her feet. She let out a defiant scream and transformed into her true self. Her skin became dark green and shimmered in the light from above. Her hands turned into talons and her face became smooth. Her eyes transformed into obsidian and her nose disappeared, leaving two small slits. She screamed again, revealing rows of sharp teeth.

Tara searched frantically for her gun as Lilith descended on her. Tara only had moments to react as Lilith grabbed at her legs. She rolled to her left, barely missing Lilith's talons. She scrambled to her feet, still searching for her weapon.

"Lose something, detective?" Lilith asked as she bent down and picked up Tara's .45. She began to laugh maniacally. Lilith aimed the gun at Tara but her talons couldn't find the trigger. Tara ran as fast as she could and bulldozed straight into Lilith's abdomen. Lilith let out an oomph as both of them crashed into the floor. Lilith's grip on the gun waned and Tara grabbed at it.

Lilith squeezed Tara around her left arm her talons pierced her skin. Tara let out a painful scream as blood seeped through the wounds. Lilith pulled sideways and Tara toppled over onto her back. Lilith got up swiftly. She gazed down at herself and tsked.

"Look at what you did to my dress," she screamed. "Do you know how hard it is to get blood out of anything? It's ruined for sure." She shook her head and tsked again. Tara scrambled backward as Lilith walked closer to her. Lilith's black eyes were like daggers as she clutched Tara's leg and, with surprising strength, flung her through the air. Tara let out an oomph of pain as she landed hard on her side and rolled into a body.

Tara laid there, dazed for a moment. The air had been knocked out of her and she concentrated on trying to breathe. She tried to get to her feet, but found it difficult. She braced herself, using the body on the floor for leverage and got to her knees. She looked over her shoulder and saw Lilith advancing toward her stake.

Tara mustered up all her strength and forced herself to her feet. She searched again for her gun and finally spotted it lying next to a masked body in a floral dress. She ran as fast as her legs would allow and plucked it from the floor.

"Lilith!" She screamed as she took aim. Lilith managed to find her stake and was now making her way to Dominik.

"Give it up, dear," Lilith uttered. "You've lost. The sacrifices have already been made! My goddess will be reborn and I will get my family back!"

"Not if I can help it," Tara warned and fired. The bullet left the .45 and shot Lilith in the left shoulder. The force of the impact sent Lilith backward and blood exploded behind her. She let out a surprising grunt as her left arm released the Dradogian and it went flying before coming down and shattering into pieces.

Lilith cupped her shoulder with her right arm but cackled madly. The light of the Dradogian exploded with such force that Tara had to shield her eyes. Green mist swirled around the shattered crystal.

"It is done!" Lilith cackled again. "The Dradogian is broken. The barrier is down!" She clasped her talons together and cheered gleefully. Tara, with utter horror on her face, realized what she had done. She frowned, staring at the mist. "Now, there is just one thing left to do," Lilith whispered to herself. She whirled around and limped to Dominik, stake at the ready.

Tara lunged at her, tackling her to the ground, but Lilith was ready. She used Tara's own momentum and sent her flying over her. Tara landed on top of a couple bodies.

"Stupid girl," Lilith screamed impatiently. Lilith raised her hands and uttered some words in a language Tara had never heard before. Water droplets began to form just above Lilith's palms. They grew in size as Lilith continued her chant. The water began to swirl into a massive ball. Lightning crackled inside the ball and Tara heard the boom of thunder.

Tara ran toward Lilith just as she threw the ball of water. Tara braced herself for the impact. Just as the water would have collided with her, the ball exploded, sending waves of water around Tara, leaving her untouched.

Lilith's shark like jaw gaped open at the sight. "How," she managed to say before Tara tackled her to the ground. She punched Lilith in the face, causing the slits to stream blood. Lilith roared in agony as Tara kept hitting her. Lilith tried to grab at Tara but her shoulder wound wouldn't allow it.

Tara clasped Lilith's head with both hands and banged it against the floor over and over again. Lilith let out a muffled scream before falling into unconsciousness. Tara gave her one last punch before the green mist hit her in the chest.

Tara rose high into the air and was turning over and over. The air was suddenly gone and she fought to breathe. Her chest became heavy as if someone had hit her hard with a metal bat. She writhed in agony as the mist swirled in and out of her suspended body. Fissures repeatedly broke through her skin and instantly healed. Then as quickly as it had happened, it had stopped. She collapsed down hard on the floor with a loud thud. She too fell unconscious.

Chapter 33

Tara's eyes bolted open as Bethany Sloan shook her gently. "Oh, thank god," Bethany exclaimed. "I thought you might have been dead." She bent down and hugged Tara tightly who winced in pain by her embrace. "Sorry," She said and quickly let go.

Tara's body felt like it had been hit by a semi. She tried to speak but her mouth was dry. She mustered up enough energy to lick her chapped lips, but that was all she could do.

"Are you alright?" Bethany asked. Tara managed a slight nod, and it hurt to move. Her head was pounding and her heart was thudding against her chest. Every muscle ached and she knew she would be sore for days to come. What the hell happened, she thought to herself. "Can you sit?"

Tara tried to get up, but she was glued in place. With Bethany's help, she managed to get into a sitting position without falling over and braced herself on her hands. Tara noticed Dominik was standing near her, and she was glad to see that Lilith hadn't finished him off. She looked past him and a small gasp escaped her lips as she saw the dead ballroom guests getting to their feet.

"You saved us," Dominik stated calmly.

Tara licked her lips and managed a slight nod. "You're welcome," she said with a hoarse voice

"But I don't understand," Bethany said. "What happened?"

"I can explain that," came a woman's voice. Tara managed to look beyond Bethany to see Vita waltzing toward them. She stopped just in front of Dominik. "Detective Bancroft gave me a call about an hour ago. She told me Lilith was behind your son's disappearance and was planning on killing everyone at the ball tonight with poison."

Dominik and Bethany exchanged worried glances. "You mean Lilith killed my son?"

"No," Tara whispered. "Eric's not dead." Tara tried to get to her feet but fell down. She grabbed onto Bethany's shoulder's and holstered herself up, leaning into Bethany for support. She told them as best as her voice would manage what happened over at Lilith's house. Dominik's mask of emotion faltered and his eyes narrowed into slits as he found out Eric had betrayed them.

"Eric tried to kill us?" Bethany asked as if she couldn't believe it. A tear filled her eye and she quickly wiped it away. Tara sympathized and squeezed her hand gently.

"How did you know she would try to poison us?" Dominik asked her.

"She mentioned that you Sloan's have poisoned this world enough and that it was your turn to see how you like it."

"So Tara called me for help," Vita interrupted. "I deduced that she could only poison everyone one of two ways. The first would be to put it in the ventilation system. But that didn't make sense. She would be poisoned along with everyone else. The next would be to put her poison in the food or drink. So I snuck to the kitchens and called out the poison."

"What do you mean you called out the poison?" Bethany asked.

"I forced the poison out of the food and into this," Vita answered, raising a small vial of reddish liquid. "It's a simple spell if you know what you're doing. Lucky for all of us that I happen to know what I'm doing."

"Then why was I knocked out?" Bethany asked her. "If you knew that Lilith was up to something, why didn't you tell us so we could all stop her?"

"Ah," Vita said. "I replaced the poison with a sleeping draught. I wanted Lilith to think that she had succeeded in her plan until Tara could show up and stop her."

"How did you know I would?"

"Call it intuition," Vita replied, then winked.

"Your intuition almost got me staked," Dominik said serenely. Vita became still and slowly glanced into Dominik's eyes. "Lucky for you that your intuition was right. Explain to me why you didn't come to me immediately?"

Vita stared at him with abject terror. She opened her mouth to speak, then closed it. She blinked before taking in a deep breath. "I'm sorry I didn't include you, sir, but an animal is most dangerous when it's cornered. If Lilith found out her plan hadn't worked, who knows what harm she could have done. This way everyone survived and no one was seriously hurt."

"I beg to differ," Tara stated. All eyes turned to her as she tried to move. Vita walked up beside her and uttered a few words in Latin. She made a hand gesture and Tara's body filled with a warmness she hadn't experienced before. Suddenly the aching stopped. She could move freely.

Tara was in the process of thanking Vita when a high pitched voice echoed over hers. "What the hell is going on here, Sloan?" Isis Thompson stomped her way over to them. She wore a pink cut off dress with a black floral pattern that now had a purple stain down the front. "Look at my dress! It's ruined! I hope you're paying my dry cleaning!"

Bethany turned to her in anger. "My father didn't do this! If you want someone to blame, then blame that bitch!" Bethany pointed to Lilith's unconscious body. Isis glanced over at Lilith and then at Tara. A look of confusion spread over her face. The crowd behind her started pointing and whispering to each other. As Tara scanned the crowd, she saw the same confused look on most of them. No one knew what had happened.

"I think it's time to address the guests, don't you?" Vita asked Dominik.

"I think that's wise, witch," Anton Wright said appearing beside Isis. He wore a large black tuxedo with a blue tie. The tux clashed with his mangy beard and frazzled hair. His scar stood out prominently against the color of the tie. Isis nodded her agreement.

Troy Lynch hurried over to them in a brown suit that matched his eyes. "The crowd is getting restless, Sloan," he told them. "Whatever you're gonna do, it better be quick or they will eat you alive." Tara wondered if he meant that literally.

The whispers turned into a loud uproar as many of the guests began accusing their neighbors. Some began fighting amongst themselves and Tara watched helplessly as the crowd's fear and anger spread like a tidal wave.

"Vita. If you will," Dominik said calmly. Vita nodded her head, then raised her hands above her. She whispered something in Latin, then clapped her hands. A thunderous boom echoed throughout the ballroom and everyone covered their ears. Tara's head felt like it was going to explode and it took effort to stay on her feet.

The chatter died immediately as the crowd quivered and coward backward in fear. They turned their attention to Dominik.

"Ladies and Gentlemen," Dominik walked forward slowly as he addressed them. "I know you all are frightened by this unexpected change in events, but rest assured, you are all safe now."

"What happened to us?" A young man dressed in an outlandish green suit asked. The crowd murmured their agreement and demanding answers. Dominik raised his hands and the crowd quieted down.

"We are in the process of finding that out ourselves," he explained. "As it is, I am afraid the ball is over for now." More murmurs erupted and Dominik spoke over them. "I ask each and every one of you to meet with your leader tonight to discuss this event. We will know more by then."

The crowd roared in protest. They wanted answers now and wouldn't take no as one of them. Dominik turned to Vita and nodded. She clapped her hands once again and the boom echoed throughout the room. Everyone hushed at once.

"We can debate this here and now, but since your leaders stand beside me on this matter, I think it wise you follow their wishes. To go against them could have disastrous consequences for you." The crowd shrank back slightly.

Tara was awestruck at how much control Dominik had over them all. What would happen if someone didn't follow their leader's instructions? She shuddered to think. Seems the crowd did as well as their faces trembled with fear.

After scanning the crowd, Dominik seized the chance to gain control again. "Please, give us the opportunity to find out what has transpired. We will tell you all everything, later on, tonight. I promise you that."

A few members whispered amongst themselves, but most nodded their compliance. Seems Dominik's threat had worked. They were more afraid of their leaders than what happened to them tonight. Tara didn't know if that was a good thing.

Dominik turned to Bethany. "Bethany, can you please escort our guests out?" Bethany started to protest but Dominik's eyes narrowed on her and she thought better of it. She rolled her eyes in defiance, then turned pleasantly toward the crowd.

"If you will each follow me; I will show you out." She weaved into the crowd and they turned to follow as she swept by. One by one, the crowd diminished, whispering and murmuring to each other.

Dominik, Vita, Troy, Isis, and Anton stayed behind with Tara. As the crowd hurried out the door, Anton spoke. "What the hell happened?"

"That's a good question," Troy replied. Isis nodded.

"I think it best to let the detective tell you," Dominik answered. "You all have met Detective Bancroft, I assume?" They nodded and all eyes turned to Tara. She hated being put on the spot. "Detective, please tell us what has happened."

Tara swallowed loudly and began telling them about interviewing each of them. She left out the Tarot card reading and the bird attack. Vita seemed to nod in response to her omission. She told them about the shapeshifter David and how he had been tricked into turning into Eric, but left Curtis out of it. She guessed he wouldn't want Isis to find out he was gay that way. When she told them about the car crash and Jacob being chained up, Isis's face turned from skeptical into worrisome.

"Is he alright?" she asked apprehensively.

"He's at the hospital now," Tara replied. "Yvette is looking after him." She continued her story about how Yvette saved her from Eric and how they locked him up in the basement. Dominik's face was utterly neutral throughout her story, but she was guessing he was dealing with some serious heartache.

She told them about calling Vita for help and arriving at the ball. "Once I got here, I thought Lilith had succeeded. You all were dead. She had the Dradogian in one hand and a stake in the other." She told them about fighting with Lilith and how the Dradogian shattered. Their jaws dropped open at the premise of the Dradogian being destroyed.

She told them about Lilith throwing her water ball at her and how it seemed to have hit an invisible force field. Vita beamed at her. "So my necklace worked?"

"What?" Tara asked.

"My necklace I gave you. I told you while you wear it, no magical harm can come to you." Vita smiled brightly. "Sensing a magical attack, the necklace made it to where the water ball exploded around you instead of hitting you."

"Ah," Tara finally understood. "Good deal." She continued her story. She recalled what happened after tackling Lilith and how the mist of the Dradogian enveloped her. Vita held a hand to her mouth.

"You saved us," Isis stated with shock in her voice.

"Anton smiled. "You are strong, like Ogres." He patted her on the back, congratulating her, which nearly sent her flying, but Vita held her still.

"Thank you, Tara," Troy told her. "On behalf of all the wolves, thank you." Dominik nodded his appreciation, then turned to look at Lilith's unconscious body. The rest of them followed suit.

"What do we do with her?" Isis asked Dominik. "I'd like to skin her for having a part in one of my shapeshifter's death."

"You can't!" Tara protested. "She needs to answer in a court of law."

Anton sneered loudly. "You are funny, human," he said. "I didn't know humans could be funny."

"I'm not joking," Tara retorted. "She needs to stand trial for her crimes. She almost committed genocide!"

"And how do you explain that to a human jury?" Dominik asked. Tara didn't know what to say. Dominik continued, "Do you feel that a human cell could hold the queen of the sirens?"

Tara thought about it. She pictured Lilith transforming into her siren form and throwing water balls at the other inmates. She wouldn't be able to lock her up, not without exposing the supernatural world. Unless…

"Vita? Do you think you could do some sort of witchy woo and keep her locked into her human form?"

"You can't be serious?" Isis shouted. "That's absurd!"

Vita ignored Isis's outburst. "I might have been able to, but the Dradogian was destroyed." Isis seemed to relax a bit. Her eyes fixated on Lilith with murderous intentions. "Why don't you try it, detective?"

"What?" Tara asked. The rest turned to look at her.

Vita continued. "If I'm right about the Dradogian, then I believe you have the power to hold Lilith's form." Tara stared at her quizzically. What was she talking about? She was human and possessed no magical ability. How could she keep Lilith locked up in a human form? The rest of the group seemed to be thinking the same thing.

"You think the Dradogian became a part of her," Dominik stated solemnly. Troy gasped. Isis let out a tsk.

"Don't be absurd!" Isis told them. "The Dradogian can't become a part of anyone. It's magical energy. That crystal barely held its power." She laughed uneasily.

"Something happened, though," Anton replied, studying Tara. "The Dradogian has never collided with a human before. At least not that I am aware of." Vita nodded in agreement.

"According to the Conservation of Energy, energy cannot be created nor destroyed. It can only be altered from one form to another." She swallowed hard enough for Tara to hear it. "It might simply have transferred itself into a new host."

"No fucking way!" Tara screamed. "I feel the same. If I held the Dradogian, wouldn't I be able to feel it?" Everyone turned toward Vita as if she was the expert on such matters. Tara continued. "Besides, I was wearing your necklace. I thought no magical means could harm me."

"Vita shrugged sympathetically. "I'm not sure, to be honest. As Anton said, this is an unprecedented event. I made the necklace with the power of the Dradogian. Maybe once the crystal was broken, it sensed a part of it on you and needed a place to go."

"So mist can sense things, now?" Tara asked. She wasn't sure why she was angry, but she was. She didn't want to be anything but human. If the Dradogian altered her in some way, what did that mean? Was she still her?

"There is one way to settle this," Troy stated. They turned to look at him. "I say we let the detective try. If she succeeds in holding Lilith in human form, then we know the Dradogian is a part of her now."

Isis cleared her throat. She opened her mouth to say something, but closed it. Anton nodded his agreement. "Seems the choice is up to you, detective," Dominik said. Tara bit her lip.

There is no way, she thought to herself. I'm a normal human. But a nagging feeling started in the pit of her stomach. It spread like wildfire over her as she thought about it logically. What if Vita was right? What if the Dradogian did transfer its power to her?

She gave Dominik a nod and he stepped aside, revealing Lilith's body on the floor. Tara really did a number on her. Lilith's face was covered in blood and her dress was soaked through. She was still in her siren form and the blood clashed against her dark green skin.

Tara knelt beside her. Vita did the same. "What do I have to do?" Tara asked.

"Close your eyes and concentrate on Lilith," Vita guided. "See her as she is when she is human." Tara obeyed. She closed her eyes and pictured Lilith. She held that picture clearly in her mind. "Now push that image into Lilith," Vita took her hand and placed it on Lilith's forehead. "Here."

Tara imagined Lilith transforming back into her human self. She sensed something, an overwhelming feeling she couldn't quite explain. Her hand began to tingle. The air around her grew heavy as if she had waded into a dense smoke. It filled her lungs and she held back the urge to cough. The tingling spread throughout her body. She became dizzy again. Her head swirled and she began to hear buzzing inside her. The buzzing grew louder as if thousands of bees had built a hive in her head. She cried out as the buzzing became unbearable. Then all of a sudden, the feeling left her with a powerful jolt and she thrashed forward. She felt it pass from her and into Lilith.

Lilith cried out in pain as the energy passed into her, then she began to change rapidly back into her human form. Tara didn't see it, not exactly. She sensed it happening. She heard gasps as the remaining ballroom members watched in shock and horror. Tara collapsed into Vita's right shoulder, completely exhausted. Panting heavily, Tara opened her eyes. Lilith was completely human.

"How can this be?" Isis asked with a quiver in her voice. She looked down at Tara as if seeing her for the first time. Behind her eyes, Tara noticed something hidden there. It was fear.

"She holds the Dradogian," Dominik said blankly. The other remaining masters stood quietly over her. None of them knew what to say. Silence filled the ballroom. It was deafening.

Lilith woke up gasping for breath. Everyone looked into Lilith's startled eyes. Seeing everyone standing over her, Lilith began to cry.

Chapter 34

Tara walked quietly to Jacob's hospital room, or rather her room, as Jacob still appeared to be her. When she arrived at the hospital, many orderlies and nurses let out startled cries upon seeing her walk by. She told the nurse at the front desk she was there to see her twin sister. The woman gave her a suspicious glance, but told her which room she was in.

Tara knocked lightly on the door and walked in to see Jacob lying on the bed hooked up to tubing. She let out a surprised gasp at seeing her body like that. Jacob's neck, or rather her neck to be more precise, was bandaged with gauze. He had bruises and welts over his face and arms from the car crash. But at least he was alive.

Yvette was sleeping in a chair next to him and Tara didn't know if she should wake her. Jacob was sleeping as well and she thought it best to return in the morning. She turned to leave when she heard her voice call out to her.

"I'm glad to see you are alive," Jacob said behind her voice. She whirled around to see herself staring at her. She put on her best sympathetic smile.

"Same to you, partner," she whispered. She walked over and gently squeezed his hand. "You had me worried there for a while." Jacob tried to sit up, and Tara gently helped as much as she was able.

"Tell me you caught the bitch," he said and it came out harsh and raspy. Tara smiled weakly and nodded.

"It's over. We can now return home without fear of being ambushed."

"Good," he said. "I miss my bed." He coughed a couple of times and gently rubbed his bandaged neck.

"You look like hell," she told him.

"You mean you look like hell, don't you?" He winked at her and she blushed.

Yvette woke up, startled. She looked around as if she had forgotten where she was until she saw both Tara's staring at her. "Detective Bancroft, you're here."

Tara nodded. "Thanks for staying with him." Yvette pursed her lips and nodded.

"My mother? Is she...?"

"She's alive, Yvette," Tara answered. Yvette let out a breath she hadn't realized she'd been holding and closed her eyes. She nodded her thanks.

"The others?" Jacob asked, his face full of concern.

Tara smiled and squeezed his hand once more. "Everyone's alive. Including your mother." Jacob beamed at her. A silent tear rolled down his cheek.

"What happened?" Yvette asked, her full attention on Tara.

Tara turned and shut the door. She wanted to explain what transpired away from listening ears. She recalled the night's events while both Jacob and Yvette listened with rapt attention. Yvette squinted her face when Tara told them she had to shoot Lilith. Tara apologized for it but Yvette held her hand up.

"It's alright, detective. I understand."

"Still, it is your mother," Tara whispered sympathetically.

Yvette shrugged indifferently. "We cannot choose our family, nor are we responsible for their actions. Her pain turned into anger and she let it get the best of her. Those actions had consequences, whether good or bad, and she has to live with it. You did the right thing in stopping her."

Tara nodded her understanding and continued her story. When she finished, both were staring at her with gaping mouths. Tara shifted uncomfortably waiting for one of them to process everything.

"You hold the Dradogian?" Jacob asked behind wide eyes. Tara nodded silently. She still couldn't believe it herself. She felt the same but somehow, she was different. She had no idea what that meant for the future. "Vita said she would help me channel its power, should I ever need to use it, but I just want it out of me."

"Is that possible?" Yvette asked. "If you and the Dradogian are blended, it might be in your DNA. Transferring it out of you might not be possible." Tara shrugged.

Silence filled the hospital room once more. Then Jacob laughed in Tara's voice, "I wish I could have seen my mother's face when you turned Lilith back to her human form!"

Tara cracked a smile. "She was pretty shocked." Both laughed loudly at that. Yvette stared at them in wonderment.

"What happened after the ball?" Yvette asked once the laughter subsided. "To my mother, I mean?"

"I arrested her. After everyone realized I held the Dradogian inside me, no one seemed to have the will to try to stop me. I think they were worried I'd turn them into a toad or something."

"So she's in a human prison?" Jacob asked. Tara nodded. "Is that wise? She can't shift but she knows about all of us. What if she spills her guts out?"

"So what if she does?" Tara asked. "She was arrested for the murder of Eric Sloan and for trying to poison a bunch of people. If she mentions anything without being able to use her powers, it will just sound like utter nonsense; the ravings of a lunatic. Who would believe her?"

"And what of Eric?" Yvette asked.

"I don't know. Dominik sent someone to bring him home. I didn't stick around to find out if they got him. I had more important matters to deal with." She gave Jacob a broad smile.

A knock at the door startled them all. The door opened a crack and Isis Thompson peered inside. "Am I interrupting?"

Jacob's eyes widened in shock. He was speechless as the door widened and Isis walked in followed by Curtis holding Rhea. Adam came up the rear.

"Jakey!" Rhea yelled. Curtis put her down and she half ran, half jumped onto Jacob. He winced in pain but smiled as she hugged him tightly.

"Rhea, get down!" Isis ordered, picking her up and handing her back to Curtis. She struggled a little but put her arms around Curtis's neck for support.

"My, my," Adam said. "Don't you look like death hung over." Curtis shot him a warning glance.

"What are you all doing here?" Jacob asked behind Tara's voice. He was still stunned to see them all. Isis turned to the real Tara.

"You didn't tell him?"

"I was getting to it, but you got here before I could," Tara replied. She shifted her stance in defense.

"Tell me what?"

Adam smiled, and it was cynical. "Oh, can I tell him, mother? I can't wait to see the look on his face. He'll probably die of a heart attack here and now!" Tara shot him a disapproving glance. He winked back at her. Isis held up her hand and he became perfectly still.

"Tell me what?" Jacob repeated.

"Well, after I stopped Lilith, your mother and I had a little chat," Tara said. Isis walked up to Jacob and squeezed his hand. A faint glow emanated around their cupped hands.

"I thanked your partner for saving our lives." Isis looked at Tara then back down at Jacob. "I asked her if there was anything I could do to repay her. You know how I hate being in someone's debt."

Jacob nodded. "Okay...," he said, still unclear as to what was happening.

"I told her there was only one thing I wanted in return," Tara stated in an almost bored like tone, examining her nails. Then she turned to Jacob with a big smile. "For you to be free to rejoin your family."

Jacob gasped. His eyes widened and his jaw dropped. Adam snickered at the expression on his face but quickly stopped when Isis looked at him. "You mean...,"

Isis nodded. "You are no longer an exile." She bent down and gave him a hug. "Welcome home, Jacob."

"Welcome back, brother," Curtis said, nodding to him. Rhea shrieked with glee.

"Although I liked you better when you were verboten, I have to admit it'll be nice to see you without all that pesky sneaking around," Adam said. Isis turned on him quick. "Only joking, mother. Yay, your son is back." Isis's eyes narrowed, but turned back to Jacob. Tara noticed Adam's forehead had started to sweat. She smiled at his discomfort.

Yvette cleared her throat. She stood up as everyone looked at her. "I think that's my cue to leave." She gave Jacob a nod and patted him on his arm. "I'm glad you're going to be alright." She walked to the door.

"I should leave too," Tara told them.

"Aw, but the party's just getting started," Adam said, playfully. "I was going to braid Jacob's hair while Curtis did his makeup. We were going to take funny pictures and post them all over the internet!" Curtis turned and slugged his brother in the arm. Adam let out a small gasp and rubbed it. Rhea giggled madly.

"That's enough, boys," Isis warned. They stopped immediately. She turned to Tara. "Thank you for getting him to the hospital." Isis grabbed Tara around the shoulders and hugged her tight.

Tara turned a deep shade of pink. "You're welcome?" She replied awkwardly, then turned to Jacob. He was smiling wryly at her and if he hadn't looked as bad as he did, she would have slugged him in the arm.

"I'll stop by tomorrow to check on you," she told him once Isis let go. He nodded his appreciation.

"See you tomorrow, Tara." She walked out with Yvette. They walked in silence for a brief moment before Yvette stopped.

"Thank you for not killing my mother," She said sheepishly. "I know it could not have been easy after everything."

"Killing the woman who wanted to murder a bunch of people? Who kidnapped me and wanted some goddess to possess me? Naw," Tara jested. "Why would I want to do that?"

Yvette cracked a shrewd smile. "You're a good woman," she told Tara, who just shrugged. Her cell phone rang, causing her to jump at the sound. Tara fished it out of her pocket and held up a finger to Yvette as she answered.

"Detective, it's Dominik Sloan," Tara was surprised to be hearing from him so soon.

"Is everything alright, Mr. Sloan?" She asked.

"Everything's fine. I was just wondering if you had a moment to talk. Could you come to the house tonight?"

Tara was physically and mentally exhausted. All she wanted to do was crawl into her own bed and sleep for a week. "Can this wait until tomorrow?"

"It could, detective," he replied. "But I believe it would be better tonight given everything that has happened. I'll have Walter make you some tea."

"Alright," Tara replied shaking her head. "I'll be over as soon as I can."

"See you then, detective." He hung up.

"What was that about?" Yvette asked.

"That was Mr. Sloan. He wants to see me tonight about something," Tara told her. "Not sure what."

"Now?" Yvette glanced at her watch. "At this hour? He does realize that you're not a vampire, right?"

Tara shrugged. "Can I get a ride?"

Tara sat inside the library next to the blazing fire Walter had turned on inside the fireplace. He placed a tray of tea on the table and Dominik uttered his thanks. Walter bowed his head and headed for the door. Dominik poured tea into a Victorian floral pattern tea cup and handed it to Tara.

"Thank you for coming in so late," Dominik said once Walter had left. "I can imagine that you are extremely exhausted after these last few days." Tara nodded and took a sip of her tea. It tasted sweet and herby. Dominik continued. "I asked you here because the council has a proposition for you."

"The council," Tara said aloud. "Go on."

"We would like to offer you a seat on the council."

Tara nearly dropped her teacup. "What?" She asked. That makes no sense. I'm human, she thought. Why would they want a human on a council full of monsters?

"I can see that I've caught you off guard," Dominik said.

"Just a little, yes," she said truthfully. "Why do you want me? I don't know enough about your laws and regulations to be of any help." Dominik smiled at her pleasantly. "I'm human."

"That is why we want you, detective. Because you are human."

"Come again?" She asked.

"You saved us tonight. You saved all of us. You didn't have to, but you did. A human, with no magical ability, took down the queen of the sirens and saved all of Seattle's supernatural creatures." He took a sip of his tea. "You know of our kind and have fought to protect us."

She held up her hand to stop him. "I was just doing my job. Anyone would have done the same."

"Maybe," he replied. "Maybe not. In any case, none of us had a clue as to what Lilith was up to until it was too late."

"Yeah, well in my experience, evil masterminds rarely let people in on their plans," Tara told him.

He smiled again. "That is what I'm talking about. You have experience with these sorts of things and have remained unafraid. You are smart and determined. The council could use someone with your specific expertise."

She thought about it. Besides being human, she wouldn't have allowed Jacob's last partner to be drained just for being his lover. She wouldn't have been able to exile him for falling in love with a human. It just seemed like a bad idea.

"I heard what you did to Jacob's last partner," she stated flatly. "You all have a way of thinking that is foreign to me. I wouldn't be able to hold my tongue if you all made decisions I wouldn't agree with."

"That would be another reason to join, wouldn't it?" he argued. "You could be the voice of reason against the sea of uncertainty. You are human, with a human mind and heart. We do not have such understandings. Not anymore. But you do."

Tara didn't know what to say. She changed the subject. "Did you find Eric at Lilith's house?"

Dominik became slack and his face was hidden behind his usual neutral mask. "No," he replied stoically. "Seems the cage in the basement wasn't meant to hold vampires." She let out a tiny gasp. "We will find him eventually."

"And when you do?" Tara asked. "What will you do to him?"

Dominik smiled again. "Well, detective, that depends on you, doesn't it? I mean, you know what the council is capable of. What do you think they would want to happen to him?"

Tara stared blankly into her teacup. She knew they would want him killed. Would Dominik allow that to happen to his own son? Would she allow that if she could prevent it? Dominik continued. "Join the council, Tara, and you could use your influence to sway the council members."

Tara took a long swig of her tea, finished it, then nodded. Dominik smiled brightly. What have I gotten myself into, she thought? She already regretted her decision.

Epilogue

When she arrived at her place after leaving Dominik's house, she noticed a bouquet of red roses laying against her doorway. They were from Brandon Brooks. The card attached said, "Dinner? Friday Night? See you soon." She smelled the roses as she walked in and couldn't help but smile. At least some men know how to woo a woman.

Tara felt good to be in her own bed again, not that she had gotten used to it within the week she had moved to Seattle, but it was hers and it was comfortable. Exhausted from the last couple of nights, Tara fell asleep immediately.

Over the next week, Jacob was ordered to take some time off. Chief Martinez did not want him pulling any stitches out or causing him more pain, so Tara was partnerless. She managed to finally pick an office, a corner office with a view of the Puget Sound. There were worse views to have.

Eric Sloan was still in the wind. She wasn't happy about that, but when a 350-year-old vampire goes into hiding, what can you do? Dominik swore he had his people searching for him, but did warn her that it was entirely possible that he had left Seattle altogether. Good riddance to bad rubbish.

The barrier around Seattle was still down. Vita and her coven wanted Tara to help them channel the Dradogian inside her. She was all for it since she didn't want to run into any unexpected visitors anytime soon. Vita warned her that the process could take several meetings before Tara could tap into the power. She was willing and focused but so far, no luck.

Yvette took a sample of her DNA and gave Tara the bad news. The Dradogian had indeed bonded with her. There was no way of transferring it out of her. Not without killing her in the process. The best thing she could do was learn to manage it.

Life had returned to a semblance of normalcy, considering green mist was bonded within her. Cynthia had convinced her to come to a get together after work at her place. Tara really didn't feel up to it, but before she knew it, everyone at the precinct knew about it and she had to go. Tara was told to bring a friend, so she asked Brandon. He accepted instantly. She already regretted saying yes.

Bethany and Tara had gone shopping for dresses a few times over the course of the week. Bethany explained that she couldn't wear her stuffy old uniform to the council meetings. Tara allowed her to be her own personal dress up doll. Bethany did have exquisite taste. Bethany mentioned that she and Tina had made up. It's funny how mass genocide puts things into perspective.

Officer Robertson seemed to be back to his comical ways. Since finding out about the car crash, he seemed to have forgotten the night at the diner. He even helped Tara move her desk around her office. She was liking him more and more.

Yvette had taken charge of the sirens, although that was not a permanent position. She explained to Tara that there needed to be a consensus vote on the matter. Who knew sirens were so democratic?

Yvette and Tara ate lunch together pretty regularly. Tara liked Yvette and considered her not just a colleague, but a true friend. As far as she could tell, Yvette was the exact opposite of her mother.

Lilith was causing quite the ruckus being locked up. According to one of the guards, Officer Smith, a black woman with a no-nonsense attitude, Lilith was "cuckoo for cocoa puffs," They ran a psyche test on Lilith and the therapist said she was a schizophrenic suffering from mass delusions. He suggested she be transferred to a psychiatric hospital. Tara agreed, but they were waiting on the paperwork.

A few days after the ball, Tara was walking around at Pike's Place Market. She loved seeing the fresh fruit and vegetables, even in late October. She felt great knowing that so many people had healthy lifestyles in Seattle.

Her phone rang and she picked it up on the third ring. It was officer Smith. "Detective, I think you better come in," she said. Something in the way she said it unnerved her.

"Why?" Tara asked her. "Is everything okay?" Officer Smith was silent. "Smith? You there?"

"Lilith has managed to escape!" officer Smith replied quickly. "I don't know how. One minute she was there in her cell. The next, she was gone. It was as if she just vanished"

Tara's mouth dropped to the floor. Many tourists passed her by without giving her a second glance, but some noticed her disconcerting expression. "I'm on my way!" she hung up.

She ran to the precinct. By the time she arrived at Lilith's cell, the place was crawling with cops and CSI's searching for clues as to how she managed to escape. She found officer Smith and questioned her.

"What happened?"

Officer Smith cleared her throat. "She was there when I went to the bathroom. When I returned, she was just gone!" Officer Smith looked frightened. There would be hell to pay and she would be the one to pay it. Tara sympathized with her, but had to keep a clear head. They needed to figure out what happened, and fast.

"There's more," Smith told her. "Lying on the bed was this." Officer Smith handed Tara a sealed manila envelope addressed to her. Tara took the envelope and examined it. It was blank except for her full name written in Calligraphy. She stuffed the note in her pocket. "Aren't you going to read it?"

"Later," Tara told her, frowning. "Right now, I want to know how the hell she escaped."

Every cop down inside the jail cell searched for clues as to how Lilith managed to leave unnoticed. They came up with nothing. Even the video cameras came up empty as they happened to glitch at the time. Strange coincidence.

It was late by the time Tara arrived at her apartment. She took off her jacket and the manila envelope fell to the floor. She scooped it up and examined it again. Should she open it? What she should have done was log it into evidence, but since it came from the queen of the sirens, who knows what it would say.

She stood in the hallway and decided to open it. A card with a black floral pattern lay inside. She took it out and opened the card. In giant black calligraphy, one word stood prominently in the middle of the card. "Soon."

Soon what? Tara thought. Her heart jumped into her throat as she heard a large caw echo out of the card. She dropped it and recoiled backward as the card floated to the floor. It then caught on fire and burst into flames.

Made in the USA
Columbia, SC
14 December 2019